Tomorrow is another world . . .

In Poul Anderson's "The Only Game in Town," an organization that tries to stop people from warping the past shows that it not only knows how to enforce the rules, it knows how to break them, too . . .

In "Playing the Game," Jack Dann and Gardner Dozois demonstrate that not only is it impossible to go home again, it may be impossible to even *find* it . . .

Damon Knight's poignant, bittersweet "What Rough Beast" shows one man can make a difference, in more ways than you thought possible . . .

R. A. Lafferty's "Thus We Frustrate Charlemagne" is a sharp, funny cautionary tale about altering the past—and how sometimes it's better to leave well enough alone . . .

And Howard Waldrop's "Calling Your Name" is a wry, compassionate look at how the little things in life count so much, they can change everything—including the world itself . . .

Edited by Jack Dann & Gardner Dozois

FUTURES PAST

edited by
JACK DANN & GARDNER DOZOIS

ACE BOOKS, NEW YORK

THE BERKLEY PUBLISHING GROUP
Published by the Penguin Group
Penguin Group (USA) Inc.
375 Hudson Street, New York, New York 10014, USA
Penguin Group (Canada), 90 Eglinton Avenue East, Suite 700, Toronto, Ontario M4P 2Y3, Canada
(a division of Pearson Penguin Canada Inc.)
Penguin Books Ltd., 80 Strand, London WC2R 0RL, England
Penguin Group Ireland, 25 St. Stephen's Green, Dublin 2, Ireland (a division of Penguin Books Ltd.)
Penguin Group (Australia), 250 Camberwell Road, Camberwell, Victoria 3124, Australia
(a division of Pearson Australia Group Pty. Ltd.)
Penguin Books India Pvt. Ltd., 11 Community Centre, Panchsheel Park, New Delhi—110 017, India
Penguin Group (NZ), Cnr. Airborne and Rosedale Roads, Albany, Auckland 1310, New Zealand
(a division of Pearson New Zealand Ltd.)
Penguin Books (South Africa) (Pty.) Ltd., 24 Sturdee Avenue, Rosebank, Johannesburg 2196,
South Africa

Penguin Books Ltd., Registered Offices: 80 Strand, London WC2R 0RL, England

FUTURES PAST

An Ace Book / published by arrangement with the editors

PRINTING HISTORY
Ace mass-market edition / November 2006

Copyright © 2006 by Jack Dann and Gardner Dozois.
A complete listing of individual copyrights can be found on page v.
Cover art by axb group. Cover design by Rita Frangie.
Text design by Stacy Irwin.

ISBN: 0-441-01454-2

ACE
Ace Books are published by The Berkley Publishing Group,
a division of Penguin Group (USA) Inc.,
375 Hudson Street, New York, New York 10014.
ACE and the "A" design are trademarks belonging to Penguin Group (USA) Inc.

PRINTED IN THE UNITED STATES OF AMERICA

10 9 8 7 6 5 4 3 2 1

Contents

Preface

EVERY MOMENT OF every day, a thousand possible futures die unborn around us, a thousand corners not turned, a thousand roads not taken. We've all wondered, What would have happened if we'd gotten to that party late and so never met the person whom, in this universe, later became our spouse? What if we hadn't driven down that particular street at just the right time to collide with another car going across an intersection? What if we *had* managed to get to the airport in time to make that flight, the one that crashed?

And what's true of our own personal lives is true of history as well, of course: a thousand corners not turned, a thousand roads not taken. The fate of nations depends on the outcome of battles, which, as Shakespeare has shown us, can depend on whether or not a horse throws a horseshoe, or, in one memorable example from the American Civil War, whether or not a staff officer decided to have a cigar after dinner. What has become increasingly evident, over the past few decades, as we've learned about Chaos Theory and the Butterfly Effect (that busy, frenetically flailing insect that causes hurricanes in the Gulf by flapping its wings in Peru) and the Sensitive Dependence on Initial Conditions, is how *small* a change is needed to alter everything. How completely the entire structure of history could change once you tamper with one small brick in the foundation upon which everything else is built— the difference in one course of bricks altering the shape of the next, which alters the next, and so on; a cascade of changes building upon changes, until the structure you get is radically different than the one you *would* have ended up with, if that first brick hadn't been changed.

In the pages of the anthology that follow, sixteen of science fiction's most expert dreamers will show you what happens when people (often people with only the very best of intentions) deliberately set out to change the world by going back and turning one of those unturned corners, taking one of those roads not taken . . . actively *changing* things, so that the Mongols discover the New World instead of the Europeans, or the American Revolution never happens, or ruthless industrialists take over eighteenth-century Salzburg and set up refineries and cracking towers in the town square . . . exploring what would happen if you woke up one day to find yourself in a different life from the one you remember, or lost among the billion worlds of probability, unable to find your way home . . . if you had to meddle, with sabotage and murder, to provoke World War I, or if refugees from the future returned to destroy your past and replace it with another . . . or if someone from another time took over your body in order to kill someone . . . or if you were forced to hide from ruthless immortals who were implacably chasing you through every second of recorded history . . . or if the most casual touch of your hand changed everything in the world around you, whether you wanted it to or not . . .

Changing worlds. Worlds where the stuff of history is so mutable that it melts and reforms like wax under heat and pressure, and the universe you wake up in might not be the one in which you went to sleep—or the one in which you'll wake tomorrow.

Enjoy!

Aristotle and the Gun

L. Sprague de Camp

The late L. Sprague de Camp was a seminal figure, one whose career spanned almost the entire development of modern fantasy and SF. Much of the luster of the "Golden Age" of *Astounding* during the late '30s and the '40s is due to the presence in those pages of de Camp, along with his great contemporaries Robert A. Heinlein, Theodore Sturgeon, and A. E. Van Vogt. At the same time, for *Astounding*'s sister fantasy magazine, *Unknown*, he helped to create a whole new modern style of fantasy writing—funny, whimsical, and irreverent, including such classics as "The Wheels of If," "The Gnarly Man," "Nothing in the Rules," "The Hardwood Pile," and (written in collaboration with Fletcher Pratt), the famous "Harold Shea" stories, which would later be collected as *The Complete Enchanter*. In science fiction, he was the author of *Lest Darkness Fall*, in my opinion one of the three or four best Alternate Worlds novels ever written, as well as the at-the-time highly controversial novel *Rogue Queen*, and a body of expertly crafted short fiction such as "Judgment Day," "Divide and Rule," and "A Gun for Dinosaur."

"Aristotle and the Gun," published in 1956, would prove to

be de Camp's last science fiction short story for more than a decade. After this, he would devote his energies to turning out a long sequence of critically-acclaimed historical novels (including *The Bronze God of Rhodes* and *An Elephant for Aristotle*, two of my favorite historical novels) and, like Isaac Asimov (and at about the same time), a number of nonfiction books on scientific and technical topics. He would not return to writing fantasy and SF to any significant degree until the mid-1970s, and, although his presence enriched several other fields, it was sorely missed in ours. Still, if de Camp *had* to stop writing science fiction for a time, this was a good story to go out with—de Camp at the height of his powers, writing in his usual vivid, erudite, and slyly witty way about some of the subjects—and the historical personages—that interested him the most, and demonstrating how worlds can irrevocably change whether you want them to or not.

De Camp's other books include *The Glory That Was, The Search for Zei, The Tower of Zanid, The Great Fetish, The Honorable Barbarian*, and, with Fletcher Pratt, *The Land of Unreason*. His short fiction has been collected in *The Best of L. Sprague de Camp, A Gun for Dinosaur*, and *The Purple Pterodactyls*. His most recent books are the posthumous collections *Aristotle and the Gun and Other Stories*, and *Years in the Making: The Time-Travel Stories of L. Sprague de Camp*, and the novel omnibus *The Complete Enchanter*.

From: Sherman Weaver, Librarian
The Palace
Paumanok, Sewanhaki
Sachimate of Lenape
Flower Moon 3, 3097

To: Messire Markos Koukidas
Consulate of the Balkan Commonwealth
Kataapa, Muskhogian Federation

My dear Consul:

You have no doubt heard of our glorious victory at Ptaksit, when our noble Sachim destroyed the armored chivalry of the Mengwe by the brilliant use of pikemen and archery. (I suggested it to him years ago, but never mind.) Sagoyewatha and most of his Senecas fell, and the Oneidas broke before our countercharge. The envoys from the Grand Council of the Long House arrive tomorrow for a peace-pauwau. The roads to the South are open again, so I send you my long-promised account of the events that brought me from my own world into this one.

If you could have stayed longer on your last visit, I think I could have made the matter clear, despite the language difficulty and my hardness of hearing. But perhaps, if I give you a simple narrative, in the order in which things happened to me, truth will transpire.

Know, then, that I was born into a world that looks like this one on the map, but is very different as regards human affairs. I tried to tell you of some of the triumphs of our natural philosophers, of our machines and discoveries. No doubt you thought me a first-class liar, though you were too polite to say so.

Nonetheless, my tale is true, though for reasons that will appear I cannot prove it. I was one of those natural philosophers. I commanded a group of younger philosophers, engaged in a task called a *project,* at a center of learning named Brookhaven, on the south shore of Sewanhaki twenty parasangs east of Paumanok. Paumanok itself was known as Brooklyn, and formed part of an even larger city called New York.

My project had to do with the study of space-time. (Never mind what that means but read on.) At this center we had learned to get vast amounts of power from sea water by what we called a fusion process. By this process we could concentrate so much power in a small space that we could warp the entity called space-time and cause things to travel in time as our other machines traveled in space.

When our calculations showed that we could theoretically hurl an object back in time, we began to build a machine for testing this hypothesis. First we built a small pilot model. In this we sent small objects back in time for short periods.

We began with inanimate objects. Then we found that a rabbit or rat could also be projected without harm. The time-translation would not be permanent; rather, it acted like one of these rubber balls the Hesperians play games with. The object would stay in the desired time for a period determined by the power used to project it and its own mass, and would then return spontaneously to the time and place from which it started.

We had reported our progress regularly, but my chief had other matters on his mind and did not read our reports for many months. When he got a report saying that we were completing a machine to hurl human beings back in time, however, he awoke to what was going on, read our previous reports, and called me in.

"Sherm," he said, "I've been discussing this project with Washington, and I'm afraid they take a dim view of it."

"Why?" said I, astonished.

"Two reasons. For one thing, they think you've gone off the reservation. They're much more interested in the Antarctic Reclamation Project and want to concentrate all our appropriations and brain power on it.

"For another, they're frankly scared of this time machine of yours. Suppose you went back, say, to the time of Alexander the Great and shot Alexander before he got started? That would change all later history, and we'd go out like candles."

"Ridiculous," I said.

"What, what *would* happen?"

"Our equations are not conclusive, but there are several possibilities. As you will see if you read Report No. 9, it depends on whether space-time has a positive or negative curvature. If positive, any disturbance in the past tends to be ironed out in subsequent history, so that things become more and more nearly identical with what they would have been anyway. If negative, then events will diverge more and more from their original pattern with time.

"Now, as I showed in this report, the chances are overwhelmingly in favor of a positive curvature. However, we intend to take every precaution and make our first tests for short periods, with a minimum—"

"That's enough," said my superior, holding up a hand. "It's very interesting, but the decision has already been made."

"What do you mean?"

"I mean Project A-257 is to be closed down and a final report written at once. The machines are to be dismantled, and the group will be put to work on another project."

"What?" I shouted. "But you can't stop us just when we're on the verge—"

"I'm sorry, Sherm, but I can. That's what the ABC decided at yesterday's meeting. It hasn't been officially announced, but they gave me positive orders to kill the project as soon as I got back here."

"Of all the lousy, arbitrary, benighted—"

"I know how you feel, but I have no choice."

I lost my temper and defied him, threatening to go ahead with the project anyway. It was ridiculous, because he could easily dismiss me for insubordination. However, I knew he valued my ability and counted on his wanting to keep me for that reason. But he was clever enough to have his cake and eat it.

"If that's how you feel," he said, "the section is abolished here and now. Your group will be broken up and assigned to other projects. You'll be kept on at your present rating with the title of consultant. Then when you're willing to talk sense, perhaps we can find you a suitable job."

I stamped out of his office and went home to brood. I ought now to tell you something of myself. I am old enough to be objective, I hope. And, as I have but a few years left, there is no point in pretense.

I have always been a solitary, misanthropic man. I had little interest in or liking of my fellow man, who naturally paid me back in the same coin. I was awkward and ill at ease in company. I had a genius for saying the wrong thing and making a fool of myself.

I never understood people. Even when I watched and

planned my own actions with the greatest care, I never could tell how others would react to them. To me men were and are an unpredictable, irrational, and dangerous species of hairless ape. While I could avoid some of my worst gaffes by keeping my own counsel and watching my every word, they did not like that either. They considered me a cold, stiff, unfriendly sort of person when I was only trying to be polite and avoid offending them.

I never married. At the time of which I speak, I was verging on middle age without a single close friend and no more acquaintances than my professional work required.

My only interest, outside my work, was a hobby of the history of science. Unlike most of my fellow philosophers, I was historically minded, with a good smattering of a classical education. I belonged to the History of Science Society and wrote papers on the history of science for its periodical *Isis*.

I went back to my little rented house, feeling like Galileo. He was a scientist persecuted for his astronomical theories by the religious authorities of my world several centuries before my time, as Georg Schwartzhorn was a few years ago in this world's Europe.

I felt I had been born too soon. If only the world were scientifically more advanced, my genius would be appreciated and my personal difficulties solved.

Well, I thought, why is the world not scientifically more advanced? I reviewed the early growth of science. Why had not your fellow countrymen, when they made a start toward a scientific age two thousand to twenty-five hundred years ago, kept at it until they made science the self-supporting, self-accelerating thing it at last became—in my world, that is?

I knew the answers that historians of science had worked out. One was the effect of slavery, which made work disgraceful to a free man and therefore made experiment and invention unattractive because they looked like work. Another was the primitive state of the mechanical arts: things like making clear glass and accurate measuring devices. Another was the Hellenes's fondness for spinning cosmic theories without enough facts to go on, the result of which was that most of their theories were wildly wrong.

Well, thought I, could a man go back to this period and, by applying a stimulus at the right time and place, give the necessary push to set the whole trend rolling off in the right direction?

People had written fantastic stories about a man's going back in time and overawing the natives by a display of the discoveries of his own later era. More often than not, such a time-traveling hero came to a bad end. The people of the earlier time killed him as a witch, or he met with an accident, or something happened to keep him from changing history. But, knowing these dangers, I could forestall them by careful planning.

It would do little or no good to take back some major invention, like a printing press or an automobile, and turn it over to the ancients in the hope of grafting it on their culture. I could not teach them to work it in a reasonable time; and, if it broke down or ran out of supplies, there would be no way to get it running again.

What I had to do was to find a key mind and implant in it an appreciation of sound scientific method. He would have to be somebody who would have been important in any event, or I could not count on his influence's spreading far and wide.

After study of Sarton and other historians of science, I picked Aristotle. You have heard of him, have you not? He existed in your world just as he did in mine. In fact, up to Aristotle's time our worlds were one and the same.

Aristotle was one of the greatest minds of all time. In my world, he was the first encyclopedist; the first man who tried to know everything, write down everything, and explain everything. He did much good original scientific work, too, mostly in biology.

However, Aristotle tried to cover so much ground, and accepted so many fables as facts, that he did much harm to science as well as good. For, when a man of such colossal intellect goes wrong, he carries with him whole generations of weaker minds who cite him as an infallible authority. Like his colleagues, Aristotle never appreciated the need for constant verification. Thus, though he was married twice, he said that men have more teeth than women. He never thought to ask either of his wives to open her mouth for a count. He never grasped the need for invention and experiment.

Now, if I could catch Aristotle at the right period of his career, perhaps I could give him a push in the right direction.

When would that be? Normally, one would take him as a young man. But Aristotle's entire youth, from seventeen to thirty-seven, was spent in Athens listening to Plato's lectures. I did not wish to compete with Plato, an overpowering personality who could argue rings around anybody. His viewpoint was mystical and anti-scientific, the very thing I wanted to steer Aristotle away from. Many of Aristotle's intellectual vices can be traced back to Plato's influence.

I did not think it wise to present myself in Athens either during Aristotle's early period, when he was a student under Plato, or later, when he headed his own school. I could not pass myself off as a Hellene, and the Hellenes of that time had a contempt for all non-Hellenes, who they called "barbarians." Aristotle was one of the worst offenders in this respect. Of course this is a universal human failing, but it was particularly virulent among Athenian intellectuals. In his later Athenian period, too, Aristotle's ideas would probably be too set with age to change.

I concluded that my best chance would be to catch Aristotle while he was tutoring young Alexander the Great at the court of Philip the Second of Macedon. He would have regarded Macedon as a backward country, even though the court spoke Attic Greek. Perhaps he would be bored with bluff Macedonian stag-hunting squires and lonesome for intellectual company. As he would regard the Macedonians as the next thing to *barbaroi*, another barbarian would not appear at such a disadvantage there as at Athens.

Of course, whatever I accomplished with Aristotle, the results would depend on the curvature of space-time. I had not been wholly frank with my superior. While the equations tended to favor the hypothesis of a positive curvature, the probability was not overwhelming, as I claimed. Perhaps my efforts would have little effect on history, or perhaps the effect would grow and widen like ripples in a pool. In the latter case the existing world would, as my superior said, be snuffed out.

Well, at that moment I hated the existing world and would not give a snap of my fingers for its destruction. I was going to create a much better one and come back from ancient times to enjoy it.

Our previous experiments showed that I could project myself back to ancient Macedon with an accuracy of about two months temporally and a half-parasang spatially. The machine included controls for positioning the time traveler anywhere on the globe, and safety devices for locating him above the surface of the earth, not in a place already occupied by a solid object. The equations showed that I should stay in Macedon about nine weeks before being snapped back to the present.

Once I had made up my mind, I worked as fast as I could. I telephoned my superior (you remember what a telephone is?) and made my peace. I said:

"I know I was a damned fool, Fred, but this thing was my baby; my one chance to be a great and famous scientist. I might have got a Nobel Prize out of it."

"Sure, I know, Sherm," he said. "When are you coming back to the lab?"

"Well—uh—what about my group?"

"I held up the papers on that, in case you might change your mind. So if you come back, all will go on organization-wise as before."

"You want that final report on A-257, don't you?" I said, trying to keep my voice level.

"Sure."

"Then don't let the mechanics start to dismantle the machines until I've written the report."

"No; I've had the place locked up since yesterday."

"Okay. I want to shut myself in with the apparatus and the data sheets for a while and bat out the report without being bothered."

"That'll be fine," he said.

My first step in getting ready for my journey was to buy a suit of classical traveler's clothing from a theatrical costume company. This comprised a knee-length pullover tunic or chiton, a short horseman's cloak or chlamys, knitted buskins, sandals, a broad-brimmed black felt hat, and a staff. I stopped shaving, though I did not have time to raise a respectable beard.

My auxiliary equipment included a purse of coinage of the time, mostly golden Macedonian staters. Some of these coins were genuine, bought from a numismatic supply house, but most were copies I cast myself in the laboratory at night. I made sure of being rich enough to live decently for longer than my nine weeks' stay. This was not hard, as the purchasing power of precious metals was more than fifty times greater in the classical world than in mine.

I wore the purse attached to a heavy belt next to my skin. From this belt also hung a missile-weapon called a *gun*, which I have told you about. This was a small gun, called a pistol or revolver. I did not mean to shoot anybody, or expose the gun at all if I could help it. It was there as a last resort.

I also took several small devices of our science to impress Aristotle: a pocket microscope and a magnifying glass, a small telescope, a compass, my timepiece, a flashlight, a small camera, and some medicines. I intended to show these things to people of ancient times only with the greatest caution. By the time I had slung all these objects in their pouches and cases from my belt, I had a heavy load. Another belt over the tunic supported a small purse for day-to-day buying and an all-purpose knife.

I already had a good reading knowledge of classical Greek, which I tried to polish by practice with the spoken language and listening to it on my talking machine. I knew I should arrive speaking with an accent, for we had no way of knowing exactly what Attic Greek sounded like.

I decided, therefore, to pass myself off as a traveler from India. Nobody would believe I was a Hellene. If I said I came from the north or west, no Hellene would listen to me, as they regarded Europeans as warlike but half-witted savages. If I said I was from some well-known civilized country like Carthage, Egypt, Babylonia, or Persia, I should be in danger of meeting someone who knew those countries and of being exposed as a fraud.

To tell the truth of my origin, save under extraordinary circumstances, would be most imprudent. It would lead to my being considered a lunatic or a liar, as I can guess that your good self has more than once suspected me of being.

An Indian, however, should be acceptable. At this time, the Hellenes knew about that land only a few wild rumors and the account of Ktesias of Knidos, who made a book of the tales he picked up about India at the Persian court. The Hellenes had heard that India harbored philosophers. Therefore, thinking Greeks might be willing to consider Indians as almost as civilized as themselves.

What should I call myself? I took a common Indian name, Chandra, and Hellenized it to Zandras. That, I knew, was what the Hellenes would do anyway, as they had no "tch" sound and insisted on putting Greek inflectional endings on foreign names. I would not try to use my own name, which is not even remotely Greek- or Indian-sounding. (Someday I must explain the blunders in my world that led to Hesperians being called "Indians.")

The newness and cleanliness of my costume bothered me. It did not look worn, and I could hardly break it in around Brookhaven without attracting attention. I decided that if the question came up, I should say: yes, I bought it when I entered Greece, so as not to be conspicuous in my native garb.

During the day, when not scouring New York for equipment, I was locked in the room with the machine. While my colleagues thought I was either writing my report or dismantling the apparatus, I was getting ready for my trip.

Two weeks went by thus. One day a memorandum came down from my superior, saying: "How is that final report coming?"

I knew then I had better put my plan into execution at once. I sent back a memorandum: "Almost ready for the writing machine."

That night I came back to the laboratory. As I had been doing this often, the guards took no notice. I went to the time-machine room, locked the door from the inside, and got out my equipment and costume.

I adjusted the machine to set me down near Pella, the capital of Macedon, in the spring of the year 340 before Christ in our system of reckoning (976 Algonkian). I set the auto-actuator, climbed inside, and closed the door.

THE FEELING OF being projected through time cannot really be described. There is a sharp pain, agonizing but too short to let the victim even cry out. At the same time there is the feeling of terrific acceleration, as if one were being shot from a catapult, but in no particular direction.

Then the seat in the passenger compartment dropped away from under me. There was a crunch, and a lot of sharp things jabbed me. I had fallen into the top of a tree.

I grabbed a couple of branches to save myself. The mechanism that positioned me in Macedon, detecting solid matter at the point where I was going to materialize, had raised me up above the treetops and then let go. It was an old oak, just putting out its spring leaves.

In clutching for branches I dropped my staff, which slithered down through the foliage and thumped the ground below. At least it thumped something. There was a startled yell.

Classical costume is impractical for tree-climbing. Branches kept knocking off my hat, or snagging my cloak, or poking me in tender places not protected by trousers. I ended my climb with a slide and a fall of several feet, tumbling into the dirt.

As I looked up, the first thing I saw was a burly, black-bearded man in a dirty tunic, standing with a knife in his hand. Near him stood a pair of oxen yoked to a wooden plow. At his feet rested a water jug.

The plowman had evidently finished a furrow and lain down to rest himself and his beasts when the fall of my staff on him and then my arrival in person aroused him.

Around me stretched the broad Emathian Plain, ringed by

ranges of stony hills and craggy mountains. As the sky was overcast, and I did not dare consult my compass, I had no sure way of orienting myself, or even telling what time of day it was. I assumed that the biggest mountain in sight was Mount Bermion, which ought to be to the west. To the north I could see a trace of water. This would be Lake Loudias. Beyond the lake rose a range of low hills. A discoloration on the nearest spur of these hills might be a city, though my sight was not keen enough to make out details, and I had to do without my eyeglasses. The gently rolling plain was cut up into fields and pastures with occasional trees and patches of marsh. Dry brown grasses left over from winter nodded in the wind.

My realization of all this took but a flash. Then my attention was brought back to the plowman, who spoke.

I could not understand a word. But then, he would speak Macedonian. Though this can be deemed a Greek dialect, it differed so from Attic Greek as to be unintelligible.

No doubt the man wanted to know what I was doing in his tree. I put on my best smile and said in my slow fumbling Attic: "Rejoice! I am lost, and climbed your tree to find my way."

He spoke again. When I did not respond, he repeated his words more loudly, waving his knife.

We exchanged more words and gestures, but it was evident that neither had the faintest notion of what the other was trying to say. The plowman began shouting, as ignorant people will when faced by the linguistic barrier.

At last I pointed to the distant headland overlooking the lake, on which there appeared a discoloration that might be the city. Slowly and carefully I said:

"Is that Pella?"

"*Nai, Pella!*" The man's mien became less threatening.

"I am going to Pella. Where can I find the philosopher Aristoteles?" I repeated the name.

He was off again with more gibberish, but I gathered from his expression that he had never heard of any Aristoteles. So, I picked up my hat and stick, felt through my tunic to make

sure my gear was all in place, tossed the rustic a final
"Chaire!" and set off.

By the time I had crossed the muddy field and come out on
a cart track, the problem of looking like a seasoned traveler
had solved itself. There were green and brown stains on my
clothes from the scramble down the tree; the cloak was torn;
the branches had scratched my limbs and face; my feet and
lower legs were covered with mud. I also became aware that,
to one who has lived all his life with his loins decently
swathed in trousers and underdrawers, classical costume is
excessively drafty.

I glanced back to see the plowman still standing with one
hand on his plow, looking at me in puzzled fashion. The poor
fellow had never been able to decide what, if anything, to do
about me.

When I found a road, it was hardly more than a heavily
used cart track, with a pair of deep ruts and the space between
them alternating stones, mud, and long grass.

I walked toward the lake and passed a few people on the
road. To one used to the teeming traffic of my world, Macedon seemed dead and deserted. I spoke to some of the people,
but ran into the same barrier of language as with the plowman.

Finally a two-horse chariot came along, driven by a stout
man wearing a headband, a kind of kilt, and high-laced boots.
He pulled up at my hail.

"What is it?" he said, in Attic not much better than mine.

"I seek the philosopher, Aristoteles of Stageira. Where can
I find him?"

"He lives in Mieza."

"Where is that?"

The man waved. "You are going the wrong way. Follow
this road back the way you came. At the ford across the Bot-
tiais, take the right-hand fork, which will bring you to Mieza
and Kition. Do you understand?"

"I think so," I said. "How far is it?"

"About two hundred stadia."

My heart sank to my sandals. This meant five perasangs, or
a good two days' walk. I thought of trying to buy a horse or a

chariot, but I had never ridden or driven a horse and saw no prospect of learning how soon enough to do any good. I had read about Mieza as Aristotle's home in Macedon but, as none of my maps had shown it, I had assumed it to be a suburb of Pella.

I thanked the man, who trotted off, and set out after him. The details of my journey need not detain you. I was benighted far from shelter through not knowing where the villages were, attacked by watchdogs, eaten alive by mosquitoes, and invaded by vermin when I did find a place to sleep the second night. The road skirted the huge marshes that spread over the Emathian Plain west of Lake Loudias. Several small streams came down from Mount Bermion and lost themselves in this marsh.

At last I neared Mieza, which stands on one of the spurs of Mount Bermion. I was trudging wearily up the long rise to the village when six youths on little Greek horses clattered down the road. I stepped to one side, but instead of cantering past they pulled up and faced me in a semicircle.

"Who are you?" asked one, a smallish youth of about fifteen, in fluent Attic. He was blond and would have been noticeably handsome without his pimples.

"I am Zandras of Pataliputra," I said, giving the ancient name for Patna on the Ganges. "I seek the philosopher Aristoteles."

"Oh, a barbarian!" cried Pimples. "We know what the Aristoteles thinks of these, eh, boys?"

The others joined in, shouting noncompliments and bragging about all the barbarians they would some day kill or enslave.

I made the mistake of letting them see I was getting angry. I knew it was unwise, but I could not help myself. "If you do not wish to help me, then let me pass," I said.

"Not only a barbarian, but an insolent one!" cried one of the group, making his horse dance uncomfortably close to me.

"Stand aside, children!" I demanded.

"We must teach you a lesson," said Pimples. The others giggled.

"You had better let me alone," I said, gripping my staff in both hands.

A tall handsome adolescent reached over and knocked my hat off. "That for you, cowardly Asiatic!" he yelled.

Without stopping to think, I shouted an English epithet and swung my staff. Either the young man leaned out of the way or his horse shied, for my blow missed him. The momentum carried the staff past my target and the end struck the nose of one of the other horses.

The pony squealed and reared. Having no stirrups, the rider slid off the animal's rump into the dirt. The horse galloped off.

All six youths began screaming. The blond one, who had a particularly piercing voice, mouthed some threat. The next thing I knew, his horse bounded directly at me. Before I could dodge, the annual's shoulder knocked me head over heels and the beast leaped over me as I rolled. Luckily, horses' dislike of stepping on anything squashy saved me from being trampled.

I scrambled up as another horse bore down upon me. By a frantic leap, I got out of its way, but I saw that the other boys were jockeying their mounts to do likewise.

A few paces away rose a big pine. I dodged in among its lower branches as the other horses ran at me. The youths could not force their mounts in among these branches, so they galloped round and round and yelled. Most of their talk I could not understand, but I caught a sentence from Pimples:

"Ptolemaios! Ride back to the house and fetch bows or javelins!"

Hooves receded. While I could not see clearly through the pine needles, I inferred what was happening. The youths would not try to rush me on foot, first because they liked being on horseback, and if they dismounted they might lose their horses or have trouble remounting; second, because, as long as I kept my back to the tree, they would have a hard time getting at me through the tangle of branches, and I could hit and poke them with my stick as I came. Though not an unusually tall man in my own world, I was much bigger than any of these boys.

This, however, was a minor consideration. I recognized the name "Ptolemaios" as that of one of Alexander's companions, who in my world became King Ptolemy of Egypt and founded a famous dynasty. Young Pimples, then, must be Alexander himself.

I was in a real predicament. If I stayed where I was, Ptolemaios would bring back missiles for target practice, with me as the target. I could of course shoot some of the boys with my gun, which would save me for the time being. But, in an absolute monarchy, killing the crown prince's friends, let alone the crown prince himself, is no way to achieve a peaceful old age, regardless of the provocation.

While I was thinking of these matters and listening to my attackers, a stone swished through the branches and bounced off the trunk. The small dark youth who had fallen off his horse had thrown the rock and was urging his friends to do likewise. I caught glimpses of Pimples and the rest dismounting and scurrying around for stones, a commodity with which Greece and Macedon are notoriously well supplied.

More stones came through the needles, caroming from the branches. One the size of my fist struck me lightly in the shin.

The boys came closer so that their aim got better. I wormed my way around the trunk to put it between me and them, but they saw the movement and spread out around the tree. A stone grazed my scalp, dizzying me and drawing blood. I thought of climbing, but, as the tree became more slender with height, I should be more exposed the higher I got. I should also be less able to dodge while perched in the branches.

That is how things stood when I heard hoofbeats again. This is the moment of decision, I thought. Ptolemaios is coming back with missile weapons. If I used my gun, I might doom myself in the long run, but it would be ridiculous to stand there and let them riddle me while I had an unused weapon.

I fumbled under my tunic and unsnapped the safety strap

that kept the pistol in its holster. I pulled the weapon out and checked its projectiles.

A deep voice broke into the bickering. I caught phrases: ". . . insulting an unoffending traveler . . . how know you he is not a prince in his own country? . . . the king shall hear of this . . . like newly-freed slaves, not like princes and gentlemen . . ."

I pushed towards the outer limits of the screen of pine needles. A heavy-set, brown-bearded man on a horse was haranguing the youths, who had dropped their stones. Pimples said:

"We were only having a little sport."

I stepped out from the branches, walked over to where my battered hat lay, and put it on. Then I said to the newcomer: "Rejoice! I am glad you came before your boys' play got too rough." I grinned, determined to act cheerful if it killed me. Only iron self-control would get me through this difficulty.

The man grunted. "Who are you?"

"Zandras of Pataliputra, a city in India. I seek Aristoteles the philosopher."

"He insulted us—" began one of the youths, but Brownbeard ignored him. He said:

"I am sorry you have had so rude an introduction to our royal house. This mass of youthful insolence" (he indicated Pimples) "is the Alexandros Philippou, heir to the throne of Makedonia." He introduced the others: Hephaistion, who had knocked my hat off and was now holding the others' horses; Nearchos, who had lost his horse; Ptolemaios, who had gone for weapons; and Harpalos and Philotas. He continued:

"When the Ptolemaios dashed into the house, I inquired the reason for his haste, learned of their quarrel with you, and came out forthwith. They have misapplied their master's teachings. They should not behave thus even to a barbarian like yourself, for in so doing they lower themselves to the barbarian's level. I am returning to the house of Aristoteles. You may follow."

he man turned his horse and started walking it back towards Mieza. The six boys busied themselves with catching Nearchos' horse.

I walked after him, though I had to dog-trot now and then to keep up. As it was uphill, I was soon breathing hard. I panted:

"Who—my lord—are you?"

The man's beard came round and he raised an eyebrow. "I thought you would know. I am Antipatros, regent of Makedonia."

Before we reached the village proper, Antipatros turned off through a kind of park, with statues and benches. This, I supposed, was the Precinct of the Nymphs, which Aristotle used as a school ground. We went through the park and stopped at a mansion on the other side. Antipatros tossed the reins to a groom and slid off his horse.

"Aristoteles!" roared Antipatros. "A man wishes to see you."

A man of about my own age—the early forties—came out. He was of medium height and slender build, with a thin-lipped, severe-looking face and a pepper-and-salt beard cut short. He was wrapped in a billowing himation or large cloak, with a colorful scroll-patterned border. He wore golden rings on several fingers.

Antipatros made a fumbling introduction: "Old fellow, this is—ah—what's-his-name from—ah—some place in India." He told of rescuing me from Alexander and his fellow delinquents, adding: "If you do not beat some manners into your pack of cubs soon, it will be too late."

Aristotle looked at me sharply and lisped: "It ith always a pleasure to meet men from afar. What brings you here, my friend?"

I gave my name and said: "Being accounted something of a philosopher in my own land, I thought my visit to the West would be incomplete without speaking to the greatest Western philosopher. And when I asked who he was, everyone told me to seek out Aristoteles Nikomachou."

Aristotle purred. "It is good of them to thay tho. Ahem.

Come in and join me in a drop of wine. Can you tell me of the wonders of India?"

"Yes indeed, but you must tell me in turn of your discoveries, which to me are much more wonderful."

"Come, come, then. Perhaps you could stay over a few days. I shall have many, many things to athk you."

THAT IS HOW I met Aristotle. He and I hit it off, as we said in my world, from the start. We had much in common. Some people would not like Aristotle's lisp, or his fussy, pedantic ways, or his fondness for worrying any topic of conversation to death. But he and I got along fine.

That afternoon, in the house that King Philip had built for Aristotle to use as the royal school, he handed me a cup of wine flavored with turpentine and asked:

"Tell me about the elephant, that great beast we have heard of with a tail at both ends. Does it truly exist?"

"Indeed it does," I said, and went on to tell what I knew of elephants, while Aristotle scribbled notes on a piece of papyrus.

"What do they call the elephant in India?" he asked.

The question caught me by surprise, for it had never occurred to me to learn ancient Hindustani along with all the other things I had to know for this expedition. I sipped the wine to give me time to think. I have never cared for alcoholic liquors, and this stuff tasted awful to me. But, for the sake of my objective, I had to pretend to like it. No doubt I should have to make up some kind of gibberish—but then a mental broad-jump carried me back to the stories of Kipling I had read as a boy.

"We call it a *hathi*," I said. "Though of course there are many languages in India."

"How about that Indian wild ath of which Ktesias thpeakth, with a horn in the middle of its forehead?"

"You had better call it a nose-horn (*rhinokerōs*) for that is where its horn really is, and it is more like a gigantic pig than an ass . . ."

As dinnertime neared, I made some artful remarks about

going out to find accommodations in Mieza, but Aristotle (to my joy) would have none of it. I should stay right there at the school; my polite protestations of unworthiness he waved aside.

"You mutht plan to stop here for months," he said. "I shall never, never have such a chance to collect data on India again. Do not worry about expense; the king pays all. You are—ahem—the first barbarian I have known with a decent intellect, and I get lonethome for good tholid talk. Theophrastos has gone to Athens, and my other friends come to these backlands but seldom."

"How about the Macedonians?"

"*Aiboi!* Thome like my friend Antipatros are good fellows, but most are as lackwitted as a Persian grandee. And now tell me of Patal—what is your city's name?"

Presently Alexander and his friends came in. They seemed taken aback at seeing me closeted with their master. I put on a brisk smile and said: "Rejoice, my friends!" as if nothing untoward had happened. The boys glowered and whispered among themselves, but did not attempt any more disturbance at that time.

When they gathered for their lecture next morning, Aristotle told them: "I am too busy with the gentleman from India to waste time pounding unwanted wisdom into your miserable little thouls. Go shoot some rabbits or catch some fish for dinner, but in any case begone!"

The boys grinned. Alexander said: "It seems the barbarian has his uses after all. I hope you stay with us forever, good barbarian!"

After they had gone, Antipatros came in to say good-bye to Aristotle. He asked me with gruff goodwill how I was doing and went out to ride back to Pella.

The weeks passed unnoticed and the flowers of spring came out while I visited Aristotle. Day after day we strolled about the Precinct of the Nymphs, talking, or sat indoors when it rained. Sometimes the boys followed us, listening; at other times we talked alone. They played a couple of practical jokes on me, but, by pretending to be amused when I was really furious, I avoided serious trouble with them.

I learned that Aristotle had a wife and a little daughter in another part of the big house, but he never let me meet the lady. I only caught glimpses of them from a distance.

I carefully shifted the subject of our daily discourse from the marvels of India to the more basic questions of science. We argued over the nature of matter and the shape of the solar system. I gave out that the Indians were well on the road to the modern concepts—modern in my world, that is—of astronomy, physics, and so forth. I told of the discoveries of those eminent Pataliputran philosophers: Kopernikos in astronomy, Neuton in physics, Darben in evolution, and Mendeles in genetics. (I forgot; these names mean nothing to you, though an educated man of my world would recognize them at once through their Greek disguise.)

Always I stressed *method*: the need for experiment and invention and for checking each theory back against the facts. Though an opinionated and argumentative man, Aristotle had a mind like a sponge, eagerly absorbing any new fact, surmise, or opinion, whether he agreed with it or not.

I tried to find a workable compromise between what I knew science could do on one hand and the limits of Aristotle's credulity on the other. Therefore I said nothing about flying machines, guns, buildings a thousand feet high, and other technical wonders of my world. Nevertheless, I caught Aristotle looking at me sharply out of those small black eyes one day.

"Do you doubt me, Aristoteles?" I said.

"N-no, no," he said thoughtfully. "But it does theem to me that, were your Indian inventors as wonderful as you make out, they would have fabricated you wings like those of Daidalos in the legend. Then you could have flown to Makedonia directly, without the trials of crossing Persia by camel."

"That has been tried, but men's muscles do not have enough strength in proportion to their weight."

"Ahem. Did you bring anything from India to show the skills of your people?"

I grinned, for I had been hoping for such a question. "I did fetch a few small devices," said I, reaching into my tunic and bringing out the magnifying glass. I demonstrated its use.

Aristotle shook his head. "Why did you not show me this before? It would have quieted my doubts."

"People have met with misfortune by trying too suddenly to change the ideas of those around them. Like your teacher's teacher, Sokrates."

"That is true, true. What other devices did you bring?"

I had intended to show my devices at intervals, gradually, but Aristotle was so insistent on seeing them all that I gave in to him before he got angry. The little telescope was not powerful enough to show the moons of Jupiter or the rings of Saturn, but it showed enough to convince Aristotle of its power. If he could not see these astronomical phenomena himself, he was almost willing to take my word that they could be seen with the larger telescopes we had in India.

One day a light-armed soldier galloped up to us in the midst of our discussions in the Precinct of Nymphs. Ignoring the rest of us, the fellow said to Alexander: "Hail, O Prince! The king, your father, will be here before sunset."

Everybody rushed around cleaning up the place. We were all lined up in front of the big house when King Philip and his entourage arrived on horseback with a jingle and a clatter, in crested helmets and flowing mantles. I knew Philip by his one eye. He was a big powerful man, much scarred, with a thick curly black beard going gray. He dismounted, embraced his son, gave Aristotle a brief greeting, and said to Alexander:

"How would you like to attend a siege?"

Alexander whooped.

"Thrace is subdued," said the king, "but Byzantion and Perinthos have declared against me, thanks to Athenian intrigue. I shall give the Perintheans something to think about besides the bribes of the Great King. It is time you smelled blood, youngster; would you like to come?"

"Yes, yes! Can my friends come too?"

"If they like and their fathers let them."

"O King!" said Aristotlé.

"What is it, spindle-shanks?"

"I trust thith is not the end of the prince's education. He has much yet to learn."

"No, no; I will send him back when the town falls. But he nears the age when he must learn by doing, not merely by listening to your rarefied wisdom. Who is this?" Philip turned his one eye on me.

"Zandras of India, a barbarian philothopher."

Philip grinned in a friendly way and clapped me on the shoulder. "Rejoice! Come to Pella and tell my generals about India. Who knows? A Macedonian foot may tread there yet."

"It would be more to the point to find out about Persia," said one of Philip's officers, a handsome fellow with a reddish-brown beard. "This man must have just come through there. How about it, man? Is the bloody Artaxerxes still solid on his throne?"

"I know little of such matters," I said, my heart beginning to pound at the threat of exposure. "I skirted the northernmost parts of the Great King's dominions and saw little of the big cities. I know nothing of their politics."

"Is that so?" said Redbeard, giving me a queer look. "We must talk of this again."

They all trooped into the big house, where the cook and the serving wenches were scurrying about. During dinner I found myself between Nearchos, Alexander's little Cretan friend, and a man-at-arms who spoke no Attic. So I did not get much conversation, nor could I follow much of the chatter that went on among the group at the head of the tables. I gathered that they were discussing politics. I asked Nearchos who the generals were.

"The big one at the king's right is the Parmenion," he said, "and the one with the red beard is the Attalos."

When the food was taken away and the drinking had begun, Attalos came over to me. The man-at-arms gave him his place. Attalos had drunk a lot of wine already; but, if it made him a little unsteady, it did not divert him.

"How did you come through the Great King's domain?" he asked. "What route did you follow?"

"I told you, to the north," I said.

"Then you must have gone through Orchoê."

"I—" I began, then stopped. Attalos might be laying a trap for me. What if I said yes and Orchoê was really in the south? Or suppose he had been there and knew all about the place? Many Greeks and Macedonians served the Great King as mercenaries.

"I passed through many places whose names I never got straight," I said. "I do not remember if Orchoê was among them."

Attalos gave me a sinister smile through his beard. "Your journey will profit you little, if you cannot remember where you have been. Come, tell me if you heard of unrest among the northern provinces."

I evaded the question, taking a long pull on my wine to cover my hesitation. I did this again and again until Attalos said: "Very well, perhaps you are really as ignorant of Persia as you profess. Then tell me about India."

"What about it?" I hiccuped; the wine was beginning to affect me, too.

"As a soldier, I should like to know of the Indian art of war. What is this about training elephants to fight?"

"Oh, we do much better than that."

"How so?"

"We have found that the flesh-and-blood elephant, despite its size, is an untrustworthy war beast because it often takes fright and stampedes back through its own troops. So, the philosophers of Pataliputra make artificial elephants of steel with rapid-fire catapults on their backs."

I was thinking in a confused way of the armored war vehicles of my own world. I do not know what made me tell Attalos such ridiculous lies. Partly, I suppose, it was to keep him off the subject of Persia.

Partly it was a natural antipathy between us. According to history, Attalos was not a bad man, though at times a reckless and foolish one. But it annoyed me that he thought he could pump me by subtle questions, when he was about as subtle as a ton of bricks. His voice and manner said as plainly as words:

I am a shrewd, sharp fellow; watch out for me, everybody. He was the kind of man who, if told to spy on the enemy, would don an obviously false beard, wrap himself in a long black cloak, and go slinking about the enemy's places in broad daylight, leering and winking and attracting as much attention as possible. No doubt, too, he had prejudiced me against him by his alarming curiosity about my past.

But the main cause for my rash behavior was the strong wine I had drunk. In my own world, I drank very little and so was not used to these carousals.

Attalos was all eyes and ears at my tale of mechanical elephants. "You do not say!"

"Yes, and we do even better than that. If the enemy's ground forces resist the charge of our iron elephants, we send flying chariots, drawn by gryphons, to drop darts on the foe from above." It seemed to me that never had my imagination been so brilliant.

Attalos gave an audible gasp. "What else?"

"Well—ah—we also have a powerful navy, you know, which controls the lower Ganges and the adjacent ocean. Our ships move by machinery, without oars or sails."

"Do the other Indians have these marvels, too?"

"Some, but none is so advanced as the Pataliputrans. When we are outnumbered on the sea, we have a force of tame Tritons who swim under the enemy's ships and bore holes in their bottoms."

Attalos frowned. "Tell me, barbarian, how it is that, with such mighty instruments of war, the Palalal—the Patapata—the people of your city have not conquered the whole world?"

I gave a shout of drunken laughter and slapped Attalos on the back. "We *have*, old boy, we have! You Macedonians have just not yet found out that you are our subjects!"

Attalos digested this, then scowled blackly. "You temple-thief! I think you have been making a fool of me! Of *me*! By Herakles, I ought—"

He rose and swung a fist back to clout me. I jerked an arm up to guard my face.

There came a roar of "Attalos!" from the head of the table. King Philip had been watching us.

Attalos dropped his fist, muttered something like "Flying chariots and tame Tritons, forsooth!" and stumbled back to his own crowd.

This man, I remembered, did not have a happy future in store. He was destined to marry his niece to Philip, whose first wife Olympias would have the girl and her baby killed after Philip's assassination. Soon afterwards, Attalos would be murdered by Alexander's orders. It was on the tip of my tongue to give him a veiled warning, but I forebore. I had attracted enough hostile attention already.

Later, when the drinking got heavy, Aristotle came over and shooed his boys off to bed. He said to me: "Let uth walk outside to clear our heads, Zandras, and then go to bed, too. These Makedones drink like sponges. I cannot keep up with them."

Outside, he said: "The Attalos thinks you are a Persian thpy."

"A spy? Me? In Hera's name, why?" Silently I cursed my folly in making an enemy without any need. Would I never learn to deal with this damned human species?

Aristotle said: "He thays nobody could pass through a country and remain as ignorant of it as you theem to be. *Ergo*, you know more of the Persian Empire than you pretend, but wish us to think you have nothing to do with it. And why should you do that, unleth you are yourself a Persian? And being a Persian, why should you hide the fact unleth you are on some hostile mission?"

"A Persian might fear anti-Persian prejudice among the Hellenes. Not that I am one," I hastily added.

"He need not. Many Persians live in Hellas without molestation. Take Artabazos and his sons, who live in Pella, refugees from their own king."

Then the obvious alibi came to me, long after it should have. "The fact is, I went even farther north than I said. I went around the northern ends of the Caspian and Euxine seas and so did not cross the Great King's domains save through the Bactrian deserts."

"You did? Then why did you not thay tho? If that is true, you have settled one of our hottest geographical disputes: whether the Caspian is a closed thea or a bay of the Northern Ocean."

"I feared nobody would believe me."

"I am not sure what to believe, Zandras. You are a strange man. I do not think you are a Persian, for no Persian was ever a philothopher. It is good for you that you are not."

"Why?"

"Because I *hate* Persia!" he hissed.

"You do?"

"Yeth. I could list the wrongs done by the Great Kings, but it is enough that they seized my beloved father-in-law by treachery and tortured and crucified him. People like Isokrates talk of uniting the Hellenes to conquer Persia, and Philippos may try it if he lives. I hope he does. However," he went on in a different tone, "I hope he does it without dragging the cities of Hellas into it, for the repositories of civilization have no busineth getting into a brawl between tyrants."

"In India," said I sententiously, "we are taught that a man's nationality means nothing and his personal qualities everything. Men of all nations come good, bad, and indifferent."

Aristotle shrugged. "I have known virtuouth Persians, too, but that monstrouth, bloated empire . . . No state can be truly civilized with more than a few thousand citizens."

There was no use telling him that large states, however monstrous and bloated he thought them, would be a permanent feature of the landscape from then on. I was trying to reform, not Aristotle's narrow view of international affairs, but his scientific methodology.

Next morning King Philip and his men and Aristotle's six pupils galloped off towards Pella, followed by a train of baggage mules and the boys' personal slaves. Aristotle said:

"Let us hope no chance sling-thtone dashes out Alexandros' brains before he has a chance to show his mettle. The boy has talent and may go far, though managing him is like trying to plow with a wild bull. Now, let us take up the question of atoms again, my dear Zandras, about which you have been talking thuch utter rubbish. First, you must admit that if a thing exists, parts of it must also exist. Therefore there is no thuch thing as an indivisible particle . . ."

Three days later, while we were still hammering at the question of atoms, we looked up at the clatter of hooves. Here came Attalos and a whole troop of horsemen. Beside Attalos rode a tall swarthy man with a long gray beard. This man's appearance startled me into thinking he must be another time traveler from my own time, for he wore a hat, coat, and pants. The mere sight of these familiar garments filled me with homesickness for my own world, however much I hated it when I lived in it.

Actually, the man's garb was not that of one from my world. The hat was a cylindrical felt cap with ear flaps. The coat was a brown knee-length garment, embroidered with faded red and blue flowers, with trousers to match. The whole outfit looked old and threadbare, with patches showing. He was a big craggy-looking fellow, with a great hooked nose, wide cheekbones, and deep-set eyes under bushy, beetling brows.

They all dismounted, and a couple of grooms went around collecting the bridles to keep the horses from running off. The soldiers leaned on their spears in a circle around us.

Attalos said: "I should like to ask your guest some more philosophical questions, O Aristoteles."

"Ask away."

Attalos turned, not to me, but to the tall graybeard. He said something I did not catch, and then the man in trousers spoke to me in a language I did not know.

"I do not understand," I said.

The graybeard spoke again, in what sounded like a different tongue. He did this several times, using a different-sounding speech each time, but each time I had to confess ignorance.

"Now you see," said Attalos. "He pretends not to know Persian, Median, Armenian, or Aramaic. He could not have traversed the Great King's dominions from east to west without learning at least one of these."

"Who are you, my dear sir?" I asked Graybeard.

The old man gave me a small dignified smile and spoke in Attic with a guttural accent. "I am Artavazda, or Artabazos as the Hellenes say, once governor of Phrygia but now a poor pensioner of King Philippos."

This, then, was the eminent Persian refugee of whom Aristotle had spoken.

"I warrant he does not even speak Indian," said Attalos.

"Certainly," I said, and started off in English: *"Now is the time for all good men to come to the aid of the party. Four score and seven years ago our fathers brought forth—"*

"What would you call that?" Attalos asked Artavazda.

The Persian spread his hands. "I have never heard the like. But then, India is a vast country of many tongues."

"I was not—" I began, but Attalos kept on:

"What race would you say he belonged to?"

"I know not. The Indians I have seen were much darker, but there might be light-skinned Indians for aught I know."

"If you will listen, General, I will explain," I said. "For most of the journey I was not even in the Persian Empire. I crossed through Bactria and went around the north of the Caspian and Euxine seas."

"Oh, so now you tell another story?" said Attalos. "Any educated man knows the Caspian is but a deep bay opening into the Ocean River to the north. Therefore you could not go around it. So, in trying to escape, you do but mire yourself deeper in your own lies."

"Look here," said Aristotle. "You have proved nothing of the sort, O Attalos. Ever thince Herodotos there have been those who think the Caspian a closed thea—"

"Hold your tongue, Professor," said Attalos. "This is a matter of national security. There is something queer about this alleged Indian, and I mean to find out what it is."

"It is not queer that one who comes from unknown distant lands should tell a singular tale of his journey."

"No, there is more to it than that. I have learned that he first appeared in a treetop on the farm of the freeholder Diktys Pisandrou. Diktys remembers looking up into the tree for crows before he cast himself down under it to rest. If the Zandras had been in the tree, Diktys would have seen him, as it was not yet fully in leaf. The next instant there was the crash of a body falling into the branches, and Zandras' staff smote Diktys on the head. Normal mortal men fall not out of the sky into trees."

"Perhaps he flew from India. They have marvelous mechanisms there, he tells me," said Aristotle.

"If he survives our interrogation in Pella, perhaps he can make me a pair of wings," said Attalos. "Or better yet, a pair for my horse, so he shall emulate Pegasos. Meanwhile, seize and bind him, men!"

The soldiers moved. I did not dare submit for fear they would take my gun and leave me defenseless. I snatched up the hem of my tunic to get at my pistol. It took precious seconds to unsnap the safety strap, but I got the gun out before anybody laid a hand on me.

"Stand back or I will blast you with lightning!" I shouted, raising the gun.

Men of my own world, knowing how deadly such a weapon can be, would have given ground at the sight of it. But the Macedonians, never having seen one, merely stared at the device and came on. Attalos was one of the nearest.

I fired at him, then whirled and shot another soldier who was reaching out to seize me. The discharge of the gun produces a lightning-like flash and a sharp sound like a close clap of thunder. The Macedonians cried out, and Attalos fell with a wound in his thigh.

I turned again, looking for a way out of the circle of soldiers, while confused thoughts of taking one of their horses flashed through my head. A heavy blow in the flank staggered me. One of the soldiers had jabbed me with his spear, but my belt kept the weapon from piercing me. I shot at the man but missed him in my haste.

"Do not kill him!" screamed Aristotle.

Some of the soldiers backed up as if to flee; others poised

their spears. They hesitated for the wink of an eye, either for fear of me or because Aristotle's command confused them. Ordinarily they would have ignored the philosopher and listened for their general's orders, but Attalos was down on the grass and looking in amazement at the hole in his leg.

As one soldier dropped his spear and started to run, a blow on the head sent a flash of light through my skull and hurled me to the ground, nearly unconscious. A man behind me had swung his spear like a club and struck me on the pate with the shaft.

Before I could recover, they were all over me, raining kicks and blows. One wrenched the gun from my hand. I must have lost consciousness, for the next thing I remember is lying in the dirt while the soldiers tore off my tunic. Attalos stood over me with a bloody bandage around his leg, leaning on a soldier. He looked pale and frightened but resolute. The second man I had shot lay still.

"So that is where he keeps his infernal devices!" said Attalos, indicating my belt. "Take it off, men."

The soldiers struggled with the clasp of the belt until one impatiently sawed through the straps with his dagger. The gold in my money pouch brought cries of delight.

I struggled to get up, but a pair of soldiers knelt on my arms to keep me down. There was a continuous mumble of talk. Attalos, looking over the belt, said:

"He is too dangerous to live. Even stripped as he is, who knows but what he will soar into the air and escape by magic?"

"Do not kill him!" said Aristotle. "He has much valuable knowledge to impart."

"No knowledge is worth the safety of the kingdom."

"But the kingdom can benefit from his knowledge. Do you not agree?" Aristotle asked the Persian.

"Drag me not into this, pray," said Artavazda. "It is no concern of mine."

"If he is a danger to Makedonia, he should be destroyed at once," said Attalos.

"There is but little chance of his doing harm now," said Aristotle, "and an excellent chance of his doing us good."

"Any chance of his doing harm is too much," said Attalos. "You philosophers can afford to be tolerant of interesting strangers. But, if they carry disaster in their baggage, it is on us poor soldiers that the brunt will fall. Is it not so, Artabazos?"

"I have done what you asked and will say no more," said Artavazda. "I am but a simple-minded Persian nobleman who does not understand your Greek subtleties."

"I can increase the might of your armies, General!" I cried to Attalos.

"No doubt, and no doubt you can also turn men to stone with an incantation, as the Gorgons did with their glance." He drew his sword and felt the edge with his thumb.

"You will slay him for mere thuperstition!" walled Aristotle, wringing his hands. "At least, let the king judge the matter."

"Not superstition," said Attalos; "murder." He pointed to the dead soldier.

"I come from another world! Another age!" I yelled, but Attalos was not to be diverted.

"Let us get this over with," he said. "Set him on his knees, men. Take my sword, Glaukos; I am too unsteady to wield it. Now bow your head, my dear barbarian, and—"

In the middle of Attalos' sentence, he and the others and all my surroundings vanished. Again there came that sharp pain and sense of being jerked by a monstrous catapult . . .

I FOUND MYSELF lying in leaf mold with the pearl-gray trunks of poplars all around me. A brisk breeze was making the poplar leaves flutter and show their silvery bottoms. It was too cool for a man who was naked save for sandals and socks.

I had snapped back to the year 1981 of the calendar of my world, which I had set out from. But where was I? I should be near the site of the Brookhaven National Laboratories in a vastly improved super-scientific world. There was, however, no sign of super-science here; nothing but poplar trees.

I got up, groaning, and looked around. I was covered with bruises and bleeding from nose and mouth.

The only way I had of orienting myself was the boom of a distant surf. Shivering, I hobbled towards the sound. After a few hundred paces, I came out of the forest on a beach. This beach could be the shore of Sewanhaki, or Long Island as we called it, but there was no good way of telling. There was no sign of human life; just the beach curving into the distance and disappearing around headlands, with the poplar forest on one side and the ocean on the other.

What, I wondered, had happened? Had science advanced so fast as a result of my intervention that man had already exterminated himself by scientific warfare? Thinkers of my world had concerned themselves with this possibility, but I had never taken it seriously.

It began to rain. In despair I cast myself down on the sand and beat it with my fists. I may have lost consciousness again.

At any rate, the next thing I knew was the now-familiar sound of hooves. When I looked up, the horseman was almost upon me, for the sand had muffled the animal's footsteps until it was quite close.

I blinked with incredulity. For an instant I thought I must be back in the classical era still. The man was a warrior armed and armored in a style much like that of ancient times. At first he seemed to be wearing a helmet of classical Hellenic type. When he came closer I saw that this was not quite true, for the crest was made of feathers instead of horsehair. The nasal and cheek plates hid most of his face, but he seemed dark and beardless. He wore a shirt of scale mail, long leather trousers, and low shoes. He had a bow and a small shield hung from his saddle and a slender lance slung across his back by a strap. I saw that this could not be ancient times because the horse was fitted with a large, well-molded saddle and stirrups.

As I watched the man stupidly, he whisked the lance out of its boot and couched it. He spoke in an unknown language.

I got up, holding my hands over my head in surrender. The man kept repeating his question, louder and louder, and making jabbing motions. All I could say was "I don't understand" in the languages I knew, none of which seemed familiar to him.

Finally he maneuvered his horse around to the other side of me, barked a command, pointed along the beach the way he had come, and prodded me with the butt of the lance. Off I limped, with rain, blood, and tears running down my hide.

You know the rest, more or less. Since I could not give an intelligible account of myself, the Sachim of Lenape, Wayotan the Fat, claimed me as a slave. For fourteen years I labored on his estate at such occupations as feeding hogs and chopping kindling. When Wayotan died and the present Sachim was elected, he decided I was too old for that kind of work, especially as I was half crippled from the beatings of Wayotan and his overseers. Learning that I had some knowledge of letters (for I had picked up spoken and written Algonkian in spite of my wretched lot), he freed me and made me official librarian.

In theory I can travel about as I like, but I have done little of it. I am too old and weak for the rigors of travel in this world, and most other places are, as nearly as I can determine, about as barbarous as this one. Besides, a few Lenapes come to hear me lecture on the nature of man and the universe and the virtues of the scientific method. Perhaps I can light a small spark here after I failed in the year 340 B.C.

When I went to work in the library, my first thought was to find out what had happened to bring the world to its present pass.

Wayotan's predecessor had collected a considerable library that Wayotan had neglected, so that some of the books had been chewed by rats and others ruined by dampness. Still, there was enough to give me a good sampling of the literature of this world, from ancient to modern times. There were even Herodotos' history and Plato's dialogues, identical with the versions that existed in my own world.

I had to struggle against more language barriers, as the European languages of this world are different from, though related to, those of my own world. The English of today, for instance, is more like the Dutch of my own world, as a result of England's never having been conquered by the Normans.

I also had the difficulty of reading without eyeglasses. Luckily, most of these manuscript books are written in a large, clear hand. A couple of years ago I did get a pair of glasses, imported from China, where the invention of the printing press has stimulated their manufacture. But, as they are a recent invention in this world, they are not so effective as those of mine.

I rushed through all the history books to find out when and how your history diverged from mine. I found that differences appeared quite early. Alexander still marched to the Indus but failed to die at thirty-two on his return. In fact he lived fifteen years longer and fell at last in battle with the Sarmatians in the Caucasus Mountains.

I do not know why that brief contact with me enabled him to avoid the malaria mosquito that slew him in my world. Maybe I aroused in him a keener interest in India than he would otherwise have had, leading him to stay there longer so that all his subsequent schedules were changed. His empire held together for most of a century instead of breaking up right after his death as it did in my world.

The Romans still conquered the whole Mediterranean, but the course of their conquests and the names of the prominent Romans were all different. Two of the chief religions of my world, Christianity and Islam, never appeared at all. Instead we have Mithraism, Odinism, and Soterism, the last an Egypto-Hellenic synthesis founded by that fiery Egyptian prophet whose followers call him by the Greek word for "savior."

Still, classical history followed the same *general* course that it had in my world, even though the actors bore other names. The Roman Empire broke up, as it did in my world, though the details are all different, with a Hunnish emperor ruling in Rome and a Gothic one in Antioch.

It is after the fall of the Roman Empire that profound differences appear. In my world there was a revival of learning that began about nine hundred years ago, followed by a scientific revolution beginning four centuries later. In your history the revival of learning was centuries later, and the scientific revolution has hardly begun. Failure to develop the compass and the full-rigged ship resulted in North America's (I mean Hesperia's) being discovered and settled via the northern route, by way of Iceland, and more slowly than in my world. Failure to invent the gun meant that the natives of Hesperia were not swept aside by the invading Europeans, but held their own against them and gradually learned their arts of iron-working, weaving, cereal-growing, and the like. Now most of the European settlements have been assimilated, though the ruling families of the Abnakis and Mohegans frequently have blue eyes and still call themselves by names like "Sven" and "Eric."

I was eager to get hold of a work by Aristotle, to see what effect I had had on him and to try to relate this effect to the subsequent course of history. From allusions in some of the works in this library I gathered that many of his writings had come down to modern times, though the titles all seemed different from those of his surviving works in my world. The only actual samples of his writings in the library were three essays, *Of Justice, On Education,* and *Of Passions and Anger*. None of these showed my influence.

I had struggled through most of the Sachim's collection when I found the key I was looking for. This was an Iberic translation of *Lives of the Great Philosophers*, by one Diomedes of Mazaka. I never heard of Diomedes in the literary history of my own world, and perhaps he never existed. Anyway, he had a long chapter on Aristotle, in which appears the following section:

> Now Aristotle, during his sojourn at Mytilene, had been an assiduous student of natural sciences. He had planned, according to Timotheus, a series of works that should correct the errors of Empedokles, Demokritos, and others of his predecessors. But, after he had removed to Macedonia and busied himself with the education of

Alexander, there one day appeared before him a traveler, Sandos of Palibothra, a mighty philosopher of India.

The Indian ridiculed Aristotle's attempts at scientific research, saying that in his land these investigations had gone far beyond anything the Hellenes had attempted, and the Indians were still a long way from arriving at satisfactory explanations of the universe. Moreover, he asserted that no real progress could be made in natural philosophy unless the Hellenes abandoned their disdain for physical labor and undertook exhaustive experiments with mechanical devices of the sort that cunning Egyptian and Asiatic craftsmen make.

King Philip, hearing of the presence of this stranger in his land and fearing lest he be a spy sent by some foreign power to harm or corrupt the young prince, came with soldiers to arrest him. But, when he demanded that Sandos accompany him back to Pella, the latter struck dead with thunderbolts all the king's soldiers that were with him. Then, it is said, mounting into his chariot drawn by winged gryphons, he flew off in the direction of India. But other authorities say that the man who came to arrest Sandos was Antipatros, the regent, and that Sandos cast darkness before the eyes of Antipatros and Aristotle, and when they recovered from their swoon he had vanished.

Aristotle, reproached by the king for harboring so dangerous a visitor and shocked by the sanguinary ending of the Indian's visit, resolved to have no more to do with the sciences. For, as he explains in his celebrated treatise *On the Folly of Natural Science*, there are three reasons why no good Hellene should trouble his mind with such matters.

One is that the number of facts that must be mastered before sound theories become possible is so vast that if all the Hellenes did nothing else for centuries, they would still not gather the amount of data required. The task is therefore futile.

Secondly, experiments and mechanical inventions are necessary to progress in science, and such work, though all very well for slavish Asiatics, who have a natural bent for it, is beneath the dignity of a Hellenic gentleman.

And, lastly, some of the barbarians have already surpassed the Hellenes in this activity, wherefore it ill becomes the Hellenes to compete with their inferiors in skills at which the latter have an inborn advantage. They should rather cultivate personal rectitude, patriotic valor, political rationality, and aesthetic sensitivity, leaving to the barbarians such artificial aids to the good and virtuous life as are provided by scientific discoveries.

This was it, all right. The author had gotten some of his facts wrong, but that was to be expected from an ancient historian.

So! My teachings had been too successful. I had so well shattered the naïve self-confidence of the Hellenic philosophers as to discourage them from going on with science at all.

I should have remembered that glittering theories and sweeping generalizations, even when wrong, are the frosting on the cake; they are the carrot that makes the donkey go. The possibility of pronouncing such universals is the stimulus that keeps many scientists grinding away, year after year, at the accumulation of facts, even seemingly dull and trivial facts. If ancient scientists had realized how much laborious fact-finding lay ahead of them before sound theories would become possible, they would have been so appalled as to drop science altogether. And that is just what happened.

The sharpest irony of all was that I had placed myself where I could not undo my handiwork. If I had ended up in a scientifically advanced world, and did not like what I found, I might have built another time machine, gone back, and somehow warned myself of the mistake lying in wait for me. But such a project is out of the question in a backward world like this one, where seamless columbium tubing, for instance, is not even thought of. All I proved by my disastrous adventure is that space-time has a negative curvature, and who in this world cares about that?

You recall, when you were last here, asking me the mean-

ing of a motto in my native language on the wall of my cell. I
said I would tell you in connection with my whole fantastic
story. The motto says: "Leave Well Enough Alone," and I
wish I had.

Cordially yours,
Sherman Weaver

Sitka

William Sanders

William Sanders makes his home in Tahlequah, Oklahoma, but his formative years were spent in the hill country of western Arkansas. He appeared on the SF scene in the early '80s with a couple of alternate-history comedies, *Journey to Fusang* (a finalist for the John W. Campbell Award) and *The Wild Blue and the Gray*. Sanders then turned to mystery and suspense, before returning to SF, this time via the short story form; his stories have appeared in *Asimov's Science Fiction*, *The Magazine of Fantasy and Science Fiction*, and numerous anthologies, earning himself a well-deserved reputation as one of the best short-fiction writers of the last decade, and winning him two Sidewise Awards for Best Alternate History story. He has also returned to novel writing, with books such as *The Ballad of Billy Badass and the Rose of Turkestan* and *The Bernadette Operations*, a new SF novel *J.*, and a mystery novel, *Smoke*. Some of his acclaimed short stories have been collected in *Are We Having Fun Yet? American Indian Fantasy Stories*. His most recent book is a historical study, *Conquest: Hernando de Soto and the Indians: 1539–1543*. Coming up is a new collection, *Is It Now Yet?* (Most of his books, including

reissues of his earlier novels, are available from Wildside Press
or on Amazon.com.)

In the sharp little story that follows, he escorts us around
the town of Sitka, which proves to be a very cold place, even in
the summertime . . . especially when world-altering change is
in the air—at any cost.

LATE IN THE afternoon, a little before sundown, the fog
moved in off the ocean and settled in over the islands and
peninsulas of the coast. It wasn't much of a fog, by the stan-
dards of Russian America in late summer; just enough to
mask the surface of the sea and soften the rough outlines of
the land.

On the waterfront in the town of New Arkhangelsk, on the
western side of the big island that the Russians called Baranof
and the natives called Sitka, two men stood looking out over
the harbor. "Perfect," one of them said. "If it'll stay like this."

The other man looked at him. "Perfect, Jack? How so?"

The first man flung out a hand. "Hell, just look. See how
it's hanging low over the water?"

The other man turned back toward the harbor, following
his gesture. He stood silently for a moment, seeing how the
fog curled around the hulls of the anchored ships while leaving their upper works exposed. The nearest, a big deepwater
steamer, was all but invisible down near the waterline, yet her
masts and funnels showed clear and black against the hills beyond the harbor, and the flag of the Confederate States of
America was clearly recognizable at her stern.

"Perfect," the man called Jack said again. "Just enough to
hide a small boat, but not enough to hide a ship. Less chance
of a mistake."

He was a powerfully built young man with curly blond hair
and a tanned, handsome face. His teeth flashed white in the
fading light. "After all," he said, "we don't want to get the
wrong one, do we, Vladimir?"

The man called Vladimir, whose last name was Ulyanov and
who sometimes called himself Lenin, closed his eyes and shud-

dered slightly. "No, that would be very bad." His English was excellent but strongly accented. "Don't even joke about it."

"Don't worry," the younger man said. "We'll get her for you."

"Not for me. You know better than that."

"Yeah, all right. For the cause." Jack slapped him lightly on the upper arm, making him wince. "Hey, I'm a good socialist too. You know that."

"So you have assured me," Lenin said dryly. "Otherwise I might suspect—"

He stopped suddenly as a pair of long-bearded Orthodox monks walked past. Jack said, "What," and then, "Oh, hell. Vladimir, don't you ever relax? I bet they don't even speak English."

Lenin looked after the two black-robed figures and shook his head. "Two years away from the twentieth century," he murmured, "and still the largest country in the world is ruled by medieval superstition. . . ."

He turned to the younger man. "We shouldn't be standing here like this. It looks suspicious. And believe me," he said as Jack started to speak, "to the people we are dealing with, *everything* looks suspicious. Trust me on this."

He jerked his head in the direction of a nearby saloon. "Come," he said. "Let us have a drink, Comrade London."

As THE TWO men started down the board sidewalk, a trio of dark-faced women suddenly appeared from the shadows and fell in alongside, smiling and laughing. One of them grabbed Jack's arm and said something in a language that was neither English nor Russian. "For God's sake," Jack said, and started to pull free. "Just what we need, a bunch of Siwash whores."

"Wait." Lenin held up a hand. "Let them join us for now. With them along, no one will wonder what we are doing here."

"Huh. Yeah, all right. Good idea." Jack looked at the three women. They weren't bad-looking in a shabby sort of way. The one holding his arm had red ribbons in her long black hair. He laughed. "Too bad I'm going to be kind of busy this evening. Give them a bath, they might be good for some fun."

Lenin's nose twitched slightly. "You're not serious."

"Hell, no. I may be down on my luck but I'm still a white man."

Lenin winced. "Jack, I've got to talk to you some time about your—"

The saloon door swung open and a couple of drunken Cossacks staggered out, leaning on the unpainted timber wall for support. When they were past, Lenin led the way through the narrow doorway and into a long, low-ceilinged, poorly lit room full of rough wooden tables and benches where men, and a few women, sat drinking and talking and playing cards. An old man rested on a tall stool near the door, playing a slow minor-key tune on an accordion. The air was dense with smoke from cheap *mahorka* tobacco.

"There," Lenin said. "In the back, by the wall, where we can watch the door."

He strode up to the bar, pushing past a group of sailors in the white summer uniform of the Imperial German navy, and came back a moment later carrying a bottle and a couple of glasses. "One minute," he said, setting the glasses down and pouring, while Jack dragged up a bench and sat down. "I've got an idea."

Stepping over to the next table, Lenin beckoned to the three women. They looked blank. "Come," he said, in Russian and then in English, and at last they giggled in unison and moved over to join him. "Here." He set the bottle in the center of the table, making exaggerated sit-down motions with his free hand. "*Sadityes'*. You sit here," he said, speaking very slowly. He touched the bottle. "You can have this. *Ponimaitye?*"

As they seated themselves, with another flurry of giggles, Lenin came back and sat down across from Jack. "There," he said. "That's the only table in the place close enough for anyone to overhear us. Better to have it occupied by harmless idiots."

Jack snorted. "For God's sake, Vladimir!"

"Laugh if you like," Lenin said. "I don't take risks. Already I have been arrested—"

"Me too."

"Pardon me." Lenin's voice was very flat. "You have been arrested by stupid American policemen, who beat you and threw you in a cell for a few days and then made you leave town and forgot about you. You have been detained briefly, at a military outpost, for prospecting for gold without a permit. You have no idea what a Cheka interrogation is like. Or," he said, "what it is like to live under the eyes of a vigilant and well-organized secret police force and their network of informers."

He lifted his glass. "What is that American idiom? 'The walls have ears,' yes? In the Russian Empire they have both ears and eyes—and feet, to run and tell the men with the big boots what you say and do. Until you have been stepped on by those boots, you have no business to laugh at the caution of those who have."

AT THE NEXT table the woman with the red ribbons in her hair said, "I'm looking at him and I still don't believe it."

She said it in a language that was not spoken anywhere in that world.

The woman beside her pushed back her own hair, which was done up in thick braids that hung down to the swell of her bosom under her trade-blanket coat. She said in the same language, "Well, he *was* one of the great figures of history, for better or worse."

"Not Lenin," the woman with the red ribbons said impatiently. "Jack London. He's gorgeous. The pictures didn't even come close."

Across the table, the third woman was doing something with one of the seashell ornaments that dangled from her ears. She looked over at the men's table for a moment and then smiled and nodded without speaking.

"Hand me that bottle," the one with the red ribbons said. "I think I'm in love."

• • •

"OF COURSE," LENIN said, "for me things did perhaps work out for the best. Siberia wasn't pleasant, but it gave me time to think, to organize my ideas. And then the authorities decided to send some of the Siberian exiles even farther away, to this remote American outpost of the empire, and in time this presented . . . possibilities."

Jack gave a meaningless grunt and reached for his own glass, staring off across the room. The German sailors were clustered around the accordion player, who was trying to accompany them on "Du, Du Liegst Mir Am Herzen." Some of the Russians were giving them dirty looks but they didn't seem to notice.

"That's right," Jack muttered. "Sing, have yourselves a good time. Get drunk, find some whores, get skinned in a rigged card game. Just for God's sake don't go back to the ship tonight."

THE WOMAN WITH the red ribbons said, "He looks a lot younger. Than Lenin, I mean."

"Only six years' difference in their ages," the woman with the braids said. "But you're right. Or rather, Lenin looks older—"

"Sh." The other woman raised a finger, still fiddling with her seashell ear pendants. "Quiet. I've almost—there. There." She dropped her hands to her lap and sat back. "Locked on and recording."

"All right," the woman with the red ribbons said. She reached up and pushed back her hair with a casual-looking motion, her hand barely brushing the area of her own ear. A moment later the woman beside her did something similar.

"Oh," the one with the red ribbons said. "Yes. Nice and clear. All this background noise, too, I'm impressed."

The one with the braids said, "Speaking of background noise, we need to generate some. We're being too quiet. We're supposed to be cheap whores drinking free vodka. Time to laugh it up again."

•   •   •

LENIN GLANCED OVER at the next table as the three women broke into another fit of noisy giggles. "They seem to be making inroads on that bottle," Lenin said. "If you want any more, you'd better go get it before they finish it off."

"They're welcome to it," Jack said. He looked at his own glass and grimaced. "Damn vodka tastes like something you'd rub on a horse. How the hell do you people stand it?"

"Practice."

"Yeah, well, better you than me. What I'd give for a taste of good old honest John Barleycorn."

"It's available," Lenin said. "Though probably not in a place like this. It's just very expensive, like everything else not made in Russia, thanks to the exorbitant import duties. Another blessing from our beloved official bureaucracy."

"Tell me about it," Jack said. "Came up here figuring to dig some gold, make a little something for myself instead of always being broke on my ass. Found out foreigners have to have a special permit to prospect or even to travel in the interior, no way to get it without paying off a bunch of crooks behind government desks. So I said the hell with it."

"And you were caught"

"Yep. Damn near went to jail, too, but by then I'd hit just enough pay dirt to be able to grease a certain Cossack officer. And here I am, broke on my ass again and a long way from home. I'm telling you, Vladimir," he said, "if you wanted somebody to blow up that bunch of greedy sons of bitches who run things here, I'd be your man and I wouldn't charge a nickel to do it."

He rubbed his face and sighed. "Instead I'm about to go blow the bottom out of a German battleship and kill a bunch of people who never did me any harm, all for the sake of the great workers' revolution. How about that?"

THE THREE WOMEN exchanged looks. The one with the red ribbons said. "No." She squeezed her eyes shut. *"No."*

"So it's true." The woman with the seashell ear pendants shook her head. "Incredible."

"Watch it," the one with the braids said, breaking into a

broad sloppy smile. "Lenin's already nervous—see, he's looking around again. Act drunk, damn it."

"That's easy," the woman with the red ribbons said, reaching for the vodka bottle. "After hearing that, I *need* a drink."

"IN FACT," LENIN said, "you are doing it for the price of a ticket back to your own country. Not that I question your socialist convictions, but right now you would blow up your own mother—"

Jack's hand shot across the table and clamped down on Lenin's forearm. "Don't you ever speak to me about my mother," he said thickly. "You got that?"

Lenin sat very still. His face had gone pale and there were pain lines at the corners of his mouth. "Yes," he said in a carefully even voice. "Yes, I apologize."

"Okay, then." Jack let go and gulped at his drink. "Just watch it."

Lenin rubbed his forearm. After a moment he said, "Go easy on that vodka. You're going to need a clear head and steady hands tonight."

Jack gave a short, harsh laugh. "Save your breath. Even I'm not fool enough to tie one on when I'm going to be handling dynamite in the dark. Make a mistake with that much giant, it'd be raining Jack London for a week. Mixed up with a couple of Aleut paddlers, too, they'd never get the pieces sorted out."

He sipped his drink again, more cautiously. "Not that it's all that tricky a job," he added. "Nothing to it, really. Come alongside the *Brandenburg*, just forward of her aft turret, so we're next to the powder magazine. Arm the mine, start the timer—neat piece of work there, your pal Iosif knows what he's doing—and ease the whole thing up against the hull till the magnets take hold, being careful not to let it clang. Take the forked stick and slide the mine down under the waterline, below the armor belt, and then tell the boys to high-tail it. Hell, anybody could do it."

He grinned crookedly. "When you get right down to it, you only need me to make sure we get the right ship. Those Aleuts are the best paddlers in the world, but they wouldn't know the *Brandenburg* from the *City of New Orleans*."

THE WOMAN WITH the braids said, "You know, I never believed it. I got into some pretty hot arguments, in fact. 'Ridiculous' was one of the milder words I used."

The one with the seashell ear pendants said, "Well, you were hardly alone. All the authorities agree that Jack London's involvement in the *Brandenburg* affair is merely a romantic legend, circulated by a few revisionist crackpots. I don't know any responsible scholar who takes it seriously."

She chuckled softly. "And oh, is the shit going to fly in certain circles when we get back! I can hardly wait."

"NOT QUITE TRUE," Lenin said. "I also need you to make sure that our aboriginal hirelings don't change their minds and run away home with their advance money. If they haven't already done so."

"Oh, they wouldn't do that. See," Jack said, "they think it's a Russian ship we're after."

Lenin's eyebrows went up. "You told them that?"

"Hell, I had to tell them something. So they'll be there. The way they hate Russians, they wouldn't pass up a chance like this. Christ," Jack said, "I know we did some rotten things to the Indians in the States, but compared to what your people did to those poor devils . . ."

"Oh, yes. The exploitation of native peoples, here and in Asia, has been one of the worst crimes of the Tsarist state."

"Yeah, well," Jack said, "all I'm saying, the boys will do their job and I'll do mine. Quit worrying about it."

"HEY," THE WOMAN with the braids said. "Go easy on that stuff. You're going to make yourself sick."

"I'm already sick," the woman with the red ribbons said. "Just thinking about it, sitting here listening to them talk about it, seeing it about to happen, I'm as sick as I've ever been my life. Aren't you?"

• • •

"Now what happens after that," Jack said, "whether things turn out the way you want, I can't guarantee. I'll sink the ship for you, but if it doesn't get you your war, don't come to me wanting a refund."

Lenin's lips twitched in what was very nearly a smile. "That," he said, "is perhaps the surest part of the entire business. Believe me, nothing is more predictable than the reaction of the Kaiser to the sinking of one of his precious warships in a Russian port."

"Really? I don't know as much as I should about things like that," Jack admitted. "Foreign rulers and all, I need to read up . . . but I can see how it would make him pretty mad. Mad enough to go to war, though?"

"Wilhelm will be furious," Lenin said. "But also secretly delighted. At last he will have a pretext for the war he has wanted for so long."

Jack frowned. "He's crazy?"

"Not mad, no. Merely a weakling—a cripple and, according to rumor, a homosexual—determined to prove his manhood by playing the great warrior."

"Ah." Jack nodded slowly. "A punk trying to pick a fight to show he's not a punk. Yeah, I know the kind. Saw a good many of them when I was riding the rails."

"Even so. Wilhelm has been looking for a fight ever since ascending the throne. Since no one has so far obliged him, he contents himself with playing the bully."

Lenin nodded in the direction of the German sailors, who were now roaring out "Ach, Du Lieber Augustin" in somewhat approximate harmony. "As for example this little 'goodwill cruise,'" he said. "This series of visits to various ports by a *Hochseeflotte* battleship. Nothing but a crude show of force to impress the world."

"Showing everybody who's the boss?"

"Exactly. And therefore its destruction will be taken as a response to a challenge."

"Hm. Okay, you know more about it than I do." Jack shrugged. "Still seems pretty strange, though, starting a war hoping your own country will get whipped."

"I don't like it," Lenin said. "I am Russian, after all, and this isn't easy for me. But there is no better breeding ground for revolution than a major military defeat. Look at France."

"The Communards lost, didn't they?"

"True. They made mistakes, from which we have learned."

"IF HE SAYS anything about omelettes and eggs," the woman with the red ribbons said through her teeth, "I'm going to go over there and beat his brains out with this bottle. Screw the mission and screw non-interference and screw temporal paradox. I don't care. I'll kill him."

JACK SAID, "You know, the joke's really going to be on you if Russia wins."

"Not much chance of that. Russia's armed forces are a joke, fit only to keep the Tatars in line and occasionally massacre a village of Jews. The officers are mostly incompetent buffoons, owing their rank to family connections rather than ability. The troops are badly trained, and their equipment is decades out of date. The German military on the other hand, are very nearly as good as they think they are."

"Russia's a big country, though."

"Yes. A big country with too much territory to protect. A German offensive in the west, a Japanese attack in the east—it will be too much. You'll see."

"You're awfully sure the Japs are going to come into it."

"Comrade London," Lenin said softly, "where do you think our funds come from? Who do you think is paying for this business tonight?"

THE THREE WOMEN stared at one another. "Now that," the one with the braids said after a moment, "is going to knock *everyone* on their butts."

"THE JAPS ARE bankrolling us?" Jack said incredulously. "For God's sake, why?"

"They have territorial ambitions in Asia. Russia has become an obstacle. A war in Europe would create opportunities."

"Damn." Jack looked unhappy. "I don't know if I like that part. Working for Orientals against white—all right, all right," he said quickly, seeing Lenin's expression. "I didn't say I wouldn't do it. All I want is to get back home. I don't really care if I have to go to work for the Devil."

He looked at Lenin over the rim of his glass. "If I haven't already. . . ."

"OH, DEAR," THE woman with the braids said. "He does have some unfortunate racial attitudes, doesn't he?"

"So did Ernest Hemingway," the one with the red ribbons said without looking up from the bottle. "And I thought we were going to have to peel you off him with a steam hose."

"THE INTERESTING QUESTION," Lenin said, "is whether the other European countries will become involved. The French may well decide that this is an opportunity to settle old scores with Germany. The others, who knows? This could turn into a general conflict, like nothing since Napoleon."

"What the hell. As long as the United States doesn't get involved," Jack said. "And that's not going to happen. We've just barely *got* an army, and they're still busy with the Indians. The Confederates, now, they just might be crazy enough to get in on it."

"If the war spreads, so much the better," Lenin said. "Because if it spreads, so will the revolution."

He took out a heavy, silver pocket watch and snapped it open. "And now I think we should be going. It is still several hours, but we both have things we must do."

He started to push himself back from the table. Jack said, "Wait. Just one more thing."

Lenin sank back onto the bench. Jack said, "See, I've been thinking. Suppose somebody were to hire somebody to do something against the law. And maybe the man doing the hiring was the cautious type, and wanted to make sure the other bastard didn't get talkative afterward. Maybe the law might catch him and beat the story out of him, maybe he might just get drunk and shoot his mouth off. I mean, you never know, do you?"

Jack's voice was casual, his expression bland; he might have been asking about a good place to eat.

"But when the job involves a bomb," he said, "then there's one sure way to make sure the man never talks, isn't there? With the little added bonus that you don't have to pay him. Not," he added quickly, "that I'm suggesting anything. I don't really think you'd do something like that. Not to a good old revolutionary comrade."

He leaned forward, staring into Lenin's eyes. "But just in case I'm wrong, you might be interested to know that a few things have been written down and left in safe hands, and if I don't make it back tonight there are some people who will be reading them with deep interest by this time tomorrow."

Lenin sat unmoving, returning the younger man's stare, for perhaps five seconds. Then he laughed out loud. "*Nu, molodyets!*" He slapped the table with his palm. "Congratulations, Comrade London. At last you are learning to think like a Russian."

"Looks like they're leaving," the woman with the braids said. "Do we follow them, or—"

The woman with the red ribbons said, "I can't stand this."

Suddenly she was on her feet, moving very fast, brushing past Lenin and grabbing Jack by the arms, pushing him back against the wall. "Listen," she said, speaking quickly but with great care, "listen, you mustn't do this. You're about to start the most terrible war in your world's history. Millions of people will die and nothing will come of it but suffering and destruction. Listen," she said again, her voice rising. "You have a great talent—"

Jack stood looking down at her, open-mouthed, as her voice grew higher and louder. "Damn!" he said finally. "Vladimir, did you ever hear the like? Sorry, honey." He reached up and pulled her hands away, not roughly. "Me no speak Tlingit, or whatever the hell that is."

He grinned and slapped her bottom. "Run along, now. Big white brothers got heap business."

And to Lenin, "Give her a few kopecks, would you, or she'll follow me like a hound pup. And then let's get out of here."

THE WOMAN WITH the red ribbons said, "But I *heard* myself speaking English!"

They were climbing slowly up a hillside above the town of New Arkhangelsk. It was dark now, but the stars gave a good deal of light and the fog didn't reach this high.

The woman with the shell ear pendants, walking in the lead, said without looking around, "That's how it works. Don't ask me why. Some quirk of the conditioning program."

"It was covered in training," the third woman said. "Don't tell me you forgot something that basic. But then as much vodka as you put away, it's a wonder you can remember where you left your own ass . . . you didn't take the anti-intoxicants, did you?"

"They make my skin itch."

"Gods." The woman with the braids raised her hands in a helpless flapping motion. "You're a menace, you know? One of these days we're going to stop covering for you."

"No, we won't," the woman in the lead said. "We'll cover for her this time—going to be a job doctoring the recording, but I can do it—and we'll keep on covering for her. For the same reason she's helped cover for us, when we lost it or just blew it. The same reason everyone covers for their partners. Because when you're out on the timelines there's no one else you can depend on and when you're back home there's no one else who really knows what it was like."

She stopped. "Hold on. It's getting a little tricky."

She took out a pair of oddly shaped goggles and slipped them on. "All right," she said. "Stay close behind me. It shouldn't be much farther."

THE ALEUTS WERE waiting in the shadow of a clump of cedars as Jack came walking down the beach. *"Zdras'tye,"* one of them said, stepping out and raising a hand. "We ready. Go now?"

"*Da.* Go now." Jack's gold-field Russian was even worse than their pidgin. "Uh, *gdye baidarka?*"

"*Von tam.*" The man gestured and Jack saw it now, a long, low black shape pulled up on the shore.

"*Harasho.*" Jack made a come-on gesture and the two men followed him down to the water's edge. His boots made soft crunching sounds in the damp sand. Theirs made none at all.

Together they lifted the big three-man sea kayak and eased it out until it floated free. Jack slid the heavy pack off his back, while the two Aleuts began the elaborate process of cleaning their feet and clothing, getting rid of any sand that might damage the boat's sealskin covering.

The forward paddler said cheerfully, "We go kill Russians, *da?*"

"Oh, yes," Jack said in English. "More than you know, you poor ignorant bastard. More than you'll ever know."

THE WOMAN WITH the red ribbons said, "I'm sorry. I let it get to me and I'm sorry." She turned her head to look at the other two. "It's just the stupid stinking *waste* of it all."

They were well up on the hillside now, sitting on the trunk of a fallen tree, facing out over the dark fog-blanketed harbor. It was the last hour before midnight.

The woman with the seashell ear pendants said, "It was a dreadful war, all right. One of the worst in all the lines—"

"Not that. All right, that too, but I meant him. Jack London," the woman with the red ribbons said. "You know what happens to him after this. He's going to ruin himself with drink and then shoot himself in another five years, and never write anything in a class with his best work from the other lines. And now we know why, don't we?"

"Guilt? Yes," the woman with the seashell ear pendants said. "Probably. But that's just it. He *is* going to do those things, just as he *is* going to sink the *Brandenburg* tonight, because he's already *done* them and there's nothing you can do about it."

She raised a hand and stroked the red-ribboned hair. "And that's what gets to you, isn't it? The inevitability. That's what gets to all of us. That's why we burn out so soon."

The woman with the braids said, "How many known time-lines are there, now, that have been mapped back this far?"

"I don't know." The woman with the seashell ear pendants shrugged. "Well over a hundred, the last I heard."

"And so far not a single one where it didn't happen. One way or another, a huge and bloody world war always breaks out, invariably over something utterly stupid, some time within the same twenty-year bracket. Talk about inevitability."

"I know all that," the woman with the red ribbons said. "But this is the first time I've had to watch it happening. With someone I cared about getting destroyed by it."

She put an arm around the woman beside her and laid her head on her shoulder, making the seashell ear pendants clack softly. "How much longer?" she said.

"Not long. Any time now."

They sat looking out into the darkness, watching for the tall flame that would mark the end of yet another world.

The Only Game in Town

Poul Anderson

If you're going to have people traveling back in time and changing the present by altering the past, then it makes sense that eventually an organization would evolve to try to *stop* them. That's the premise behind Poul Anderson's famous "Time Patrol" stories, such as the taut and fast-paced adventure that follows, in which it's demonstrated that even those who enforce the rules sometimes have to know when to break them . . .

One of the best-known writers in science fiction, the late Poul Anderson made his first sale in 1947, while he was still in college, and in the course of his subsequent fifty-four-year career published almost a hundred books (in several different fields, as Anderson wrote historical novels, fantasies, and mysteries, in addition to SF), sold hundreds of short pieces to every conceivable market, and won seven Hugo Awards, three Nebula Awards, and the Tolkein Memorial Award for life achievement.

In spite of his high output of fiction, Anderson somehow managed to maintain an amazingly high standard of literary quality as well, and by the mid '60s was also on his way to becoming one of the most honored and respected writers in the genre. At one point during this period (in addition to nonrelated work, and lesser series such as the "Hoka" stories he was writing in collaboration with Gordon R. Dickson), Anderson was running three of the most popular and prestigious series in science fiction *all at the same time*: the Technic History series detailing the exploits of the wily trader Nicholas Van Rijn (which includes novels such as *The Man Who Counts*, *The Trouble Twisters*, *Satan's World*, *Mirkheim*, *The People of the Wind*, and collections such as *Trader to the Stars* and *The Earth Book of Stormgate*); the extremely popular series relating the adventures of interstellar secret agent Dominic Flandry, probably the most successful attempt to cross science fiction with the spy thriller, next to Jack Vance's Demon Princes novels (the Flandry series includes novels such as *A Circus of Hells*, *The Rebel Worlds*, *The Day of Their Return*, *Flandry of Terra*, *A Knight of Ghosts and Shadows*, *A Stone in Heaven*, and *The Game of Empire*, and collections such as *Agent of the Terran Empire*); and, my own personal favorite, a series that took us along on assignment with the agents of the Time Patrol (including the collections *The Guardians of Time*, *Time Patrolman*, *The Shield of Time*, and *The Time Patrol*).

When you add to this amazing collection of memorable titles the impact of the best of Anderson's nonseries novels, work such as *Brain Wave*, *Three Hearts and Three Lions*, *The Night Face*, *The Enemy Stars*, and *The High Crusade*, all of which was being published in *addition* to the series books, it becomes clear that Anderson dominated the late '50s and the pre–New Wave '60s in a way that only Robert A. Heinlein, Isaac Asimov, and Arthur C. Clarke could rival. Anderson, in fact, would continue to be an active and dominant figure for the rest of the twentieth century and on into the next, continuing to produce strong and innovative work until the very end of his life, winning the John W. Campbell Award for his novel *Genesis* just months before his death in 2001.

Anderson's other books (among *many* others) include: *The Broken Sword*, *Tau Zero*, *A Midsummer Tempest*, *Orion Shall*

*Rise, The Boat of a Million Years, Harvest of Stars, The Fleet
of Stars, Starfarers,* and *Operation Luna.* His short work has
been collected in *The Queen of Air and Darkness and Other
Stories, Fantasy, The Unicorn Trade* (with Karen Anderson),
Past Times, The Best of Poul Anderson, Explorations, and *All
One Universe.* Anderson died in 2001. The last book published
in his lifetime was the novel *Genesis.* Two novels, *Mother of
Kings* and *For Love and Glory,* and a new collection, *Going For
Infinity,* have been published posthumously.

1

JOHN SANDOVAL DID not belong to his name. Nor did it
seem right that he should stand in slacks and aloha shirt before an apartment window opening on midtwentieth-century
Manhattan. Everard was used to anachronism, but the dark
hooked face confronting him always seemed to want
warpaint, a horse, and a gun sighted on some pale thief.

"Okay," he said. "The Chinese discovered America. Interesting, but why does the fact need my services?"

"I wish to hell I knew," Sandoval answered.

His rangy form turned about on the polar-bear rug, which
Bjarni Herjulfsson had once given to Everard, until he was
staring outward. Towers were sharp against a clear sky; the
noise of traffic was muted by height. His hands clasped and
unclasped behind his back.

"I was ordered to co-opt an Unattached agent, go back
with him and take whatever measures seemed indicated," he
went on after a while. "I knew you best, so . . ." His voice
trailed off.

"But shouldn't you get an Indian like yourself?" asked
Everard. "I'd seem rather out of place in thirteenth-century
America."

"So much the better. Make it impressive, mysterious. . . . It
won't be too tough a job, really."

"Of course not," said Everard. "Whatever the job actually
is."

He took pipe and tobacco pouch from his disreputable-

smoking jacket and stuffed the bowl in quick, nervous jabs.
One of the hardest lessons he had had to learn, when first re-
cruited into the Time Patrol, was that every important task
does not require a vast organization. That was the characteris-
tic twentieth-century approach; but earlier cultures, like
Athenian Hellas and Kamakura Japan—and later civilizations
too, here and there in history—had concentrated on the development of individual excellence. A single graduate of the Patrol Academy (equipped, to be sure, with tools and weapons
of the future) could be the equivalent of a brigade.

But it was a matter of necessity as well as aesthetics. There
were all too few people to watch over all too many thousands
of years.

"I get the impression," said Everard slowly, "that this is not
a simple rectification of extratemporal interference."

"Right," said Sandoval in a harsh voice. "When I reported
what I'd found, the Yuan milieu office made a thorough investigation. No time travelers are involved. Kublai Khan thought
this up entirely by himself. He may have been inspired by
Marco Polo's accounts of Venetian and Arab sea voyages, but
it was legitimate history, even if Marco's book doesn't mention anything of the sort."

"The Chinese had quite a nautical tradition of their own,"
said Everard. "Oh, it's all very natural. So how do we come
in?"

He got his pipe lit and drew hard on it. Sandoval still
hadn't spoken, so he asked, "How did you happen to find this
expedition? It wasn't in Navajo country, was it?"

"Hell, I'm not confined to studying my own tribe," Sandoval answered. "Too few Amerinds in the Patrol as is, and
it's a nuisance disguising other breeds. I've been working on
Athabascan migrations generally." Like Keith Denison, he
was an ethnic Specialist, tracing the history of peoples who
never wrote their own so that the Patrol could know exactly
what the events were that it safeguarded.

"I was working along the eastern slope of the Cascades,
near Crater Lake," he went on. "That's Lutuami country, but I
had reason to believe an Athabascan tribe I'd lost track of had

passed that way. The natives spoke of mysterious strangers coming from the north. I went to have a look, and there the expedition was, Mongols with horses. I checked their back trail and found their camp at the mouth of the Chehalis River, where a few more Mongols were helping the Chinese sailors guard the ships. I hopped back upstairs like a bat out of Los Angeles and reported."

Everard sat down and stared at the other man. "How thorough an investigation did get made at the Chinese end?" he said. "Are you absolutely certain there was no extratemporal interference? It could be one of those unplanned blunders, you know, whose consequences aren't obvious for decades."

"I thought of that too, when I got my assignment," Sandoval nodded. "I even went directly to Yuan milieu HQ in Khan Baligh—Cambaluc, or Peking to you. They told me they'd checked it clear back to Genghis's lifetime, and spatially as far as Indonesia. And it was all perfectly okay, like the Norse and their Vinland. It simply didn't happen to have gotten the same publicity. As far as the Chinese court knew, an expedition had been sent out and had never returned, and Kublai decided it wasn't worthwhile to send another. The record of it lay in the Imperial archives, but was destroyed during the Ming revolt, which expelled the Mongols. Historiography forgot the incident."

Still Everard brooded. Normally he liked his work, but there was something abnormal about this occasion.

"Obviously," he said, "the expedition met a disaster. We'd like to know what. But why do you need an Unattached agent to spy on them?"

Sandoval turned from the window. It crossed Everard's mind again, fleetingly, how little the Navajo belonged here. He was born in 1930, had fought in Korea and gone through college on the G.I. bill before the Patrol contacted him, but somehow he never quite fitted the twentieth century.

Well, do any of us? Could any man with real roots stand knowing what will eventually happen to his own people?

"But I'm not supposed to spy!" Sandoval exclaimed. "When I'd reported, my orders came straight back from

Danellian headquarters. No explanation, no excuses, the naked command: to arrange that disaster. To revise history myself!"

2

ANNO DOMINI ONE Thousand Two Hundred Eighty:

The writ of Kublai Khan ran over degrees of latitude and longitude; he dreamed of world empire, and his court honored any guest who brought fresh knowledge or new philosophy. A young Venetian merchant named Marco Polo had become a particular favorite. But not all peoples desired a Mongol overlord. Revolutionary secret societies germinated throughout those several conquered realms lumped together as Cathay. Japan, with the Hojo family an able power behind the throne, had already repelled one invasion. Nor were the Mongols unified, save in theory. The Russian princes had become tax collectors for the Golden Horde; the Il-Khan Abaka sat in Baghdad.

Elsewhere, a shadowy Abbasid Caliphate had refuge in Cairo; Delhi was under the Slave Dynasty; Nicholas III was Pope; Guelphs and Ghibbelines were ripping up Italy; Rudolf of Habsburg was German Emperor, Philip the Bold was King of France, Edward Longshanks ruled England. Contemporaries included Dante Alighieri, Joannes Duns Scotus, Roger Bacon, and Thomas the Rhymer.

And in North America, Manse Everard and John Sandoval reined their horses to stare down a long hill.

"The date I first saw them is last week," said the Navajo. "They've come quite a ways since. At this rate, they'll be in Mexico in a couple of months, even allowing for some rugged country ahead."

"By Mongol standards," Everard told him, "they're proceeding leisurely."

He raised his binoculars. Around him, the land burned green with April. Even the highest and oldest beeches fluttered gay young leaves. Pines roared in the wind, which blew down off the mountains cold and swift and smelling of melted snow, through a sky where birds were homebound in such flocks that they could darken the sun. The peaks of the Cascade range seemed to float in the west, blue-white, distant, and holy. Eastward the foothills tumbled in clumps of forest and meadow to a valley, and so at last, beyond the horizon, to prairies thunderous under buffalo herds.

Everard focused on the expedition. It wound through the open areas, more or less following a small river. Some seventy men rode shaggy, dun-colored, short-legged, long-headed Asian horses. They led pack animals and remounts. He identified a few native guides, as much by their awkward seat in the saddle as by their physiognomy and clothing. But the newcomers held his attention most.

"A lot of pregnant mares toting packs," he remarked, half to himself. "I suppose they took as many horses in the ships as they could, letting them out to exercise and graze wherever they made a stop. Now they're breeding more as they go along. That kind of pony is tough enough to survive such treatment."

"The detachment at the ships is also raising horses," Sandoval informed him. "I saw that much."

"What else do you know about this bunch?"

"No more than I've told you, which is little more than you've now seen. And that record that lay for a while in Kublai's archives. But you recall, it barely notes that four ships under the command of the Noyon Toktai and the scholar Li Tai-Tsung were dispatched to explore the islands beyond Japan."

Everard nodded absently. No sense in sitting here and rehashing what they'd already gone over a hundred times. It was only a way of postponing action.

Sandoval cleared his throat. "I'm still dubious about both of us going down there," he said. "Why don't you stay in reserve, in case they get nasty?"

"Hero complex, huh?" said Everard. "No, we're better off together. I don't expect trouble anyhow. Not yet. Those boys are much too intelligent to antagonize anyone gratuitously. They've stayed on good terms with the Indians, haven't they?

And we'll be a far more unknown quantity. . . . I wouldn't
mind a drink beforehand, though."

"Yeh. And afterward, too!"

Each dipped in his saddlebag, took out a half-gallon canteen and hoisted it. The Scotch was pungent in Everard's
throat, heartening in his veins. He clucked to his horse and
both Patrolmen rode down the slope.

A whistling cut the air. They had been seen. He maintained
a steady pace toward the head of the Mongol line. A pair of
outriders closed in on either flank, arrows nocked to their
short powerful bows, but did not interfere.

I suppose we look harmless, Everard thought. Like Sandoval, he wore twentieth-century outdoor clothes: hunting
jacket to break the wind, hat to keep off the rain. His own outfit was a good deal less elegant than the Navajo's Abercrom-
bie & Fitch special. They both bore daggers for show, Mauser
machine pistols and thirtieth-century stun-beam projectors for
business.

The troop reined in, so disciplined that it was almost like
one man halting. Everard scanned them closely as he neared.
He had gotten a pretty complete electronic education in an
hour or so before departure—language, history, technology,
manners, morals—of Mongols and Chinese and even the local
Indians. But he had never before seen these people close up.

They weren't spectacular: stocky, bowlegged, with thin
beards and flat, broad faces that shone greased in the sunlight.
They were all well equipped, wearing boots and trousers, lam-
inated leather cuirasses with lacquer ornamentation, conical
steel helmets that might have a spike or plume on top. Their
weapons were curved sword, knife, lance, compound bow.
One man near the head of the line bore a standard of gold-
braided yak tails. They watched the Patrolmen approach, their
narrow dark eyes impassive.

The chief was readily identified. He rode in the van, and a
tattered silken cloak blew from his shoulders. He was rather
larger and even more hard-faced than his average trooper,
with a reddish beard and almost Roman nose. The Indian
guide beside him gaped and huddled back; but Toktai Noyon

held his place, measuring Everard with a steady carnivore look.

"Greeting," he called, when the newcomers were in earshot. "What spirit brings you?" He spoke the Lutuami dialect, which was later to become the Klamath language, with an atrocious accent.

Everard replied in flawless, barking Mongolian: "Greeting to you, Toktai son of Batu. The Tengri willing, we come in peace."

It was an effective touch. Everard glimpsed Mongols reaching for lucky charms or making signs against the evil eye. But the man mounted at Toktai's left was quick to recover a schooled self-possession. "Ah," he said, "so men of the Western lands have also reached this country. We did not know that."

Everard looked at him. He was taller than any Mongol, his skin almost white, his features and hands delicate. Though dressed much like the others, he was unarmed. He seemed older than the Noyon, perhaps fifty. Everard bowed in the saddle and switched to North Chinese: "Honored Li Tai-Tsung, it grieves this insignificant person to contradict your eminence, but we belong to the great realm farther south."

"We have heard rumors," said the scholar. He couldn't quite suppress excitement. "Even this far north, tales have been borne of a rich and splendid country. We are seeking it that we may bring your Khan the greeting of the Kha Khan, Kublai son of Tuli, son of Genghis; the earth lies at his feet."

"We know of the Kha Khan," said Everard, "as we know of the Caliph, the Pope, the Emperor, and all lesser monarchs." He had to pick his way with care, not openly insulting Cathay's ruler but still subtly putting him in his place. "Little is known in return of us, for our master does not seek the outside world, nor encourage it to seek him. Permit me to introduce my unworthy self. I am called Everard and am not, as my appearance would suggest, a Russian or Westerner. I belong to the border guardians."

Let them figure out what that meant.

"You didn't come with much company," snapped Toktai.

"More was not required," said Everard in his smoothest voice.

"And you are far from home," put in Li.

"No farther than you would be, honorable sirs, in the Kirghiz marches."

Toktai clapped a hand to his sword hilt. His eyes were chill and wary. "Come," he said. "Be welcome as ambassadors, then. Let's make camp and hear the word of your king."

3

THE SUN, LOW above the western peaks, turned their snowcaps tarnished silver. Shadows lengthened down in the valley, the forest darkened, but the open meadow seemed to glow all the brighter. The underlying quiet made almost a sounding board for such noises as existed: rapid swirl and cluck of the river, ring of an ax, horses cropping in long grass. Woodsmoke tinged the air.

The Mongols were obviously taken aback at their visitors and this early halt. They kept wooden faces, but their eyes would stray to Everard and Sandoval and they would mutter formulas of their various religions—chiefly pagan, but some Buddhist, Moslem, or Nestorian prayers. It did not impair the efficiency with which they set up camp, posted guard, cared for the animals, prepared to cook supper. But Everard judged they were more quiet than usual. The patterns impressed on his brain by the educator called Mongols talkative and cheerful as a rule.

He sat cross-legged on a tent floor. Sandoval, Toktai, and Li completed the circle. Rugs lay under them, and a brazier kept a pot of tea hot. It was the only tent pitched, probably the only one available, taken along for use on ceremonial occasions like this. Toktai poured *kumiss* with his own hands and offered it to Everard, who slurped as loudly as etiquette demanded and passed it on. He had drunk worse things than fermented mare's milk, but was glad that everyone switched to tea after the ritual.

The Mongol chief spoke. He couldn't keep his tone

smooth, as his Chinese amanuensis did. There was an instinctive bristling: what foreigner dares approach the Kha Khan's man, save on his belly? But the words remained courteous: "Now let our guests declare the business of their king. First, would you name him for us?"

"His name may not be spoken," said Everard. "Of his realm you have heard only the palest rumors. You may judge his power, Noyon, by the fact that he needed only us two to come this far, and that we needed only one mount apiece."

Toktai grunted. "Those are handsome animals you ride, though I wonder how well they'd do on the steppes. Did it take you long to get here?"

"No more than a day, Noyon. We have means."

Everard reached in his jacket and brought out a couple of small gift-wrapped parcels. "Our lord bade us present the Cathayan leaders with these tokens of regard."

While the paper was being removed, Sandoval leaned over and hissed in English: "Dig their expressions, Manse. We goofed a bit."

"How?"

"That flashy cellophane and stuff impresses a barbarian like Toktai. But notice Li. His civilization was doing calligraphy when the ancestors of Bonwit Teller were painting themselves blue. His opinion of our taste has just nosedived."

Everard shrugged imperceptibly. "Well, he's right, isn't he?"

Their colloquy had not escaped the others. Toktai gave them a hard stare, but returned to his present, a flashlight, which had to be demonstrated and exclaimed over. He was a little afraid of it at first, even mumbled a charm; then he remembered that a Mongol wasn't allowed to be afraid of anything except thunder, mastered himself, and was soon as delighted as a child. The best bet for a Confucian scholar like Li seemed to be a book, the *Family of Man* collection, whose diversity and alien pictorial technique might impress him. He was effusive in his thanks, but Everard doubted if he was overwhelmed. A Patrolman soon learned that sophistication exists at any level of technology.

Gifts must be made in return: a fine Chinese sword and a bundle of sea-otter pelts from the coast. It was quite some time before the conversation could turn back to business. Then Sandoval managed to get the other party's account first.

"Since you know so much," Toktai began, "you must also know that our invasion of Japan failed several years ago."

"The will of heaven was otherwise," said Li, with courtier blandness.

"Horse apples!" growled Toktai. "The stupidity of men was otherwise, you mean. We were too few, too ignorant, and we'd come too far in seas too rough. And what of it? We'll return there one day."

Everard knew rather sadly that they would, and that a storm would destroy the fleet and drown who knows how many young men. But he let Toktai continue:

"The Kha Khan realized we must learn more about the islands. Perhaps we should try to establish a base somewhere north of Hokkaido. Then, too, we have long heard rumors about lands farther west. Fisherman are blown off course now and then, and have glimpses; traders from Siberia speak of a strait and a country beyond. The Kha Khan got four ships with Chinese crews and told me to take a hundred Mongol warriors and see what I could discover."

Everard nodded, unsurprised. The Chinese had been sailing junks for hundreds of years, some holding up to a thousand passengers. True, these craft weren't as seaworthy as they would become in later centuries under Portuguese influence, and their owners had never been much attracted by any ocean, let alone the cold northern waters. But still, there were some Chinese navigators who would have picked up tricks of the trade from stray Koreans and Formosans, if not from their own fathers. They must have a little familiarity with the Kuriles, at least.

"We followed two chains of islands, one after another," said Toktai. "They were bleak enough, but we could stop here and there, let the horses out, and learn something from the natives. Though the Tengri know it's hard to do that last, when you may have to interpret through six languages! We did find out that there are two mainlands, Siberia and another, which come so close together up north that a man might cross in a skin boat, or walk across the ice in winter sometimes. Finally we came to the new mainland. A big country; forests, much game and seals. Too rainy, though. Our ships seemed to want to continue, so we followed the coast, more or less."

Everard visualized a map. If you go first along the Kuriles and then the Aleutians, you are never far from land. Fortunate to avoid the shipwreck, which had been a distinct possibility, the shallow-draft junks had been able to find anchorage even at those rocky islands. Also, the current urged them along, and they were very nearly on a great-circle course. Toktai had discovered Alaska before he quite knew what had happened. Since the country grew ever more hospitable as he coasted south, he passed up Puget Sound and proceeded clear to the Chehalis River. Maybe the Indians had warned him the Columbia mouth, farther on, was dangerous—and, more recently, had helped his horsemen cross the great stream on rafts.

"We set up camp when the year was waning," said the Mongol. "The tribes thereabouts are backward, but friendly. They gave us all the food, women, and help we could ask for. In return, our sailors taught them some tricks of fishing and boatbuilding. We wintered there, learned some of the languages, and made trips inland. Everywhere were tales of huge forests and plains where herds of wild cattle blacken the earth. We saw enough to know the stories were true. I've never been in so rich a land." His eyes gleamed tigerishly. "And so few dwellers, who don't even know the use of iron."

"Noyon," murmured Li warningly. He nodded his head very slightly toward the Patrolmen. Toktai clamped his mouth shut.

Li turned to Everard and said, "There were also rumors of a golden realm far to the south. We felt it our duty to investigate this, as well as explore the country in between. We had not looked for the honor of being met by your eminent selves."

"The honor is all ours," Everard purred. Then, putting on

his gravest face: "My lord of the Golden Empire, who may not be named, has sent us in a spirit of friendship. It would grieve him to see you meet disaster. We come to warn you."

"What?" Toktai sat up straight. One sinewy hand snatched for the sword, which, politely, he wasn't wearing. "What in the hells is this?"

"In the hells indeed, Noyon. Pleasant though this country seems, it lies under a curse. Tell him, my brother."

Sandoval, who had a better speaking voice, took over. His yarn had been concocted with an eye to exploiting that superstition that still lingered in the half-civilized Mongols, without generating too much Chinese skepticism. There were really two great southern kingdoms, he explained. Their own lay far away; its rival was somewhat north and east of it, with a citadel on the plains. Both states possessed immense powers, call them sorcery or subtle engineering, as you wished. The northerly empire, Badguys, considered all this territory as its own and would not tolerate a foreign expedition. Its scouts were certain to discover the Mongols before long, and would annihilate them with thunderbolts. The benevolent southern land of Goodguys could offer no protection, could only send emissaries warning the Mongols to turn home again.

"Why have the natives not spoken of these overlords?" asked Li shrewdly.

"Has every little tribesman in the jungles of Burma heard about the Kha Khan?" responded Sandoval.

"I am a stranger and ignorant," said Li. "Forgive me if I do not understand your talk of irresistible weapons."

Which is the politest way I've ever been called a liar, thought Everard. Aloud: "I can offer a small demonstration, if the Noyon has an animal that may be killed."

Toktai considered. His visage might have been scarred stone, but sweat filmed it. He clapped his hands and barked orders to the guard who looked in. Thereafter they made small talk against a silence that thickened.

A warrior appeared after some endless part of an hour. He said that a couple of horsemen had lassoed a deer. Would it serve the Noyon's purpose? It would. Toktai led the way out, shouldering through a thick and buzzing swarm of men. Everard followed, wishing this weren't needful. He slipped the rifle stock onto his Mauser. "Care to do the job?" he asked Sandoval.

"Christ, no."

The deer, a doe, had been forced back to camp. She trembled by the river, the horsehair ropes about her neck. The sun, just touching the western peaks, turned her to bronze. There was a blind sort of gentleness in her look at Everard. He waved back the men around her and took aim. The first slug killed her, but he kept the gun chattering till her carcass was gruesome.

When he lowered his weapon, the air felt somehow rigid. He looked across all the thick bandy-legged bodies, the flat, grimly controlled faces; he could smell them with unnatural sharpness, a clean odor of sweat and horses and smoke. He felt himself as nonhuman as they must see him.

"That is the least of the arms used here," he said. "A soul so torn from the body would not find its way home."

He turned on his heel. Sandoval followed him. Their horses had been staked out, the gear piled close by. They saddled, unspeaking, mounted, and rode off into the forest.

4

THE FIRE BLAZED up in a gust of wind. Sparingly laid by a woodsman, in that moment it barely brought the two out of shadow—a glimpse of brow, nose, and cheekbones, a gleam of eyes. It sank down again to red and blue sputtering above white coals, and darkness took the men.

Everard wasn't sorry. He fumbled his pipe in his hands, bit hard on it and drank smoke, but found little comfort. When he spoke, the vast soughing of trees, high up in the night, almost buried his voice, and he did not regret that either.

Nearby were their sleeping bags, their horses, the scooter—antigravity sled cum space-time hopper—which had brought them. Otherwise the land was empty; mile upon mile, human fires like their own were as small and lonely as stars in the universe. Somewhere a wolf howled.

"I suppose," Everard said, "every cop feels like a bastard occasionally. You've just been an observer so far, Jack. Active assignments, such as I get, are often hard to accept."

"Yeh." Sandoval had been even more quiet than his friend. He had scarcely stirred since supper.

"And now this. Whatever you have to do to cancel a temporal interference, you can at least think you're restoring the original line of development." Everard fumed on his pipe. "Don't remind me that 'original' is meaningless in this context. It's a consoling word."

"Uh-huh."

"But when our bosses, our dear Danellian supermen, tell *us* to interfere . . . We know Toktai's people never came back to Cathay. Why should you or I have to take a hand? If they ran into hostile Indians or something and were wiped out, I wouldn't mind. At least, no more than I mind any similar incident in that Goddamned slaughterhouse they call human history."

"We don't have to kill them, you know. Just make them turn back. Your demonstration this afternoon may be enough."

"Yeah. Turn back . . . and what? Probably perish at sea. They won't have an easy trip home—storm, fog, contrary currents, rocks—in those primitive ships meant mostly for rivers. And we'll have set them on that trip at precisely that time! If we didn't interfere, they'd start home later, the circumstances of the voyage would be different. . . . Why should we take the guilt?"

"They could even make it home," murmured Sandoval.

"What?" Everard started.

"The way Toktai was talking, I'm sure he plans to go back on a horse, not on those ships. As he's guessed, Bering Strait is easy to cross; the Aleuts do it all the time. Manse, I'm afraid it isn't enough simply to spare them."

"But they aren't going to get home! We know that!"

"Suppose they do make it." Sandoval began to talk a bit louder and much faster. The night wind roared around his words. "Let's play with ideas awhile. Suppose Toktai pushes on southeastward. It's hard to see what could stop him. His men can live off the country, even the deserts, far more handily than Coronado or any of those boys. He hasn't terribly far to go before he reaches a high-grade neolithic people, the agricultural Pueblo tribes. That will encourage him all the more. He'll be in Mexico before August. Mexico's just as dazzling now as it was—will be—in Cortez's day. And even more tempting: the Aztecs and Toltecs are still settling who's to be master, with any number of other tribes hanging around ready to help a newcomer against both. The Spanish guns made, will make, no real difference, as you'll recall if you've read Diaz. The Mongols are as superior, man for man, as any Spaniard. . . . Not that I imagine Toktai would wade right in. He'd doubtless be very polite, spend the winter, learn everything he could. Next year he'd go back north, proceed home, and report to Kublai that some of the richest, most gold-stuffed territory on earth was wide open for conquest!"

"How about the other Indians?" put in Everard. "I'm vague on them."

"The Mayan New Empire is at its height. A tough nut to crack, but a correspondingly rewarding one. I should think, once the Mongols got established in Mexico, there'd be no stopping them. Peru has an even higher culture at this moment, and much less organization than Pizarro faced; the Quechua-Aymar, the so-called Inca race, are still only one power down there among several.

"And then, the land! Can you visualize what a Mongol tribe would make of the Great Plains?"

"I can't see them emigrating in hordes," said Everard. There was that about Sandoval's voice that made him uneasy and defensive. "Too much Siberia and Alaska in the way."

"Worse obstacles have been overcome. I don't mean they'd pour in all at once. It might take them a few centuries to start mass immigration, as it will take the Europeans. I can imagine a string of clans and tribes being established in the course of some years, all down western North America. Mexico and Yucatan get gobbled up—or, more likely, become khanates.

The herding tribes move eastward as their own population grows and as new immigrants arrive. Remember, the Yuan dynasty is due to be overthrown in less than a century. That'll put additional pressure on the Mongols in Asia and go elsewhere. And Chinese will come here too, to farm and to share in the gold."

"I should think, if you don't mind my saying so," Everard broke in softly, "that you of all people wouldn't want to hasten the conquest of America."

"It'd be a different conquest," said Sandoval. "I don't care about the Aztecs; if you study them, you'll agree that Cortez did Mexico a favor. It'd be rough on other, more harmless tribes too—for a while. And yet, the Mongols aren't such devils. Are they? A Western background prejudices us. We forget how much torture and massacre the Europeans were enjoying at the same time.

"The Mongols are quite a bit like the old Romans, really. Same practice of depopulating areas that resist, but respecting the rights of those who make submission. Same armed protection and competent government. Same unimaginative, uncreative national character; but the same vague awe and envy of true civilization. The *Pax Mongolica*, right now, unites a bigger area, and brings more different peoples into stimulating contact, than that piddling Roman Empire ever imagined.

"As for the Indians—remember, the Mongols are herdsmen. There won't be anything like the unsolvable conflict between hunter and farmer that made the white man destroy the Indian. The Mongol hasn't got race prejudices, either. And after a little fighting, the average Navajo, Cherokee, Seminole, Algonquin, Chippewa, Dakota, will be glad to submit and become allied. Why not? He'll get horses, sheep, cattle, textiles, metallurgy. He'll outnumber the invaders, and be on much more nearly equal terms with them than with white farmers and machine-age industry. And there'll be the Chinese, I repeat, leavening the whole mixture, teaching civilization and sharpening wits. . . .

"Good God, Manse! When Columbus gets here, he'll find

his Grand Cham all right! The Sachem Khan of the strongest nation on earth!"

Sandoval stopped. Everard listened to the gallows creak of branches in the wind. He looked into the night for a long while before he said, "It could be. Of course, we'd have to stay in this century till the crucial point was past. Our own world wouldn't exist. Wouldn't ever have existed."

"It wasn't such a hell of a good world anyway," said Sandoval, as if in dream.

"You might think about your . . . oh . . . parents. They'd never have been born either."

"They lived in a tumbledown hogan. I saw my father crying once, because he couldn't buy shoes for us in winter. My mother died of TB."

Everard sat unstirring. It was Sandoval who shook himself and jumped to his feet with a rattling kind of laugh. "What have I been mumbling? It was just a yarn, Manse. Let's turn in. Shall I take first watch?"

Everard agreed, but lay long awake.

5

THE SCOOTER HAD jumped two days futureward and now hovered invisibly far above to the naked eye. Around it, the air was thin and sharply cold. Everard shivered as he adjusted the electronic telescope. Even at full magnification, the caravan was little more than specks toiling across green immensity. But no one else in the Western Hemisphere could have been riding horses.

He twisted in the saddle to face his companion. "So now what?"

Sandoval's broad countenance was unreadable. "Well, if our demonstration didn't work—"

"It sure as hell didn't! I swear they're moving south twice as fast as before. Why?"

"I'd have to know all of them a lot better than I do, as individuals, to give you a real answer, Manse. But essentially it must be that we challenged their courage. A warlike culture, nerve and hardihood its only absolute virtues . . . what choice have they got but to go on? If they retreated before a mere threat, they'd never be able to live with themselves."

"But Mongols aren't idiots! They didn't conquer everybody in sight by bull strength, but by jolly well understanding military principles better. Toktai should retreat, report to the Emperor what he saw, and organize a bigger expedition."

"The men at the ships can do that," Sandoval reminded. "Now that I think about it, I see how grossly we underestimated Toktai. He must have set a date, presumably next year, for the ships to try and go home if he doesn't return. When he finds something interesting along the way, like us, he can dispatch an Indian with a letter to the base camp."

Everard nodded. It occurred to him that he had been rushed into this job, all the way down the line, with never a pause to plan it as he should have done. Hence this botch. But how much blame must fall on the subconscious reluctance of John Sandoval? After a minute Everard said: "They may even have smelled something fishy about us. The Mongols were always good at psychological warfare."

"Could be. But what's our next move?"

Swoop down from above, fire a few blasts from the forty-first-century energy gun mounted in this timecycle, and that's the end. . . . No, by God, they can send me to the exile planet before I'll do any such thing. There are decent limits.

"We'll rig up a more impressive demonstration," said Everard.

"And if it flops too?"

"Shut up! Give it a chance!"

"I was just wondering." The wind harried under Sandoval's words. "Why not cancel the expedition instead? Go back in time a couple of years and persuade Kublai Khan it isn't worthwhile sending explorers eastward. Then all this would never have happened."

"You know Patrol regs forbid us to make historical changes."

"What do you call this we're doing?"

"Something specifically ordered by supreme HG. Perhaps

to correct some interference elsewhere, elsewhen. How should I know? I'm only a step on the evolutionary ladder. They have abilities a million years hence that I can't even guess at."

"Father knows best," murmured Sandoval.

Everard set his jaws. "The fact remains," he said, "the court of Kublai, the most powerful man on earth, is more important and crucial than anything here in America. No, you rang me in on this miserable job, and now I'll pull rank on you if I must. Our orders are to make these people give up their exploration. What happens afterward is none of our business. So they don't make it home. We won't be the proximate cause, any more than you're a murderer if you invite a man to dinner and he has a fatal accident on the way."

"Stop quacking and let's get to work," rapped Sandoval.

Everard sent the scooter gliding forward. "See that hill?" He pointed after a while. "It's on Toktai's line of march, but I think he'll camp a few miles short of it tonight, down in that little meadow by the stream. The hill will be in his plain view, though. Let's set up shop on it."

"And make fireworks? It'll have to be pretty fancy. Those Cathayans know about gunpowder. They even have military rockets."

"Small ones. I know. But when I assembled my gear for this trip, I packed away some fairly versatile gadgetry, in case my first attempt failed."

The hill bore a sparse crown of pine trees. Everard landed the scooter among them and began to unload boxes from its sizeable baggage compartments. Sandoval helped, wordless. The horses, Patrol trained, stepped calmly off the framework stalls that had borne them and started grazing along the slope.

After a while the Indian broke his silence. "This isn't my line of work. What are you rigging?"

Everard patted the small machine he had half assembled. "It's adapted from a weather-control system used in the Cold Centuries era upstairs. A potential distributor. It can make some of the damnedest lightning you ever saw, with thunder to match."

"Mmm . . . the great Mongol weakness." Suddenly Sandoval grinned. "You win. We might as well relax and enjoy this."

"Fix us a supper, will you, while I put the gimmick together? No fire, naturally. We don't want any mundane smoke. . . . Oh, yes, I also have a mirage projector. If you'll change clothes and put on a hood or something at the appropriate moment, so you can't be recognized, I'll paint a mile-high picture of you, half as ugly as life."

"How about a PA system? Navajo chants can be fairly alarming, if you don't know it's just a *yeibichai* or whatever."

"Coming up!"

The day waned. It grew murky under the pines; the air was chill and pungent. At last Everard devoured a sandwich and watched through his binoculars as the Mongol vanguard checked that campsite he had predicted. Others came riding in with their day's catch of game and went to work cooking. The main body showed up at sundown, posted itself efficiently, and ate. Toktai was indeed pushing hard, using every daylight moment. As darkness closed down, Everard glimpsed outposts mounted and with strung bows. He could not keep up his own spirits, however hard he tried. He was bucking men who had shaken the earth.

Early stars glittered above snowpeaks. It was time to begin work.

"Got our horses tethered, Jack? They might panic. I'm fairly sure the Mongol horses will! Okay, here goes." Everard flipped a main switch and squatted by the dimly lit control dials of his apparatus.

First there was the palest blue flicker between earth and sky. Then the lightnings began, tongue after forked tongue leaping, trees smashed at a blow, the mountainsides rocking under their noise. Everard threw out ball lightning, spheres of flame, which whirled and curvetted, trailing sparks, shooting across to the camp and exploding above it till the sky seemed white hot.

Deafened and half blinded, he managed to project a sheet of fluorescing ionization. Like northern lights the great ban-

ners curled, bloody red and bone white, hissing under the repeated thunder cracks. Sandoval trod forth. He had stripped to
his pants, daubed clay on his body in archaic patterns; his face
was not veiled after all, but smeared with earth and twisted
into something Everard would not have known. The machine
scanned him and altered its output. That which stood forth
against the aurora was taller than a mountain. It moved in a
shuffling dance, from horizon to horizon and back to the sky,
and it wailed and barked in a falsetto louder than thunder.

Everard crouched beneath the lurid light, his fingers stiff
on the control board. He knew a primitive fear of his own; the
dance woke things in him that he had forgotten.

Judas priest! If this doesn't make them quit . . .

His mind returned to him. He even looked at his watch.
Half an hour . . . give them another fifteen minutes, in which
the display tapered off . . . They'd surely stay in camp till
dawn rather than blunder wildly out in the dark, they had that
much discipline. So keep everything under wraps for several
hours more, then administer the last stroke to their nerves by
a single electric bolt smiting a tree right next to them. . . .
Everard waved Sandoval back. The Indian sat down, panting
harder than his exertions seemed to warrant.

When the noise was gone, Everard said, "Nice show,
Jack." His voice sounded tinny and strange in his ears.

"I hadn't done anything like that for years," muttered Sandoval. He struck a match, startling noise in the quietness. The
brief flame showed his lips gone thin. Then he shook out the
match and only his cigarette end glowed.

"Nobody I knew on the reservation took that stuff seriously," he went on after a moment. "A few of the older men
wanted us boys to learn it to keep the custom alive, to remind
us we were still a people. But mostly our idea was to pick up
some change by dancing for tourists."

There was a longer pause. Everard doused the projector
completely. In the murk that followed, Sandoval's cigarette
waxed and waned, a tiny red Algol.

"Tourists!" he said at last.

After more minutes: "Tonight I was dancing for a purpose. It meant something. I never felt that way before."

Everard was silent.

Until one of the horses, which had plunged at its halter's end during the performance and was still nervous, whinnied.

Everard looked up. Night met his eyes. "Did you hear anything, Jack?"

The flashlight beam speared him.

For an instant he stared blinded at it. Then he sprang erect, cursing and snatching for his stun pistol. A shadow ran from behind one of the trees. It struck him in the ribs. He lurched back. The beam gun flew to his hand. He shot at random.

The flashlight swept about once more. Everard glimpsed Sandoval. The Navajo had not donned his weapons again. Unarmed, he dodged the sweep of a Mongol blade. The swordsman ran after him. Sandoval reverted to Patrol judo. He went to one knee. Clumsy afoot, the Mongol slashed, missed, and ran straight into a shoulder block to the belly. Sandoval rose with the blow. The heel of his hand jolted upward to the Mongul's chin. The helmeted head snapped back. Sandoval chopped a hand at the Adam's apple, yanked the sword from its owner's grasp, turned, and parried a cut from behind.

A voice yammered above the Mongol yipping, giving orders. Everard backed away. He had knocked one attacker out with a bolt from his pistol. There were others between him and the scooter. He circled to face them. A lariat curled around his shoulders. It tightened with one expert heave. He went over. Four men piled on him. He saw half a dozen lance butts crack down on Sandoval's head, then there wasn't time for anything but fighting. Twice he got to his feet, but his stun gun was gone by now, the Mauser was plucked from its holster—the little men were pretty good at *yawara*-style combat themselves. They dragged him down and hit him with fists, boots, dagger pommels. He never quite lost consciousness, but he finally stopped caring.

6

TOKTAI STRUCK CAMP before dawn. The first sun saw his troop wind between scattered copses on a broad valley floor. The land was turning flat and arid, the mountains to the right farther away, fewer snowpeaks visible and those ghostly in a pale sky.

The hardy small Mongol horses trotted ahead—plop of hoofs, squeak and jingle of harness. Looking back, Everard saw the line as a compact mass; lances rose and fell, pennants and plumes and cloaks fluttered beneath, and under that were the helmets, with a brown slit-eyed face and a grotesquely painted cuirass visible here and there. No one spoke, and he couldn't read any of those expressions.

His brain felt sandy. They had left his hands free, but lashed his ankles to the stirrups, and the cord chafed. They had also stripped him naked—sensible precaution, who knew what instruments might be sewn into his garments?—and the Mongol garb given him in exchange was ludicrously small. The seams had had to be slit before he could even get the tunic on.

The projector and the scooter lay back at the hill. Toktai would not take any risks with those things of power. He had had to roar down several of his own frightened warriors before they would even agree to bring the strange horses, with saddle and bedroll, riderless among the pack mares.

Hoofs thudded rapidly. One of the bowmen flanking Everard grunted and moved his pony a little aside. Li Tai-Tsung rode close.

The Patrolman gave him a dull stare. "Well?" he said.

"I fear your friend will not waken again," answered the Chinese. "I made him a little more comfortable."

But lying strapped on an improvised litter between two ponies, unconscious . . . Yes, concussion, when they clubbed him last night. A Patrol hospital could put him to rights soon enough. But the nearest Patrol office is in Cambaluc, and I can't see Toktai letting me go back to the scooter and use its radio. John Sandoval is going to die here, six hundred and fifty years before he was born.

Everard looked into cool brown eyes, interested, not unsympathetic, but alien to him. It was no use, he knew; arguments that were logical in his culture were gibberish today; but one had to try. "Can you, at least, not make Toktai understand what ruin he is going to bring on himself, on his whole people, by this?"

Li stroked his fork beard. "It is plain to see, honored sir, your nation has arts unknown to us," he said. "But what of it? The barbarians—" He gave Everard's Mongol guards a quick glance, but evidently they didn't understand the Sung Chinese he used—"took many kingdoms superior to them in every way but fighting skill. Now already we know that you, ah, amended the truth when you spoke of a hostile empire near these lands. Why should your king try to frighten us away with a falsehood, did he not have reason to fear us?"

Everard spoke with care: "Our glorious emperor dislikes bloodshed. But if you force him to strike you down—"

"Please." Li looked pained. He waved one slender hand, as if brushing off an insect. "Say what you will to Toktai, and I shall not interfere. It would not sadden me to return home; I came only under Imperial orders. But let us two, speaking confidentially, not insult each other's intelligence. Do you not see, eminent lord, that there is no possible harm with which you can threaten these men? Death they despise; even the most lingering torture must kill them in time; even the most disgraceful mutilation can be made as naught by a man willing to bite through his tongue and die. Toktai sees eternal shame if he turns back at this stage of events, and a good chance of eternal glory and uncountable wealth if he continues."

Everard sighed. His own humiliating capture had indeed been the turning point. The Mongols had been very near bolting at the thunder show. Many had groveled and wailed (and from now on would be all the more aggressive, to erase that memory). Toktai charged the source as much in horror as defiance; a few men and horses had been able to come along. Li himself was partly responsible: scholar, skeptic, familiar with sleight-of-hand and pyrotechnic displays, the Chinese had helped hearten Toktai to attack before one of those thunderbolts did strike home.

The truth of the matter is, son, we misjudged these people. We should have taken along a Specialist, who'd have an intuitive feeling for the nuances of this culture. But no, we assumed a brainful of facts would be enough. Now what? A Patrol relief expedition may show up eventually, but Jack will be dead in another day or two. . . . Everard looked at the stony warrior face on his left. *Quite probably I'll be also. They're still on edge. They'd sooner scrag me than not.*

·And even if he should (unlikely chance!) survive to be hauled out of this mess by another Patrol band—it would be tough to face his comrades. An Unattached agent, with all the special privileges of his rank, was expected to handle situations without extra help. Without leading valuable men to their deaths.

"So I advise you most sincerely not to attempt any more deceptions."

"What?" Everard turned back to Li.

"You do understand, do you not," said the Chinese, "that our native guides did flee? That you are now taking their place? But we expect to meet other tribes before long, establish communication. . . ."

Everard nodded a throbbing head. The sunlight pierced his eyes. He was not astonished at the ready Mongol progress through scores of separate language areas. If you aren't fussy about grammar, a few hours suffice to pick up the small number of basic words and gestures; thereafter you can take days or weeks actually learning to speak with your hired escort.

". . . and obtain guides from stage to stage, as we did before," continued Li. "Any misdirection you may have given will soon be apparent. Toktai will punish it in most uncivilized ways. On the other hand, faithful service will be rewarded. You may hope in time to rise high in the provincial court, after the conquest."

Everard sat unmoving. The casual boast was like an explosion in his mind.

He had been assuming the Patrol would send another force. Obviously *something* was going to prevent Toktai's return. But was it so obvious? Why had this interference been ordered at all, if there were not—in some paradoxical way his twentieth-century logic couldn't grasp—an uncertainty, a shakiness in the continuum right at this point?

Judas in hell! Perhaps the Mongol expedition was going to succeed! Perhaps all the future of an American Khanate, which Sandoval had not quite dared dream of . . . was the real future.

There are quirks and discontinuities in space-time. The world lines can double back and bite themselves off, so that things and events appear causelessly, meaningless flutters soon lost and forgotten. Such as Manse Everard, marooned in the past with a dead John Sandoval, after coming from a future that never existed as the agent of a Time Patrol that never was.

7

AT SUNDOWN THEIR unmerciful pace had brought the expedition into sagebrush and greasewood country. The hills were steep and brown; dust smoked under hoofs; silvery-green bushes grew sparse, sweetening the air when bruised but offering little else.

Everard helped lay Sandoval on the ground. The Navajo's eyes were closed, his face sunken and hot. Sometimes he tossed and muttered a bit. Everard squeezed water from a wetted cloth past the cracked lips, but could do nothing more.

The Mongols established themselves more gaily than of late. They had overcome two great sorcerers and suffered no further attack, and the implications were growing upon them. They went about their chores chattering to each other, and after a frugal meal they broke out the leather bags of *kumiss*.

Everard remained with Sandoval, near the middle of camp. Two guards had been posted on him, who sat with strung bows a few yards away but didn't talk. Now and then one of them would get up to tend the small fire. Presently silence fell on their comrades, too. Even this leathery host was tired; men rolled up and went to sleep, the outposts rode their rounds drowsy-eyed, other watch-fires burned to embers while stars kindled overhead, a coyote yelped across miles. Everard covered Sandoval against the gathering cold; his own low flames showed rime frost on sage leaves. He huddled into a cloak and wished his captors would at least give him back his pipe.

A footfall crunched dry soil. Everard's guards snatched arrows for their bows. Toktai moved into the light, his head bare above a mantle. The guards bent low and moved back into shadow.

Toktai halted. Everard looked up and then down again. The Noyon stared a while at Sandoval. Finally, almost gently, he said: "I do not think your friend will live to next sunset."

Everard grunted.

"Have you any medicines that might help?" asked Toktai. "There are some queer things in your saddlebags."

"I have a remedy against infection, and another against pain," said Everard mechanically. "But for a cracked skull, he must be taken to skillful physicians."

Toktai sat dawn and held his hands to the fire. "I'm sorry we have no surgeons along."

"You could let us go," said Everard without hope. "My chariot, back at the last camp, could get him to help in time."

"Now you know I can't do that!" Toktai chuckled. His pity for the dying man flickered out. "After all, Eburar, you started the trouble."

Since it was true, the Patrolman made no retort.

"I don't hold it against you," went on Toktai. "In fact, I'm still anxious to be friends. If I weren't, I'd stop for a few days and wring all you know out of you."

Everard flared up. "You could try!"

"And succeed, I think, with a man who has to carry medicine against pain." Toktai's grin was wolfish. "However, you may be useful as a hostage or something. And I do like your nerve. I'll even tell you an idea I have. I think maybe you don't belong to this rich southland at all. I think you're an adventurer, one of a little band of shamans. You have the southern king in your power, or hope to, and don't want strangers interfering." Toktai spat into the fire. "There are old stories about that sort of thing, and finally a hero overthrew the wizard. Why not me?"

Everard sighed. "You will learn why not, Noyon." He wondered how correct that was.

"Oh, now." Toktai clapped him on the back. "Can't you tell me even a little? There's no blood feud between us. Let's be friends."

Everard jerked a thumb at Sandoval.

"It's a shame, that," said Toktai, "but he would keep on resisting an officer of the Kha Khan. Come, let's have a drink together, Eburar. I'll send a man for a bag."

The Patrolman made a face. "That's no way to pacify me!"

"Oh, your people don't like *kumiss*? I'm afraid it's all we have. We drank up our wine long ago."

"You could let me have my whisky." Everard looked at Sandoval again, and out into night, and felt the cold creep inward. "God, but I could use that!"

"Eh?"

"A drink of our own. We had some in our saddlebags."

"Well . . ." Toktai hesitated. "Very well. Come along and we'll fetch it."

The guards followed their chief and their prisoner, through the brush and the sleeping warriors, up to a pile of assorted gear also under guard. One of the latter sentries ignited a stick in his fire to give Everard some light. The Patrolman's back muscles tensed—arrows were aimed at him now, drawn to the barb—but he squatted and went through his own stuff, careful not to move fast. When he had both canteens of Scotch, he returned to his own place.

Toktai sat down across the fire. He watched Everard pour a shot into the canteen cap and toss it off. "Smells odd," he said.

"Try." The Patrolman handed over the canteen.

It was an impulse of sheer loneliness. Toktai wasn't such a

bad sort. Not in his own terms. And when you sit by your dying partner, you'd bouse with the devil himself, just to keep from thinking. The Mongol sniffed dubiously, looked back at Everard, paused, and then raised the bottle to his lips with a bravura gesture.

"Whoo-oo-oo!"

Everard scrambled to catch the flask before too much was spilled. Toktai gasped and spat. One guardsman nocked an arrow, the other sprang to lay a hard hand on Everard's shoulder. A sword gleamed high. "It's not poison!" the Patrolman exclaimed. "It's only too strong for him. See, I'll drink some more myself."

Toktai waved the guards back and glared from watery eyes. "What do you make that of?" he choked. "Dragon's blood?"

"Barley." Everard didn't feel like explaining distillation. He poured himself another slug. "Go ahead, drink your mare's milk."

Toktai smacked his lips. "It does warm you up, doesn't it? Like pepper." He reached out a grimy hand. "Give me some more."

Everard sat still for a few seconds. "Well?" growled Toktai.

The Patrolman shook his head. "I told you, it's too strong for Mongols."

"What? See here, you whey-faced son of a Turk—"

"On your head be it, then. I warn you fairly, with your men here as witnesses, you will be sick tomorrow."

Toktai guzzled heartily, belched, and passed the canteen back. "Nonsense. I simply wasn't prepared for it, the first time. Drink up!"

Everard took his time. Toktai grew impatient. "Hurry along there. No, give me the other flask."

"Very well. You are the chief. But I beg you, don't try to match me draught for draught. You can't do it."

"What do you mean, I can't do it? Why, I've drunk twenty men senseless in Karakorum. None of your gutless Chinks, ei-

ther: they were all Mongols." Toktai poured down a couple of
ounces more.

Everard sipped with care. But he hardly felt the effect anyway, save as a burning along his gullet. He was too tightly
strung. Suddenly he was glimpsing what might be a way out.

"Here, it's a cold night," he said, and offered his canteen to
the nearest guardsman. "You lads have one to keep you
warm."

Toktai looked up, a trifle muzzily. "Good stuff, this," he
objected. "Too good for . . ." He remembered himself and
snapped his words off short. Cruel and absolute the Mongol
Empire might be, but officers shared equally with the hum-
blest of their men.

The warrior grabbed the jug, giving his chief a resentful
look, and slanted it to his mouth. "Easy, there," said Everard.
"It's heady."

"Nothin's heady to me." Toktai poured a further dose into
himself. "Sober as a bonze." He wagged his finger. "That's the
trouble bein' a Mongol. You're so hardy you can't get drunk."

"Are you bragging or complaining?" said Everard. The
first warrior fanned his tongue, resumed a stance of alertness,
and passed the bottle to his companion. Toktai hoisted the
other canteen again.

"Ahhh!" He stared, owlish. "That was fine. Well, better get
to sleep now. Give him back his liquor, men."

Everard's throat tightened. But he managed to leer. "Yes,
thanks, I'll want some more," he said. "I'm glad you realize
you can't take it."

"Wha'd'you mean?" Toktai glared at him. "No such thing
as too much. Not for a Mongol!" He glugged afresh. The first
guardsman received the other flask and took a hasty snort before it should be too late.

Everard sucked in a shaken breath. It might work out after
all. It might.

Toktai was used to carousing. There was no doubt that he
or his men could handle *kumiss*, wine, ale, mead, *kvass*, that
thin beer miscalled rice wine—any beverage of this era.
They'd know when they'd had enough, say goodnight, and

walk a straight line to their bedrolls. The trouble was, no sub-stance merely fermented can get over about 24 proof—the process is stopped by its waste product—and most of what they brewed in the thirteenth century ran well under 5 percent alcohol, with a high foodstuff content to boot.

Scotch whisky is in quite a different class. If you try to drink that like beer, or even like wine, you are in trouble. Your judgment will be gone before you've noticed its absence, and consciousness follows soon after.

Everard reached for the canteen held by one of the guards. "Give me that!" he said. "You'll drink it all up!"

The warrior grinned and took another long gulp, before passing it on to his fellow. Everard stood up and made an undignified scrabble for it. A guard poked him in the stomach. He went over on his backside. The Mongols bawled laughter, leaning on each other. So good a joke called for another drink.

When Toktai folded, Everard alone noticed. The Noyon slid from a cross-legged to a recumbent position. The fire sputtered up long enough to show a silly smile on his face. Everard squatted wire-tense.

The end of one sentry came a few minutes later. He reeled, went on all fours, and began to jettison his dinner. The other one turned, blinking, fumbling after a sword. "Wha's mat-tuh?" he groaned. "Wha' yuh done? Poison?"

Everard moved.

He had hopped over the fire and fallen on Toktai before the last guard realized it. The Mongol stumbled forward, crying out. Everard found Toktai's sword. It flashed from the scab-bard as he bounded up. The warrior got his own blade aloft. Everard didn't like to kill a nearly helpless man. He stepped close, knocked the other weapon aside, and his fist clopped. The Mongol sank to his knees, retched, and slept.

Everard bounded away. Men stirred in the dark, calling. He heard hoofs drum, one of the mounted sentries racing to in-vestigate. Somebody took a brand from an almost extinct fire and whirled it till it flared. Everard went flat on his belly.

A warrior pelted by, not seeing him in the brush. He glided

toward deeper darknesses. A yell behind him, a machine-gun
volley of curses, told that someone had found the Noyon.

Everard stood up and began to run.

The horses had been hobbled and turned out under guard
as usual. They were a dark mass on the plain, which lay gray-
white beneath a sky crowded with sharp stars. Everard saw
one of the Mongol watchers gallop to meet him. A voice
barked: "What's happening?"

He pitched his answer high. "Attack on camp!" It was only
to gain time, lest the horseman recognize him and fire an arrow.
He crouched, visible as a hunched and cloaked shape. The
Mongol reined in with a spurt of dust. Everard sprang.

He got hold of the pony's bridle before he was recognized.
Then the sentry yelled and drew sword. He hewed downward.
But Everard was on the left side. The blow from above came
awkwardly, easily parried. Everard chopped in return and felt
his edge go into meat. The horse reared in alarm. Its rider fell
from the saddle. He rolled over and staggered up again, bel-
lowing. Everard already had one foot in a pan-shaped stirrup.
The Mongol limped toward him, blood running black in that
light from a wounded leg. Everard mounted and laid the flat
of his own blade on the horse's crupper.

He got going toward the herd. Another rider pounded to intercept him. Everard ducked. An arrow buzzed where he had
been. The stolen pony plunged, fighting its unfamiliar burden.
Everard needed a minute to get it under control again. The
archer might have taken him then, by coming up and going at
it hand to hand. But habit sent the man past at a gallop, shooting. He missed in the dimness. Before he could turn, Everard
was out of night view.

The Patrolman uncoiled a lariat at the saddlebow and
broke into the skittish herd. He roped the nearest animal,
which accepted it with blessed meekness. Leaning over, he
slashed the hobbles with his sword and rode off, leading the
remount. They came out the other side of the herd and started
north.

A stern chase is a long chase, Everard told himself inap-
propriately. *But they're bound to overhaul me if I don't lose*

'em. Let's see, if I remember my geography, the lava beds lie northwest of here.

He cast a glance behind. No one pursued yet. They'd need a while to organize themselves. However . . .

Thin lightnings winked from above. The cloven air boomed behind them. He felt a chill, deeper than the night cold. But he eased his pace. There was no more reason for hurry. That must be Manse Everard—

—who had returned to the Patrol vehicle and ridden it south in space and backward in time to this same instant.

That was cutting it fine, he thought. Patrol doctrine frowned on helping oneself thus. Too much danger of a closed causal loop, or of tangling past and future.

But in this case, I'll get away with it. No reprimands, even. Because it's to rescue Jack Sandoval, not myself. I've already gotten free. I could shake pursuit in the mountains, which I know and the Mongols don't. The time-hopping is only to save my friend's life.

Besides, (an upsurging bitterness) *what's this whole mission been, except the future doubling back to create its own past? Without us, the Mongols might well have taken over America, and then there'd never have been any us.*

The sky was enormous, crystalline black; you rarely saw that many stars. The Great Bear flashed above hoar earth; hoofbeats rang through silence. Everard had not felt so alone before now.

"And what am I doing back there?" he asked aloud.

The answer came to him, and he eased a little, fell into the rhythm of his horses and started eating miles. He wanted to get this over with. But what he must do turned out to be less bad than he had feared.

Toktai and Li Tai-Tsung never came home. But that was not because they perished at sea or in the forests. It was because a sorcerer rode down from heaven and killed all their horses with thunderbolts, and smashed and burned their ships in the river mouth. No Chinese sailor would venture onto those tricky seas in whatever clumsy vessel could be built here; no Mongol would think it possible to go home on foot.

Indeed, it probably wasn't. The expedition would stay, marry
into the Indians, live out their days. Chinook, Tlingit, Nootka,
all the potlatch tribes, with their big seagoing canoes, lodges
and copperworking, furs and cloths and haughtiness . . . well,
a Mongol Noyon, even a Confucian scholar might live less
happily and usefully than in creating such a life for such a
race.

Everard nodded to himself. So much for that. What was
harder to take than the thwarting of Toktai's bloodthirsty ambitions was the truth about his own corps; which was his own
family and nation and reason for living. The distant supermen
turned out to be not quite such idealists after all. They weren't
merely safeguarding a perhaps divinely ordained history that
led to them. Here and there they, too, meddled, to create their
own past. . . . Don't ask if there ever was any "original"
scheme of things. Keep your mind shut. Regard the rutted
road mankind had to travel, and tell yourself that if it could be
better in places, in other places it could be worse.

"It may be a crooked game," said Everard, "but it's the
only one in town."

His voice came so loud, in that huge rime-white land, that
he didn't speak any more. He clucked at his horse and rode a
little faster northward.

Playing the Game

Jack Dann and Gardner Dozois

Here's a quiet little story that demonstrates that not only is it impossible to go home again, it may be impossible even to *find* it . . .

Gardner Dozois was the editor of *Asimov's Science Fiction* magazine for twenty years, and also edits the annual anthology series *The Year's Best Science Fiction*, now up to its *Twenty-Second Annual Collection.* He's won the Hugo Award fifteen times as the year's Best Editor, won the *Locus* Award thirty times, and has won the Nebula Award twice for his own short fiction. He is the author or editor of more than a hundred books, the most recent of which are *The Best of the Best: Twenty Years of The Year's Best Science Fiction*, *Galileo's Children: Tales of Science vs. Superstition*, a reissue of his novel *Strangers*, and a new collection of his own short fiction, *Morning Child and Other Stories*. Born in Salem, Massachusetts, he has now lived for thirty-four years in Philadelphia.

Jack Dann is a multiple award–winning author who is the author or editor of more than sixty books, including the novels *Junction, Starhiker, The Man Who Melted, High Steel* (with

Jack C. Haldeman), *Counting Coup, The Silent*, and the international bestseller *The Memory Cathedral*. His many short stories have been collected in *Timetipping, Visitations*, and *Jubilee*. His anthologies include *Wandering Stars, More Wandering Stars, In the Field of Fire* (edited with Jeanne Van Buren), *Dreaming Down Under* (edited with Janeen Webb), *Gathering the Bones* (edited with Dennis Etchison and Ramsey Campbell), and a long series of anthologies edited with Gardner Dozois. He won the Nebula Award for his novella "Da Vinci Rising," and has also won the Ditmar Award. His most recent books are a new novel, *The Rebel: An Imagined Life of James Dean*, and a new collection of his works in collaboration with other authors, *The Fiction Factory*. Coming up is a new collection, *Promised Land*. Born in the United States, he now makes his home in Australia.

THE WOODS THAT edged the north side of Manningtown belonged to the cemetery, and if you looked westward toward Endicott, you could see marble mausoleums and expensive monuments atop the hills. The cemetery took up several acres of carefully mown hillside and bordered Jefferson Avenue, where well-kept wood-frame houses faced the rococo painted headstones of the Italian section.

West of the cemetery there had once been a district of brownstone buildings and small shops, but for some time now there had been a shopping mall there instead; east of the cemetery, the row of dormer-windowed old mansions that Jimmy remembered had been replaced by an ugly brick school building and a fenced-in schoolyard where kids never played. The cemetery itself, though—that never changed; it had always been there, exactly the same for as far back as he could remember, and this made the cemetery a pleasant place to Jimmy Daniels, a refuge, a welcome island of stability in a rapidly changing world where change itself was often unpleasant and sometimes menacing.

Jimmy Daniels lived in Old Town most of the time, just down the hill from the cemetery, although sometimes they lived in Passdale or Southside or even Durham. Old Town was a quiet residential neighborhood of whitewashed narrow-fronted houses and steep cobbled streets that were lined with oak and maple trees. Things changed slowly there also, unlike the newer districts downtown, where it seemed that new parking garages or civic buildings popped out of the ground like mushrooms after a rain. Only rarely did a new building appear in Old Town, or an old building vanish. For this reason alone, Jimmy much preferred Old Town to Passdale or Southside, and was always relieved to be living there once again. True, he usually had no friends or school chums in the neighborhood, which consisted mostly of first- and second-generation Poles who worked for the Mannington shoe factories, which had recently begun to fail. Sometimes, when they lived in Old Town, Jimmy got to play with a lame Italian boy who was almost as much of an outcast in the neighborhood as Jimmy was, but the Italian boy had been gone for the last few days, and Jimmy was left alone again. He didn't really mind being alone all that much—most of the time, anyway. He was a solitary boy by nature.

The whole Daniels family tended to be solitary, and usually had little to do with the close-knit, church-centered life of Old Town, although sometimes his mother belonged to the PTA or the Ladies' Auxiliary, and once Jimmy had been amazed to discover that his father had joined the Rotary Club. Jimmy's father usually worked for Weston Computers in Endicott, although Jimmy could remember times, unhappier times, when his father had worked as a CPA in Johnson City or even as a shoe salesman in Vestal. Jimmy's father had always been interested in history, that was another constant in Jimmy's life, and sometimes he did volunteer work for the Catholic Integration League. He never had much time to spend with Jimmy, wherever they lived, wherever he worked; that was another thing that didn't change. Jimmy's mother usually taught at the elementary school, although sometimes she worked as a typist at home, and other times—the bad times again—she stayed at home and took "medicine" and didn't work at all.

That morning when Jimmy woke up, the first thing he

realized was that it was summer, a fact testified to by the
brightness of the sunshine and the balminess of the air that
came in through the open window, making up for his memory of yesterday, which had been gray and cold and dour. He
rolled out of bed, surprised for a moment to find himself on
the top tier of a bunk bed, and plumped down to the floor
hard enough to make the soles of his feet tingle; at the last
few places they had lived, he hadn't a bunk bed, and he
wasn't used to waking up that high off the ground. Sometimes he had trouble finding his clothes in the morning, but
this time it seemed that he had been conscientious enough to
hang them all up the night before, and he came across a blue
shirt with a zigzag green stripe that he had not seen in a long
time. That seemed like a good omen to him, and cheered him.
He put on the blue shirt, then puzzled out the knots he could
not remember leaving in his shoelaces. Still blinking sleep
out of his eyes, he hunted futilely for his toothbrush; it always took a while for his mind to clear in the mornings, and
he could be confused and disoriented until it did, but eventually memories began to seep back in, as they always did, and
he sorted through them, trying to keep straight which house
this was out of all the ones he had lived in, and where he kept
things here.

Of course. But who would ever have thought that he'd
keep it in an old coffee can under his desk!

Downstairs, his mother was making French toast, and he
stopped in the archway to watch her as she cooked. She was
a short, plump, dark-eyed, olive-complexioned woman who
wore her oily black hair pulled back in a tight bun. He
watched her intently as she fussed over the hot griddle, noticing her quick nervous motions, the irritable way she patted at
loose strands of her hair. Her features were tightly drawn, her
nose was long and straight and sharp, as though you could
cut yourself on it, and she seemed all angles and edges today.
Jimmy's father had been sitting sullenly over his third cup of
coffee, but as Jimmy hesitated in the archway, he got to his
feet and began to get ready for work. He was a thin man with
a pale complexion and a shock of wiry red hair, and Jimmy

bit his lip in disappointment as he watched him, keeping well back and hoping not to be noticed. He could tell from the insignia on his father's briefcase that his father was working in Endicott today, and those times when his father's job was in Endicott were among the times when both of his parents would be at their most snappish in the morning.

He slipped silently into his chair at the table as his father stalked wordlessly from the room, and his mother served him his French toast, also wordlessly, except for a slight, sullen grunt of acknowledgment. This was going to be a bad day—not as bad as those times when his father worked in Manningtown and his mother took her "medicine," not as bad as some other times that he had no intention of thinking about at all, but unpleasant enough, right on the edge of acceptability. He shouldn't have given in to tiredness and come inside yesterday, he should have kept playing the Game . . . Fortunately, he had no intention of spending much time here today.

Jimmy got through his breakfast with little real difficulty, except that his mother started in on her routine about why didn't he call Tommy Melkonian, why didn't he go swimming or bike riding, he was daydreaming his summer away, it wasn't natural for him to be by himself all the time, he needed friends, it hurt her and made her feel guilty to see him moping around by himself all the time . . . and so on. He made the appropriate noises in response, but he had no intention of calling Tommy Melkonian today, or of letting her call for him. He had only played with Tommy once or twice before, the last time being when they lived over on Clinton Street (Tommy hadn't been around before that), but he didn't even *like* Tommy all that much, and he certainly wasn't going to waste the day on him. Sometimes Jimmy had given in to temptation and wasted whole days playing jacks or kick-the-can with other kids, or going swimming, or flipping baseball cards; sometimes he'd frittered away a week like that without once playing the Game. But in the end he always returned dutifully to playing the Game again, however tired of it all he sometimes became. And the Game had to be played alone.

Yes, he was definitely going to play the Game today; there was certainly no incentive to hang around here; and the Game seemed to be easier to play on fine, warm days anyway, for some reason.

So as soon as he could, Jimmy slipped away. For a moment he confused this place with the house they sometimes lived in on Ash Street, which was very similar in layout and where he had a different secret escape route to the outside, but at last he got his memories straightened out. He snuck into the cellar while his mother was busy elsewhere, and through the back cellar window, under which he had placed a chair so that he could reach the cement overhang and climb out onto the lawn. He cut across the neighbors' yards to Charles Street and then over to Floral Avenue, a steep macadam dead-end road. Beyond was the start of the woods that belonged to the cemetery. Sometimes the mud hills below the woods would be guarded by a mangy black and brown dog that would bark, snarl at him, and chase him. He walked faster, dreading the possibility.

But once in the woods, in the cool brown and green shade of bole and leaf, he knew he was safe, safe from everything, and his pace slowed. The first tombstone appeared, half buried in mulch and stained with green moss, and he patted it fondly, as if it were a dog. He was in the cemetery now, where it had all begun so long ago. Where he had first played the Game.

Moving easily, he climbed up toward the crown of woods, a grassy knoll that poked up above the surrounding trees, the highest point in the cemetery. Even after all he had been through, this was still a magic place for him; never had he feared spooks or ghouls while he was here, even at night, although often as he walked along, as now, he would peer up at the gum-gray sky, through branches that interlocked like the fingers of witches, and pretend that monsters and secret agents and dinosaurs were moving through the woods around him, that the stunted azalea bushes concealed pirates or orcs . . . But these were only small games, mood-setting exercises to prepare him for the playing of the Game itself, and they fell away from him like a shed skin as he came out onto the grassy knoll and the landscape opened up below.

Jimmy stood entranced, feeling the warm hand of the sun on the back of his head, hardly breathing, listening to the chirruping of birds, the scratching of katydids, the long, sighing rush of wind through oak and evergreen. The sky was blue and high and cloudless, and the Susquehanna River gleamed below like a mirror snake, burning silver as it wound through the rolling, hilly country.

SLOWLY, HE BEGAN to play the Game. How had it been, that first time that he had played it, inadvertently, not realizing what he was doing, not understanding that he was playing the Game or what Game he was playing until after he had already started playing? How had it been? Had everything looked like this? He decided that the sun had been lower in the sky that day, that the air had been hazier, that there had been a mass of clouds on the eastern horizon, and he flicked through mental pictures of the landscape as if he were rifling through a deck of cards with his thumb, until he found one that seemed to be right. Obediently, the sky grew darker, but the shape and texture of the clouds were not right, and he searched until he found a better match. It had been somewhat colder, and there had been a slight breeze . . .

So far it had been easy, but there were more subtle adjustments to be made. Had there been four smokestacks or five down in Southside? Four, he decided, and took one away. Had that radio tower been on the crest of that particular distant hill? Or on *that* one? Had the bridge over the Susquehanna been nearer or farther away? Had that Exxon sign been there, at the corner of Cedar Road? Or had it been an Esso sign? His blue shirt had changed to a brown shirt by now, and he changed it further, to a red pinstriped shirt, trying to remember. Had that ice cream stand been there? He decided that it had not been. His skin was dark again now, although his hair was still too straight . . . Had the cemetery fence been a wrought-iron fence or a hurricane fence? Had there been the sound of a factory whistle blowing? The smell of sulphur in the air? Or the smell of pine . . . ?

He worked at it until dark; and then, drained, he came back down the hill again.

The shopping mall was still there, but the school and schoolyard had vanished this time, to be replaced by the familiar row of stately, dormer-windowed old mansions. That usually meant that he was at least close. The house was on Schubert Street this evening, several blocks over from where it had been this morning, and it was a two-story, not a three-story house, closer to his memories of how things had been before he'd started playing the Game. The car outside the house was a '78 Volvo—not what he remembered, but closer than the '73 Buick from this morning. The windshield bore an Endicott parking sticker, and there was some Weston Computer literature tucked under the eyeshade, all of which meant that it was probably safe to go in; his father wouldn't be a murderous drunk this particular evening.

Inside the parlor, Jimmy's father looked up from his armchair, where he was reading Fuller's *Decisive Battles of the Western World*, and winked. "Hi, sport," he said, and Jimmy replied, "Hi, Dad." At least his father was a black man this time, as he should be, although he was much fatter than Jimmy ever remembered him being, and still had this morning's kinky red hair, instead of the kinky black hair he should have. Jimmy's mother came out of the kitchen, and she was thin enough now, but much too tall, with a tiny upturned nose, blue eyes instead of hazel, hair more blond than auburn . . .

"Wash up for dinner, Jimmy," his mother said, and Jimmy turned slowly for the stairs, feeling exhaustion wash through him like a bitter tide. She wasn't *really* his mother, they weren't *really* his parents. He had come a lot closer than this before, lots of other times . . . But always there was some small detail that was wrong, that proved that this particular probability-world out of the billions of probability-worlds was *not* the one he had started from, was not *home*.

Still, he had done much worse than this before, too. At

least this wasn't a world where his father was dead, or an atomic war had happened, or his mother had cancer or was a drug addict, or his father was a brutal drunk, or a Nazi, or a child molester . . . This would do, for the night . . . He would settle for this, for tonight . . . He was so tired . . .

In the morning, he would start searching again.

Someday, he would find them.

Killing the Morrow

Robert Reed

It's a commonplace that the past creates the future; in the chilling story that follows, we see what happens when the future tries to create the future. . . .

Robert Reed sold his first story in 1986, and quickly established himself as one of the most prolific of today's young writers, particularly at short fiction lengths, seriously rivaled for that position only by authors such as Stephen Baxter and Brian Stableford. And—also like Baxter and Stableford—he manages to keep up a very high standard of quality *while* being prolific, something that is not at all easy to do. Reed stories such as "Sister Alice," "Brother Perfect," "Decency," "Savior," "The Remoras," "Chrysalis," "Whiptail," "The Utility Man," "Marrow," "Birth Day," "Blind," "The Toad of Heaven," "Stride," "The Shape of Everything," "Guest of Honor," "Waging Good," and "Killing the Morrow," among at least a half-dozen others equally as strong, count as among some of the best short work produced by anyone in the '80s and '90s; many of his best stories were assembled in his first collection, *The Dragons of Springplace*. He is equally prolific as a novelist, having turned out ten novels since the end of the '80s, including *The Lee*

Shore, The Hormone Jungle, Black Milk, The Remarkables, Down the Bright Way, Beyond the Veil of Stars, An Exaltation of Larks, Beneath the Gated Sky, Marrow, and *Sister Alice,* plus a novella chapbook, *Mere.* His most recent books are a new novel, *The Well of Stars,* and a new collection, *The Cuckoo's Boys.* Reed lives with his family in Lincoln, Nebraska.

YOU KNOW, I'VE heard my share of disembodied voices. I'm accustomed to their fickle, sometimes bizarre demands. But tonight's voice is different, clear as gin and utterly compelling. I must listen. Sitting inside my old packing crate, my worldly possessions at arm's length, I am fed instructions that erase everything familiar and prosaic. Yet I cannot resist, can't offer even a token resistance, now crawling out of my little house and rising, my heart pounding as the last shreds of sanity are lost to me.

I've lived in this alleyway for eight months, yet I don't look back. I'm in poor physical condition and my shoes are worn through, but I walk several miles without rest, without complaint. And there are others, too: the streets are full of silent walkers. They exhibit a calmness, a liquid orderliness, that would disturb the healthy observer. Yet I barely notice the others. I want a specific street, which I find, turning right and following it for another mile. The tall buildings fall away into trim working-class houses. Another street beckons. I start to read the numbers on mailboxes. The house I want is on a corner, lit up and its front door left open. I step inside without ringing the bell, thinking that the place looks familiar . . . as if I've been here before, or maybe seen it in dreams. . . .

My new life begins.

More than most people, I have experience with radical change, with the vagaries of existence. Tonight's change is simply more sudden and more tightly orchestrated than those of the past. I'm here for a reason, no doubt about it. There's some grand cause that will be explained in due time. And meanwhile, there's pleasure: for the first time in years, existence has a palatable purpose, authority, and as astonishing as it seems, a genuine beauty.

An opened can of warming beer is set on the coffee table. I pick it up and sniff, then set it down again, which is uncharacteristic for me. An enormous television is in the corner, the all-sports channel still broadcasting, nothing to see but an empty court and arena. The game was canceled without fuss. Somehow I know that nobody will ever again play that particular sport, that it was rendered extinct in an instant. Yet any sense of loss is cushioned by the Voice. It makes me crumble onto a lumpy sofa, listening and nodding, eyes fixed on nothing.

Tools are in the garage, I'm told. I carry them into the living room, arranging them according to their use. Then armed with a short rusty crowbar I head upstairs, finding the bathroom and a big steel bathtub, and with the crowbar I start to batter the mildewed tile and plaster, startled cockroaches fleeing the light.

After a little while the front door opens, closes.

I go downstairs, part of me curious. A handsome woman is waiting for me, offering a thin smile. She's dressed in quality clothes, and she's my age but with much less mileage. That smile of hers is hopeful, even enthusiastic, but beneath it is a much-hidden sense of terror.

What's her name? I wonder. But I won't ask.

Nor does she ask about me.

With two backs available, we start to clear the living room of furniture and the dusty old carpeting. By now the television has gone blank. I unplug it, and together we carry it to the curb. Electronics are an important resource. Our neighbors— mismatched couples like ourselves—are doing the same job, stereos and microwave ovens and televisions stacked and covered carefully with plastic. Firearms make smaller, secondary piles. Then around midnight a large truck arrives. I'm dragging out the last of the carpeting, pausing long enough to watch a crew of burly men loading everything into the long trailer. One of them seems familiar. He was a police officer, wasn't he? I remember him. He bullied me on several occasions for the fun of it. And now we are equals, animosity nothing but a luxury. I manage to wave at him. No response. Then

I return to the house, never hurrying. Rain begins to fall, fat cold drops striking the back of my neck, and with them comes a fatigue, sudden and profound, that leaves my legs shaking and my breath coming in little wet gulps.

The Voice has already told us to sleep when it's needed. The woman and I move upstairs, climbing into the same bed without undressing. Nudity is permitted. Many things are permitted, we've been told. But I can't help thinking of the woman's terror as I lie beside her, looking as I do, unshaved and filthy, wearing sores and months of grime. It's better to do nothing, I decide. Just to sleep.

"Good night," I whisper.

She isn't crying, but when she says, "Sleep well," I hear her working not to cry, the words tight and slow. Was she married in her former life? She doesn't wear any rings, yet she seems like a person who would enjoy, even demand marriage. She's awake for more than an hour, lying as motionless as possible, her ordinary old parts struggling to find some reason for the bizarre things that are happening now.

I feel pity.

Yet for the most part, I like these changes. The bed is soft, the sheets almost clean. I lie awake out of contentment, listening to the rain on the roof and thinking about my packing crate in the alleyway—feeling no fondness at all for that dead past.

I DREAM OF grass, astonishing as that seems.

Of an apeman.

No, that's a lousy term. *Hominid* is more appropriate. The creature walks under a bright tropical sky, minding its own narrow business. A male, I realize. I'm sitting in the future, watching it from ground level and feeling waves of excitement. Here is an ancestor of the human species, naked and lovely, and it doesn't even notice me, strolling past and out of sight. I have seen through time, changing nothing. Aren't I a clever ape? I ask myself.

Not clever enough, a voice warns me.

A quiet, almost whispered voice.

•   •   •

WE DIVIDE OUR jobs according to ability. Being somewhat stronger than the woman, I work to dislodge the bathtub from the wall, then lever it into the hallway and shove it down the splintering wooden stairs. And meanwhile the woman has cleaned the living room a dozen times, at least, the windows covered with foil and the air heavy with chlorine.

Vans and small trucks begin to deliver equipment. Thermostats and filters have been adapted from local stocks, I suppose. More sophisticated machinery arrives later. Jugs of thick clear fluid are stacked in the darkest corner. Perfect cleanliness isn't mandatory, yet the woman struggles to keep the room surgically clean, hoping that the Voice will applaud her efforts.

She's first to say, "The Voice comes from the future."

Obviously, yes.

"From the distant future," she adds.

I can't guess dates, but it seems likely.

"And this is a womb," she remarks, pointing at the old bathtub. "Here is where the future will be born."

The Voice speaks differently to different people, it seems. I assumed that the tub was an elaborate growth chamber, but how exactly does one grow the future?

Taking me by the waist, she says, "It'll be like our own child."

I make affirmative sounds, but something feels wrong.

"I love you," she assures me.

"I love you," I lie. Nothing is as vital to her as her illusions of the loving family.

Does the Voice know that?

In the night, between work and sleep, she invites me to her side of the bed. It's been a long time. My performance is less than sterling, but at least the experience is pleasant, building new bonds. Then afterward we cuddle under the sheets, whisper in secret tones, then drift off into a fine, deep sleep, dreams coming from the darkness.

RAIN FALLS IN my dreams.

Motion, I learn, is matter shaped by the hand of Chaos.

Tiny variations in wind and moisture will conspire to ignite or extinguish entire storms. And no conceivable machine or mind can know every fluctuation, every inspiration. It's not even possible to predict which minuscule event will produce the perfect day, leaving millions of lives changed, the fundamental shape of everything warped ever so slightly. . . .

Suppose you can reach back in time, says my dream voice. Suppose you're aware of the dangers in changing what was, but you have ego enough to accept the risks. Channeling vast energies, you create your windows entirely from local materials. It is thermally identical to the surrounding ground. You limit your study to a few useful moments. All you allow yourself is a camera and transmitter, intricate but indistinguishable from the local sand and grit. The hominid can stare at the window. He can stomp on it. He can fling it, eat it, or simply ignore it. But nothing, nothing, nothing he can do will make it behave as anything but the perfect grain of dirty quartz.

And yet, says the dream voice.

Despite your hard work and cleverness, there is some telling impact. Perhaps heat leaked from the mechanism, atoms jostled by their touch. Or perhaps its optical energies were imperfectly balanced, excess photons added to or taken away from the local environment. There would be no way to know what went wrong. But the consequences will spread, becoming apparent, growing from nothing until they encompass everything.

The universe, I'm learning, is incomprehensibly fragile.

How can any person, any intelligence, hope to put *everything* back where it belongs?

A YOUNG MAN delivers foodstuffs and other general supplies, coming twice a week, and sometimes he lingers on the porch, telling me what he has seen around town. Factories and warehouses have been refurbished, he says. Old people and eerily patient children work and live inside them. Some of the factories make the machines that fill my living room/nursery. But the majority of the products are stranger. He grins, describing brilliant lights and tiny power plants, robots and more robots. Isn't it all amazing? Wondrous? And fun?

I nod. Astonishment does seem like the day's most abundant product.

The woman dislikes my chatting with the young man. She feels that he's a poor worker, obviously not paying ample attention to the Voice. For the first time, for just an instant, I wonder if the Voice doesn't touch people with equal force. For instance, the woman claims to hear it all of the time, her initial terror replaced with energy and commitment, or at least the nervous desire to please it. But for me there are long periods of silence, of relative peace. It's the woman who wakes first in the morning. It's the woman who loses track of time and hunger, scrubbing the floor until her hands bleed. And she's the one who snaps at the delivery boy, telling him:

"You're not helping us at all!"

To which he says, "Except I am." At once, without hesitation, he says, "Part of my job is to tell others what I see, to keep them aware of what's being done. How else can you know? You can't go anywhere. Your job is to stay put, and you're doing that perfectly."

The logic has its impact. She retreats with a growl, her anger helping her to polish the bathtub for the umpteenth time.

I wonder, in secret, if the delivery boy is telling the truth.

Or is he a clever liar?

And how can I wonder about such things? Just considering the possibility of subterfuge is a kind of subterfuge. Particularly when I find myself admiring the boy's courage.

In secret.

THE PAST HAS been changed, I learn in my sleep.

Small events have evolved into mammoth ones.

Perhaps an excess heat caused an instability that altered the precise pattern of raindrops in a summer shower. Hominids made love in the rain. It's not that they wouldn't have had rain, but it's the delicate impact of thousands of raindrops that matter. Eggs and sperm are extraordinarily sensitive, I'm learning. Change any parameter—the instant of ejaculation; the angle of thrust; the simplest groan of thanks—and a different sperm will find its target. Even the drumming of raindrops will jostle the testicles enough, now and again, and produce different offspring. Which in turn means a different human evolution.

The species isn't altered appreciably. People remain people, good and not. Nor is the character of history changed. Humankind will master the same tools, then warfare and the intricacies of nation-states. What matters is that the specific faces will change, and the names, every historical figure erased along with every anonymous one, an enormous wavelike disruption racing out through time.

In order to kill myself, I don't have to kill my grandpa.

I just have to tickle his hairy balls.

THEY BRING THE embryo in, of all things, an old florist's van.

Each house on our street gets its own embryo, and the Voice fills everyone with a sense of honor and duty. We've sealed the bathtub's drain, then filled it with the heavy fluids. Tubes pump in oxygen. The workers connect the embryo to a plastic umbilical, then I help the woman check every dial and sensor, making certain that the tiny smear of living tissue is healthy.

It doubles in size, that day and every day, hands and feet showing before the end of the week. It's not growing like any human, but maybe that's a consequence of the fluids. Or synthetic genes. Or maybe all the generations of evolution between him and me.

The woman shivers, weeps. Holding herself, she announces, "At least one of us has to stay with it now. Always."

In case of some unlikely, unforeseen problem, yes. We can pick up the telephone, emergency services waiting to troubleshoot.

"Night and day," she says, with a thrill.

I'll give her the night shift, I decide.

"This is our child," she claims, repeating what the Voice

tells her. Her own voice is stiff and dry. Unabashedly fanatical. "Don't you think he's lovely, darling?"

But he's not my child, or my grandchild, either. For an instant, I consider mentioning my dreams of Africa and the vagaries of time . . . but then I think again, some piece of me guessing that this woman has had no such dreams.

"Isn't he lovely?" she asks again.

I say, "Lovely," without feeling.

Yet the word itself is enough for her. She nods and smiles, her face lit up with the injected joy.

THE PAST IS a sea, I dream. A great flat mirror of a sea. Standing on the present, on a low shoreline, I carelessly throw a grain of sand over my shoulder. Its impact is tiny, too tiny to observe, but the resulting wave is growing, a small ripple becoming a mountainous wall rushing straight at me.

What can I do? Flee into the future? But with each step the future becomes the present, and I can never run so far that the wave won't catch me, utterly and forever dissolving my existence.

But there is one answer. Pack a bag, bend at the knees, and wait. Wait, then leap. With care and a certain desperate fearlessness, I can launch myself over the wave, evading it entirely. Then I'll fall again, tumbling onto the calm past, creating a second obliterating wave, but my own life saved regardless.

Fuck the costs.

OUR "CHILD" IS less childlike with each passing day.

Even the woman is having difficulty sounding like the proud parent.

Curled in a fetal position, this citizen from the future resembles a middle-aged man, comfortably plump and shockingly hairy, lost in sleep while his memories are placed inside his newly minted mind.

I can't help but notice, his brain is huge.

I sit alone with him in the morning and again in the early evening, nothing to do but watch his slumber as well as the humming and clicking machines. It's ironic that this creature, having his existence threatened by the most trivial event, is now employing the coarsest tomfoolery to save his ass. The entire Earth must be involved. Every human and every resource is being marshaled to meet some rigorous schedule. This is an invasion; and like any invasion, success hinges on the beachhead.

The future is attempting to leap over its extinction, very little room for error.

And I'm beginning to notice how the Voice, busy speaking to this superman's mind, speaks less and less to me.

The Voice has its limits, of course.

Yet at night my dreams persist, that different voice showing me wonders as fascinating as anything in my waking life.

THE DELIVERY BOY begins to arrive at irregular intervals, but never as often as before.

"To save gas," he claims, always smiling. But that smile has a satirical bite to it. "And from now on, sorry. There's no more meat or eggs."

For health reasons, perhaps. Or the invaders could be vegetarians.

"Let me look at yours," says the boy, stepping indoors for the first time. He doesn't wait for approval, walking up to the bathtub and staring at the sleeping shape. "I wonder what he's like. When he's finished, I mean."

I have no idea. And that bothers me.

"Of course he'll be grateful for your help. I'm sure of that."

I'm nervous. It's against every rule to have visitors. What if the woman wakes early and finds the boy here? What if a neighbor reports me? Touching a shoulder, I try easing him toward the door, asking in a whisper, "What have you seen lately?"

He mentions giant machines that have rolled to the north. Bright lights show at night, and there's rumbling that might mean construction. A new city is being built, he hears. From others.

I ask about the people who built those rolling machines. Where have they gone?

"They've been reassigned, of course. There's always work to be done somewhere. Always, always."

He smiled at me, the message in his eyes.

Then we reach the door, and again he stands on the porch, telling me, "Once a week, and I don't know which day. No meat, no eggs. And that's a lovely boy you've got there. A real darling."

I WASH MYSELF daily, using a shower in the basement. Rationing my soap, I've managed to stay clean for six months in a row. My loose-fitting clothes come from the closets and drawers. When they're gone, I put the soiled ones in the sun, cleaning them with light and heat.

I wanted to seem more attractive to the woman, and for a little while she was responding.

But now she has doubts about sex, always distracted, needing to be in some position that leaves her able to monitor the dials. More and more she complains about being tired or disinterested. The man-child's presence makes her edgy. I wish she'd become pregnant, except of course a pregnancy would be a problem. A division of allegiances. But then I realize that if the Voice can speak to a mind, interfacing with its network of interlocking neurons, then shouldn't it be able to speak to glands as well? Couldn't it put all of our bothersome sperm and eggs to sleep?

One night, waking alone in bed, I feel a powerful desire to make love to a woman. I come downstairs and ask permission, and the woman's response is a sharp "Not here, no!" Which leads me to suggest that she abandon her post for a few minutes. I promise to hurry, and where's the harm?

She gasps, moans, and nearly collapses. "I can't do *that*."

We'll never couple again. I know it, and it both saddens and relieves me. Alone, I feel free. An old reflex lets me wonder where I could find someone else. A lady more amiable, someone that I've selected for myself.

Beginning tomorrow morning, the woman sleeps in the

living room, on sheets and pillows spread over the clean hard floor.

She won't leave me alone at my post.

She has a bucket next to the door where she pisses and shits. And when she looks at me, in those rare moments, nothing can hide her total scorn.

THIS IS MY last lucid dream.

I'm standing on the beach, sand without color and a wall of radiant ocean water roaring toward me. And a woman appears. Like the man in my bathtub, she has an elongated skull and a superior intellect, but her face is completely human, showing a mixture of fear and empathy, as well as a sturdy strength born of convictions.

"We think they are wrong," she begins. "Please remember this. Not all of us are like *them*."

I nod, trying to describe my appreciation.

But she interrupts, telling me, "This is all we can do for you."

I can't recognize her language, yet I understand every word.

"Best wishes," she says.

Then she begins to cry.

I try to embrace her. I step forward and open my arms . . . but then the water is on me, the beach and her dissolving into atoms . . . and my hands struggle to reassemble her from memory, the task impossible for every good reason. . . .

A NEW DELIVERY boy arrives.

Perhaps ten years old, he needs to make two trips from his station wagon, carrying the minimal groceries to the porch and no farther. I'm standing on my porch waiting for the second load. Fresh air feels pleasant. The lawn has grown shaggy and seedy, the old furniture and carpeting rotting without complaint amidst the greenness. A quick calculation tells me that this is late autumn, early winter. The trees should have changed and lost their leaves by now. Yet the world smells and tastes like spring, both climate and vegetation under some kind of powerful control.

The boy struggles with a numbered sack. Not only is he small, he looks malnourished. But he brings my food with a fanatical sense of purpose, and when I ask about the other boy, the older boy, he merely replies:

"He's done."

What does that mean?

"Done," he repeats, angry not to be understood.

Hearing our voices, the woman wakes and comes to the door. "Get back in here," she snaps. "I'm warning you!"

One last look at the improved world, then I retreat, taking both sacks with me. Meanwhile the boy fires up the station wagon, black smoke dispersing in all directions. He looks silly, that fierce little head peering through the steering wheel. He pulls into the next driveway, and I wonder who lives in that house. And what do they dream about?

The woman is complaining about my attitudes, my carelessness. Everything. I'm a safer subject than the lousy quality of today's barley and rice.

"Come here," she tells me.

Perhaps I will, perhaps I won't.

"Or I'll pick up the phone and complain," she threatens.

She won't. First of all, I terrify her. What if I extracted some kind of vengeance in response? And secondly, the thought of being entirely alone must disturb her. I know it whenever I stare at her, making her shrink away. As much as she hates me, without my presence she might forget that she's genuinely alive.

THE FUTURE DOOMED itself.

Then it packed its bags, intending to save itself.

But like a weather system, the future is too large and chaotic to be of one mind, holding to a single outcome. Some of its citizens argued that they didn't have the right to intrude on the past. "Why should we supplant these primitive people?" they asked. "We screwed up, and if we were any sort of hominids, we would accept our fate and be done with it."

But most of their species felt otherwise. And by concentrating the energies of two earths, present and past, they felt there was a better than good chance of success.

Unaware of the secret movement in their midst.

Never guessing that there was a second surreptitious Voice.

ALARMS WAKE ME, and I rush downstairs just as the man-child is born. With a slow majesty, he sits up in the bathtub, the thick fluids sliding off his slick and hairy body. The beep-beep of the alarms quit, replaced with a scream from the woman. "Look at you," she says. "Oh, look at you!"

The man couldn't look more pissed, coughing until his lungs clear, then screwing up his face, saying something in that future language. A nearby machine activates itself, translating his words. "I want water. Cold water. Get me water."

"I'll get it," I say.

The woman is too busy grinning and applauding herself. "You're a darling lovely man, sir. And I took care of you. Almost entirely by myself, I did."

The man-child speaks again.

"I'm still thirsty," the machine reports, both voices impatient.

In the kitchen, propped next to the back door, is the same crow bar that I used on the bathtub. That's what I bring him. A useful sense of rage has been building, probably from the beginning; this stranger and his ilk have destroyed my world. It's only fair, only just, to take the steel bar in my hands and swing, striking him before he has the strength or coordination to fight me.

The woman wails and moans, too stunned to move.

That elongated skull is paper-thin, demolished with the first blow and its jellylike contents scattered around the room.

Too late, she grabs at me, trying to wrestle the crowbar from my hands. I throw her to the floor, considering a double homicide. But that wouldn't be right. Even when she picks up the phone and begs for help, I can't bring myself to kill her. Instead I demolish the wall above her head, startling her, and when she crawls away I lift the receiver, grinning as I calmly tell whoever is listening, "You're next, friend. Your time is just about done."

OUTDOORS IS THE smell of sweet chemicals and smoke. Strange robotic craft streak overhead, probably heading for crisis points. They ignore me. Maybe too much is happening; maybe their mechanisms were sabotaged at the factory. Either way, I'm left to move up the street, entering each house and killing the just-born invaders where I find them. It's messy, violent work, but in one living room I find the "parents" slain, presumably by their thankless "child." The ceiling creaks above their bodies. I climb the stairs on my toes, catching the murderer as she tries on spare clothes, pants around her knees and no chance for her to grab her bloody softball bat.

From then on I'm a demon, focused and confident and very nearly tireless.

Finishing my block, I start for the next one. Rounding the corner of a house, I come face-to-face with a stout woman wielding a fire axe. The two of us pause, then smile knowingly. Then we join forces. Toward dawn, taking a break from our gruesome work, I think to ask:

"What's your name?"

"Laverne," she replies, with a lifelong embarrassment. "And yours?"

"Harold," I confess, pleased that I can remember it after so long. "Good to meet you, and Laverne is a lovely name."

Later that day, she and I and twenty other new friends find the invaders barricaded inside a once-gorgeous mansion. Once it's burned to the ground, the city is liberated.

Where now?

Laverne suggests, "How about north? I once heard that they were building something in that direction."

I hug her, no words needed just now.

WE NAME OUR daughter Unique.

The three of us are living in a city meant for the extinct future, in a shelter made from scraps and set between empty buildings. The buildings themselves are tall and clean, yet somehow very lonely edifices. They won't admit us, but they won't fight us either. And the climate remains ideal. Gardens thrive wherever the earth shows, and our neighbors are scarce and uniformly pleasant.

One night I speak to my infant daughter, telling her that perhaps someday she'll learn how to enter the buildings. Or better, tear them down and use their best parts.

She acts agreeable, babbling something in her baby language. Laverne stretches out before me, naked and agreeable in a different sense. With a sly grin, she asks:

"Care to ride the chaos, darling?"

Always and gladly, thank you. And together, with every little motion, we change the universe in ways we happily cannot predict.

Thus We Frustrate Charlemagne

R. A. Lafferty

The late R. A. Lafferty started writing in 1960, at the relatively advanced age (for a new writer, anyway) of forty-eight, and in the years before his retirement in 1987 and his eventual death, he published some of the freshest and funniest short stories ever written in the genre, as well as a string of vivid and unforgettable books such as the novels *Past Master*, *The Devil Is Dead*, *The Reefs of Earth*, *Okla Hannali*, *The Fall of Rome*, *Arrive At Easterwine*, and *The Flame Is Green*, and landmark collections such as *Nine Hundred Grandmothers*, *Strange Doings*, *Does Anyone Else Have Something Further to Add?*, *Golden Gate and Other Stories*, *Ringing the Changes*, *Iron Star*, *Lafferty In Orbit*, *Iron Tears*, and *The Early Lafferty*. Lafferty won the Hugo Award in 1973 for his story "Eurema's Dam," and in 1990 received the World Fantasy Award, the prestigious Life Achievement Award. He died in 2002.

Here he delivers a sharp and funny cautionary tale for those determined to alter the past to improve the present—maybe sometimes it's better to leave well-enough *alone* . . .

"WE'VE BEEN ON some tall ones," said Gregory Smirnov of the Institute, "but we've never stood on the edge of a bigger one than this, nor viewed one with shakier expectations. Still, if the calculations of Epiktistes are correct, this will work."

"People, it will work," Epikt said.

This was Epiktistes the Ktistec machine? Who'd have believed it? The main bulk of Epikt was five floors below them, but he had run an extension of himself up to this little penthouse lounge. All it took was a cable, no more than a yard in diameter, and a functional head set on the end of it.

And what a head he chose! It was a sea-serpent head, a dragon head, five feet long and copied from an old carnival float. Epikt had also given himself human speech of a sort, a blend of Irish and Jewish and Dutch comedian patter from ancient vaudeville. Epikt was a comic to his last para-DNA relay when he rested his huge, boggle-eyed, crested head on the table there and smoked the biggest stogies ever born.

But he was serious about this project.

"We have perfect test conditions," the machine Epikt said as though calling them to order. "We set out basic texts, and we take careful note of the world as it is. If the world changes, then the texts should change here before our eyes. For our test pilot, we have taken that portion of our own middle-sized city that can be viewed from this fine vantage point. If the world in its past-present continuity is changed by our meddling, then the face of our city will also change instantly as we watch it.

"We have assembled here the finest minds and judgments in the world: eight humans and one Ktistec machine, myself. Remember that there are nine of us. It might be important."

The nine finest minds were: Epiktistes, the transcendent machine who put the "K" in Ktistec; Gregory Smirnov, the large-souled director of the Institute; Valery Mok, an incandescent lady scientist: her over-shadowed and over-intelligent husband Charles Cogsworth; the humorless and inerrant Glasser; Aloysius Shiplap, the seminal genius; Willy McGilly, a man of unusual parts (the seeing third finger on his left hand he had picked up on one of the planets of Kapteyn's Star) and no false modesty; Audifax O'Hanlon; and Diogenes Pontifex.

The latter two men were not members of the Institute (on account of the Minimal Decency Rule), but when the finest minds in the world are assembled, these two cannot very well be left out.

"We are going to tamper with one small detail in past history and note its effect," Gregory said. "This has never been done before openly. We go back to an era that has been called 'A patch of light in the vast gloom,' the time of Charlemagne. We consider why that light went out and did not kindle others. The world lost four hundred years by that flame expiring when the tinder was apparently ready for it. We go back to that false dawn of Europe and consider where it failed. The year was 778, and the region was Spain. Charlemagne had entered alliance with Marsilies, the Arab king of Saragossa, against the Caliph Abd ar-Rahmen of Cordova. Charlemagne took such towns as Pamplona, Huesca and Gerona and cleared the way to Marsilies in Saragossa. The Caliph accepted the situation. Saragossa should be independent, a city open to both Moslems and Christians. The northern marches to the border of France should be permitted their Christianity, and there would be peace for everybody.

"This Marsilies had long treated Christians as equals in Saragossa, and now there would be an open road from Islam into the Frankish Empire. Marsilies gave Charlemagne thirty-three scholars (Moslem, Jewish and Christian) and some Spanish mules to seal the bargain. And there could have been a cross-fertilization of cultures.

"But the road was closed at Roncevalles where the rearguard of Charlemagne was ambushed and destroyed on its way back to France. The ambushers were more Basque than Moslems, but Charlemagne locked the door at the Pyrenees and swore that he would not let even a bird fly over that border thereafter. He kept the road closed, as did his son and his grandsons. But when he sealed off the Moslem world, he also sealed off his own culture.

"In his latter years he tried a revival of civilization with a ragtag of Irish half-scholars, Greek vagabonds and Roman copyists who almost remembered an older Rome. These weren't enough to revive civilization, and yet Charlemagne came close with them. Had the Islam door remained open, a real revival of learning might have taken place then rather than four hundred years later. We are going to arrange that the ambush at Roncevalles did not happen and that the door between the two civilizations was not closed. Then we will see what happens to us."

"Intrusion like a burglar bent," said Epikt.

"Who's a burglar?" Glasser demanded.

"I am," Epikt said. "We all are. It's from an old verse. I forget the author; I have it filed in my main mind downstairs if you're interested."

"We set out a basic text of Hilarius," Gregory continued. "We note it carefully, and we must remember it the way it is. Very soon, that may be the way it *was*. I believe that the words will change on the very page of this book as we watch them. Just as soon as we have done what we intend to do."

The basic text marked in the open book read:

> The traitor, Gano, playing a multiplex game, with money from the Cordova Caliph, hired Basque Christians (dressed as Saragossan Mozarabs) to ambush the rear-guard of the Frankish force. To do this it was necessary that Gano keep in contact with the Basques and at the same time delay the rear-guard of the Franks. Gano, however, served both as guide and scout for the Franks. The ambush was effected. Charlemagne lost his Spanish mules. And he locked the door against the Moslem world.

That was the text by Hilarius.

"When we, as it were, push the button (give the nod to Epiktistes), this will be changed," Gregory said. Epikt, by a complex of devices that he has assembled, will send an Avatar (partly of mechanical and partly of ghostly construction), and something will have happened to the traitor Gano along about sundown one night on the road to Roncevalles."

"I hope the Avatar isn't expensive," Willy McGilly said.

"When I was a boy we got by with a dart whittled out of slip-pery elm wood."

"This is no place for humor," Glasser protested. "Who did you, as a boy, ever kill in time, Willy?"

"Lots of them. King Wu of the Manchu, Pope Adrian VII, President Hardy of our own country, King Marcel of Auvergne, the philosopher Gabriel Toeplitz. It's a good thing we got them. They were a bad lot."

"But I never heard of any of them, Willy," Glasser insisted.

"Of course not. We killed them when they were kids."

"Enough of your fooling, Willy," Gregory cut it off.

"Willy's not fooling," the machine Epikt said. "Where do you think I got the idea?"

"Regard the world," Aloysius said softly. "We see our own middle-sized town with half a dozen towers of pastel-colored brick. We will watch it as it grows or shrinks. It will change if the world changes."

"There's two shows in town I haven't seen," Valery said. "Don't let them take them away! After all, there are only three shows in town."

"We regard the Beautiful Arts as set out in the reviews here, which we have also taken as basic texts," Audifax O'Hanlon said. "You can say what you want to, but the arts have never been in meaner shape. Painting is of three schools only, all of them bad. Sculpture is the heaps-of-rusted-metal school and the obscene tinker-toy effects. The only popular art, graffiti on mingitorio walls, has become unimaginative, stylized and ugly.

"The only thinkers to be thought of are the dead Teilhard de Chardin and the stillborn Sartre, Zielinski, Aichinger. Oh well, if you're going to laugh there's no use going on."

"All of us here are experts on something," Cogsworth said. "Most of us are experts on everything. We know the world as it is. Let us do what we are going to do and then look at the world."

"Push the button, Epikt!" Gregory Smirnov ordered.

From his depths, Epiktistes the Ktistec machine sent out an Avatar, partly of mechanical and partly of ghostly construction. Along about sundown on the road from Pamplona to Roncevalles, on August 14 of the year 778, the traitor Gano was taken up from the road and hanged on a carob tree, the only one in those groves of oak and beech. And all things thereafter were changed.

"DID IT WORK, Epikt? Is it done?" Louis Lobachevski demanded. "I can't see a change in anything."

"The Avatar is back and reports his mission accomplished," Epikt stated. "I can't see any change in anything either."

"Let's look at the evidence," Gregory said.

The thirteen of them, the ten humans and the Ktistec, Chresmoeidec and Proaisthematic machines, turned to the evidence with mounting disappointment.

"There is not one word changed in the Hilarius text," Gregory grumbled, and indeed the basic text still read:

> The king Marsilies of Saragossa, playing a multiplex game, took money from the Caliph of Cordova for persuading Charlemagne to abandon the conquest of Spain (which Charlemagne had never considered and couldn't have effected), took money from Charlemagne in recompense for the cities of the Northern marches being returned to Christian rule (though Marsilies himself had never ruled them); and took money from everyone as toll on the new trade passing through his city. Marsilies gave up nothing but thirty-three scholars, the same number of mules and a few wagonloads of book-manuscripts from the old Hellenistic libraries. But a road over the mountains was opened between the two worlds; and also a sector of the Mediterranean coast became open to both. A limited opening was made between the two worlds, and a limited reanimation of civilization was affected in each.

"No, there is not one word of the text changed," Gregory grumbled. "History followed its same course. How did our experiment fail? We tried, by a device that seems a little cloudy now, to shorten the gestation period for the new birth. It would not be shortened."

"The town is in no way changed," said Aloysius Shiplap. "It is still a fine large town with two dozen imposing towers of varicolored limestone and midland marble. It is a vital metropolis, and we all love it, but it is now as it was before."

"There are still two dozen good shows in town that I haven't seen," Valery said happily as she examined the billings. "I was afraid that something might have happened to them."

"There is no change at all in the Beautiful Arts as reflected in the reviews here that we have taken as basic texts," said Audifax O'Hanlon. "You can say what you want to, but the arts have never been in finer shape."

"It's a link of sausage," said the machine Chresmoeidy.

"'Nor know the road who never ran it thrice,'" said the machine Proaisth. "That's from an old verse; I forget the author; I have it filed in my main mind in England if you're interested."

"Oh yes, it's the three-cornered tale that ends where it begins," said the machine Epiktistes. "But it is good sausage, and we should enjoy it; many ages have not even this much."

"What are you fellows babbling about?" Audifax asked without really wanting to know. "The art of painting is still almost incandescent in its bloom. The schools are like clustered galaxies, and half the people are doing some of this work for pleasure. Scandinavian and Maori sculpture are hard-put to maintain their dominance in the field where almost everything is extraordinary. The impassioned-comic has released music from most of its bonds. Since speculative mathematics and psychology have joined the popular performing arts, there is considerably more sheer fun in life.

"There's a piece here on Pete Teilhard putting him into context as a talented science fiction writer with a talent for outre burlesque. The Brainworld Motif was overworked when he tackled it, but what a shaggy comic extravaganza he did make of it! And there's Muldoom, Zielinski, Popper, Gander, Aichinger, Whitecrow, Hornwhanger—we owe so much to the juice of the cultists! In the main line there are whole congeries and continents of great novels and novelists.

"An ever popular art, graffiti on rningitorio walls, maintains its excellence. Travel Unlimited offers a ninety-nine-day art tour of the world keyed to the viewing of the exquisite and hilarious miniatures on the walls of its own restrooms. Ah, what a copious world we live in!"

"It's more grass than we can graze," said Willy McGilly. "The very bulk of achievement is stupefying. Ah, I wonder if there is subtle revenge in my choice of words. The experiment, of course, was a failure, and I'm glad. I like a full world."

"We will not call the experiment a failure since we have covered only a third of it," said Gregory. "Tomorrow we will make our second attempt on the past. And, if there is a present left to us after that, we will make a third attempt the following day."

"Shove it, good people, shove it," the machine Epiktistes said. "We will meet here again tomorrow. Now you to your pleasures, and we to ours."

THE PEOPLE TALKED that evening away from the machines where they could make foolish conjectures without being laughed at.

"Let's pull a random card out of the pack and go with it," said Louis Lobachevski. "Let's take a purely intellectual crux of a little later date and see if the changing of it will change the world."

"I suggest Ockham," said Johnny Konduly.

"Why?" Valery demanded. "He was the last and least of the medieval schoolmen. How could anything he did or did not do affect anything?"

"Oh no, he held the razor to the jugular," Gregory said. "He'd have severed the vein if the razor hadn't been snatched from his hand. There is something amiss here, though. It is as though I remembered when things were not so stark with Ockham, as though, in some variant, Ockham's Terminalism did not mean what we know that it did mean."

"Sure, let's cut the jugular," said Willy. "Let's find out the logical termination of Terminalism and see just how deep Ockham's razor can cut."

"We'll do it," said Gregory. "Our world has become something of a fat slob; it cloys; it has bothered me all evening. We will find whether purely intellectual attitudes are of actual effect. We'll leave the details to Epikt, but I believe the turning point was in the year 1323 when John Lutterell came from Oxford to Avignon where the Holy See was then situated. He brought with him fifty-six propositions taken from Ockham's Commentary on the Sentences, and he proposed their condemnnation. They were not condemned outright, but Ockham was whipped soundly in that first assault, and he never recovered. Lutterell proved that Ockham's nihilism was a bunch of nothing. And the Ockham thing did die away, echoing dimly through the little German courts where Ockham traveled peddling his wares, but he no longer peddled them in the main markets. Yet his viewpoint could have sunk the world, if indeed, intellectual attitudes are of actual effect."

"We wouldn't have liked Lutterell," said Aloysius. "He was humorless and he had no fire in him, and he was always right. And we would have liked Ockham. He was charming, and he was wrong, and perhaps we will destroy the world yet. There's a chance that we will get our reaction if we allow Ockham free hand. China was frozen for thousands of years by an intellectual attitude, one not nearly so unsettling as Ockham's. India is hypnotized into a queer stasis that calls itself revolutionary, and which does not move—hypnotized by an intellectual attitude. But there was never such an attitude as Ockham's."

So they decided that the former chancellor of Oxford, John Lutterell, who was always a sick man, should suffer one more sickness on the road to Avignon in France, and that he should not arrive there to lance the Ockham thing before it infected the world.

"LET'S GET ON with it, good people," Epikt rumbled the next day. "Me, I'm to stop a man getting from Oxford to Avignon in the year 1323. Well, come, come, take your places, and let's get the thing started." And Epiktistes' great sea-serpent head glowed every color as he puffed on a seven-branched pooka-dooka and filled the room with wonderful smoke.

"Everybody ready to have his throat cut?" Gregory asked cheerfully.

"Cut them," said Diogenes Pontifex, "but I haven't much hope for it. If our yesterday's essay had no effect, I cannot see how one English schoolman chasing another to challenge him in an Italian court in France, in bad Latin, nearly seven hundred years ago, on fifty-six points of unscientific abstract reasoning, can have effect."

"We have perfect test conditions here," said the machine Epikt. "We set out a basic text from Cobblestone's *History of Philosophy*. If our test is effective, then the text will change before our eyes. So will every other text, and the world.

"We have assembled here the finest minds and judgments in the world," the machine Epiktistes said, "ten humans and three machines. Remember that there are thirteen of us. It might be important."

"Regard the world," said Aloysius Shiplap. "I said that yesterday, but it is required that I say it again. We have the world in our eyes and in our memories. If it changes in any way, we will know it."

"Push the button, Epikt," said Gregory Smirnov.

From his depths, Epiktistes the Ktistec machine sent out an Avatar, partly of mechanical and partly of ghostly construction. And along about sundown on the road from Mende to Avignon in the old Languedoc district of France, in the year 1323, John Lutterell was stricken with one more sickness. He was taken to a little inn in the mountain country, and perhaps he died there. He did not, at any rate, arrive at Avignon.

"DID IT WORK, Epikt? Is it done?" Aloysius asked.

"Let's look at the evidence," said Gregory.

The four of them, the three humans and the ghost Epikt, who was a kachenko mask with a speaking tube, turned to the evidence with mounting disappointment.

"There is still the stick and the five notches in it," said Gregory. "It was our test stick. Nothing in the world is changed."

"The arts remain as they were," said Aloysius. "Our picture here on the stone on which we have worked for so many seasons is the same as it was. We have painted the bears black, the buffalos red and the people blue. When we find a way to make another color, we can represent birds also. I had hoped that our experiment might give us that other color. I had even dreamed that birds might appear in the picture on the rock before our very eyes."

"There's still rump of skunk to eat and nothing else," said Valery. "I had hoped that our experiment would have changed it to haunch of deer."

"All is not lost," said Aloysius. "We still have the hickory nuts. That was my last prayer before we began our experiment. 'Don't let them take the hickory nuts away,' I prayed."

They sat around the conference table that was a large flat natural rock, and cracked hickory nuts with stone fist-hammers. They were nude in the crude, and the world was as it had always been. They had hoped by magic to change it.

"Epikt has failed us," said Gregory. "We made his frame out of the best sticks, and we plaited his face out of the finest weeds and grasses. We chanted him full of magic and placed all our special treasures in his cheek pouches. So, what can the magic mask do for us now?"

"Ask it, ask it," said Valery. They were the four finest minds in the world—the three humans, Gregory, Aloysius, and Valery (the *only* humans in the world unless you count those in the other valleys), and the ghost Epikt, a kachenko mask with a speaking tube.

"What do we do now, Epikt?" Gregory asked. Then he went around behind Epikt to the speaking tube.

"I remember a woman with a sausage stuck to her nose," said Epikt in the voice of Gregory. "Is that any help?"

"It may be some help, " Gregory said after he had once more taken his place at the flat-rock conference table. "It is from an old (what's old about it? I made it up myself this morning) folk tale about the three wishes."

"Let Epikt tell it," said Valery. "He does it so much better than you do." Valery went behind Epikt to the speaking tube and blew smoke through it from the huge loose black-leaf uncured stogie that she was smoking.

"The wife wastes one wish for a sausage," said Epikt in the voice of Valery. "A sausage is a piece of deer-meat tied in a piece of a deer's stomach. The husband is angry that the wife has wasted a wish, since she could have wished for a whole deer and had many sausages. He gets so angry that he wishes the sausage might stick to her nose forever. It does, and the woman wails, and the man realized that he had used up the second wish. I forget the rest."

"You can't forget it, Epikt!" Aloysius cried in alarm. "The future of the world may depend on your remembering. Here, let me reason with that damned magic mask!" And Aloysius went behind Epikt to the speaking tube.

"Oh yes, now I remember," Epikt said in the voice of Aloysius. "The man used the third wish to get the sausage off his wife's nose. So things were the way they had been before."

"But we don't want it the way it was before!" Valery howled. "That's the way it is now, rump of skunk to eat, and me with nothing to wear but my ape cape. We want it better. We want deer skins and antelope skins."

"Take me as a mystic or don't take me at all," Epikt signed off.

"Even though the world has always been so, yet we have intimations of other things," Gregory said. "What folk hero was it who made the dart? And of what did he make it?"

"Willy McGilly was the folk hero," said Epikt in the voice of Valery, who had barely got to the speaking tube in time, "and he made it out of slippery elm wood."

"Could we make a dart like the folk hero Willy made?" Aloysius asked.

"We gotta," said Epikt.

"Could we make a slinger and whip it out of our own context and into—"

"Could we kill an Avatar with it before he killed somebody else?" Gregory asked excitedly.

"We sure will try," said the ghost Epikt, who was nothing but a kachenko mask with a speaking tube. "I never did like those Avatars."

You *think* Epikt was nothing but a kachenko mask with a speaking tube! There was a lot more to him than that. He had red garnet rocks inside him and real sea salt. He had powder made from beaver eyes. He had rattlesnake rattles and armadillo shields. He was the first Ktistec machine.

"Give me the word, Epikt," Aloysius cried a few moments later as he fitted the dart to the slinger.

"Fling it! Get that Avatar fink!" Epikt howled.

ALONG ABOUT SUNDOWN in an unnumbered year, on the Road from Nowhere to Eom, an Avatar fell dead with a slippery elm dart in his heart.

"Did it work, Epikt? Is it done?" Charles Cogsworth asked in excitement. "It must have. I'm here. I wasn't in the last one."

"Let's look at the evidence," Gregory suggested calmly.

"Damn the evidence!" Willy McGilly cussed. "Remember where you heard it first."

"Is it started yet?" Glasser asked.

"Is it finished?" Audifax O'Hanlon questioned.

"Push the button, Epilkt!" Diogenes barked. "I think I missed part of it. Let's try again."

"Oh, no, no!" Valery forbade. "Not again. That way is rump of skunk and madness."

The Game of Blood and Dust

Roger Zelazny

Here's a dazzling little story that shows that although the gods may play with our lives and change the world around us as they will, even They still have to play by the *rules*. . . .

Like a number of other writers, the late Roger Zelazny began publishing in 1962 in the pages of Cele Goldsmith's *Amazing*. This was the so-called "Class of '62," whose membership also included Thomas M. Disch, Keith Laumer, and Ursula K. Le Guin. Everyone in that "class" would eventually achieve prominence, but some of them would achieve it faster than others, and Zelazny's subsequent career would be one of the most meteoric rises in the history of SF. The first Zelazny story to attract wide notice was "A Rose for Ecclesiastics," published in 1963 (it was later selected by vote of the SFWA membership to have been one of the best SF stories of all time). By the end of that decade, he had won two Nebula Awards, two Hugo Awards (for *This Immortal* and for his best-known novel, *Lord of Light*) and was widely regarded as one of the two most important American SF writers of the sixties (the other was Samuel R. Delany). By the end of the '70s, although his critical acceptance as an important science fiction writer had dimmed, his long series of novels about the enchanted land of Amber—beginning with *Nine Princes in Amber*—had made him one of the most popular and best-selling fantasy writers of our time, and inspired the founding of worldwide fan clubs and fanzines. Zelazny won another Nebula and a Hugo Award in 1976 for his novella "Home Is the Hangman;" another Hugo in 1986 for his novella "24 Views of Mt. Fuji, by Hosiki;" and a final Hugo in 1987 for his story "Permafrost." In addition to the multivolume Amber series, his other books include the novels *The Dream Master, Isle of the Dead, Jack of Shadows, Eye of Cat, Doorways in the Sand, Today We Choose Faces, Bridge of Ashes, To Die in Italbar,* and *Roadmarks,* and the collections *Four for Tomorrow, The Doors of His Face, The Lamps of His Mouth, and Other Stories, The Last Defender of Camelot,* and *Frost and Fire.* Zelazny died in 1995. A tribute anthology to Zelazny, featuring stories by authors who had been inspired by his work, *Lord of the Fantastic,* was published in 1998.

> *"I am Blood—I go first."*
> *"I am Dust—I follow you."*

THEY DRIFTED TOWARD the Earth, took up stations at its Trojan points.

They regarded the world, its two and a half billions of people, their cities, their devices.

After a time, the inhabitant of the forward point spoke:

"I am satisfied."

There was a long pause, then, "It will do," said the other, fetching up some strontium-90.

Their awareness met above the metal.

"Go ahead," said the one who had brought it.

The other insulated it from Time, provided antipodal pathways, addressed the inhabitant of the trailing point: "Select."

"That one."

The other released the stasis. Simultaneously, they became aware that the first radioactive decay particle emitted fled by way of the opposing path.

"I acknowledge the loss. Choose."

"I am Dust," said the inhabitant of the forward point. "Three moves apiece."

"And I am Blood," answered the other. "Three moves. Acknowledged."

"I choose to go first."

"I follow you. Acknowledged."

They removed themselves from the temporal sequence and regarded the history of the world.

Then Dust dropped into the Paleolithic and raised and uncovered metal deposits across the south of Europe.

"Move one completed."

Blood considered for a timeless time then moved to the second century B.C. and induced extensive lesions in the carotids of Marcus Porcius Cato where he stood in the Roman Senate, moments away from another "Carthago delenda est."

"Move one completed."

Dust entered the fourth century A.D. and injected an air bubble into the bloodstream of the sleeping Julius Ambrosius, the Lion of Mithra.

"Move two completed."

Blood moved to eighth-century Damascus and did the same to Abou Iskafar, in the room where he carved curling alphabets from small, hard blocks of wood.

"Move two completed."

Dust contemplated the play.

"Subtle move, that."

"Thank you."

"But not good enough, I feel. Observe."

Dust moved to seventeenth-century England and, on the morning before the search, removed from his laboratory all traces of the forbidden chemical experiments that had cost Isaac Newton his life.

"Move three completed."

"Good move. But I think I've got you."

Blood dropped to early nineteenth-century England and disposed of Charles Babbage.

"Move three completed."

Both rested, studying the positions.

"Ready?" said Blood.

"Yes."

They reentered the sequence of temporality at the point they had departed.

It took but an instant. It moved like the cracking of a whip below them . . .

They departed the sequence once more, to study the separate effects of their moves now that the general result was known. They observed:

The south of Europe flourished. Rome was founded and grew in power several centuries sooner than had previously been the case. Greece was conquered before the flame of Athens burned with its greatest intensity. With the death of Cato the Elder the final Punic War was postponed. Carthage also continued to grow, extending her empire far to the east and the south. The death of Julius Ambrosius aborted the Mithraist revival and Christianity became the state religion in Rome. The Carthaginians spread their power throughout the middle east. Mithraism was acknowledged as their state religion. The clash did not occur until the fifth century. Carthage itself was destroyed, the westward limits of its empire pushed back to Alexandria. Fifty years later, the Pope called for a crusade. These occurred with some regularity for the next century and a quarter, further fragmenting the Carthaginian empire while sapping the enormous bureaucracy which had grown up in Italy. The fighting fell off, ceased, the lines were drawn, an economic depression swept the Mediterranean area. Outlying districts grumbled over taxes and conscription, revolted. The general anarchy that followed the wars of secession settled down into a dark age reminiscent of that in the initial undisturbed sequence. Off in Asia Minor, the printing press was not developed.

"Stalemate till then, anyway," said Blood.

"Yes, but look what Newton did."

"How could you have known?"

"That is the difference between a good player and an inspired player. I saw his potential even when he was fooling around with alchemy. Look what he did for their science, single-handed—everything! Your next move was too late and too weak."

"Yes. I thought I might still kill their computers by destroying the founder of International Difference Machines, Ltd."

Dust chuckled.

"That was indeed ironic. Instead of an IDM 120, the *Beagle* took along a young naturalist named Darwin."

Blood glanced along to the end of the sequence where the radioactive dust was scattered across a lifeless globe.

"But it was not the science that did it, or the religion."

"Of course not," said Dust. "It is all a matter of emphasis."

"You were lucky. I want a rematch."

"All right. I will even give you your choice: Blood or Dust?"

"I'll stick with Blood."

"Very well. Winner elects to go first. Excuse me."

DUST MOVED TO second-century Rome and healed the carotid lesions that had produced Cato's cerebral hemorrhage.

"Move one completed."

Blood entered eastern Germany in the sixteenth century and induced identical lesions in the Vatican assassin who had slain Martin Luther.

"Move one completed."

"You are skipping pretty far along."

"It is all a matter of emphasis."

"Truer and truer. Very well. You saved Luther. I will save Babbage. Excuse me."

An instantless instant later Dust had returned.

"Move two completed."

Blood studied the playing area with extreme concentration. Then, "All right."

Blood entered Chevvy's Theater on the evening in 1865 when the disgruntled actor had taken a shot at the president of the United States. Delicately altering the course of the bullet in midair, he made it reach its target.

"Move two completed."

"I believe that you are bluffing," said Dust. "You could not have worked out all the ramifications."

"Wait and see."

Dust regarded the area with intense scrutiny.

"All right, then. You killed a president. I am going to save one—or at least prolong his life somewhat. I want Woodrow Wilson to see that combine of nations founded. Its failure will mean more than if it had never been—and it *will* fail.—Excuse me."

Dust entered the twentieth century and did some repair work within the long-jawed man.

"Move three completed."

"Then I, too, shall save one."

Blood entered the century at a farther point and assured the failure of Leon Nozdrev, the man who had assassinated Nikita Khrushchev.

"Move three completed."

"Ready, then?"

"Ready."

They reentered the sequence. The long whip cracked. Radio noises hummed about them. Satellites orbited the world. Highways webbed the continents. Dusty cities held their points of power throughout. Ships clove the seas. Jets slid through the atmosphere. Grass grew. Birds migrated. Fishes nibbled.

Blood chuckled.

"You have to admit it was very close," said Dust.

"As you were saying, there is a difference between a good player and an inspired player."

"You were lucky, too."

Blood chuckled again.

They regarded the world, its two and a half billions of people, their cities, their devices . . .

After a time, the inhabitant of the forward point spoke:

"Best two out of three?"

"All right. I am Blood. I go first."

". . . And I am Dust. I follow you."

Calling Your Name

Howard Waldrop

Here's a wry and compassionate look at the proposition that sometimes it's the little things that count—and when they *do*, they count for a whole hell of a lot. In fact, they can change everything . . . including the world itself.

Howard Waldrop is widely considered to be one of the best short-story writers in the business, and his famous story "The Ugly Chickens" won both the Nebula and the World Fantasy Awards in 1981. His work has been gathered in the collections: *Howard Who?*, *All About Strange Monsters of the Recent Past: Neat Stories by Howard Waldrop*, *Night of the Cooters: More Neat Stories by Howard Waldrop*, and *Going Home Again*. Waldrop is also the author of the novel *The Texas-Israeli War: 1999*, in collaboration with Jake Saunders, and of two solo novels, *Them Bones* and *A Dozen Tough Jobs*. He is at work on a new novel, tentatively entitled *The Moon World*. His most recent books are the print version of his collection *Dream Factories and Radio Pictures* (formerly available only in downloadable form online), the chapbook *A Better World's in Birth!*, and a collection of his stories written in collaboration with various other authors, *Custer's Last Jump and Other Col-*

laborations. Coming up is a new chapbook collection. Having
lived in Washington State for a number of years, Waldrop recently moved back to his former hometown of Austin, Texas.

> *All my life I've waited*
> *for someone to ease the pain*
> *All my life I've waited*
> *for someone to take the blame*

> —from "Calling Your Name"
> by Janis Ian

I REACHED FOR the switch on the band saw.

THEN I WOKE up with a crowd forming around me.
    And I was in my own backyard.

IT TURNS OUT that my next-door neighbor had seen me fall
out of the storage building I use as a workshop and had called
911 when I didn't get up after a few seconds.

ONCE, LONG AGO in college, working in Little Theater. I'd
had a light bridge lowered to set the fresnels for *Blithe Spirit,*
just after the Christmas semester break. Some idiot had left a
hot male 220 plug loose, and as I reached up to the iron
bridge, it dropped against the bar. I'd felt that, all over, and I
jumped backward about fifteen feet.
    A crowd started for me, but I let out some truly blazing
oath that turned the whole stage violet-indigo blue and they
disappeared in a hurry. Then I yelled at the guys and girl in the
technical booth to kill everything onstage, and spent the next
hour making sure nothing else wasn't where it shouldn't
be. . . .
    That's while I was working thirty-six hours a week at a
printing plant, going to college full-time and working in the
theater another sixty hours a week for no pay. I was also dat-
ing a foul-mouthed young woman named Susan who was

brighter than me. Eventually something had to give—it was my stomach (an ulcer at twenty) and my relationship with her.

She came back into the theater later that day, and heard about the incident and walked up to me and said, "Are you happy to see me, or is that a hot male 220-volt plug in your pocket?"

That shock, the 220, had felt like someone shaking my hand at 2700 rpm while wearing a spiked glove and someone behind me was hammering nails in my head and meanwhile they were piling safes on me. . . .

When I'd touched the puny 110 band saw, I felt nothing.

Then there were neighbors and two EMS people leaning over me upside down.

"What's up, Doc?" I asked.

"How many fingers?" he asked, moving his hand, changing it in a slow blur.

"Three, five, two,"

"What's today?"

"You mean Tuesday, or May 6th?"

I sat up.

"Easy," said the lady EMS person. "You'll probably have a headache."

The guy pushed me back down slowly. "What happened?"

"I turned on the band saw. Then I'm looking at you."

He got up, went to the corner of the shed and turned off the breakers. By then the sirens had stopped, and two or three firefighters and the lieutenant had come in the yard.

"You okay, Pops?" he asked.

"I think so," I said. I turned to the crowd. "Thanks to whoever called these guys." Then the EMS people asked me some medical stuff, and the lieutenant, after looking at the breakers, went in the shed and fiddled around. He came out.

"You got a shorted switch," he said. "Better replace it."

I thanked Ms. Krelboind, the neighbor lady, everybody went away, and I went inside to finish my cup of coffee.

MY DAUGHTER MAUREEN pulled up as I drank the last of the milk skim off the top of the coffee.

She ran in.

"Are you all right, Dad?"

"Evidently," I said.

Her husband, Bob, was a fireman. He usually worked over at Firehouse #2, the one on the other side of town. He'd heard the address the EMS had been called to on the squawk box, and had called her.

"What happened?"

"Short in the saw," I said. "The lieutenant said so, officially."

"I mean," she repeated, "are you sure you're all right?"

"It was like a little vacation," I said. "I needed one."

SHE CALLED HER husband, and I made more coffee, and we got to talking about her kids—Vera, Chuck and Dave, or whichever ones are hers—I can't keep up. There's two daughters, Maureen and Celine, and five grandkids. Sorting them all out was my late wife's job. She's only been gone a year and a month and three days.

We got off onto colleges, even though it would be some years before any of the grandkids needed one. The usual party schools came up. "I can see them at Sam Houston State in togas," I said.

"I'm *just real sure* toga parties will come back," said Mo.

Then I mentioned Kent State.

"Kent State? Nothing ever happens there," she said.

"Yeah, right," I said, "like the nothing that happened after Nixon invaded Cambodia. All the campuses in America shut down. They sent the Guard in. They shot four people down, just like they were at a carnival."

She looked at me.

"Nixon? What did Nixon have to do with anything?"

"Well, he *was* the president. He wanted 'no wider war.' Then he sent the Army into Cambodia and Laos. It was before your time."

"Daddy," she said, "I don't remember *much* American history. But Nixon was never president. I think he was vice president under one of those old guys—was it Eisenhower? Then he tried to be a senator. Then he wanted to be president, but someone whipped his ass at the convention. Where in that was he *ever* president? I know Eisenhower didn't die in office."

"What the hell are you talking about?"

"You stay right here," she said, and went to the living room. I heard her banging around in the bookcase. She came back with Vol 14 of the set of 1980s encyclopedias I'd bought for $20 down and $20 a month, seems like paying for about fifteen years on them. . . . She had her thumb in it, holding a place. She opened it on the washing machine lid. "Read."

The entry was on Nixon, Richard Milhous, and it was shorter than it should have been. There was the HUAC and Hiss stuff, the Checkers speech, the vice presidency and re-election, the Kennedy-Nixon debates, the loss, the Senate attempt, the "won't have Dick Nixon to kick around anymore" speech, the law firm, the oil company stuff, the death from phlebitis in 1977—

"Where the hell did you get this? It's *all wrong.*"

"It's yours, Dad. It's your encyclopedia. You've had them twenty years. You bought them for us to do homework out of. Remember?"

I went to the living room. There was a hole in the set at Vol 14. I put it back in. Then I took out Vol 24 UV and looked up Vietnam, War in. There was WWII, 1939–1945, then French Colonial War 1945–1954, then America in 1954–1970. Then I took down Vol II and read about John F. Kennedy (president, 1961–1969).

"Are you better now, Daddy?" she asked.

"No. I haven't finished reading a bunch of lies yet, I've just begun."

"I'm sorry. I know the shock hurt. And things haven't been good since Mom . . . But this really isn't like you."

"I know what happened in the Sixties! I was there! Where were you?"

"Okay, okay. Let's drop it. I've got to get back home; the kids are out of school soon."

"All right," I said. "It was a shock—not a nasty one, not my first, but maybe if I'm careful, my last."

"I'll send Bill over tomorrow on his day off and he can help you fix the saw. You know how he likes to futz with machinery."

"For gods sakes, Mo, it's a bad switch. It'll take two minutes to replace it. It ain't rocket science!"

She hugged me, went out to her car and drove off.

Strange that she should have called her husband Bob, Bill.

No wonder the kids struggled at school. Those encyclopedias sucked. I hope the whole staff got fired and went to prison.

I WENT DOWN to the library where they had *Britannicas*, *World Books*, old *Compton's*. Everybody else in the place was on, or waiting in line for, the Internet.

I sat down by the reference shelves and opened four or five encyclopedias to the entries on Nixon. All of them started Nixon, Richard Milhous, and then in brackets (1913–1977).

After the fifth one, I got up and went over to the reference librarian, who'd just unjammed one of the printers. She looked up at me and smiled, and as I said it, I knew I should not have, but I said. "All your encyclopedias are wrong."

The smile stayed on her face.

And then I thought *Here's a guy standing in front of her; he's in his fifties; he looks a little peaked, and he's telling her all her reference books are wrong. Just like I once heard a guy, in his fifties, a little peaked, yelling at a librarian that some book in the place was trying to tell him that Jesus had been a Jew!*

What would *you* do?

Before she could do anything, I said, "Excuse me."

"Certainly," she said.

I left in a hurry.

MY SON-IN-LAW CAME over the next morning when he should have been asleep.

He looked a little different (His ears were longer. It took a little while to notice that was it.) and he seemed a little older, but he looked pretty much the same as always.

"Hey. Mo sent me over to do the major overhaul on the band saw."

"Fuck it," I said. "It's the switch. I can do it in my sleep."

"She said she'd feel better if you let me do it."

"Buzz off."

He laughed and grabbed one of the beers he keeps in my refrigerator. "Okay, then," he said. "can I borrow a couple of albums to tape? I want the kids to hear what real music sounds like."

He had a pretty good selection of 45s, albums and CDs, even some shellac 78s. He's got a couple of old turntables (one that plays 16 rpm, even). But I have some stuff on vinyl he doesn't.

"Help yourself," I said. He went to the living room and started making noises opening cabinets.

I MENTIONED THE Who.

"Who?"

"Not who. The Who."

"What do you mean, who?"

"Who. The rock group. *The* Who."

"Who?"

"No, no. The rock group, which is named The Who."

"What is this," he asked. "Abbott and Hardy?"

"Well get to that later," I said. "Same time as the early Beatles. That . . ."

"Who?"

"Let me start over. Roger Daltry. Pete Townsend. John Entwistle. Keith—"

"The High Numbers!" he said. "Why didn't you say so?"

"A minute ago. I said they came along with the early Beatles and you said—"

"Who?"

"Do *not* start."

"There is no rock band called the Beetles," he said with authority.

I looked at him. "Paul McCartney . . ."

He cocked his head, gave me a go-on gesture.

". . . John Lennon, George Harri . . ."

"You mean the Quarrymen?" he asked.

". . . son, Ringo Starr."

"You mean Pete Best and Stuart Sutcliffe," he said.

"Sir Richard Starker. Ringo Starr. From all the rings on his fingers."

"The Quarrymen. Five guys. They had a few hits in the early Sixties. Wrote a shitpot of songs for other people. Broke up in 1966. Boring old farts since then—tried comeback albums, no back to come to. Lennon lives in a trailer in New Jersey. God knows where the rest of them are."

"Lennon's dead," I said. "He was assassinated at the Dakota Apartments in NYC in 1981 by a guy who wanted to impress Jodie Foster."

"Well, then, CNTV's got it all wrong, because they did a where-are-they-now thing a couple of weeks ago, and he looked pretty alive to me. He talked a few minutes and showed them some Holsteins or various other moo-cows, and a reporter made fun of them, and Lennon went back into the trailer and closed the door."

I knew they watched a lot of TV at the firehouse.

"This week they did one on ex-President Kennedy. It was his eighty-fourth birthday or something. He's the one that looked near-dead to me—they said he's had Parkinson's since the Sixties. They only had one candle on the cake, but I bet like Popeye these days, he had to eat three cans of spinach just to blow it out. His two brothers took turns reading a proclamation from President Gore. It looked like he didn't know who *that* was. His mom had to help him cut the cake. Then his wife, Marilyn, kissed him. He seemed to like *that*."

I SAT THERE quietly a few minutes.

"In your family," I asked, "who's Bill?"

He quit thumbing through the albums. He took in his breath a little too loudly. He looked at me.

"Edward," he said. "*I'm* Bill."

"Then who's Bob?"

"Bob was what they called my younger brother. He lived

two days. He's out at Kid Heaven in Greenwood. You, me and Mo went out there last Easter. Remember?"

"Uh, yeah," I said.

"Are you sure you're okay, after the shock, I mean?"

"Fit as a fiddle," I said, lying through my teeth.

"You sure you don't need help with the saw?"

"It'll be a snap."

"Well, be careful."

"The breakers are still off."

"Thanks for the beer," he said, putting a couple of albums under his arm and going toward the door.

"Bye. Go get some sleep," I said.

I'll have to remember to call Bob, Bill.

Mo was back, in a hurry.

"What is it, Dad? I've never seen Bill so upset."

"I don't know. Things are just so mixed up. In fact, they're wrong."

"What do you mean, wrong? I'm really worried about you now, and so's Bill."

I've never been a whiner, even in the worst of times.

"Oh, Dad," she said. "Maybe you should go see Doc Adams, maybe get some tests done. See if he can't recommend someone . . ."

"You mean, like I've got Alzheimer's? I don't have Alzheimer's! It's not me, it's the world that's off the trolley. Yesterday—I don't know, it's like everything I thought I knew is wrong. It's like some Mohorovic discontinuity of the mind. Nixon was president. He had to resign because of a break-in at the Watergate Hotel, the Democratic National Headquarters, in 1972. I have a bumper sticker somewhere: 'Behind Every Watergate Is A Milhous.' It was the same bunch of guys who set up Kennedy in 1963. It was . . ."

I started to cry. Maureen didn't know whether to come to me or not.

"Are you thinking about Mom?" she asked.

"Yes," I said. "Yes, I'm thinking about your mother."

Then she hugged me.

• • •

I DON'T KNOW what to say.

I'm a bright enough guy. I'm beginning to understand,
though, about how people get bewildered.

On my way from the library after embarrassing myself, I
passed the comic book and poster shop two blocks away.
There were reproduction posters in one window; the famous
one of Clark Gable and Paulette Goddard with the flames of
Atlanta behind them from *Mules in Horses' Harnesses*; Fred
MacMurray and Jack Oakie in *The Road to Morroco*, and
window cards from James Dean in *Somebody Up There Likes
Me*, along with *Giant* and *East of Eden*.

I came home and turned on the oldies station. It wasn't
there, one like it was somewhere else on the dial.

It was just like Bo—Bill said. The first thing I heard was
The Quarrymen doing "*Gimme Deine Hande*." I sat there for
two hours, till it got dark, without turning on the lights, listening. There were familiar tunes by somebody else, called
something else. There were the right songs by the right people. Janis I. Fink seemed to be in heavy rotation, three songs
in the two hours, both before and after she went to prison, according to the DJ. The things you find out on an oldies station . . .

I heard no Chuck Berry, almost an impossibility.

Well, I will try to live here. I'll just have to be careful finding my way around in it. Tomorrow, after the visit to the doc,
it's back to the library.

Before going to bed, I rummaged around in my "Important
Papers" file. I took out my old draft notice.

It wasn't from Richard Nixon, like it has been for the last
thirty-two years. It was from Barry Goldwater. (Au + H_2O =
1968?)

THE PSYCHIATRIST SEEMED like a nice enough guy. We
talked a few minutes about the medical stuff Doc Adams had
sent over; work, the shock, what Mo had told the doc.

"Your daughter seems to think you're upset about your environment. Can you tell me why she thinks that?"

"I think she means to say I told her this was not the world I was born in and have lived in for fifty-six years," I said.

He didn't write anything down in his pad.

"It's all different," I said. He nodded.

"Since the other morning, everything I've known all my life doesn't add up. The wrong people have been elected to office. History is different. Not just the politics-battles-wars stuff, butt also social history, culture. There's a book of social history by a guy named Furnas. I haven't looked, but I bet that's all different, too. I'll get it out of the library today. *If* it's there. *If* there's a guy named Furnas anymore."

I told him some of the things that were changed—just in two days' worth. I told him it—some of it anyway—was fascinating, but I'm sure I'll find scary stuff sooner or later. I'd have to learn to live with it, go with the flow.

"What do you think happened?" he asked.

"What is this, *The Sopranos*?"

"Beg pardon?" he asked.

"Oh. *Oh.* You'd like it. It's a TV show about a Mafia guy who, among other things, goes to a shrink—a lady shrink. It's on HBO."

"HBO?"

"*Sorry.* A cable network."

He wrote three things down on his pad.

"Look. Where I come from . . . I know that sounds weird. In Lindner's book . . ."

"Lindner?"

"Lindner. *The Fifty-Minute Hour.* Best-seller. 1950s."

"I take it by the title it was about psychiatry. *And* a best-seller?"

"*Let me start over.* He wrote the book they took the title *Rebel Without A Cause* from—but *that* had nothing to do with the movie . . ."

He was writing stuff down now, fast.

"It's getting deeper and deeper, isn't it?" I asked.

"Go on. *Please.*"

"Lindner had a patient who was a guy who thought he lived on a far planet in an advanced civilization—star-spanning galaxy-wide stuff. Twenty years before *Star Wars*. Anyway . . ."

He wrote down two words without taking his eyes off me.

"In my world," I said, very slowly and carefully, looking directly at him, "there was a movie called *Star Wars* in 1977 that changed the way business was done in Hollywood.

"Okay," he said.

"This is not getting us anywhere!" I said.

And then he came out with the most heartening timing I'd heard in two days. He said, "What do you mean *we, kemo sabe?*"

Well, we laughed and laughed, and then I tried to tell him, *really* tell him, what I thought I knew.

THE PAST WAS another country, as they say; they did things differently there.

The more I looked up, the more I needed to look up. I had twelve or fifteen books scattered across the reference tables.

Now I know how conspiracy theorists feel. It's not just the Trilateral Commission or Henry Kissinger (a minor ARC/NRC official *here*) and the Queen of England and Area 51 and the Grays. It's like history has ganged up on me, as an individual, to drive me bugfuck. I don't have a chance. The more you find out the more you need to explain . . . how much more you need to find out . . . it could never end.

Where did it change?

We are trapped in history like insects in amber, and it is hardening all around me.

Who am I to struggle against the tree sap of Time?

THE PSYCHIATRIST HAS asked me to write down and bring in everything I can think of—anything: presidents, cars, wars, culture. He wants to read it ahead of time and schedule two full hours on Friday.

You can bet I don't feel swell about this.

•   •   •

MY OTHER DAUGHTER, Celine, is here. I had *tried* and *tried*
and *tried*, but she'd turned out to be a Christian in spite of *all*
my work.

She is watching me like a hawk, I can tell. We were never
as close as Maureen and me; she was her mother's daughter.

"How are you feeling?"

"Just peachy," I said. "Considering."

"Considering *what*?" Her eyes were very green, like her
mother's had been.

"If you don't mind, I'm pretty tired of answering questions. *Or* asking them."

"You ought to be more careful with those tools."

"This is not about power tools, or the shock," I said. "I
don't know what Mo told you, but I have been *truly* discomfited these last few days."

"Look, Daddy," she said. "I don't care what the trouble is,
we'll find a way to get you through it."

"You couldn't get me through it, unless you've got a couple of thousand years on rewind."

"What?"

"Never mind. I'm just tired. And I have to go to the hardware store and get a new switch for the band saw, before I
burn the place down, or cause World War III or something.
I'm *sure* they have hardware stores here, or *I* wouldn't have
power tools."

She looked at me like I'd grown tentacles.

"Just kidding," I said. "Loosen up, Celine. Think of me
right now as your old, tired father. I'll learn my way around
the place and be right as rain . . ."

Absolutely no response.

"I'm being ironic," I said, "I have always been noted for
my sense of humor. Remember?"

"Well, yes. Sort of."

"Great!" I said. "Let's go get some burgers at McDon-
ald's!"

"Where?"

"I mean Burger King," I said. I'd passed one on the way

back from the library. "Sounds good, Dad." She said, "Let *me* drive."

I HAVE LIVED in this house for twenty-six years. I was born in the house across the street. In 1957, my friend Gino Ballantoni lived here, and I was over here every day, or just about, for four years, till Gino's father's aircraft job moved to California. I'd always wanted it, and after I got out of the Army, I got it on the GI Bill.

I know its every pop and groan, every sound it makes day or night, the feel of the one place the paint isn't smooth, on the inside doorjamb trim of what used to be Mo's room before it was Celine's. There's one light switch put on upside down I never changed. The garage makeover I did myself; it's what's now the living room.

I love this place. I would have lived here no matter what.

I tell myself history wasn't different enough that this house isn't still a vacant lot, *or* an apartment building. That's, at least, something to hang on to.

I noticed the extra sticker inside the car windshield. Evidently, we now have an emissions-control test in this state, too. I'll have to look in the phone book and find out where to go, as this one expires at the end of the mouth.

And also, on TV, when they show news from New York, there's still the two World Trade Center Towers.

You can't be *too* careful about the past.

THE PSYCHIATRIST CALLED to ask if someone could sit in on the double session tomorrow—he knew it was early, but it was special—his old mentor from whatever Mater he'd Alma'd at; the guy was in a day early for some shrink hoedown in the Big City and wanted to watch his star pupil in action. He was asking all the patients tomorrow, he said. The old doc wouldn't say anything, and you'd hardly know he was there.

"Well, I got enough troubles, what's one more?"

He thanked me.

That's what did it for me. This was not going to stop. This was not something that I could be helped to work through,

like bedwetting or agoraphobia or the desire to eat human
flesh. It was going to go on forever, here, until I died.

Okay, I thought. Let's get out Occam's Famous Razor and
cut a few Gordian Knots. Or somewhat, as the logicians used
to say.

I WENT OUT to the workshop where everybody thinks it all
started.

I turned on the outside breakers. I went inside. This time I
closed the door. I went over and turned on the bandsa

AFTER I GOT up off the floor, I opened the door and stepped
out into the yard. It was near dark, so I must have been out an
hour or so.

I turned off the breakers and went into the house through
the back door and through the utility room and down the hall
to the living room bookcase. I pulled out Vol 14 of the encyclopedia and opened it.

Nixon, Richard Milhous, it said (1913–1994). A good long
entry.

There was a sound from the kitchen. The oven door opened
and closed.

"What have you been doing?" asked a voice.

"There's a short in the band saw I'll have to get fixed," I
said. I went around the corner.

It was my wife, Susan. She looked a little older, a little
heavier since I last saw her, it seemed. She still looked pretty
good.

"Stand there where I can see you," I said.

"We were having a fight before you wandered away, remember?"

"Whatever it was," I said, "I was wrong. You were right.
We'll do whatever it is you want."

"Do you even remember what it was we were arguing
about?"

"No," I said. "Whatever. It's not important. The problems
of two people don't amount to a hill of beans in—"

"Cut the Casablanca crap," said Susan. "Jodie and Susie Q

want to bring the kids over next Saturday and have Little
Eddy's birthday party here. You wanted peace and quiet here,
and go somewhere else for the party. That was the argument."

"I wasn't cut out to be a grandpa," I said. "But bring 'em
on. Invite the neighbors! Put out signs on the street! Annoy an
old man here!' "

Then I quieted down. "Tell them we'd he happy to have the
party here," I said.

"Honestly, Edward," said Susan, putting the casserole on
the big trivet. It was *her* night to cook. "Sometimes I think
you'd forget your ass if it weren't glued on."

"Yeah, sure," I said. "I've damn sure forgotten what peace
and quiet was like. And probably lots of other stuff, too."

"Supper's ready," said Susan.

What Rough Beast

Damon Knight

Here's a poignant and bittersweet story that shows us that sometimes one man can change everything around him—in more ways than you'd think.

A multitalented professional whose career as writer, editor, critic, and anthologist spanned almost fifty years, Damon Knight was a major shaping force in the development of modern science fiction. He wrote the first important book of SF criticism, *In Search of Wonder*, and won a Hugo Award for it. He was the founder of the Science Fiction Writers of America, co-founder of the prestigious Milford Writer's Conference, and, with his wife, writer Kate Wilhelm, was involved in the creation of the *Clarion* workshop for new young writers. He was the editor of *Orbit*, the longest running original anthology series in the history of American science fiction, and also produced important works of genre history such as *The Futurians* and *Turning Points*, as well as dozens of influential reprint anthologies. Knight was also highly influential as a writer, and may well be one of the finest short story writers ever to work in the genre. His books include the novels *A for Anything*, *The Other Foot*, *Hell's Pavement*, *The Man in the Tree*, *CV*, *A Rea-*

sonable World, Why Do Birds, Humptey Dumptey: An Oval, and the collections *Rule Golden and Other Stories, Turning On, Far Out, The Best of Damon Knight,* and *One Side Laughing.*

MR. FRANK SAID to me, "Hey you. Get that corner cleaned up." He was a big man with red face, mouth always open little bit, wet lips always pulling back suddenly over little yellow teeth. This I remember, late at night, just after rush from theaters and before bars close. Place was empty, all sick light on the tiles and brown tabletops. Outside, dark and wet. People going by with coat collars turned up and faces gray like rain.

On corner table was some dishes, some food spilled. I cleaned up, put dishes in kitchen sink on top of big stack, then came back to Mr. Frank. He was cutting tomato for sandwiches, using his knife too quick and hard. Tip of his big pink thumb was white from holding knife.

I said to him, "Mr. Frank, I work here three weeks and you call me 'Hey, you.' My name is Kronski. If it is too hard to remember, say Mike. But not 'Hey, you.' "

He looked down on me, with lips twitching away from yellow teeth. Sides of his nose turned yellow-white, like I saw before when he was mad. And his knife went cut. He sucked air between teeth, and grabbed his hand. I saw the blood coming out dark as ink where he sliced the side of his thumb. Blood was dripping on board and pieces of tomato. It was deep cut, bleeding hard. He said through teeth, "Now look what you made me do. Christ!"

From other end of counter, Mr. Harry called out, "What's the matter?" He started toward us—a thin man, bald, with big eyes blinking all time like afraid.

Was my fault. I went quickly to Mr. Frank, but he pushed me away with his elbow. "Get off of me, you creep!"

Now Mr. Harry looked at Mr. Frank's thumb and he whistled, then turned and went to the medicine box on wall. Mr. Frank was holding his wrist and cursing. From the cashier's desk at front of cafeteria, Mr. Wilson the night manager was coming; I heard his footsteps click on the tiles.

Mr. Harry was trying to put a bandage on, but it would not stick. Mr. Frank pushed him out of the way, shouting, "God damn it!" and pulled the medicine box off wall. Always bleeding.

I got quickly a fork and handkerchief, not clean, but best I could do. I tied a knot in the handkerchief, and tried to put it around Mr. Frank's wrist, but he pushed me away again.

"Give me that," says Mr. Harry, and he took from me the fork and handkerchief. Now Mr. Frank was leaning back against coffee machine looking white, and Mr. Harry slipped the handkerchief over his wrist. In coffee machine I saw myself, like shadow standing—no face, just blackness—and I looked other way.

Always was blood, over counter, duckboards, steam tables, everything. Mr. Harry tried to tighten the fork, but he dropped it and I picked up. He took it saying, "Get out of the way, will you?" and started to turn the handkerchief.

"Better call a hospital," says Mr. Wilson's voice behind me. Then, "Look out!"

Mr. Frank had his eyes turned up and mouth open. His knees started to bend and then he was falling, and Mr. Harry tried to catch, but too late, and he also went down.

Mr. Wilson was going around end of counter, so I went the other way to telephone.

Was in my pocket, no dimes. I thought to go back and ask, but it would take minute. I thought maybe Mr. Frank would die because I was not quick. So I put fingers in the metal hole where coin is supposed to come back, and was no coin there; but I felt deeper, down where turning place was, and I found it and I turned. Then, was a dime lying in coin hole. So I took it and put in top of telephone. I called ambulance for Mr. Frank.

Then I went back to where he was lying, and they were by his side squatting, and Mr. Wilson looked up and said, "Did you call that hospital?" I say yes, but without stopping he said, "Well, get out of my way then. Harry, you take the feet and we'll straighten him out a little."

I could see Mr. Frank's red shirt front, and hand wrapped now in gauze, also red, with tourniquet around his wrist. He was lying without moving. To lose blood is for some not easy.

I went to stand at end of the counter, out of way. I was feeling very bad for Mr. Frank. I saw he was mad, and I knew he was cutting with knife, as it was my fault.

After long while came a policeman, and he looked on Mr. Frank, and I told how it happened. Mr. Harry and Mr. Wilson also told, but they did not see from beginning. Then came ambulance, and I ask Mr. Wilson if I can go with Mr. Frank to hospital. So he said, "Go on, I don't care. We won't need you here after tonight anyhow, Kronski." He looked on me from bright glasses. He was gray-haired man, very neat, who always spoke cheerful but thought suspicious. I liked Mr. Harry, and even Mr. Frank, but him I could never like.

So I was fired. Not new feeling for me. But I thought how in a year, two years, or even sooner, those men would forget I was ever alive.

I was working in place three nights, night shift, cleaning up tables and stacking dishes in sink for dishwasher. It is not enough to make a place different because you are there. But if you make no difference, you are not living.

AT THE HOSPITAL, they wheeled Mr. Frank up indoors and took him in elevator. Hospital woman asked me questions and wrote down on a big paper, then policeman came again, and was more questions.

"Your name is Michael Kronski, right? Been in this country long?"

"Since twenty years." But I told a lie, was only one month. Policeman said, "You didn't learn English very good, did you?"

"For some is not easy."

"You a citizen?"

"Sure."

"When naturalized?"

I said, "Nineteen forty-five." But was a lie.

He asked more questions, was I in army, how long belong to union, where I worked before, and always I would lie. Then he closed book.

"All right, you stick around till he comes to. Then if he says there was no assault, you can go on home."

In hospital was quiet like grave. I sat on hard bench. Sometimes doors opened, doctors shoes squeaked on floor. Then telephone went *brr* very quiet, hospital woman picked up and talked so I could not hear. She was blonde, I think from bottle, with hard lines in cheeks.

She put down telephone, talked to policeman for minute, then he came over to me. "Okay, they fixed him up. He says he did it himself. You a friend of his?"

"We work together. *Did* work. Is something I can do?"

"They're going to let him go, they need the bed. But somebody ought to go home with him. I got to get back on patrol."

"I will take him to his home, yes."

"Okay." He sat down on bench, looked on me. "Say, what kind of an accent is that, anyhow? You chesky?"

"No." I would say yes, but this man had the face of a Slav. I was afraid he should be Polish. Instead, I told different lie. "Russian. From Omsk."

"No," he said slow, looking on me hard, and then spoke some words in Russian. I did not understand, it was too different from Russiche, so I said nothing.

"Nyet?" asked policeman, looking on me with clear gray eyes. He was young man, big bones in cheeks and jaw, and lines of smiling around mouth.

Just then came down the elevator with Mr. Frank and nurse. He had a big white bandage on hand. He looked on me and turned away.

Policeman was writing in his book. He looked on me again. He said something more in Russian. I did not know the words, but one of them was like word for "pig" in Russiche. But I said nothing, looked nothing.

Policeman scratched his head. "You say you're from Russia, but you don't get the language. How come?"

I said, "Please, when we leave Russia, I was young boy. In house we speaking only Yiddish."

"Yeah? *Ir zent ah Yidishe' yingl?*"

"*Vi den?*"

Now was better, but still he did not look happy. "And you only spoke Yiddish in the home?"

"Sometimes French. My mother spoke French, also my aunt."

"Well—that might account for it, I guess." He closed book and put away. "Look, you got your naturalization papers on you?"

"No, is home in box."

"Well, hell, you ought to carry them on you. Times like these. You remember what I said. All right, take it easy now."

I looked up, and was no Mr. Frank. I went quickly to desk. "Where did he go?"

Woman said very cold, "I don't know what you mean." Each word separate, like to child.

"Mr. Frank, was just here."

She said, "Down the hall, the payment office." And pointed with yellow pencil over her shoulder.

I went, but in hall I stopped to look back. Policeman was leaning over desk to talk with woman, and I saw his book in pocket. I knew there would be more questions, maybe tomorrow, maybe next week. I took long breath, and closed eyes. I reached down where turning place of book was. I found it, and turned. I felt it happen.

Policeman never noticed; but next time he would look in book, would be no writing about me in it. Maybe would be empty pages, maybe something else written.

He would remember, but without writing is no good.

Mr. Frank was by window in hall, pale in face, arguing with man in office. I came up, I heard him say, "Twenty-three bucks, ridiculous."

"It's all itemized, sir." Man inside pointed to piece of paper in Mr. Frank's hand.

"Anyway, I haven't got that much."

I say quickly, "I will pay." I took out money, almost all I have in purse.

"I don't want your money," said Mr. Frank. "Where would you get twenty-three bucks? Let the workmen's pay for it."

"Please, for me is pleasure. Here, you take." I pushed money at man behind window.

"Twenty-three seventeen." I gave him the change.

"All right, give him the God damn money," said Mr. Frank, and turned away.

Man behind the window stamped bill and gave me. I quickly caught up Mr. Frank and we went outdoors. Mr. Frank could not walk straight. I took his elbow. First he pushed me away, but then he let me.

"THAT'S IT," SAID Mr. Frank. Was street of old thin houses with stone steps coming down like they stick out all their tongues. I paid the taxi driver, and helped Mr. Frank up steps. "What floor you live?"

"Fourth. I can make it."

But I said, "No, I help you," and we went up stairs. Mr. Frank was very weak, very tired, and now his lips did not pull back over teeth anymore.

We went in kitchen and Mr. Frank sat down by table under the sour yellow light. He leaned his head on hand. "I'm all right. Just let me alone now, okay?"

"Mr. Frank, you are tired. Eat something now, then sleep."

He did not move. "What sleep? In three hours I got to be on my day job."

I looked on him. Now I understand why was cutting so hard with knife, why was so quick anger.

"How long you worked two jobs?" I say.

He leaned back in chair and put his hand with white bandage on the table. "Year and a half."

"Is no good. You should quit one job."

"You don't know a thing about it."

I wanted to ask something more, but then opened a door, and I saw someone in bathrobe standing. A voice said, "Pop?" Was young girl's voice.

Mr. Frank answered her, and I said quick, "Well, I will go then. Goodbye." And while the girl was coming into kitchen one way, I was going out other. I saw only face, pale, and brown hair, and I thought she was tall.

Downstairs I found mailbox with Mr. Frank's name, and apartment number, and over door was number of house. I wrote on piece of paper, thinking when I go home I would make some money and send him by mail. From me he would not take, but if he finds in mailbox, is like from God, he must take it and give thanks.

On street, dawn was coming up, gray and cold. In gutter was papers blowing.

SINCE I WAS small boy in Novo Russie—what they call here Canada, but it is all different—always I could see where every thing in world, even every stone and stick, had shadow in past and in future. To me is hard thing to understand that other people only see what is *now*.

Sometimes I would say to my brother Misha when he would hurt himself, "But didn't you *see* that it would happen?" And because I was stubborn, sometimes I would even say this when I saw that he would hit me because I said it.

But then I learned also to reach, not with hands but with mind. And in darkness where something could be or not be, I learned to turn it so that it is different. At first I did it without knowing, when I was very sick, and frightened that I would die. Without knowing it I reached, and turned, and suddenly I was not sick. Doctor was not believing, and my mother prayed a long time before icon, because she thought God had saved my life.

Then I learned I could do it. When I did badly in school, or if something else I did not like would happen, I could reach and turn, and change it. Little by little, I was changing pieces of world.

At first was not so bad, because I was young boy and I only did things for myself, my own pleasure.

But then I was growing up, and it was making me sad to see how other people were unhappy. So then I would begin to change more. My father had a bad knee; I made it well. Our cow broke her neck and died. And I made her alive again.

First I was careful, then not so careful. And at last they saw that I did it.

Then everyone said I was going to be a saint, they prayed over me, and big men talked to me so much that I believed it.

And I worked miracles.

Then one day I began to see that what I do is bad. I made so many patches in world that it was not world anymore, but mistake. If you would try to make chair better by many patches, putting a piece oak wood here, and piece cherry wood there, until all was patches, you would make a worse chair than before.

So I saw every day that I was only making more patches, but I would not let myself know that it was bad. And at last I could not bear it, and I reached back far, I changed not little bit but whole country. I reached back before I was born, and I turned, and I changed it.

And when I looked up, all world around me was different—houses, fields, people.

My father's house was not there. My mother, my brothers, my sisters, they were all gone; and I could not bring them back.

Then for the first time, I knew what I was.

NEXT DAY AFTER Mr. Frank's accident, I found a new room. It was time for me to move anyway; in old room was becoming everything black so I could not see it. My new room was on second floor, not bad—maple furniture, oilcloth on table, washbowl, like usual, I moved in, and then I remembered about Mr. Frank and I took a dollar bill, my last one, and reached back and turned where man could have given me five-dollar-bill by mistake. Always it is possible this should happen, even if only once in hundred times. So I turned where it did happen, and in my hand was five-dollar-bill. Then I turned again where instead of five it is ten; and then instead of ten, ten one-dollar bills. And so I went on turning until I had three hundred dollars in ten-dollar bills. And in drug store I bought envelope and stamps, and wrote Mr. Frank's address on envelope, "Mr. Frank Verney, Apartment 4B." When I put bills inside envelope, they are already becoming dark so I cannot read the numbers. This money is no good for me, I will always make mistakes if I try to spend it; but for Mr. Frank it would be all right.

Next day I was angry with myself, and I lay on bed doing nothing. I told myself it would be no good to get different job, which I knew; but I did not tell myself without job I would be like dead man, which I also knew.

Next day, I went on Greenwich Avenue walking. Sky was deep blue over the building roofs. The sun was shining warm, and all buildings looked surprised and sad, as if they would say, "I am dirty, but is best I can do."

Here, in this same place, I have seen droshkies. Also steam cars, quiet, with white puffing like man smoking a pipe very quick. I have seen people all dressed in black, and people in many colors like parrots. I know how wide is the world God made. Is so big, so deep, that heart turn small to feel it. But I would say to God, "Why did you not make a world smaller? More like man?"

I went home, and in hall the door of Mr. Brennan was standing open, the one they called landlord, but he was only janitor, and Mr. Brennan was in doorway looking. He was a man with frozen face, mouth tight like he taste lemon, and eyes always big. I said, "Hello, Mr. Brennan," but he said nothing, only looked while I went up the stairs. Behind him I saw his wife, small brown-haired woman with too much rouge.

I went in the room, and inside was policeman.

My heart was hurting chest, and I was so weak that I must lean against door. Policeman was same one that was at hospital before. He was sitting in my good chair, with hands on knees. The light was not good, but I saw his gray eyes burning.

"Shut that door."

I did it.

"Come over here."

I went.

"Okay, take everything out of your pockets and throw it on the bed."

I took out wallet, money, handkerchief and so on. My hands were shaking.

"Sit down."

I sat on wooden chair while he picked up the wallet and looked inside. Always was heart pounding, and hard to breathe.

Policeman said, "I've been looking for you for three days. My wife thinks I'm nuts. I must have tried every rooming house in Chelsea before I hit this one." He looked on me, with nostrils big.

"Nothing like this ever happened to me before," he said. "When I went to make my report out, it was all gone. Pretty soon I began to wonder if I dreamed the whole thing."

He looked at cards from my wallet, then opened his book hard on knee, and wrote. Then he threw the wallet back on bed, and said, "All right, now what's your real name?"

"I told you before, Michael Kronski."

"You told me plenty. Where are you from?"

"Odessa, Russia."

"Didn't you tell me Omsk before?"

"No, Odessa." He was right, I said Omsk, but I was too frightened to make up new lie.

"Who sent you here?"

"Nobody. Maybe God."

He leaned and slapped me across mouth with his hand. "Don't give me that sacrilegious crap."

I jumped, and my chest got tight, harder to breathe. Inside was something like balloon wanting to burst.

I said, "Please, you make mistake."

"How did you do that trick to me?"

"If you would let me explain—"

"Well?" He waited, then slapped my face again. My body was trying to go through back of chair.

"Let's have it. By God, I'll get it out of you. Where are you from? What are you here for?" He slapped me again.

I said, "Don't," but already was inside me like a bursting. I felt big weight roll over inside, then nothing.

Yellow light was shining on empty chair.

Was no policeman. No one in room but me.

I was weak all over like a baby. With the hitting I could not think, could not stop it. Now I have reached back, maybe thirty years, I have made policeman not born.

Once more, I have killed a man.

I was crying. I thought, if only he would not have hit me in face. But it was me that made him so frightened that he must hit. It was me, my fault, always my fault.

To reach back again for same turning place is foolish, because I know I cannot do it, but I tried. Was like reaching where is nothing, like empty shelf in old dusty closet.

I sat in chair, looking at walls. Then I could not bear it. I went downstairs, past Mr. Brennan and wife still in doorway watching. My knees were weak. I went like a drunk man.

I knew they would go up to my room and find no policeman, and would think I do not know what, but I had no time to worry. I went out in the street, looking for something.

My jaw was shaking, like cold, teeth going click. My hands, arms were shivering, and knees weak. But I must hurry. I crossed big avenue, running; then I was in quiet street with many old stone houses. In the street was playing two little girls with a ball.

While I stood looking, around corner came a car, too fast, tipping on wheels. I heard tires shout, and car was coming so quick that I could do nothing but stand and watch.

In street, little girls began to run. One had dark pigtails tied with pieces white ribbon, and her dress was blue and white. The other had blonde curly hair, and she was wearing pink dress. I saw their legs flashing, and I saw the ball rolling very slowly across street.

Then the car hit sideways into another car parked by sidewalk, and it made a sound like hammer hitting tin cans. The car bounced away, still coming, and I saw driver, young man with blonde hair, bouncing in seat. Car was red, with no top. He was turning the wheel as hard as he could, but the car went by little girl with pigtails and just touched her going by, and she was down in street, not moving.

Then car hit fire plug on other side of street, and stopped. All up and down street was sound of hit metal. In the car, young man was leaning over wheel. Then I saw him straighten up, I look around. In doorways and windows now was people.

Now I was beginning to run. Now came a woman out of basement, and she was screaming, "Jeannie!" But now the red car backed up away from fire plug, and the young man was twisting wheel quick, and now was grinding sound, and then red car jumped down street again, past me so close I felt the wind, and saw young man's red eyes. Then he was gone around the corner.

In middle of street was people gathering. Woman still screaming at top of voice, more people running from doorways. I did not see the girl anymore.

I could not run. I was sick inside. I bent over with hands on belly; inside my head was still shouting the tires, and red car still coming sidewise down street, to hit car, bang, hit girl, hit fire plug, bang.

Inside was reaching, turning. I felt the whole street, sky, turning all together. Then I was lying on cold pavement with ringing sound in my head.

When I looked up, I saw face hanging in the sky, men and women all looking down on me. Closer was two little girls. One blonde, pink dress, one dark pigtails, blue and white dress.

Woman's voice said, "Jeannie, go on now. Get in the house." Girl with dark pigtails turned slowly and went away, looking back over her shoulder to me. It was the same girl that I saw lying in street; but now she was not hurt, not dirty, not even frightened, only curious.

Then I began to understand. Without knowing it I had reached and turned where car would not hit girl, but would hit me instead. And now there was blood on pavement—but it was mine.

I closed my eyes, then opened them again. To lie on pavement was good, was like growing to earth. Overhead was sky very big, and here was peace. All day long would be people walking on this street, but how many would lie down?

If I was hurt, I did not feel it, only numb place on side of head. I pushed myself up on one elbow and with other hand tried to feel my head if it was broken. Then was hands helping me to sit up, even though I did not know I wanted to do it. I heard someone say "hospital."

I said, "No. No hospital." On side of head was only a cut, not big. To show them I was all right, I stood up. But could not stand straight, and with many hands they helped me.

"Where do you want to go? Where do you live?"

For minute, I could not remember. So often I move, I forget easily the old addresses and sometimes the new ones too. Always I tell myself to write down new address, and I never do it, but I felt in my pockets anyway. I found little piece of paper, squeezed together.

My fingers would not hold it, and so a man took it away from me, and opened it up, and read an address. It was man with new white cap on, like for golfing. He had face brown like coffee, and gold tooth. What he read did not sound right, but I saw paper, and it was my writing.

"Mister, don't you want to come inside and have a cup of coffee first?"

I said, "No, please—just want to go home."

Young man with many pimples said, "It's just up the block."

So they took me one on each side, with my arms around their necks, and we started. I thought we were going wrong way, but maybe it was short cut. Then we start to go up high stone stairway into building, and I stop and say, "No. Wrong house."

Man looked at paper again and said, "Two twelve east? This is it. Apartment 4B. See, it says right here." He showed me the paper, but I could not read what it said, only that the handwriting was mine.

Also we did not walk long enough to get back to my house; but I knew that I had seen this house before. And I could not understand it; except that I think in back of my mind, I did understand.

Man with white cap said, "Well, it must be somebody that knows him, anyway. Let's take him up." So we went up the stairs.

Then we knocked on a door, and I saw face of young woman, surprised, looking through crack. Then they were talking, and after minute door opened all the way, and they helped me in through kitchen, and narrow hall, then brown living room and they put me in a chair. Now my head was hurting. But I saw young woman, brown hair, tall, in blue dress. Then they were lifting me, putting me down on soft bed. Then I remember smell of perfume, and soft hands lifting head, giving me pills to take and glass of water. Then perhaps I sleep, because when I looked up, was no one in room.

Outside window by bed was iron fire escape, and then deep courtyard, gray stone, with clotheslines across and white clothes hanging. Clotheslines curved down, beautiful. Light came from somewhere, not bright, and clothes swung a little bit from wind. Was quiet, peaceful. Was best time of day in city, when people are working, not so crowded in buildings. Light was quiet and gray; bed where I was lying smelled good for laundry.

While I was looking, I heard small noise from next room, and turned my head. Young woman came in, tall, with hands together. She had brown hair soft and shiny, not curled straw like so many; face very clean and young, but also very big. She had a wide mouth, and I wanted to see her smile, because if teeth were good, she would be beautiful.

She said, "Mr. Kronski? Is that right?"

I nodded yes, still looking at her. Now I saw little bit in her past, not clear, but what I saw I did not like.

"I thought you must be." She smiled a little, just enough to show teeth white. "I wasn't sure, but you had our address in your pocket."

"Yes." Now I knew: she was Mr. Frank's daughter.

Then I must have made a face, because she said, "Are you all right? Does your head hurt?"

I said no, head was all right. With my fingers now I could feel where she had put a gauze bandage around my head, but even without feeling I could tell that underneath was nothing wrong: no cut, nothing. In sleep I had made myself well. Always, all my life it was so. On my whole body is no mark, no scar, not even pimple.

Now I was trying not to look on her, because I could see also a little bit the future, and I was afraid. But she sat down and said, "Mr. Kronski, if you're sure you're feeling all right—"

I said rough, "You want to know if I sent money to your father."

She said, "Well—the writing on the envelope looked the same. Did you?"

"Yes. I will tell you. I sent it."

"That was pretty nice of you. You know?"

"No, foolish. Now you are going to tell me you need more money, much more than I sent."

Her eyes opened big. "How did you know that?"

"Never mind, I know."

She was pale, but now pink. She got up and said, "You seem to think people are all alike."

"No, everyone different, but all foolish like me. I ran away from you so hard, I got myself knocked down on your street, with your address in pocket."

She looked on me and said, "I don't think I get that. What do you mean, about running away from me?"

I said, "I did not want to help you. But now is no more use running." Was hard to talk, because throat was swollen up. I held out my hand and said, "Please. Let me see your shoulder."

She went stiff all over, and one hand jumped to the shoulder of her blue dress. She looked on me with big eyes, bright and mad, "Did my father—?"

"No," I said, shaking my head hard, "he didn't tell me nothing, but I know. Don't you see that I know? Now let me see it."

She was again pink, and trying not to weep from shame.

She sat down, still holding her shoulder, and did not look on me.

I said, "If you want I will help you. Do you understand? Now let me see."

She did not understand, but she looked on me. Eyes pink and wet, face swollen, not pretty. Was hard to look on her so, but I did it. After a minute she took a hard breath and turned away from me, and began to unbutton her dress in back.

I had my hands in fists, and I looked on them. After minute I heard her turn and say, "All right."

I looked, and she had pulled away the blue dress from one shoulder. By her neck, was skin smooth and like cream. But on the shoulder and across the chest was skin hard and white, standing up in strings and lumps, like something that had melted and boiled, and then hardened.

She had her head down, and eyes shut, crying. I was crying also, and inside was a big hurt trying to get out. I touched her with my hand, and said, "My dear."

She jumped when hand touched her, but then sat still. I felt under my fingertips cold skin, tough like lizard. Inside me was big hurt jumping, I could not hold in very long. I rubbed her very easy, very slow with my fingers, looking and feeling where was inside the wrong skin. Was not easy to do. But if I did not do it this way, then I knew I would do it without wanting, all at once, and it would be worse.

To make well all at once is no good. Each cell must fit with next cell. With my fingertips I felt where down inside the bottom part of bad skin was, and I made it turn, and change to good skin, one little bit at a time.

She held still and let me do it. After a while she said, "It was a fire, two years ago. Dad left a blowtorch lit, and I moved it, and there was a can of plastic stuff with the top off. And it went up—"

I said, "Not to talk. Not necessary. Wait. Wait." And always I rubbed softly the bad skin.

But she could not bear to have me rub without talking, and she said, "We couldn't collect anything. It said right on the can, keep away from flame. It was our fault. I was in the hospital twice. They healed it, but it just grew back the same way. It's what they call keloid tissue."

I said, "Yes, yes, dear one, I know."

Now was one layer on the bottom, soft skin instead of hard; and she moved a little in the chair, and said in a small voice, "It feels better."

Under my fingertips the skin was still hard, but now more soft than before. When I pushed it, was not like lizard any more, but like glove.

I worked, and she forgot to be ashamed until it came a noise of door opening at front of apartment. She sat up straight, looking around and then on me. Her face got pink again, she grabbed my wrist. "What are you doing?" Her voice was thin and not real.

In a minute I knew she would jump up and pull her dress together, and then she would run out of room, so whatever happened, it would not be her fault.

But I could not let her do it. I was also ashamed, and my ears like on fire, but to stop now was impossible. I said loud, "No, sit down." I held her in the chair, and kept my fingers on her skin. I did not look up, but I heard a man's feet come into room.

I heard Mr. Frank say, "Hey, you. What do you think you're up to?"

And the girl was trying to get up again, but I held her still, and I said, "Look. Look." With tears running down my cheeks.

Under my fingers was a little piece of good, soft skin, smooth like cream. While I moved my fingers, slowly that place got bigger. She looked down, and she forgot to breathe.

Over her shoulder, I saw Mr. Frank come nearer, with face mad and wondering. He said once more, "Hey," with lips pulling back hard over teeth, and then he looked on the shoulder of his daughter. He blinked his eyes like not believing, and then looked again. He put his hand on it, quick, hard, and then took away like burned.

Now was changing more fast the rest of skin. Was like rubbing from a window the frost. Still they were not moving, the daughter and Mr. Frank, and then he went down on his knees beside the chair with arm around her and arm around me holding so hard that it hurt, and we were all three tight together, all three hot wet faces.

IN LIVING ROOM was radio, so loud you could not think, and people laughing. I was sitting by table in kitchen when Mr. Frank came out with glass in his hand, and fell against table, and sat down hard. His face was red like from steam bath. He looked on me and said, "Well, there you are. I thought you got lost in the john or something. Well, why don't you join the party, for Christ sake? Get in there and have a little fun."

I said, "I'm feeling tired. Would like to just sit quietly for while."

He blinked and said, "Sure. You do whatever you want. You're the greatest, Mike, you know that? You just sit there and take it easy, old buddy." He looked in his drink, and shook ice cubes, and then drank what was in bottom and put it down. "You know," he said, "two years I had that hanging over me. Two years, would you believe it?" He shook his head. "I use to belong to a bowling club. Had to give that up. Use to go out bowling every Tuesday night. Sold all my fishing stuff, too—never got much for it. Had to take the telephone out. You know we were living on franks and beans? Over two hundred bucks a week coming in, and living on franks and beans. Every cent went to the doctors. For two years. I don't take no credit, what the hell, I done the damage. And I paid for it, too." He reached for bottle on cabinet, and poured more whisky in glass. He drank some and put it down.

"You know she was engaged to a fellow. I never liked him. His name was Ernest. Ernest Nixon, he worked for a bank. But, she thought she loved him and all that. Then come her accident, and we never saw him again. I broke that up, all right. And don't you think she ever let me forget it." He held up glass. "You want some of this?"

I said, "No, thank you. It makes me sick in stomach."

"Too bad." He drank again. "Funny you can't fix a thing like that, I mean, after what you done for Anne."

I said, "I could fix it, but to me is not worth the trouble."

"Oh, yeah?" He nodded without interest, and then looked up. "Mean you can fix other stuff? Like if anybody got sick?"

"Some things I can fix. But not germ disease, because is too many little germs. But sometimes cancers I can fix, and things where body is not working right."

He put down his glass. "Cancer? You kidding? Yeah, you're kidding, you can't fix no cancer." He drank again.

"No, not kidding."

"Cut it out, will you? If you could do that, you'd be a millionaire, not a busboy."

Just then door from outside opened and two girls came in giggling, Anne and her girlfriend Loraine. Anne said, "Poppa, look?" They were both wearing pretty dresses, and Anne held open little jacket to show how low was neck of dress. Where bad skin was on her chest, was now only brown place you could hardly see—tanned from sun, because if not for her accident, she would have been at beach many times in bathing suit. And even this she had powdered now so it did not show. "A strapless!" she said. "Oh, you just don't know what it *means*!" In her eyes was tears. She kissed him, and then leaned over and kissed me also on forehead. Her lips were warm and greasy with lipstick, which I did not like. Then she and other one were rustling down hall toward where radio was going.

Mr. Frank stood up, holding on to chair. He said, "Excuse me a minute. Be right back." He went down the hall.

I sat and listened to radio too loud with music I did not understand. After long time, Mr. Frank came back, bumping into one side of hall and then other, with behind him Mr. Pete, the round bald one who always smiled. Mr. Frank sat down in chair so hard I thought he would break it, and Mr. Pete tried to help him but he said, "I'm all right."

Mr. Pete sat down on other side and put his hand on my shoulder. "Well, how you doing, boy?"

"All right."

"Frank here was just telling me, you have some kind of a

secret where you cure cancer, is that right?" He smiled on me, with teeth gray and wet.

"I can cure it," I said. I moved away little bit.

But he kept his hand on my shoulder. "Well, like how do you do it? I mean, do you say some words, or what?"

"Is hard to explain."

He nodded, smiling, and said to Mr. Frank, "See, Frank, a four-flusher. I seen them before. When he says it's hard to explain, that means he can't do it."

He turned to me and said, "Is that right?" On his breath was liquor. His head was bald and shiny brown under light.

I said, "I can do it."

"Well, you don't sound like you can do it. Look, can you do it or not?" He moved little closer to me. "I mean, like if you can do it, do it, or if you can't do it, shut up." Always smiling.

Mr. Frank sat up straight and said, "What have you, got a cancer? What's he going to cure, for Christ's sake? Don't be such a jerk, will you, for Christ's sake?"

Mr. Pete said, "Look. I got a wart, see?" He held up hand. There was a brown wrinkled wart on thumb. "Now if he can cure a cancer, it stands to reason he can cure a wart, don't it?"

"Oh, don't be such a jerk, Pete." Mr. Frank was frowning and rolling himself from side to side in chair. "Come on now, I don't like it." He leaned forward suddenly and took hold of my arm. "You and me are buddies, right, Mike?"

"Sure, Mr. Frank."

"You bet. So don't be such a jerk, Pete, I don't like it." He sat back and closed his eyes.

Mr. Pete was still holding up hand with wart. He was smiling, but not so wide. He said, "Okay, how about it?"

I said, "For wart is not worth it, and already I had a hard day, I am tired—"

"No, now," said Mr. Pete, holding wart in my face, "you said you could do it, and I want to see you do it. Come on, boy, let's see you cure that wart. Go ahead, make her disappear. Go ahead."

I looked on his face, and he was very hating man, very

quiet and smiling, but always looking for reason to hurt someone. And I saw in his past a shadow that made me feel bad in stomach.

Now my heart was again jumping hard in chest, and I was afraid it would be again like with policeman. So I reached, and turned where there was no wart. And it was gone.

Mr. Pete jumped like hit, and grabbed his hand. Mr. Frank had eyes open and watching, and I saw him rub his own thumb, where was small bandage. But he was not thinking about it, he was looking on Mr. Pete's hand. Then they both looked on me.

Mr. Pete swallowed and said, "He did it, by God."

"Gone?"

"Look here. You can't even see where it was."

Mr. Pete looked on me again with small bright eyes, and smile almost gone. "I don't know about this. I got to think." He rubbed his thumb, looked on it and then rubbed again. I smelled him sour and I knew he was afraid. He said, "There's possibilities in it, Frank."

"Aw, he's kidding you. Why ain't he a millionaire, then? He's nothing but a lousy busboy. It's all a load of crap."

I said, "I could do it, but I would not. Sometimes I can help, like with Anne. But if I would cure everybody who is sick, first it would be like whirlpool, everyone coming, fighting. I could make well forty, fifty people a day, that is nothing. It is like throwing one piece bread to hundred people who are starving. Believe me, I have seen it and I know. You cannot imagine what ugliness, how terrible is a world where all life, all happiness depends on one man."

But I stopped, because I saw they were looking on me but not listening. When I stopped, Mr. Pete got up and went around table to Mr. Frank. He bent down to whisper in his ear.

Then I thought it would be better if I should go, and I got up and went to the door. But with a crash of chair on floor they came after me, one on each side, both with red faces and liquor breath, and held my arms.

"Come on!" said Mr. Pete, and they made me walk across

kitchen, down hall, and they opened bedroom door and pushed me in.

They were both breathing hard. Mr. Pete stood in doorway and took knife out of pocket, and showed me the blade. "Listen," he said, "one peep out of you, and this. Understand?"

I said nothing. They backed out of door and closed it, and I heard a click.

In room it was dark then, but I found string hanging from ceiling and turned on light. It was one lightbulb, dim and sad. One wooden chair was in room, one bureau, and one little folding bed with thin mattress and Indian blanket on it. In air was smell of spray to kill insects.

I turned out light again and sat down on bed in the dark. Then I was very tired, and I lay down. After little while I heard voices and footsteps in hall, and then in kitchen, and door slammed. Then I heard only Anne's voice sounding mad asking some questions, and Mr. Frank and Mr. Pete answering, and then after while radio was turned off and it was quiet.

I lay still and closed eyes, but could not rest. First my leg would jump, then neck, then hand. And always I would think of Mr. Pete and Mr. Frank sitting in kitchen, under sick yellow light, with their wet eyes looking on me.

Then sometimes I would remember shiny black streets empty at night, and walls of brick and soot, and the faces of the people gray as they went down stairs into subway.

After long time, when house was quiet, I got up and went to door. Underneath in crack I could see light, very thin. I tried door and it would open little way, then click on something and stop. It was not a lock, but a bolt outside, the kind that slides across and then down into a slot.

I reached, and turned to make the bolt not be there. Then I opened door little by a little, and looked out. Hall was dark, only a little bit light coming from underneath kitchen door, which was now closed. Other way, all was black in living room, but I heard someone breathing slow.

Kitchen door also was closed by bolt, and this bolt also I removed. Carefully I opened door and looked in.

Mr. Pete was asleep in chair, leaning back against wall in

corner. He was partly against wall, partly against front door, so it could not open without hitting his chair. His head was hanging, and he was breathing loud. Every so often he would start to lean too far off the chair, and then he would pull himself back with a jerk, and his breathing would be quiet. Then, noisy again, and he would lean, and so on. He was frowning, and looked worried.

I went quietly across floor. The front door was closed with a big spring lock, also a bolt, and a chain. To open them would be easy, but then if I would open door, it would knock down Mr. Pete's chair and wake him up. So I reached, and turned to where whole door was not hung. And it flickered and disappeared. A cold air began to flow in through open doorway, and I stepped out into the hall.

When I was at the top of stairs, I heard a crash and a yell from inside apartment. I looked up as I started down stairs, and I saw Mr. Pete in doorway, with eyes big. When he saw me he ducked back behind the doorway, and then I saw him coming out again, and suddenly was a flash of fire and a sound like house breaking apart. Then I was falling downstairs. In my shoulder, slowly, was a feeling like someone would have hit me with a stick.

I was lying with my head downstairs, feet up. The stairs were full of that noise that made in my ears a pain, and whole building was going slowly around. Then I saw over the railing Mr. Pete's gray face looking down on me, and I saw his hand move, and inside me the fear came bursting up, and then suddenly was a black hole over my head. No Mr. Pete, no hallway, all vanished.

I was feeling sick, and dizzy. Now when I moved I felt pain in my shoulder, and in my mind I said, "He shot me. I am shot." I put my hand on place, and there was blood.

For minutes I could not see, and I thought I would faint. Then upstairs I heard feet running, and dimly saw Mr. Frank standing on edge of hallway, where beginning of hole was, and trying not to fall over. He was in pajamas, top part open. When I saw him, the fear came up again, and then he was gone, like candle going out.

Downstairs I heard doors banging, voices. I was trying to feel inside shoulder and find bullet, but there was no bullet, only hole. Then I started to fix wound, but it was too hard, I could not think with all the voices calling, and feet running in hallways. Then I heard Anne: "Pop! Pop!" And I saw her on edge of hallway upstairs, in blue bathrobe and pajamas. She was looking at hole in floor, holding on to railing with one hand, and with other brushing back her hair from face. I said, "Go back," and then she saw me but did not hear. She said, "Mike!" and began to move sideways along railing, putting her feet in spaces between the bars.

She got safely to top of stairs and came down quickly. "Mike, what *happened*? Gee, are you hurt? Let me—"

I said, "Shot. Trying to fix it, but—Must get out." I tried to get up, and she helped me. "Mike, where's Pop? Oh, look out, you're bleeding!"

I got my feet down where should be, and stood up holding on to wall. Anne tried to help, but did not like to touch side where I was bleeding.

I said, "Don't worry, doesn't matter," and I started down stairs holding wall with one hand, and her arm with other. Still I was trying to fix bullet hole, little by little, but could not do much, only close up to make the blood stop.

Going down the next flight we met two men in bathrobes coming up. They began to ask questions, and one tried to help me and make Anne go back, but I pushed him away. Now my shoulder was hurting, but we went down, past more people in doorways, until finally we were in bottom hallway, and Anne helped me push open the big door to outside. And cool air was blowing in our faces.

I went down stone steps slow, holding on. I tried not to think, not feel, only lean against the cold stone and make well my hurt shoulder.

Behind me Anne's voice said, "Mike, should I get a doctor?"

"No, wait, I can fix." Looking up street to avenue I could see the red eyes of traffic lights, and it was so quiet that when the lights changed to green, I could hear the click all way from corner.

Still, inside me was the fear pushing to get out. I heard Anne coming downstairs behind me, and each footstep I heard like a touch on my skin. She came and looked on my face, and began to say something.

Then doors of houses opened bang, and again I was like shot: I saw a man standing in doorway with legs apart and mouth open—but only a flicker, and then doorway turned black and melted away. The man was gone. Inside house, was a rain of plaster falling into hallway like a cave: and a dirty cloud puffed out of hole where doors had been.

In my ears was pain, on my knees cold stone. Inside house, I heard a woman scream. Then the stairs shook like thunder with feet coming down; and I could not help it, the fear came up inside me again. And it was quiet inside house. Except for patter of dropping things.

Anne was calling in my ear, "Mike, Mike, what is it?" Holding my arm till it hurt.

But I could not speak to her, because from few blocks away I heard a sound that made my skin cold. It was a siren of police car—coming nearer.

Then once more the bursting inside me, bigger than before; and the siren stopped like cut off with knife.

Then there was a rumble that shook street, and a cloud of dust crawled up over tops of buildings. Anne was shouting in my ear; I could not hear what she said.

I was seeing in my mind where buildings were cut in half, with people falling out.

I could not stop it. I put my hands over ears, but no good, I heard window opening, and my head jerked up; but all I saw was bricks flying from hole in building behind me. They winked out in middle of air, and never hit sidewalk. Then— one, two—the fear bulged again inside me, and there was nothing left of that building—not a brick, not a scream, only empty lot, color of ashes.

Anne said, in hoarse voice, "Mike—"

But across the street was doors opening, and people standing . . . and then, nothing. Darkness. Empty lots, and dark backs of buildings on next street. The wind was blowing a piece white paper, like bird with broken wing. And we looked on it.

Then I heard in the air a sound like police car a million times bigger. It was air raid siren, howling, in pain, shaking the streets, up and down, up, down. I could not stand it, and there was inside me like explosion, and that sound also stopped.

Stillness came whispering down the street.

But it was no more a street, only flat gray land as far as I could look. Not a tree, not even weed, only rock. Where minute ago we were in bottom of the street, like bugs in a crack, now we could see the edge of the world, and over us was the whole sky.

Now, slowly, like one muscle unclenching after another, my fear went away.

I listened. Under stillness was no sound, not even cricket; only more stillness, deep and deep. Across the land came a cold strong wind, and it passed us and went on.

"What happened?" said Anne. Her voice was flat and dull.

I said, "I killed them. Some I killed. Some cut in pieces. And the rest I made go away."

She looked on me, and after minute whispered, long and slow, "Why?"

"I was afraid." I listened to that word, waiting for it to echo like hand slapped on a wall, but it only floated away into darkness.

She said, "But what happened—to all the buildings? The—"

"I turned to where they were not built. Where was no city, and even no life. Now is a city on a world of gray rock, like this."

"I don't understand."

I said, "The way I fix your shoulder. I turned each little bit to where your accident never happened. Many worlds, many Annes. It is to me like breathing. I could always do it, even when I did not want to do it."

She did not seem to understand. She looked on me and said politely, "How is your shoulder?"

I felt, and it was whole again. "When I am asleep, or sometimes if I am very frightened, it is like inside me a small frightened child. Anything that is wrong with me, or anything it is afraid of, it will fix. To hurt other people—it does not know, it does not care."

She shook her head, looking past me. "It was all here, just a minute ago. Gee, I was sound asleep. Then I heard this big noise, and Pop got up and ran outside and then I got up too, and went to see—" She laughed. "I just can't believe it. I mean, it was all here." She looked around, and said, "Oh," with her hand to mouth.

"What?"

"I just thought, Queens is gone too. That's where Phil lived." I saw her eye shine. "He's a boy where I work. He kept asking me for dates, and I liked him, but— Gee, I'll never know, will I? And Pop—"

She put face down into her hands and her body began to shake. Deep, hurting sounds came up from her belly. And it kept going on. I could not bear to listen, and I went close and said, "Anne, don't cry. I will do anything, anything to help you."

Still she wept, and between crying she said to me, "Why couldn't you kill yourself instead!"

I said, "Once I tried it. But inside would not let me. And I woke up, and I was alive."

She was still weeping, and only to comfort her, I said, "All must die sometime, Anne, but to me is not easy."

She raised her head and looked on me, blind with crying. I said, "If I try to bring back a world where something has made me afraid, that frightened child will not let me. I tell you with shame, that it is stronger than me. And it never forgets. I could do for you only two things. Either I could take you over there"—I pointed—"where is still other cities—Philadelphia, Boston—"

She said in thick voice, "What's the other one?"

"I could turn where is another world, and another city—

not New York, but it would be as much like New York as I could make."

"Pop?" she asked.

"No. There will be no one that you knew, because I must turn before they were born. But you are young, pretty, you will make friends—"

She wiped her eyes with sleeve. "Will they build New York up again?"

"In this world? They will build it, yes, but never in your life would it be the same. Also there will be hard times for a while, even if you would go to California. I tell you truth, so you will know. To lose such a city, is like to a man to lose his arm. There will be shock, and much unhappiness."

"I lived here all my life," she said. "What would this other place be like?"

I said, "I will reach back and turn where simple thing was different—maybe one man president of country instead of another man. From this will be all things a little bit different— there will be different people born, and even different buildings built. But it will look like New York to you, and you will soon feel at home in it. That I promise."

She found handkerchief in her pocket, and turned away. "Don't look at me."

Now I knew she would be better, so I went little bit away and sat looking across gray plain, where ash-colored sky was turning slowly to a little bit green and pale gold.

"I'm sorry."

I turned to her. She was sitting straight, with hands in lap. "I'll take the other place you talked about. Can you do it right now?"

"Yes." I reached back, feeling for place to turn. It was easy to find one, but not so easy to pick right one. After minute I said, "Ready."

I reached and turned. And like a light going on in dark room, so quick it hurt the eyes, around us was a street with high buildings of red brick: and down at corner, traffic lights were turning green, and a long car went by with swish of tires on pavement. Street lights were yellow and dusty, and sky was again black. Under the stillness was small sounds everywhere, and in air was smell of burned gasoline.

I heard Anne say, very small, "Oh."

It was almost like old street. Small different things wherever you look, but from corner of eye, almost the same.

I said, "You will need some money," and I stepped to curb. I reached, and turned one small part of gutter, like deck of cards, until I found place where money was dropped. I picked it up, it was a dollar bill, but in middle was a different face. Then I turned to where it was a five instead, and then a ten, and so on until there was five hundred dollars. And I gave it to her, but she was holding robe tight around her and looking if anyone should see her not dressed. "Wait," I said, "I will fix it."

Under stone stairway was cellar entrance with railing, and garbage cans. I climbed over railing, and turned until I found place where was a coat thrown away. It was lying beside garbage can, a fur coat, with fur rubbed off some places, but better than bathrobe. I climbed back, and gave it to her, and she put it on.

"Now what?" she said, trying to smile.

Up at corner, lights were red, and I saw a taxi, a yellow one with sign on top lit. I stood at curb and waved, and I saw driver's head turn, and then lights were yellow, then green, and the taxi came curving around. It rolled up to us and stopped. The driver looked at us out of his window without saying anything. He was young, with long, pale chin, and he was chewing gum. He saw me and he saw Anne in her bad fur coat, with bedroom slippers on her feet, but he did not look away with politeness, or stare with rudeness; he did not care.

I opened the door for her, and she got in. "Take her to a good hotel," I told driver, "quiet, not too expensive." I started to close door, but she held out her hand.

"Aren't you coming too?"

The driver was listening, but I said, "Anne, this is not a world for me. If I would stay here, it would be same as last time. Better I should go now, and not take chances."

She said, "Go where?"

"Somewhere."

"What's the use, if it always turns out the same?"

"It will not always be the same. Somewhere I know God has made a place, even for me."

On her forehead was pain. She touched my hand and said, "Mike, Mike—"

Then I closed door slowly. "Goodbye. Please go on now, driver."

She was rolling down her window as taxi made a metal sound, and gray smoke came out of tail pipe, and taxi began to roll away down empty street; and Anne's head came out of window looking back, getting smaller, and I saw her hand waving; then taxi turned corner and she was gone.

I did not think to lose her would be so hard.

But if I would have stayed with her now, first from loneliness and then from being grateful, she would have grown to need me. Other bad things there would be, but this worst of all.

At least I had not done that to her, to spoil her by making myself a little demon who would do miracles, whenever a pot would boil over or a fingernail was broken.

Over roofs of buildings the sky was turning a bright, clear blue between streamers of purple-gray cloud. There was no use to wait anymore. I was tired, but I could rest where I was going.

I took long breath, and reached back deep and far, farther than ever before—two thousand years or little bit less. I was thinking that maybe all my trouble was because I was trying to stay close to my own world, and always to be traveling around it even though I could never go back. If I must wander, why not go far?

I found place, where if one man was not born, all world would be different. And I turned.

The buildings jumped like flames and disappeared. Then, under that same sky, there was another city.

Cold gray buildings climbing one behind another, all with peaked doors and windows, very big, and with domes of yellow stone or of powdery blue copper. Across the brightening sky was an airplane drifting—not cross-shaped, but round. The street was of cobblestones.

I was standing inside a little park with a railing of stone carved like loops of cloth. Behind me was a pedestal of stone, and two statues, one of handsome young man in a hat with no brim, carrying a torch in his arms. And the other just the same, but with torch upside down. They looked down on me with blank stone eyes.

Is it you? they seemed to say.

And I, looking back, said, *Is it here?*

But we could not answer each other; and I left them standing there, and went into the city.

O Brave Old World!

Avram Davidson

As the sly and witty story that follows demonstrates, there's no detail so small that it can't cause a cascade of events that will totally change the world—including something as mundane as whether or not you like a country's *cuisine*. . . .

For many years, the late Avram Davidson was one of the most eloquent and individual voices in science fiction and fantasy, and there were few writers in any literary field who could match his wit, his erudition, or the stylish elegance of his prose. During his long career, Davidson won the Hugo, the Edgar, and the World Fantasy Awards, and his short work was assembled in landmark collections such as *The Best of Avram Davidson*, *Or All the Seas with Oysters*, *The Redward Edward Papers*, *Collected Fantasies*, and *The Adventures of Doctor Esterhazy*. His novels include the renowned *The Phoenix and the Mirror*, *Masters of the Maze*, *Rogue Dragon*, *Peregrine: Primus*, *Rork!*, *Clash of Star Kings*, and *Vergil In Averno*, and a novel in collaboration with Grania Davis, *Marco Polo and the Sleeping Beauty*. Since his death in 1993, his posthumously published books include a collection of his erudite and witty essays, *Adventures in Unhistory*, the collections *The Avram Davidson*

Treasury, Limekiller!, The Other Nineteenth Century, and
*Everyone Has Somebody in Heaven: Essential Jewish Tales of
the Spirit*, plus the novel *The Scarlet Fig*.

ALL MORNING LONG the bells had been ringing, those bells,
which had been for a while silenced so that the sound of them
might instantly signal if enemy troops were to land. But, by
common consent and by clerical permission, they now sounded
something else entirely. The reddish-gray-haired man looked
up from the sheet of parchment, of which he must by now, it
seemed, know every letter, so often had he scanned it. Im-
mersed though he was in his text and his thoughts, still he
lifted his head at length and spoke.

"It sounds as though every church in the city is ringing its
bells," he murmured.

The friend and countryman who had so long and so often
stood by his side, figuratively and literally, said, "Yes and
even in the suburbs . . . the Liberties, as they call them here."

The reddish-gray-haired man made a soft, musing noise,
turned again to the document, then half-raised his head once
more. "One might call them liberty bells, then," he said. Another thought brought his head all the way up. "What was it,"
he asked, "that text from Scripture—you recall, don't you?—
on the bell in Philadelphia?"

His friend and countryman considered, nodded. " 'Pro-
claim liberty throughout the land—' "

"Aye, liberty. The Jews had a word for it. And 'unto all the
inhabitants thereof,' aye. . . ." He nodded, sighed. "Philadelphia," he said.

"Williamsburg."

"Richmond."

"The Chickahominy."

"The Rapahannock."

At the door, a burly, tousle-headed fellow, cheeks stubby
and shirt (none too fresh) open at his shaggy breast, looked in,
listened. His face showed a mixture of impatience and compassion. Often had he listened to these and other refugees re-
counting, as a litany, the names of their towns and provinces.

(One could not always tell them apart.) Sometimes the names of the New World (perhaps Brave, perhaps just Bold) merely echoed the names of the Old. (O servant exalted above the master!) Sometimes they seemed a concatenation of barbarous sybilants and gutterals from the aboriginal tongues. Ah, well. To duty.

"Are you quite ready for us, then?" he asked the two. They turned.

"Ah, Charles. I should think—"

"Ah, Charles. Just one more moment. A last look. You understand."

"Of course. Of course. No wish to rush you. " He coughed; he raised his eyebrows. The reddish-gray-haired man went back to his text. The friend moved quietly and, gently and tactfully (he was not always quiet, or gentle, or tactful) eased the newcomer away.

"He won't be much longer at it, I promise. I know."

"Yes, yes. You've known him a long time."

"Since his hair was quite red."

Arm in arm they moved out into the corridor. There, all was controlled turmoil. Country squires and yeoman farmers with mud on their boots spoke confidentially to craftsmen smelling of machine oil and the forge. Bishops, white sleeved, listened with modified majesty to inferior clergy, all in black save for the white bands at the neck. And a member of the old peerage, head covered with a wig of archaic cut, nodded to the comments of an old man wrapped in a ragged—and still, technically, illegal—tartan. It was as least as likely that this last anachronism had crossed, recently and hastily, from long exile in France, than that he had descended from Scotland. The Estates, as the Scottish parliament was called since the revisions of the Act of Union, had done little more with the use of their regained powers than to pass innumerable acts of outlawry and attainder upon each other. But this, too, would soon enough pass away.

Very, very soon, in fact.

On seeing the two approach, one gentleman, evidently in a condition of total confusion as well as in court dress (court dress, sword and all), buttonholed the burly fellow with an agitated air.

"Where will it end, Charles?" he asked. "Where will it all end?"

"All's well that ends well," was the half-muttered reply, then added, after a moment's recollection, "Doctor."

As though needing no more than this acknowledgment of his profession, the doctor at once said, "As to where it all began, why, say I, it all began with the fatal tennis ball. Or, if I may be permitted to say it—" here he glanced around, defiantly "—the insufficiently fatal tennis ball."

"Water under the bridge," Charles muttered, tugged a watch out, glanced, then muttered again, "Water under the bridge. . . . London Bridge. . . ."

But the medical man's phrase was overheard, was appreciated, was at once repeated and passed from mouth to mouth. *The insufficiently fatal tennis ball. . . .*

And the bells rang out and the bells rang on. St. Paul's, St. Martin's, St. Clemens, Bow, St. Mary-le-Bone. . . .

The insufficiently fatal tennis ball. . . .

THE STUARTS, AS even the handful of still-unreconstructed Jacobites would needs admit, the Stuarts had had their faults. But they had not hated their heirs. That is, the Jameses and the Charleses had not hated one another. Anne, to be sure, now, Anne—Anne had certainly shown no fondness for, first, Sophia, Dowager Electress of Hanover, and for Sophia's son, George. But they were only Anne's distant cousins, and were far off in what someone later was to term "a despicable Electorate." Poor Anne! Last of the Stuarts actually to occupy the throne, thirteen (thirteen!) pregnancies, and no heir to outlive her, she might have been (and was) excused for not wishing the sight or presence of her so-distant kin.

But it was left for the kin themselves to exemplify the phrase of Elizabeth, her sentiment that "she could not bear to hear the mention of a Successor." And yet, even so, Elizabeth, too, had had some reason. Had she not? "The Queen of Scots hath a bonny Babe, and I am but a barren stock." Thus Elizabeth. But what reason had the sovereigns of the House of Hanover for hating, and for so hating, their own heirs? Heirs who were of their own bodies lawfully begotten—and lawfully present. Had not George I, at a court levee, publicly cursed his son, the future George II, forbidding him thenceforth to attend cabinet meetings, cabinet meetings from which, there no longer being any interpreter whom German George felt he could trust, the king thenceforth absented himself from. (And a good thing, too, said many.)

Even this, however, had faded beside the subsequent hatred of George II for his own heir, Frederick, Prince of Wales. The English, not used to the sort of thing which was evidently traditional in Hanover, the English had murmured, "Poor Fred. . . ." Poor Fred, indeed. The king could not, after all, immure the Prince of Wales in a palace prison, however much he called him "scoundrel." Nor could he cut his son off from revenues which either had been voted as "supply" by Act of Parliament, or accrued by ancient English law and custom, via the duchies of Cornwall and Lancaster. However much he thought and called him "fool."

Frederick, Prince of Wales, was, however, subject to all the coldness, the scorn, hatred, spleen and exclusion of which his father, George II, was capable. He was left to molder in his own petty counter-court, attended only by those politicians who were not merely out of favor but entertained no hopes of ever being again in favor while George lived. The prince was left to admire the poems of Pope. And he was left to play tennis.

It was the blow upon or near the breastbone, the blow from a hard-struck tennis ball, which gave the princely physician a concern. "I fear me," the meddlesome apothecary had murmured, "I fear me that this blow might be the occasion of an imposthume. And that, should Your Royal Highness suffer at some future date from a severe cold . . . an inflammation on the lungs . . ."

"Is nothing to be done?" inquired the prince, somewhat languid from opium and ipecac. "Am I so soon to leave nine orphans? [There had been, after all, one other thing in which

the king was powerless to constrain him.] Should we send for
the chaplain?" But the physician-in-ordinary was not ready to
send for the chaplain.

"I should propose to bleed Your Royal Highness once
again," he said. The Prince of Wales, however, was not ready
to be bled once again. "Then I should propose to purge Your
Royal Highness once again." But the Prince absolutely refused to be purged once again.

The physician-in-ordinary threw up his hands. "In that
case," he said. And stopped. "In that case . . . In that case, I
must recommend . . . in fact. . . . In that case," he said, firmly,
"I indeed must insist upon Your Royal Highness taking a long
and immediate change of air."

As was to be expected, the king managed to contain his
grief.

"A change of air? Vhere?" he demanded.

"The Isle of Wight has been suggested, Your Majesty."

"Der Isle of *Vhat?*" A map was brought and the Isle of
Wight pointed out to the king, who was pleased to give a
grunt, interpreted as a Gracious Assent.

However and however.

"His Royal Highness does not, it seems, desire to go to the
Isle of Wight."

The king had been playing backgammon with his mistress
and already felt bored with this interfering subject.

"*Teufelsdreck!* Dhen vhere he vants to go?" It was inti-
mated that the prince had expressed a preference for either
Hanover or France as the scene of his recuperation. The king
gave a shout of rage and kicked the backgammon board across
the room. Hanover! Never! Hanover. . . . In Hanover. . . . In
Hanover the air was sweeter, the water purer, the food better,
the populace more loyal ("—than in England" being understood). Hanover was reserved for the king himself to go to for
changes of air. And as for *France*—

"He vould intrigue vhit der French king! He vould efen intrigue vhit der pretender!" It was pointed out to him that the
pretender now lived in Italy, and rather meanly, on a papal
pension. But the king would hear no arguments. Once let

Frederick set foot upon the Continent, why, what would prevent his going even to Italy? *"Der force of graffity, maybe?"* he screamed, with immense sarcasm.

"Nein! Nein! He can go to der Isle of Vight—or he can go to Hell—und—und—if he doesn't vant to go to Hell, den he can go to America!"

At this, the royal mistress was unwise enough to allow a snort of laughter to escape her lips. The entire court waited breathlessly for the lightnings. But the king, having had his attention called to the fact of his having made a joke, abruptly decided to enjoy it. His hard-bitten little red face grew redder still, and the court, breathing inward sighs of relief, joined in the now royally permissable laughter.

And on this merry gale, the prince's vessel was wafted out to sea.

First aboard the *Anna Maria* was the royal and proprietarial governor. His cocked hat showing above the railing as he climbed the ladder, he was demanding, "Have ye got me snuff with ye? Have ye got me madeira? Have ye brought me mail, me newsletters?" With a heave and a ho he clambered on deck, looked all around. "Have ye got any pretty wenches that have come to seek their fortunes in the new-found world? Have ye—" And here his face, which had just that moment focused on a slender and somewhat pale passenger, underwent an absolutely fascinating transformation.

"Your Royal Highness!" he bawled, and did not so much fall upon his knees as on his face.

It was in this manner that Frederick, Prince of Wales, came to America.

The king, it was reported, had near had an apoplexy when he heard the news. But he had, after all, he *had* given his permission. After a fashion, no doubt, but given it he had. And in the hearing of all the court. There was, then, nothing he could do about it.

From *The Court Circular and Gazette:*

His Royal Highness the Prince of Wales, Her Royal Highness the Princess of Wales, and their Children [here followed a list], have, by Reason of His Majesty's Most
Gracious Solicitude, engaged upon a visit to the American
Plantations, in order that His Royal Highness may recruit
his Health.

No member of the royal family had ever before set foot
upon the soil of the American plantations ("the colonies," as
it was now becoming fashionable to call them). And, suddenly, in one stroke, here were eleven of them! They moved
into the home of the royal and proprietarial governor, the r.
and p.g. moved into the house of the lieutenant-governor and
the lieutenant-governor moved into an inn. The governor's
home was, for the Americas, palatial. But it was, after all,
crowded with all of them there. It was *damned* crowded!

"Let's build a little house," the prince suggested. "Eh, my
dearest? Shall we build a little house along the river? Is that
not a capital suggestion?" The princess thought that it *was* a
capital suggestion. All her life, after all, she had lived in
houses built for others. The notion that she might now have a
voice in designing one for her own use fell upon her ears like
harpsichord music played by an orchestra of angels. The
house was to be on the Delaware River, and not on the
Thames? Bless you, it might have been on the Styx for all she
cared! And in the meanwhile . . . in the meanwhile . . . for it
was crowded in the governor's house . . . well, what about a
visitation of the *other* colonies?

And so it was arranged. The youngermost ones of the royal
infants remained in Pennsylvania with their nurses; the eldest
of the royal infants accompanied their royal parents. New Jersey and New York had heard with curiosity what they now be-
held with enthusiasm. Connecticut had been cool, but the
coolness was now warmed. Massachusetts, New Hampshire
and Rhode Island and Providence plantations had, in fact,
been skeptical about the whole thing: who knew but that it
was some sort of a flummery tale concocted down there in
Pennsylvany? What would a prince be doing in America, any-

way? It was all obviously, or half-obviously, a sort of granny's tale. Prince? There was no—

And then, thunderation! *Here he was!*

And would you just look-see what he was *do*ing!

Previous examples of British officialdom had merely sniffed at the coarse foodstuffs of the frontier, hastily ordered their cooks to prepare some French kickshaws ("Or at least a decent dish of mutton!"). Not Fred. The capacity of Frederick for the New England dinner, boiled or otherwise, was prodigious.

"*Look* at him a-tuckin' inta the baked beans!"

"Didn't do a injustice to the hasty puddin', either!"

"*How* many bowls o' chowder and *how* many quohogs'd the prince eat down't the clambake?"

Up came the First Selectman of the Township of East Neantic, which was, so to speak, catering the affair; sweating and smiling slightly (in East Neantic they smile slightly where others would beam), he called his order for "more o'th' ha'nch o'venison fr His R'yal Highness!"

And, not very long later: "More roast beef fr the Prince o' Wales!"

In England, venison came from the King's Deer, and the king was not inclined to share. In England, one had not known that bears could be roasted; in England, one had, in fact, never even *seen* a bear!

The New Englanders looked at each other, looked at their prince—who gave them back a hearty grin, somewhat greasy about the chops—looked at each other again.

"Likes our vittles, do he? He *do!*"

"Guess we ain't sech barbarious critters after all!" they said to each other.

And they said: "Well, sir, I snum!"

"I snum!"

Even at this date one may wonder: *why* had Fred such an appetite, such a zest for things? Well, for one thing, the provinces of the New World were . . . well, they were *new!* The hand of man had not yet had time to tame them as in Europe, trim them into shape like yew hedges, turn their sparkling rivers into tame canals or drainage ditches. And, in that pure air, under that clear sky, the despised son of what a later New England writer was to call a "snuffy old drone from the German hive" seemed to enter a new youth—almost without ever having, under the cold gaze and hot scorn, almost without ever having had a previous one.

Here, no one called him "fool!"

Here, no one called him "scoundrel!"

And, perhaps best of all, here, no one called him "poor Fred!"

AFTER A WHILE, the weather commencing to turn cold, prince and princess turned south, were reunited with the royal infants in Philadelphia, examined the progress on what people were already beginning to call the Prince's Palace. . . . The Prince's Palace was not really quite ready yet. . . . Not quite ready yet, eh? Hm, well, there were colonies to the south of Pennsylvania, were there not? There certainly were! And, having heard of their sovereign's son's reception by the colonies to the north, they were restlessly waiting to show him what they could do in Delaware . . . Maryland . . . Virginia . . . North and South Carolina . . . and even in far-off Georgia, hard upon the borders of the Spanish dons.

It was all very pleasant. It was all *most* pleasant. And so, as he was bound to do, sooner or later, the king heard about it.

It is His Majesty's pleasure that the Prince should now return.

The prince did not return.

Those listless days of playing cards before a smoky fireplace under a lowering London sky, listening to the slow babble of a second-hand and second-rate set of courtiers were over. The Prince's Palace was finished now, but the prince had no intention of turning it into a copy of what he had left behind him. It was brought to his attention that what the colonies, menaced by French and Spanish and Indians, what the colonies needed was a well-regulated militia. Very well, then; he began to regulate—that is, to organize and reorganize and drill one. And, at the first occasion—another outbreak on the frontier—he led it into battle. There was no nonsense of bright, gaudy uniforms (such as his father so loved), preceded by loud-sounding brass and drums. In their native buckskin and hickory-dyed homespun, slinking through the wilderness as stealthily as Indians, the colonial troops met the enemy. And he was theirs.

More shouts of rage in far-off London. Once again the backgammon board was kicked across the room.

It is His Majesty's command that the Prince shall now return forthwith.

In tones practicedly smooth and outwardly respectful, the prince replied that his health did not, alas, permit him to return . . . just yet. And, in fact, he—but let the story follow, turn by turn.

THE KING WAS of course not without resources. And one of them was to commandeer the resources of the Prince of Wales. These were collected as soon as ever they fell due, and at once closed up in the Privy Purse. The king did not, to be sure, confiscate them. He merely neglected to forward them to the prince.

"Let der vild backvoodsmen pay Fred's bread *und* board," he said. Or was said to have said. And, so, might as well have said.

The Assembly of Pennsylvania voted the prince a subvention of a thousand pounds, Pennsylvania. The Assembly of Maryland voted a similar sum. The Virginia House of Burgesses voted him fifteen hundred. The race was on. From colony after colony the money rolled in. It rolled in—until word arrived that *His Majesty has refused the Royal Assent to the subvention.* By now the colonial temper was hotting up. What was to be done?

"The king be a-tryin' tew take our prince away from us, be he? A-tryin' to starve him out, be he? Well . . . *he bain't a-goin' tew!*"

The Selectmen and Town Meeting of East Neantic voted the prince the best three lots in the township available, and promptly voted to rent them back at the best rent possible;

they then voted to send the money forthwith; as a further act, they also voted the prince's household "twenty pecks of corn-meal, two barrels prime salt pork, a barrel of oysters, a barrel of clams, a hogshead of hominy and one of samp. . . ." The list rolled on.

"The king, he bain't able tew veto the Township of East Neantic, no, sir, not even he!"

It caught on. It caught right on. Within two months the prince's storehouses not only bulged with victualry, peltry and wampum, but he had become the largest landowner in any single colony one might care to name. There was lots of land.

COULD NOT THE prince be said to have "fled the Realm" and hence to have abdicated, as was said of James II? The cabinet dubiously said that it rather thought not. The Privy Council respectfully said, not. And even the law lords, with many a regretful harrumph, said, absolutely . . . absolutely not. Well, then, what could the king *do*? Once again the king was politely made to know that he could do—nothing.

Of course, he could die. And, of course, he did.

What happened next was compared to the Flight of the Wild Geese, the Flight of the Earls, when the leaders of the Irish almost *en masse* took to their heels and, not waiting for the completion of yet another English reconquest, took refuge on the Continent. Of course, it was not the same. It was, well, it was because no one really knew how one stood in regard to the new king. ("Frederick, by the Grace of God"; how odd it sounded! There had never been a King Frederick before. Well, there had once never been any King George before, either.) And, for that matter, no one knew how the king himself stood in regard to . . . well, anything!

The Atlantic was white with sails. London Pool was left bare of any vessel capable of crossing the ocean, and Bristol, the same. Every man with a place to lose or hope of a place to gain was posting o'er the white-waved seas. Was London the capital, still? Well . . . Parliament sat in London. But only if the king summoned it to sit. The king was, after all, still very much the Fountain of Honor . . . and of power. And each cab-

inet minister, each member of the Privy Council, each powerful marquis and viscount and earl, each of them had the
thought that if *he* were the first to bring the new king the
news, if the new king, panting for the crown, were to accompany *him* back to England. . . .

For bringing back an earlier exiled Prince of Wales, General Monk had been created Duke of Albermarle.

Historians dispute who actually was the first to bring Fred
the news. There was, after all, quite a crowd of them. They
found him—and a hard journey of it they had had, too, in finding him—they found him sitting on a split-rail fence the other
side of the Alleghenies, wearing a coonskin cap ("Sitting on a
what?) The other side of *where? Wearing a *which?*") and
buckskin breeches stained with grease and blood. They bab-
bled out their news. Their great news. And waited for the new
king to cry for his horse.

"I shan't budge," said the new king. And he spat a stream
of something which they soon learned was tobacco juice.

"I ain't a-gonna go," the king said.

He rid himself of his chaw and called—not for his horse—
for a dipper of rye whiskey. "To rense out my mouth."

Nothing was ever the same afterwards.

PARLIAMENT WAS SUMMONED to sit, and Parliament sat. A
royal and Ducal uncle opened it in the capacity of "Captain of
the Realm." *But the Privy Council was held in Philadelphia!*
True, only a Parliament could, only a House of Commons, in
fact, could vote the king "supply." But, secure in his colonial
rents and revenues, the king did not need their supply. "Ship
money"? Bless you, he had all the ships, and all the money, as
ever he could need, right where he was! London? The king
called London "a cesspool full of snobs." He said that if London did not like it, London could kiss his royal arse.

He did suggest that Parliament should make provision for
American members. Parliament was dazed, but it did not feel
itself to be as dazed as that. Parliament's term eventually expired. The king simply did not summon another one.

What he *did* summon, by and by, was a sort of American

parliament, called a Continental Congress, with the new privy
council acting as a sort of House of Lords (a prominent member of which was the First Selectman of East Neantic). The
prime minister was a colonial, a native of the American
Boston, who had moved to Philadelphia in his youth. His
name was Benjamin Franklin. The detested Navigation Acts,
so hostile to colonial manufacture and shipping, were in effect
nullified. Before long, American shipping—so much closer,
after all, to wood and sailcloth and resin and pitch, and just as
close to iron—had begun to supplant British preeminence in
the trade upon the seas.

Who does not remember the great invasion of England
planned by one Bonaparte? Who has not thrilled to the story
of the sailing of the American armada, which, under the command of John Paul Jones, swept the French from the seas in a
twinkling? Who, then, could object to the fact that American
troops now spat their tobacco juices in the streets of London?

Franklin retired and was replaced by a Virginia planter by
the name of Washington. "I detest your Party, sir," was his
common word; "your Faction, sir, I abhor." But he grew old.
(And, for that matter, so did the king.) And presently Washington stepped down, and was replaced, of course, by another
colonial. The king grew very old. But the king, though he did
not die, less and less attended to the business of state, leaving
it more and more in the hands of his first minister. And this
one was one who did by no means despise party or faction. Intrigue was middle name to him. The Americans had had little
or no experience in such matters. The power slipped bit by bit
from the hands of the old congressmen before they even noticed it. And the prime minister, securing the lord presidency
of the privy council as well, began that which some said he
had aimed at all along: a dictatorship after the old Roman
model.

The old king no longer roamed the wilderness frontier de-
lighting in the hunt and in the rough but genial banter of the
backwoodsmen. He stayed in the by now truly palatial
Prince's House—the name had stuck and would never be
changed—drinking rum cocktail and watching what were

known as minstrel shows. One by one, the old champions of liberty slipped away, slipped across the seas, took refuge in an England which their forefathers, in the name of that same liberty, had long ago left behind them.

The old king lived on and on and on.

THOUGH THE PRUDENCE of retaining the American troops in England seemed clear to many (mostly in America), the costliness of doing so was also clear. The troops could hardly go and shoot game enough to feed themselves. England grunted at the first of the new tax acts. Stamped paper was to go up, was it? Well . . . they did not like it, but, after all, it was the same both sides of the sea. One by one the Acts of Congress descended. Congress, as such, could not act for England. But the Privy Council could; it could act anywhere in the realm. An Order in Council. Another Order in Council. And another.

England, it was being said, now groaned beneath an American tyranny.

And still there was not enough money. The American troops needed new clothes. The troops were protecting England, weren't they? Well, then let the English pay for it.

To be sure, some of this expense had to be shared by American taxpayers, too. One had to step delicately here. The prime minister-president cautiously considered. What source of revenue was there which would least vex the colonies? It did not take him long to find it. After all, in all the Americas, how many folks really drank tea?

THAT HAD BEEN the back-breaking straw. The British were long suffering, slow to wrath. They were loyal. They endured the absence of their king. They had submitted to the loss of their Parliament. They had accepted the presence of what were more or less foreign troops. They had muddled through the dismal diminution of trade. But—

Raise the tax on their tea?

On TEA?

The bells tolled in the churches, but not to summon the

faithful to prayer. Fishwives and bishops, coal porters and
Whig gentry, Thames watermen and bishops, cheesemongers
and prentice boys, the beggars and the whores and the learned
Proctors of the Doctors Commons, all rose up as one.

There was an East India vessel of the Honorable Company
then in the Pool of London, laden with the newly taxed hyson,
oolong and pekoe. A mob, calling itself the Sons of Liberty
(said actually to be composed of the younger sons of younger
sons of peers), stormed the vessel and threw the tea chests into
the harbor (whence the well-sealed containers were promptly
and clandestinely pulled out, to be sold, *sub rosa* and *sub*
counter, and sans tax, by members of the Worshipful Company of Grocers). And, as though to express their opinions as
to the source of the oppressive tax, the mob had dressed themselves as Indians!

Could contempt and defiance go further?

FOR ALMOST THE first time in English history, a Parliament
met without being summoned by the hand of a sovereign. The
precedent, the so-called Convention Parliament—which had
outlawed James II and confirmed the Crown to William and
Mary—the precedent was uncertain. But when a precedent is
wanted by a people close to rebellion, any precedent will do.
They did not meet in the old Houses of Parliament, long
empty—though empty in a sense only, for the House of Commons had served for some years as a choirboys' school for
Westminster Abbey, and the Commons itself was now used as
a quartermasters warehouse for the American soldiers. They
met in the Guildhall, under the great statues of Gog and
Magog. First they repealed the old Act of Union. Then, under
a slightly different style, they reenacted it. Then they passed
resolutions. This delay was almost fatal.

The American troops, marching down Leadenhall Street in
their brave new red-white-and-blue uniforms (symbols of op-
pression), and with their newly equipped bands playing—
rashly, oh so rashly—"Yankee Doodle," were met by a
withering crossfire from the newly re-formed Trained Bands,
hiding in the thickly clustering houses. And, abandoning their

intended attack on the Guildhall, they were obliged to fall back, retreating across the Thames in the direction of South-wark.

And so, now, all day, behind the barricades, the refugee American with the reddish-gray hair had toiled over the doc-ument. And now at last he looked up, and he nodded.

They marched into the great hall. They read the document aloud as the Liberty Bells rang out, proclaiming liberty throughout the land, unto all the inhabitants thereof. And when the words were reached, "RESOLVED, *That these United Kingdoms are, and of right, ought to be,* FREE AND INDEPENDENT"—ah, then, what a shout went up!

"Charles James Fox should be first to sign," the American said.

Charles James Fox scratched his bristly chin and shaggy chest. Shook his unkempt head. "No, sir," he declared. "You have written it, the honor of signing it first belongs to you. Let that scoundrelly American prime minister-president, let the tyrant who has driven you all from your homeland, let him see your name there for himself."

The American nodded. With a wry smile, he said to his friend, "Well, Pat, I now commit treason . . . eh?"

His friend's comment was, "If this be treason, let us make the most of it."

The other, with a sound assent, picked up the proffered pen and, in a great round hand, wrote: *"Thomas Jefferson."*

"There," he said in grim contentment. "Now Aaron Burr can read it without his spectacles. . . ."

Radiant Doors

Michael Swanwick

Michael Swanwick made his debut in 1980, and in the twenty-five years that have followed has established himself as one of science fiction's most prolific and consistently excellent writers at short lengths, as well as one of the premier novelists of his generation. He has won the Theodore Sturgeon Award and the *Asimov's* Readers Award poll. In 1991, his novel *Stations of the Tide* won him a Nebula Award as well, and in 1995 he won the World Fantasy Award for his story "Radio Waves." He's won the Hugo Award four times between 1999 and 2003, for his stories "The Very Pulse of the Machine," "Scherzo with Tyrannosaur," "The Dog Said Bow-Wow," and "Slow Life." His other books include the novels *In The Drift*, *Vacuum Flowers*, *The Iron Dragon's Daughter* (which was a finalist for the World Fantasy Award *and* the Arthur C. Clarke Award, a rare distinction!), *Jack Faust*, and, most recently, *Bones of the Earth*, plus a novella-length book, *Griffin's Egg*. His short fiction has been assembled in *Gravity's Angels*, *A Geography of Unknown Lands*, *Slow Dancing Through Time* (a collection of his collaborative short work with other writers), *Moon Dogs*, *Puck Aleshire's Abecedary*,

Tales of Old Earth, Cigar-Box Faust and Other Miniatures, and *Michael Swanwick's Field Guide to the Mesozoic Megafauna*. He's also published a collection of critical articles, *The Postmodern Archipelago*, and a book-length interview, *Being Gardner Dozois*. His most recent book is a new collection, *The Periodic Table of SF*, and he is at work on a new novel. Swanwick lives in Philadelphia with his wife, Marianne Porter. He has a website at www.michaelswanwick.com.

In the harrowing story that follows, he reassures us that if you have a time-machine at your disposal, you shouldn't worry if you run out of future—just start chewing up the *past* instead.

THE DOORS BEGAN opening on a Tuesday in early March. Only a few at first—flickering and uncertain because they were operating at the extreme end of their temporal range—and those few from the earliest days of the exodus, releasing fugitives who were unstarved and healthy, the privileged scientists and technicians who had created or appropriated the devices that made their escape possible. We processed about a hundred a week, in comfortable isolation and relative secrecy. There were videocams taping everything, and our own best people madly scribbling notes and holding seminars and teleconferences, where they debated the revelations.

Those were, in retrospect, the good old days.

In April the floodgates swung wide. Radiant doors opened everywhere, disgorging torrents of ragged and fearful refugees. There were millions of them and they had every one, to the least and smallest child, been horribly, horribly abused. The stories they told were enough to sicken anyone. I know.

We did what we could. We set up camps. We dug latrines. We ladled out soup. It was a terrible financial burden to the host governments, but what else could they do? The refugees were our descendants. In a very real sense, they were our children.

Throughout that spring and summer, the flow of refugees continued to grow. As the cumulative worldwide total ran up into the tens of millions, the authorities were beginning to panic—was this going to go on forever, a plague of human locusts that would double and triple and quadruple the population, overrunning the land and devouring all the food? What measures might we be forced to take if this kept up? The planet was within a lifetime of its loading capacity as it was. It couldn't take much more. Then in August the doors simply ceased. Somebody up in the future had put an absolute and final end to them.

It didn't bear thinking what became of those who hadn't made it through.

"MORE TALES FROM the burn ward," Shriver said, ducking through the door flap. That was what he called atrocity stories. He dumped the files on my desk and leaned forward so he could leer down my blouse. I scowled him back a step.

"Anything useful in them?"

"Not a scrap. But that's not my determination, is it? You have to read each and every word in each and every report so that you can swear and attest that they contain nothing the Commission needs to know."

"Right." I ran a scanner over the universals for each of the files, and dumped the lot in the circular file. Touched a thumb to one of the new pads—better security devices were the very first benefit we'd gotten from all that influx of future tech—and said, "Done."

Then I linked my hands behind my neck and leaned back in the chair. The air smelled of canvas. Sometimes it seemed that the entire universe smelled of canvas. "So how are things with you?"

"About what you'd expect. I spent the morning interviewing vics."

"Better you than me. I'm applying for a transfer to Publications. Out of these tents, out of the camps, into a nice little editorship somewhere, writing press releases and articles for the Sunday magazines. Cushy job, my very own cubby, and the satisfaction of knowing I'm doing some good for a change."

"It won't work," Shriver said. "All these stories simply blunt the capacity for feeling. There's even a term for it. It's called compassion fatigue. After a certain point you begin to blame the vic for making you hear about it."

I wriggled in the chair, as if trying to make myself more comfortable, and stuck out my breasts a little bit more. Shriver sucked in his breath. Quietly, though—I'm absolutely sure he thought I didn't notice. I said, "Hadn't you better get back to work?"

Shriver exhaled. "Yeah, yeah. I hear you." Looking unhappy, he ducked under the flap out into the corridor. A second later his head popped back in, grinning. "Oh, hey, Ginny—almost forgot. Huong is on sick roster. Gevorkian said to tell you you're covering for her this afternoon, debriefing vics."

"Bastard!"

He chuckled, and was gone.

I SAT INTERVIEWING a woman whose face was a mask etched with the aftermath of horror. She was absolutely cooperative. They all were. Terrifyingly so. They were grateful for anything and everything. Sometimes I wanted to strike the poor bastards in the face, just to see if I could get a human reaction out of them. But they'd probably kiss my hand for not doing anything worse.

"What do you know about midpoint-based engineering? Gnat relays? Sub-local mathematics?"

Down this week's checklist I went, and with each item she shook her head. "Prigogine engines? SVAT trance status? Lepton soliloquies?" Nothing, nothing, nothing. "Phlenaria? The Toledo incident? 'Third Martyr' theory? Science Investigatory Group G?"

"They took my daughter," she said to this last. "They did things to her."

"I didn't ask you that. If you know anything about their military organization, their machines, their drugs, their research techniques—fine. But I don't want to hear about people."

"They did things." Her dead eyes bored into mine. "They—"

"Don't tell me."

"—returned her to us midway through. They said they were understaffed. They sterilized our kitchen and gave us a list of more things to do to her. Terrible things. And a check-list like yours to write down her reactions."

"Please."

"We didn't want to, but they left a device so we'd obey. Her father killed himself. He wanted to kill her too, but the device wouldn't let him. After he died, they changed the settings so I couldn't kill myself too. I tried."

"God damn." This was something new. I tapped my pen twice, activating its piezochronic function, so that it began recording fifteen seconds earlier. "Do you remember anything about this device? How large was it? What did the controls look like?" Knowing how unlikely it was that she'd give us anything usable. The average refugee knew no more about their technology than the average here-and-now citizen knows about television and computers. You turn them on and they do things. They break down and you buy a new one.

Still, my job was to probe for clues. Every little bit con-tributed to the big picture. Eventually they'd add up. That was the theory, anyway. "Did it have an internal or external power source? Did you ever see anybody servicing it?"

"I brought it with me," the woman said. She reached into her filthy clothing and removed a fist-sized chunk of quicksil-ver with small, multicolored highlights. "Here."

She dumped it in my lap.

IT WAS AUTOMATION that did it or, rather, hyperautomation. That old bugaboo of fifty years ago had finally come to fruition. People were no longer needed to mine, farm, or man-ufacture. Machines made better administrators, more attentive servants. Only a very small elite—the vics called them simply their Owners—were required to order and ordain. Which left a lot of people who were just taking up space.

There had to be *something* to do with them.

As it turned out, there was.

That's my theory, anyway. Or, rather, one of them. I've got

a million. Hyperautomation. Cumulative hardening of the collective conscience. Circular determinism. The implicitly aggressive nature of hierarchic structures. Compassion fatigue. The banality of evil.

Maybe people are just no damn good. That's what Shriver would have said.

The next day I went zombie, pretty much. Going through the motions, connecting the dots. LaShana in Requisitions noticed it right away. "You ought to take the day off," she said, when I dropped by to see about getting a replacement PzC(15)/pencorder. "Get away from here, take a walk in the woods, maybe play a little golf."

"Golf," I said. It seemed the most alien thing in the universe, hitting a ball with a stick. I couldn't see the point of it.

"Don't say it like that. You love golf. You've told me so a hundred times."

"I guess I have." I swung my purse up on the desk, slid my hand inside, and gently stroked the device. It was cool to the touch and vibrated ever so faintly under my fingers. I withdrew my hand. "Not today, though."

LaShana noticed. "What's that you have in there?"

"Nothing. I whipped the purse away from her. "Nothing at all." Then, a little too loud, a little too blustery, "So how about that pencorder?"

"It's yours." She got out the device, activated it, and let me pick it up. Now only I could operate the thing. Wonderful how fast we were picking up the technology. "How'd you lose your old one, anyway?"

"I stepped on it. By accident." I could see that LaShana wasn't buying it. "Damn it, it was an accident! It could have happened to anyone."

I fled from LaShana's alarmed, concerned face.

Not twenty minutes later, Gevorkian came sleazing into my office. She smiled, and leaned lazily back against the file cabinet when I said hi. Arms folded. Eyes sad and cynical. That big plain face of hers, tolerant and worldly-wise. Wearing her skirt just a *smidge* tighter, a *touch* shorter than was strictly correct for an office environment.

"Virginia," she said.

"Linda."

We did the waiting thing. Eventually, because I'd been here so long I honestly didn't give a shit, Gevorkian spoke first. "I hear you've been experiencing a little disgruntlement."

"Eh?"

"Mind if I check your purse?"

Without taking her eyes off me for an instant, she hoisted my purse, slid a hand inside, and stirred up the contents. She did it so slowly and dreamily that, I swear to God, I half expected her to smell her fingers afterward. Then, when she didn't find the expected gun, she said, "You're not planning on going postal on us, are you?"

I snorted.

"So what is it?"

"What is it?" I said in disbelief. I went to the window. Zip zip zip, down came a rectangle of cloth. Through the scrim of mosquito netting the camp revealed itself: canvas as far as the eye could see. There was nothing down there as fancy as our labyrinthine government office complex at the top of the hill—what we laughingly called the Tentagon—with its canvas air-conditioning ducts and modular laboratories and cafeterias. They were all army surplus, and what wasn't army surplus was Boy Scout hand-me-downs. "Take a look. Take a goddamn fucking look. That's the future out there, and it's barreling down on you at the rate of sixty seconds per minute. You can see it and still ask me that question?"

She came and stood beside me. Off in the distance, a baby began to wail. The sound went on and on. "Virginia," she said quietly. "Ginny, I understand how you feel. Believe me, I do. Maybe the universe is deterministic. Maybe there's no way we can change what's coming. But that's not proven yet. And until it is, we've got to soldier on."

"Why?"

"Because of *them*." She nodded her chin toward the slow-moving revenants of things to come. "They're the living proof of everything we hate and fear. They are witness and testimony to the fact that absolute evil exists. So long as there's the least chance, we've got to try to ward it off."

I looked at her for a long, silent moment. Then, in a voice as cold and calmly modulated as I could make it, I said, "Take your goddamned hand off my ass."

She did so.

I stared after her as, without another word, she left.

This went beyond self-destructive. All I could think was that Gevorkian wanted out but couldn't bring herself to quit. Maybe she was bucking for a sexual harassment suit. But then again, there's definitely an erotic quality to the death of hope. A sense of license. A nicely edgy feeling that since nothing means anything anymore, we might as well have our little flings. That they may well be all we're going to get.

And all the time I was thinking this, in a drawer in my desk the device quietly sat. Humming to itself.

PEOPLE KEEP HAVING children. It seems such a terrible thing to do. I can't understand it at all, and don't talk to me about instinct. The first thing I did, after I realized the enormity of what lay ahead, was get my tubes tied. I never thought of myself as a breeder, but I'd wanted to have the option in case I ever changed my mind. Now I knew I would not.

It had been one hell of a day, so I decided I was entitled to quit work early. I was cutting through the camp toward the civ/noncom parking lot when I ran across Shriver. He was coming out of the vic latrines. Least romantic place on Earth. Canvas stretching forever and dispirited people shuffling in and out. And the smell! Imagine the accumulated stench of all the sick shit in the world, and you've just about got it right.

Shriver was carrying a bottle of Spanish champagne under his arm. The bottle had a red bow on it.

"What's the occasion?" I asked.

He grinned like Kali and slid an arm through mine "My divorce finally came through. Wanna help me celebrate?"

Under the circumstances, it was the single most stupid thing I could possibly do. "Sure," I said. "Why not?"

Later, in his tent, as he was taking off my clothes, I asked, "Just why did your wife divorce you, Shriver?"

"Mental cruelty," he said, smiling.

Then he laid me down across his cot and I let him hurt me. I needed it. I needed to be punished for being so happy and well fed and unbrutalized while all about me . . .

"Harder, God damn you," I said, punching him, biting him, clawing up blood. "Make me pay."

CAUSE AND EFFECT. Is the universe deterministic or not? If everything inevitably follows what came before, tickety-tock, like gigantic, all-inclusive clockwork, then there is no hope. The refugees came from a future that cannot be turned away. If, on the other hand, time is quanticized and uncertain, unstable at every point, constantly prepared to collapse in any direction in response to totally random influences, then all that suffering that came pouring in on us over the course of six long and rainy months might be nothing more than a phantom. Just an artifact of a rejected future.

Our future might be downright pleasant.

We had a million scientists working in every possible discipline, trying to make it so. Biologists, chaoticists, physicists of every shape and description. Fabulously dedicated people. Driven. Motivated. All trying to hold out a hand before what must be and say "Stop!"

How they'd love to get their mitts on what I had stowed in my desk.

I hadn't decided yet whether I was going to hand it over, though. I wasn't at all sure what was the right thing to do. Or the smart thing, for that matter.

Gevorkian questioned me on Tuesday. Thursday, I came into my office to discover three UN soldiers with hand-held detectors, running a search.

I shifted my purse back on my shoulder to make me look more strack, and said, "What. the hell is going on here?"

"Random check, ma'am." A dark-eyed Indian soldier young enough to be if not my son then my little brother politely touched fingers to forehead in a kind of salute. "For uptime contraband." A sewn tag over one pocket proclaimed his name to be PATHAK. "It is purely standard. I assure you."

I counted the stripes on his arm, compared them to my civilian GS-rating and determined that by the convoluted UN protocols under which we operated, I outranked him.

"Sergeant-Major Pathak. You and I both know that all foreign nationals operate on American soil under sufferance, and the strict understanding that you have no authority whatsoever over native civilians."

"Oh, but this was cleared with your Mr.—"

"I don't give a good goddamn if you cleared it with the fucking Dalai Lama! This is my office—your authority ends at the door. You have no more right to be here than I have to finger-search your goddamn rectum. Do you follow me?"

He flushed angrily, but said nothing.

All the while, his fellows were running their detectors over the file cabinet, the storage closets, my desk. Little lights on each flashed red red red. Negative negative negative. The soldiers kept their eyes averted from me. Pretending they couldn't hear a word.

I reamed their sergeant-major out but good. Then, when the office had been thoroughly scanned and the two noncoms were standing about uneasily, wondering how long they'd be kept here. I dismissed the lot. They were all three so grateful to get away from me that nobody asked to examine my purse. Which was, of course, where I had the device.

After they left, I thought about young Sergeant-Major Pathak. I wondered what he would have done if I'd put my hand on his crotch and made a crude suggestion. No, make that an order. He looked to be a real straight arrow. He'd squirm for sure. It was an alarmingly pleasant fantasy.

I thought it through several times in detail, all the while holding the gizmo in my lap and stroking it like a cat.

THE NEXT MORNING, there was an incident at Food Processing. One of the women started screaming when they tried to inject a microminiaturized identi-chip under the skin of her forehead. It was a new system they'd come up with that was

supposed to save a per-unit of thirteen cents a week in track-
ing costs. You walked through a smart doorway, it registered
your presence, you picked up your food, and a second doorway checked you off on the way out. There was nothing in it
to get upset about.

But the woman began screaming and crying and—this
happened right by the kitchens—snatched up a cooking knife
and began stabbing herself over and over. She managed to
make nine whacking big holes in herself before the thing was
wrestled away from her. The orderlies took her to Intensive,
where the doctors said it would be a close thing either way.

After word of that got around, none of the refugees would
allow themselves to be identi-cbipped. Which really pissed off
the UN peacekeepers assigned to the camp, because earlier a
couple hundred vics had accepted the chips without so much
as a murmur. The Indian troops thought the refugees were
willfully trying to make their job more difficult. There were
complaints of racism, and rumors of planned retaliation.

I spent the morning doing my bit to calm things down—
hopeless—and the afternoon writing up reports that everyone
upstream wanted to receive ASAP and would probably file
without reading. So I didn't have time to think about the device at all.

But I did. Constantly.

It was getting to be a burden.

For health class, one year in high school, I was given a ten-
pound sack of flour, which I had to name and then carry
around for a month, as if it were a baby. Bippy couldn't be left
unattended; I had to carry it everywhere or else find somebody willing to baby-sit it. The exercise was supposed to
teach us responsibility and scare us off of sex. The first thing
I did when the month was over was to steal my father's .45,
put bippy in the backyard, and empty the clip into it, shot after
shot. Until all that was left of the little bastard was a cloud of
white dust.

The machine from the future was like that. Just another
bippy. I had it, and dared not get rid of it. It was obviously
valuable. It was equally obviously dangerous. Did I really

want the government to get hold of something that could compel people to act against their own wishes? Did I honestly trust them not to immediately turn themselves into everything that we were supposedly fighting to prevent?

I'd been asking myself the same questions for—what?—four days. I'd thought I'd have some answers by now.

I took the bippy out from my purse. It felt cool and smooth in my hand, like melting ice. No, warm. It felt both warm and cool. I ran my hand over and over it, for the comfort of the thing.

After a minute, I got up, zipped shut the flap to my office, and secured it with a twist tie. Then I went back to my desk, sat down, and unbuttoned my blouse. I rubbed the bippy all over my body, up my neck, and over my breasts and around and around on my belly. I kicked off my shoes and clumsily shucked off my pantyhose. Down along the outside of my calves it went, and up the insides of my thighs. Between my legs. It made me feel filthy. It made me feel a little less like killing myself.

HOW IT HAPPENED was, I got lost. How I got lost was, I went into the camp after dark.

Nobody goes into the camp after dark, unless they have to. Not even the Indian troops. That's when the refugees hold their entertainments. They had no compassion for each other, you see—that was our dirty little secret. I saw a toddler fall into a campfire once. There were vics all around, but if it hadn't been for me, the child would have died. I snatched it from the flames before it got too badly hurt, but nobody else made a move to help it. They just stood there looking. And laughing.

"In Dachau, when they opened the gas chambers, they'd find a pyramid of human bodies by the door," Shriver told me once. "As the gas started to work, the Jews panicked and climbed over each other, in a futile attempt to escape. That was deliberate. It was designed into the system. The Nazis didn't just want them dead—they wanted to be able to feel morally superior to their victims afterward."

So I shouldn't have been there. But I was unlatching the door to my trailer when it suddenly came to me that my purse felt wrong. Light. And I realized that I'd left the bippy in the top drawer of my office desk. I hadn't even locked it.

My stomach twisted at the thought of somebody else finding the thing. In a panic, I drove back to the camp. It was a twenty-minute drive from the trailer park and by the time I got there, I wasn't thinking straight. The civ/noncom parking lot was a good quarter-way around the camp from the Tentagon. I thought it would be a simple thing to cut through. So, flashing my DOD/Future History Division ID at the guard as I went through the gate. I did.

Which was how I came to be lost.

THERE ARE NEIGHBORHOODS in the camp. People have a natural tendency to sort themselves out by the nature of their suffering. The twitchers, who were victims of paralogical reprogramming, stay in one part of the camp, and the mods, those with functional normative modifications, stay in another. I found myself wandering through crowds of people who had been "healed" of limbs, ears, and even internal organs—there seemed no sensible pattern. Sometimes our doctors could effect a partial correction. But our primitive surgery was, of course, nothing like that available in their miraculous age.

I'd taken a wrong turn trying to evade an eyeless, noseless woman who kept grabbing at my blouse and demanding money, and gotten all turned around in the process when, without noticing me, Gevorkian went striding purposefully by.

Which was so unexpected that, after an instant's shock, I up and followed her. It didn't occur to me not to. There was something strange about the way she held herself, about her expression, her posture. Something unfamiliar.

She didn't even *walk* like herself.

The vics had dismantled several tents to make a large open space surrounded by canvas. Propane lights, hung from tall poles, blazed in a ring about it. I saw Gevorkian slip between two canvas sheets and, after a moment's hesitation. I followed her.

It was a rat fight.

The way a rat fight works, I learned that night, is that first you catch a whole bunch of Norwegian rats. Big mean mothers. Then you get them in a bad mood, probably by not feeding them, but there are any number of other methods that could be used. Anyway, they're feeling feisty. You put a dozen of them an a big pit you've dug in the ground. Then you dump in your contestant. A big guy with a shaven head and his hands tied behind his back. His genitals are bound up in a little bit of cloth, but other than that he's naked.

Then you let them fight it out. The rats leap and jump and bite and the big guy tries to trample them underfoot or crush them with his knees, his chest, his head—whatever he can bash them with.

The whole thing was lit up bright as day, and all the area around the pit was crammed with vics. Some shouted and urged on one side or the other. Others simply watched intently. The rats squealed. The human fighter bared his teeth in a hideous rictus and fought in silence.

It was the creepiest thing I'd seen in a long time.

Gevorkian watched it coolly, without any particular interest or aversion. After a while it was obvious to me that she was waiting for someone.

Finally that someone arrived. He was a lean man, tall, with keen, hatchetlike features. None of the vics noticed. Their eyes were directed inward, toward the pit. He nodded once to Gevorkian, then backed through the canvas again.

She followed him.

I followed her.

They went to a near-lightless area near the edge of the camp. There was nothing there but trash, the backs of tents, the razor-wire fence, and a gate padlocked for the night.

It was perfectly easy to trail them from a distance. The stranger held himself proudly, chin up, eyes bright. He walked with a sure stride. He was nothing at all like the vics.

It was obvious to me that he was an Owner.

Gevorkian too. When she was with him that inhuman arrogance glowed in her face as well. It was as if a mask had been removed. The fire that burned in his face was reflected in hers.

I crouched low to the ground, in the shadow of a tent, and listened as the stranger said, "Why hasn't she turned it in?"

"She's unstable," Gevorkian said. "They all are."

"We don't dare prompt her. She has to turn it in herself."

"She will. Give her time."

"Time," the man repeated. They both laughed in a way that sounded to me distinctly unpleasant. Then, "She'd better. There's a lot went into this operation. There's a lot riding an it."

"She will."

I stood watching as they shook hands and parted ways. Gevorkian turned and disappeared back into the tent city. The stranger opened a radiant door and was gene.

CAUSE END EFFECT. They'd done . . . *whatever* it was they'd done to that woman's daughter just so they could plant the bippy with me. They wanted me to turn it in. They wanted our government to have possession of a device that would guarantee obedience. They wanted to give us a good taste of what it was like to be them.

Suddenly I had no doubt at all what I should do. I started out at a determined stride, but inside of nine paces I was *running*. Vics scurried to get out of my way. If they didn't move fast enough, I shoved them aside.

I had to get back to the bippy and destroy it.

WHICH WAS STUPID, stupid, stupid. If I'd kept my head down and walked slowly. I would have been invisible. Invisible and safe. The way I did it, though, cursing and screaming. I made a lot of noise and caused a lot of fuss. Inevitably, I drew attention to myself.

Inevitably, Gevorkian stepped into my path.

I stumbled to a halt.

"Gevorkian," I said feebly. "Linda, I—"

All the lies I was about to utter died in my throat when I

saw her face. Her expression. Those eyes. Gevorkian reached for me. I skipped back in utter panic, turned—and fled. Anybody else would have done the same.

It was a nightmare. The crowds slowed me. I stumbled. I had no idea where I was going. And all the time, this monster was right on my heels.

Nobody goes into the camp after dark, unless they have to. But that doesn't mean that nobody goes in after dark. By sheer good luck. Gevorkian chased me into the one part of the camp that had something that outsiders could find nowhere else— the sex-for-hire district.

There was nothing subtle about the way the vics sold themselves. The trampled-grass street I found myself in was lined with stacks of cages like the ones they use in dog kennels. They were festooned with strings of Christmas lights, and each one contained a crouched boy. Naked, to best display those mods and deformities that some found attractive. Off-duty soldiers strolled up and down the cages, checking out the possibilities. I recognized one of them.

"Sergeant-Major Pathak!" I cried. He looked up, startled and guilty. "Help me! Kill her—please! Kill her now!"

Give him credit, the sergeant-major was a game little fellow. I can't imagine what we looked like to him, one harridan chasing the other down the streets of Hell. But he took the situation in at a glance, unholstered his sidearm and stepped forward "Please," he said. "You will both stand where you are. You will place your hands upon the top of your head. You will—"

Gevorkian flicked her fingers at the young soldier. He screamed, and clutched his freshly crushed shoulder. She turned away from him, dismissively. The other soldiers had fled at the first sign of trouble. All her attention was on me, trembling in her sight like a winded doe. "*Sweet* little vic," she purred. "If you won't play the part we had planned for you, you'll simply have to be silenced."

"No," I whispered.

She touched my wrist. I was helpless to stop her. "You and

I are going to go to my office now. We'll have fun there. Hours
and hours of fun."

"Leave her be."

As sudden and inexplicable as an apparition of the Virgin,
Shriver stepped out of the darkness. He looked small and
grim.

Gevorkian laughed, and gestured.

But Shriver's hand reached up to intercept hers, and where
they met, there was an electric blue flash. Gevorkian stared
down, stunned, at her hand. Bits of tangled metal fell away
from it. She looked up at Shriver.

He struck her down.

She fell with a brief harsh cry, like that of a sea gull.
Shriver kicked her, three times, hard: In the ribs. In the stom-
ach. In the head. Then, when she looked like she might yet re-
gain her feet, "It's one of *them*!" he shouted. "Look at her!
She's a spy for the Owners! She's from the future! Owner!
Look! Owner!"

The refugees came tumbling out of the tents and climbing
down out of their cages. They looked more alive than I'd ever
seen them before. They were red-faced and screaming. Their
eyes were wide with hysteria. For the first time in my life, I
was genuinely afraid of them. They came running. They
swarmed like insects.

They seized Gevorkian and began tearing her apart.

I saw her struggle up and halfway out of their grips, saw
one arm rise up above the sea of clutching hands, like that of
a woman drowning.

Shriver seized my elbow and steered me away before I
could see any more. I saw enough, though.

I saw too much.

"Where are we going?" I asked when I'd recovered my
wits.

"Where do you think we're going?"

He led me to my office.

THERE WAS A stranger waiting there. He took out a hand-
held detector like Sergeant-Major Pathak and his men had

used earlier and touched it to himself, to Shriver, and to me. These times it flashed red, negative. "You travel through time, you pick up a residual charge," Shriver explained. "It never goes away. We've known about Gevorkian for a long time"

"US Special Security," the stranger said, and flipped open his ID. It meant diddle-all to me. There was a badge. It could have read Captain Crunch for all I knew or cared. But I didn't doubt for an instant that he was SS. He had that look. To Shriver he said, "The neutralizer."

Shriver unstrapped something glittery from his wrist—the device he'd used to undo Gevorkian's weapon—and, in a silent bit of comic bureaucratic punctilio, exchanged it for a written receipt. The security officer touched the thing with his detector. It flashed green. He put both devices away in interior pockets.

All the time, Shriver stood in the background, watching. He wasn't told to go away.

Finally, Captain Crunch turned his attention to me again. "Where's the snark?"

"Snark?"

The man removed a thin scrap of cloth from an inside jacket pocket and shook it out. With elaborate care, he pulled it over his left hand. An inertial glove. Seeing by my expression that I recognized it, he said, "Don't make me use this."

I swallowed. For an instant I thought crazily of defying him, of simply refusing to tell him where the bippy was. But I'd seen an inertial glove in action before, when a lone guard had broken up a camp riot. He'd been a little man. I'd seen him crush heads like watermelons.

Anyway, the bippy was in my desk. They'd be sure to look there.

I opened the drawer, produced the device. Handed it over. "It's a plant," I said. "They want us to have this."

Captain Crunch gave me a look that told me clear as words exactly how stupid he thought I was. "We understand more than you think we do. There are circles and circles. We have informants up in the future, and some of them are more highly placed than you'd think. Not everything that's known is made public."

"Damn it, this sucker is *evil*."

A snake's eyes would look warmer than his. "Understand this. We're fighting for our survival here. Extinction is null-value. You can have all the moral crises you want when the war is won."

"It should be suppressed. The technology. If it's used, it'll just help bring about . . ."

He wasn't listening.

I'd worked for the government long enough to know when I was wasting my breath. So I shut up.

WHEN THE CAPTAIN left with the bippy, Shriver still remained, looking ironically after him. "People get the kind of future they deserve," he observed.

"But that's what I'm saying. Gevorkian came back from the future in order to help bring it about. That means that time isn't deterministic." Maybe I was getting a little weepy. I'd had a rough day. "The other guy said there was a lot riding on this operation. They didn't know how it was going to turn out. They didn't *know*."

Shriver grunted, not at all interested.

I plowed ahead unheeding. "If it's not deterministic—if they're working so hard to bring it about—then all our effort isn't futile at all. This future can be prevented."

Shriver looked up at last. There was a strangely triumphant gleam in his eye. He flashed that roguish ain't-this-fun grin of his, and said, "I don't know about you, but some of us are working like hell to *achieve* it."

With a jaunty wink, he was gone.

The Hotel at Harlan's Landing

Kage Baker

One good thing about meddling in time is that you then have all of time in which to *hide* from the consequences of your actions. Sometimes, though, no matter how isolated and remote a location you find to hide yourself away in, it isn't nearly isolated *enough* . . .

One of the most prolific new writers to appear in the late '90s, Kage Baker made her first sale in 1997, to *Asimov's Science Fiction*, and has since become one of that magazine's most frequent and popular contributors with her sly and compelling stories of the adventures and misadventures of the time-traveling agents of the Company; of late, she's started two other linked sequences of stories there as well, one of them set in as lush and eccentric a High Fantasy milieu as any we've ever seen. Her stories have also appeared in *Realms of Fantasy*, *Sci Fiction*, *Amazing*, and elsewhere. Her critically acclaimed novels include *In the Garden of Iden*, *Sky Coyote*, *Mendoza in Hollywood*, *The Graveyard Game*, and her first fantasy novel *The Anvil of the World*. Her short fiction has been collected in *Black Projects, White Knights*, and, most recently, *Mother Aegypt and Other Stories*. Her most recent books are a chapbook novella, *The Empress of Mars*, and two new Company novels, *The Life of the World to Come* and *The Children of the Company*. In addition to her writing, Baker has been an artist, actor, and director at the Living History Center, and has taught Elizabethan English as a second language. She lives in Pismo Beach, California.

THERE WAS JUST the five of us in the bar that night.

The lumber mills were all shut down for good and there hadn't been a ship come up to the wharf in years. No more big schooners down there in the cove, with their white sails flying in at eye level to the bluff top like clouds. Dirty little steamers stayed well out on the horizon and never came in, going busily to San Francisco or Portland. Nothing to come in for, at Harlan's Landing.

All this stuff the weekenders find so cute now, the gingerbread cottages and the big emporium with its grand false front and the old hotel here—you wouldn't have thought they were much then, when they were gray wood beaten into leaning by the winter storms, paint from the boom days all peeled off. No Heritage Society to save us, no tourists with cash to spend. Nobody had cash to spend. It was 1934.

I couldn't keep the hotel open, but after the Volstead Act was repealed I opened the bar downstairs and things brightened up considerably. Our own had some place to go, had sort of a social life now, see? We come that close to being a ghost town that everybody needed to know there was still a place with the yellow lights shining out through the windows, fighting to stay alive.

And it wasn't like there was anyplace else to go anyhow, not with the logging road washed out in winter, which was the only other way to get here from the city back then. I felt I sort of owed the rest of them.

Especially I owed Uncle Jacques and Aunty Irina. I had that awful year in 1929 when Mama got the cancer and I lost Bill, that was my husband, he was one of the crew on the *San Juan*, see. They were real kind to me then. Stayed by me when I wanted to just die. Aunty Irina baked bread, and Uncle

Jacques fixed the typewriter and told me what I ought to write to the damn insurance people when they weren't going to pay. People who'll help you clean your house for a funeral twice in one year are good friends, believe you me.

Then, if Uncle Jacques hadn't kept the Sheep Canyon trail cleared we'd have had nothing to eat but venison, because there'd have been no way I could have got the buckboard through to Notley for provisions most of the time. It must have been hard work, even for him, just one man with an axe busting up those redwood snags; because of course Lanark was no use. But Uncle Jacques looked after all of us, he and Aunty Irina. They said it was a good thing to have a *human community*.

And, see, once I opened the bar, there was some place to go. Lanark didn't have to stay alone in his shack watching the calendar pages turn brown, and Miss Harlan didn't have to stay alone in her cottage hearing the surf boom and wondering if Billy was going to come walking up out of the water to haunt her. I didn't have to sit alone in my room over the lobby, thinking how my folks would scold me because I hadn't kept the brass and mahogany polished like I ought to have. And Uncle Jacques and Aunty Irina had a nice little human community they could come down and be part of for a while, so they didn't have to sit staring at each other in their place up on Gamboa Ridge.

I had it real cozy here. That potbellied stove in the corner worked then; fire inspector won't let us use it now, but I used to keep it going all night with a big basket of redwood chunks, and I lit the room up bright with kerosene lamps and moved some of the good tables and chairs down from the hotel rooms. Uncle Jacques brought me a radio he'd tinkered with, he called it a wireless, and I don't know if it ran on a battery or what it had in it, but we set it behind the bar and we could get it to pull in music and shows. We had Jack Benny for Canada Dry and Chandu the Magician, and Little Orphan Annie, and even Byrd at the South Pole sometimes.

So Uncle Jacques and Aunty Irina would dance if there was music, and Miss Harlan would sit watching them, and I'd

pour out applejack for everybody or maybe some wine. I used
to get the wine, good stuff, from a man named Andy Lopez
back in Sheep Canyon. Lanark would drink too much of it, but
at least he wasn't a mean drunk. We'd all be happy in the bar,
warm and bright like it was, though the rest of the hotel was
echoing and dark, and outside the night was black and empty
too.

And that night it was black with a Pacific gale, but not
empty. The wind was driving the sleet sideways at the windows, the wild air blustered and fought in the street like the
sailors used to on Saturday nights. Every so often the sky
would light up horizon to horizon, purple and white lightning
miles long, and for a split second there'd be the town outside
the windows like it was day but awful, with the black empty
buildings and the black gaps in the sidewalk where the boards
had rotted out, and the sea beyond breaking so high there was
spume flying up the street, blown on the storm.

You wouldn't think we'd be getting any radio reception at
all, but whatever Uncle Jacques had done to that thing, it was
picking up a broadcast from some ballroom in Chicago. And
damned if the bandleader didn't play "Stormy Weather"!
Aunty Irina pulled Uncle Jacques to his feet. He slipped his
arm around her and they two-step shuffled up and down in
front of the bar, smiling at each other. Miss Harlan watched
them, getting a little misty-eyed like she always did at anything romantic, and she sang along with the music. Lanark
was pretty sober yet and making eyes at me from his table,
and I smiled back at him because he did still use to be handsome then, in a wrecked kind of way.

He had just said, "Damn, Luisa, you throw a nice party,"
and I was just about to say something sassy back when the
music was drowned out by a *crack-crack-crack* and screech-
ing static, so awful Miss Harlan and me put our hands over
our ears, and Uncle Jacques and Aunty Irina stopped short and
stood apart, looking like a couple of greyhounds on the alert.

Then we heard the call numbers and the voice out of the
storm, telling us that some vessel called the *Argive* was in
trouble, two aboard, and could the Coast Guard help? And I

wondered how the radio had switched itself over to the marine band, but it was Uncle Jacques's radio so I guess it might have done anything. They gave their location as right off Gamboa Rock, and I felt sick then.

See it out there? That's Gamboa Rock. See the way the water kind of boils around it, even on a nice summer day like this, and that little black line of shelf trailing out from it? It used to be a ship-killer, and a man-killer too, and we all knew the *Argive* wasn't ever going to see any Coast Guard rescue, if that was where she was. Not in weather like that.

And in the next big flash of lightning we could see the poor damned thing through the windows, looked like somebody's yacht, rearing on the black water and fighting for sea room. I only saw her for a split second, but I could paint her to this hour the way she looked, almost on her beam-end with her sail flapping. Then the dark swallowed up everything again. There was just a tiny little pinprick light we could still see for a while.

The voice on the radio was high and scared and there wasn't any Coast Guard answering, and pretty soon they began begging anybody to help them. They must have been able to see our light, I guess. It would have broken your heart to have to sit there and listen, the way they were asking for lifeboats and lines, which we didn't have. We couldn't have got to them anyway.

Lanark had lurched to his feet and was staring out into the storm, and I guess he was thinking how he could have made a try of it in the *Sada* if she hadn't been rotting up on sawhorses ever since he'd lost his arm. Miss Harlan had put her fingers in her ears and was rocking back and forth, and I didn't blame her; she didn't take death too well. I was crying myself, and so was Aunty Irina, wringing her hands, and she was staring up at Uncle Jacques with a pleading look in her eyes but his face was set like stone, and he was just shaking his head. They murmured back and forth in what I guessed was their language, until he said, "You know we can't, Rinka."

He sat her down and put his arms around her to keep her there. Lanark and I took a couple of lanterns and went out into the street, but the wind nearly knocked us over and there was nothing to see out there anyway, not now. We got as far as the path down the cliff before another burst of lightning showed us the sea coming white up the stairs, and the old platform that had been below torn away with bits of it bobbing in the surge, and the spray jumping high. I think Lanark would still have tried to go down, but I pulled him away and the fool paid attention for once in his life. Coming back I near broke my leg, stepping in a hole where a plank was gone out of the sidewalk. We were gasping and staggering like we'd swum a mile by the time we got back up on the porch here.

It was lovely warm in the bar, but the voice on the radio had stopped. All that was coming through the ether now was a kind of regular beat of static, *pop-pop, pop-pop* like that, just a quiet little death knell.

I said, "We all need a drink," and poured out glasses of applejack on the house, because that was the only thing on earth I could do. Miss Harlan and Lanark came and got theirs quick enough, and he backed up to the stove to warm himself. Uncle Jacques let go of Aunty Irina and stood, only to have her reel upright and slap him hard in the face.

He rocked back on his heels. Miss Harlan was beside her right away, she said, "Oh, please don't—it's too awful—" and Aunty Irina fell back in her chair crying.

She said she was sorry, but she couldn't bear sitting there and doing nothing again, when somebody might have been saved. Lanark and I were in a hurry to tell her that nobody could have done anything, that we couldn't even get down into the cove because the stairs were washed out, so she mustn't feel too bad. Uncle Jacques brought her a glass, but she pushed it away and tried to get hold of herself. Looking up at us as though to explain, she said, "We had a child, once."

Uncle Jacques said, "Rinka, easy," but she went on:

"Adopted. My baby Jimmy. We had him for eighteen years. He wanted to enlist. We thought, well, the war's almost over, let him play soldier if he wants to. He'll be safe. There wasn't any record—but we didn't think about the Spanish influenza. He caught it in boot camp in San Diego. Never even got on the troop carrier. They had him all laid out in his uniform by the time we got there . . . Only eighteen."

Real quiet, Uncle Jacques said, "There was nothing we could have done," as though it was something he'd repeated a hundred times, and she snapped back:

"We should never have let him go! Not with that event shadow—" And she started crying again, crying and cursing. Miss Harlan offered her a handkerchief and got her to drink some of her drink, and when she was a little calmer led her off to the ladies' lavatory upstairs to powder her nose. They took one of the kerosene lanterns to find their way, because it was pitch black beyond the bar threshold. A fresh squall beat against the windows, sounding like thrown gravel.

Uncle Jacques dropped down heavy in his seat, and gulped his drink and what was left of Aunty Irina's. Lanark drank too, but he was staring at Uncle Jacques with a bewildered expression on his face. Finally Lanark said, "Your kid died during the war? But . . . *how* old are you?"

And I thought, oh, hell, because you couldn't trust Lanark with a secret when he drank; that was why we'd never told him the truth about Uncle Jacques and Aunty Irina. Uncle Jacques and I looked at each other and then he cleared his throat and said:

"Irina was talking out of her head. It was her kid brother died in boot camp. We did adopt a baby once, but he died of diphtheria. She went a little crazy over it, Lanark. Most times you wouldn't know, but tonight—"

"Oh," said Lanark, and I could see the wheels turning in his head as he decided that was why Uncle Jacques and Aunty Irina lived up there alone on Gamboa Ridge, and never had visitors or went up to the city for anything.

I said, "Have another drink, Tom," and that worked like it always did, he came right away and let me fill his glass up. It never took much to get that man to stop thinking, poor thing. Just as well too.

We turned the radio off and I had another drink myself, I was feeling so low, and Lanark drank a bit more and then said we ought to go out at first light to see if there were any bodies washed up at least, so we could bury them Christian until one of us could ride up to the Point Piedras light and have them pass the word to the Coast Guard about the wreck. Uncle Jacques roused himself from his gloom enough to say we'd need to notify the Coast Guard even if we didn't find bodies, so at least the historical record would be correct.

That was about when I saw the face outside.

I am not a screaming woman. I saw enough God-awful things in this town when it was alive to harden me up. You get some hideous accidents in a sawmill, which I'm sure those folks who eat lunch there now it's a shopping arcade would rather not know about, and a redwood log that jumps the side of the flume doesn't leave much of anybody who gets in its way. Then there's the dead hereabouts, that hooker somebody killed in Room 17 who still cries, or poor Billy Molera who used to come up from the sea and go round and round Miss Harlan's cottage at night, moaning for love of her, and leave a trail of seaweed and sand in her garden come morning. You get used to things.

But it did give me a turn, the white face out there beyond the glass, just glimpsed for a second with its black eyeholes and black gaping mouth. Where I was, perched up on my stool behind the bar, I had a good look at it, though neither Lanark nor Uncle Jacques could have seen the thing. I didn't make a sound, just slopped my drink a little.

Uncle Jacques looked up at me sharply. He said, "What's scared you?"

I wasn't going to say, but then we heard it coming up the steps.

Two, three steps from the street onto the porch, it must have crossed right here where I'm sitting now, and pushed that door open, that I hadn't bolted at night in ten years. Lanark lifted his head, just noticing it when the blast of cold air came in, and even he heard the floor creaking as it took the ten steps across the dark lobby. Then it was standing in the doorway of the bar, looking in at us.

Its wet clothes were half-shredded away. Water ran down from it onto the floor and it was white as a corpse, all right, except for the red and purple places, like crushed blackberries, where it must have been pounded on the rocks. It had taken a terrible beating. Its mouth was torn, jaw hanging open. But even while I was staring at it I saw the bruises swirling under the skin and fading, the wounds closing up. It lifted its white hand and closed its mouth; reset the jaw with a *click,* and the split cheek knit up into a red line that faded too.

Lanark gave a kind of strangled howl, not very loud, and I thought he might be having a heart attack. I thought I might be having one myself. The thing smiled at Uncle Jacques, who right then looked every year of his real age. He didn't smile back.

It pushed its wet hair from its face and it said, "I don't appreciate having to go through all this, you know."

Well, surprise. He had a live person's voice, in fact he sounded cultured, like that Back East guy who used to narrate those newsreels. Uncle Jacques didn't say anything in reply and the stranger went on to say:

"I really thought you'd come out to me. What a hole this is! The Company still hasn't a clue where you've gone; but then, they haven't got our resources."

That was when I knew what he was, and I'd a whole lot rather it'd been some reproachful ghost from the *Argive,* come to punish us for not trying to save him. Lightning flashed bright in the street, and if it had shown me a whole legion of drowned ghosts standing out there, I'd have yelled for them to come in and help us.

Uncle Jacques had slumped down in his seat, but his eyes were clear and hard as he studied the stranger. He said, "Are you from Budu?" and the stranger said:

"Of course."

Then Uncle Jacques said, "I'll surrender to Budu and nobody else. You go back and tell him that. Nobody else! I want answers from him."

The stranger smiled at that and stepped down into the room. As he came into the lamplight he looked more alive, less pale. He said, "I don't think you're in any position to call the tune, Lavalle. You know what he thinks of deserters. I can't blame you for being afraid of him, but I really think you ought to cut your losses and come quietly now. The fool mortal wrecked my boat; perhaps one of these has an automobile we can appropriate?"

Uncle Jacques shook his head, and the man said, "Too bad. We'll just have to walk out then."

"You don't understand," said Uncle Jacques, "I'm not surrendering to you. I'm giving you a message to deliver. If Budu won't come to me, tell me where he is and I'll go straight to him. Where is he, Arion?"

The man he called Arion grinned and shrugged. He said, "All right; you've caught me in a lie. The truth is, we don't know where the old man's got to. He's dropped out of sight. Labienus has been holding the rebellion together. Wouldn't you really rather surrender to him? He's quite a bit more understanding. I'd even call him tolerant, compared to old Budu, who as you know never forgave doubters and weaklings . . ."

Then Uncle Jacques demanded to know how long this person called Budu had been missing, and when Arion hemmed and hawed he cut him off short with another question, which was: "He was gone before the war, wasn't he?"

And Arion said, "Probably."

Uncle Jacques showed his teeth and said, "I knew it. I knew he'd never have given that order! Who was that behind the wheel of the archduke's car, Arion? Was that Labienus's man? The epidemic, was that Labienus too?"

His voice was louder than thunder, making the walls rattle; Lanark and I had to clutch at our ears, it hurt so. Arion had stopped smiling at him. He said, like you'd order a dog, "Control yourself! Did you really think history could be changed? Labienus simply arranged it so that things fell out to our advantage. Isn't that what the Company's always done? And be glad he developed that virus! Can you imagine how badly the mortals would be faring right now, if those twenty-two million hadn't died of influenza first? Think of all those extra mouths to be fed in the bread lines."

Uncle Jacques said, "But innocents died," and Arion just laughed scornfully and said:

"None of them are innocent."

I swear, Uncle Jacques's eyes were like two coals. He said, "My son died in that epidemic," and Arion said:

"Your *pet mortal* died. They do die. Get over it. Look at you, hiding out here on the edge of nowhere! Labienus is willing to overlook your defection. He'll offer you a much better deal than the Company might, I assure you. Unless you'd like to be deactivated? Is that what you'd prefer, to crawl back on your knees to all-merciful Zeus for oblivion?"

Uncle Jacques just told him to get out.

But Arion said, "Don't be stupid! He knows where you are. What am I going to have to do before you'll see reason?"

He looked at Lanark, who was just sitting there gaping, and then over at me. I wanted to dive behind the bar, but I knew the shotgun wouldn't stop him. Uncle Jacques said, "You're going to kill them anyway."

Arion sighed. He said, "You chose to hide behind them, Lavalle. But you can save them unnecessary suffering, you see? I'm tired, I'm cold, we've got a long walk ahead of us and I want that mortal's coat. Don't make me wait any longer than I have to, or I'll pull off his remaining arm. Let's go, shall we?"

I guess that was when Uncle Jacques took his chance. I couldn't see, because they were both suddenly moving so fast they were only blurs in the air, but things began to smash, and I threw myself down on the floor and just prayed to Jesus.

They don't fight like us. You would think, being the creatures that they are, that they'd shoot lightning at each other, or fight with flaming swords, but it sounded more like a couple of animals snarling and struggling. Once when the fight got too close to me, I saw the wall panel next to my head just burst outward in splinters, and a second later there was four long gashes there, like a bear had clawed it. You can still see it, down near the floor, where we filled it in with wood putty later.

I don't know how long it lasted. Suddenly it got a whole lot louder, as something crashed straight down through the ceiling and there was a new voice screaming, shrill as a banshee. Right after that there was a wet-sounding thud and then it was quiet.

You can bet I was cautious as I got up and peered over the bar. There was Uncle Jacques, sitting up supported by Aunty Irina kneeling beside him, and he had his hand up to his face and it looked like one of his eyes was gone. She was still snarling at Arion, who lay on the floor with his throat slashed open, and she had got a crowbar from somewhere and run it through his chest, too. There was blood everywhere.

Lanark was still where he'd been sitting, wide-eyed and white-faced. I heard footsteps above and looked up to see Miss Harlan peering down through the hole in the ceiling, and by the light of the kerosene lantern she was pretty pale too. God only knows what I looked like, but my hair had come half down and was full of dust and splinters.

I collected myself enough to say, "That's one of those people you're hiding from," to Aunty Irina. She looked up, I guess startled at the sound of a human voice, and after a moment she said yes, it was.

I found a clean rag and brought it for Uncle Jacques, who pressed it to his eye and thanked me. He got unsteadily to his feet, and I saw his coat was about half ripped off his back, just hanging in ribbons. The skin underneath seemed to be healing, though. The edges of his cuts were running together like melting wax.

I said, "At least you got the bastard," and Aunty Irina shook her head grimly. She said:

"He's just in fugue," and I looked at Arion and saw that the wound in his throat was already closing up. Aunty Irina made a disgusted noise. She drew a knife from her boot and cut his jugular again. It only bled a little this time, I guess because he didn't have a lot of blood come back to flow yet.

I asked, "What happens now?" and Uncle Jacques said hoarsely:

"We'll have to run again." He looked around at the mess of the bar and added, "I'm sorry."

Lanark began to cry then, that dry hacking men cry with, and I knew he'd been scared clean out of his mind. Aunty

Irina went over to him and took his face in both her hands and kissed him, a deep kiss like they were lovers, and then she stared into his eyes and talked to him quietly. He began to blink and look confused.

Uncle Jacques meanwhile crouched with a groan and took Arion by the feet, starting to drag him backwards toward the door.

Aunty Irina turned quickly and said, "Leave that. You just sit and repair your eye."

He said, "Okay," and sat down, breathing pretty hard. They feel pain as much as we do, you see.

What happened was that we had to do it, me and Aunty Irina, and as we were dragging the body out through the lobby Miss Harlan came down with the lantern and helped us. Every so often as we took him up the road to the sawmill, he'd start moving a little, and we'd have to stop while Aunty Irina cut him again. The wind almost blew out the lantern and the rain soaked us through. Still, we got him up there at last.

We found a couple of old rusty saws in an office, and they didn't work real well, but Aunty Irina showed us how to do it so he'd come apart in a couple of places. She explained how nothing could kill him, but the more damage we did, the longer it'd be before he could piece himself together to come after her and Uncle Jacques. So we did a lot to him. It was hard work, just three women there working by one kerosene lantern, and the rain coming through the roof the whole time in steady streams.

You don't think women could do something like that? You don't know the things we have to do, sometimes. And knowing the kind of creature he was made it easier.

Most of him we dropped down a pit, and used the old crane to send a couple of redwood logs after him, and I reckon they weighed a couple of tons apiece. I'm not telling you where we put the rest of him.

It might have been near dawn when we finished and came back, but it was still black as midnight, and the storm wasn't letting up. There was two empty bottles on the bar and Lanark had passed out on the floor. Uncle Jacques had made himself

an eyepatch. He said it'd be likely another day before he got
his eye working again.

I offered to fix them some breakfast before they set out.
They thanked me kindly but said they had better not. They
gave us some careful instructions, me and Miss Harlan, about
what to look out for and what to say to anybody else who
came looking around. They told us some other stuff, too, like
what that awful Hitler was going to do pretty soon and about
international Business Machines stocks. Cut off from the
world like we were, we couldn't make a lot of use of it, but it
was nice of them.

And they apologized. They said they'd only been trying to
make the world a better place for people, and it had all gone
wrong somehow.

I got one of Papa's coats down for Uncle Jacques, and he
shrugged out of the bloody torn one he had on. I burned it in
the stove later. It flared up in some strange colors, I tell you.

Then they walked out together into that awful night, poor
people, and we never saw them again.

When Lanark sobered up he said he didn't remember anything, but he never asked any questions either, like why there
was a hole in the ceiling or where all the blood had come
from. We cleaned up and mended as best we could. One thing
we had plenty of in this town was lumber, anyhow.

That's all. The radio worked for a few years, and when it
finally broke we couldn't fix it, so I put it away in the attic.
We missed it, especially once the war started, but maybe we
were better off not worrying about that, with what we'd been
told.

Lanark never talked about what happened in so many
words, but one time when he was sober he told me he'd figured out that Uncle Jacques and Aunty Irina must have been
Socialists, because of the way they talked, and maybe J. Edgar
Hoover had come after them. I told him he was probably right.
Anyway nobody else ever came sniffing around after them.
There was a wildfire across Gamboa Ridge a few years later,
1938 that would have been, and now there's only an old rusted
stove back in the manzanita to show where their house was.

Lanark drank more after that, but why shouldn't he, and it got so I'd have to walk him home nights to be sure he got there. Sometimes he kissed me at the door, but he was too broken up to do anything else. Eventually I'd have to go make sure he was still alive in the mornings too. One morning he wasn't. That was back in 1942, I guess.

Miss Harlan lived on a good long time in that cottage, kept Billy waiting until 1957 before she went off into the sea with him. At least, I imagine that's what happened; the door was standing open, the house all full of damp, and there was a trail of sand clear from her room down to the beach, like confetti and rice after a wedding. Nobody haunts the place now. That snooty woman sells her incenses and herbal teas out of it, but I have to say she keeps the garden nice.

So I'm the last one that knows.

I kept the bar open. Right after the war the highway was put through, and those young drifters found the shacks that didn't belong to anybody and started living in them, with their beat parties and poetry. Then later the hippies came in, and pretty soon rich people from San Francisco discovered the place, and it was all upscale after that.

Not that it's a bad thing. When Kevin and Jon offered me all that money for the hotel, I was real happy. Being the way they are, I knew they'd fix everything up beautiful, which they have too, mahogany and brass all restored so I don't have to feel guilty about it anymore. They're kind to me. I stay on in my old room and they call me Nana Luisa, and that's nice.

They sit me out here in this chair so I can watch everything going on, all along the street, and sometimes they'll bring guests and introduce me as the town's official history expert, and I get interviewed for newspapers now and then. I tell them about the old days, just the kinds of stuff they want to hear. I listen more than I talk. Mostly I just like to watch people.

It's pretty now, with the flower gardens and art galleries, and the cottages all lived in by rich folks with sports cars, and you'd never think there'd been whorehouses or saloon brawls here. The biggest noise is the town council complaining about the traffic jams we get weekends. People talk about how Harlan's Landing was such an unspoiled weekend getaway once, and how more tourists are going to ruin it. They don't know what ruin is.

I look out my window at night and there's lights in all the little houses, the *human community* all nice and cozy and thinking they're here to stay, but that cold black night out there is just as heartless as it was, and a lot bigger than they are. Anything could happen. I know. The lights could go out, dwindling one by one or all at once, and there'd be nothing but the sea and the dark trees behind us, and maybe one roomful of folks left behind, lighting a lamp in the window so they don't feel so alone.

But I don't worry much about Arion.

Even with all the restoration and remodeling, even with them selling T-shirts and kites and ice cream out of the sawmill now, nobody's ever found any of him. He's still down there, under that new redwood decking, and sometimes at night I hear him moaning, though people think it's just the wind in a sea cave. He's growing back together, or growing himself some new parts; Aunty Irina said he might do either.

He will get out one of these days, but I figure I'll be dead by the time he does. That's one of the advantages to being a mortal.

I do worry about my sweetie boys, I'm afraid this AIDS epidemic will get them. I wonder if it's something to do with that Labienus fellow, the one Uncle Jacques told me cooks up epidemics because he hates mortal folk. And I wonder if Uncle Jacques and Aunty Irina found a new place to hide, some shelter in out of the black night, and how the war for power over the Earth is going.

Because that's what it is, see. I'm not crazy, honey. It's all there in the Bible. For some have entertained angels unawares, but some folks get let in on their secrets, you follow me? And it isn't a comforting thing to know the truth about angels.

Mozart in Mirrorshades

Bruce Sterling and Lewis Shiner

Much is said in anthropological circles about the dangers of cultural contamination, a primitive culture being corrupted by contact with a more technologically advanced one, succumbing to the lure of glitzy gadgets and civilized comforts that totally disrupt the old ways of life. Much the same might happen when the future starts colonizing the past, with results that could ultimately be as dangerous for the contaminator as for the contaminatee . . .

One of the most powerful and innovative new talents to enter SF in the past few decades, Bruce Sterling sold his first story in 1976. By the end of the '80s, he had established himself, with a series of stories set in his exotic "Shaper/Mechanist" future and with novels such as the complex and Stapeldonian *Schismatrix* and the well-received *Islands in the Net* (as well as with his editing of the influential anthology *Mirrorshades: the Cyberpunk Anthology* and the infamous critical magazine *Cheap Truth*), as perhaps the prime driving force behind the revolutionary "Cyberpunk" movement in science fiction, and also as one of the best new hard science writers to enter the field in some time. His other books include a critically acclaimed non-fiction study of First Amendment issues in the world of computer networking, *The Hacker Crackdown: Law and Disorder on the Electronic Frontier*, the novels *The Artificial Kid*, *Involution Ocean*, *Heavy Weather*, *Holy Fire*, *Distraction*, and *Zeitgeist*, a novel in collaboration with William Gibson, *The Difference Engine*, an omnibus collection (it contains the novel *Schismatrix* as well as most of his Shaper/Mechanist stories) *Schismatrix Plus*, and the landmark collections *Crystal Express*, *Globalhead*, and *A Good Old-fashioned Future*. His most recent books include a nonfiction study of the future, *Tomorrow Now: Envisioning the Next Fifty Years*, and a new novel, *The Zenith Angle*. Coming up is a new collection, *Visionary in Residence*. His story "Bicycle Repairman" earned him a long-overdue Hugo in 1997, and he won another Hugo in 1999 for his story "Taklamakan."

Lewis Shiner was widely regarded as one of the most exciting new SF writers of the eighties. His stories have appeared in *The Magazine of Fantasy and Science Fiction*, *Omni*, *Oui*, *Shayol*, *Asimov's Science Fiction*, *The Twilight Zone Magazine*, *Wild Card*, and elsewhere, and have been collected in *Nine Hard Questions About the Nature of the Universe* and *The Edges of Things*. His novels include *Frontera*, *Deserted Cities of the Heart*, *Glimpses*, and the mainstream novel *Slam*. As editor, he produced the original anthology *When the Music's Over*. His novel *Glimpses* won a World Fantasy Award in 1994. His most recent novel is *Say Goodbye: The Laurie Moss Story*.

FROM THE HILL north of the city, Rice saw eighteenth-century Salzburg spread out below him like a half-eaten lunch.

Huge cracking towers and swollen, bulbous storage tanks dwarfed the ruins of the St. Rupert Cathedral. Thick white smoke billowed from the refinery's stacks. Rice could taste the familiar petrochemical tang from where he sat, under the leaves of a wilting oak.

The sheer spectacle of it delighted him. You didn't sign up for a time-travel project, he thought, unless you had a taste for incongruity. Like the phallic pumping station lurking in the

central square of the convent, or the ruler-straight elevated
pipelines ripping through Salzburg's maze of cobbled streets.
A bit tough on the city, maybe, but that was hardly Rice's
fault. The temporal beam had focused randomly in the
bedrock below Salzburg, forming an expandable bubble connecting this world to Rice's own time.

This was the first time he'd seen the complex from outside
its high chain-link fences. For two years, he'd been up to his
neck getting the refinery operational. He'd directed teams all
over the planet, as they caulked up Nantucket whalers to serve
as tankers, or trained local pipefitters to lay down line as far
away as the Sinai and the Gulf of Mexico.

Now, finally, he was outside. Sutherland, the company's
political liaison, had warned him against going into the city.
But Rice had no patience with her attitude. The smallest thing
seemed to set Sutherland off. She lost sleep over the most trivial local complaints. She spent hours haranguing the "gate
people," the locals who waited day and night outside the
square-mile complex, begging for radios, nylons, a jab of
penicillin.

To hell with her, Rice thought. The plant was up and breaking design records, and Rice was due for a little R and R. The
way he saw it, anyone who couldn't find some action in the
Year of Our Lord 1775 had to be dead between the ears. He
stood up, dusting windblown soot from his hands with a cam-
bric handkerchief.

A moped sputtered up the hill toward him, wobbling
crazily. The rider couldn't seem to keep his high-heeled,
buckled pumps on the pedals while carrying a huge portable
stereo in the crook of his right arm. The moped lurched to a
stop at a respectful distance, and Rice recognized the music
from the tape player: Symphony No. 40 in G Minor.

The boy turned the volume down as Rice walked toward
him. "Good evening, Mr. Plant Manager, sir. I am not inter-
rupting?"

"No, that's okay" Rice glanced at the bristling hedgehog
cut that had replaced the boy's outmoded wig. He'd seen the
kid around the gates; he was one of the regulars. But the

music had made something else fall into place. "You're
Mozart, aren't you?"

"Wolfgang Amadeus Mozart, your servant."

"I'll be goddamned. Do you know what that tape is?"

"It has my name on it."

"Yeah. You wrote it. Or would have, I guess I should say.
About fifteen years from now."

Mozart nodded. "It is so beautiful. I have not the English
to say how it is to hear it."

By this time most of the other gate people would have been
well into some kind of pitch. Rice was impressed by the boy's
tact, not to mention his command of English. The standard native vocabulary didn't go much beyond *radio, drugs,* and *fuck.*
"Are you headed back toward town?" Rick asked.

"Yes, Mr. Plant Manager, sir."

Something about the kid appealed to Rice. The enthusiasm, the gleam in the eyes. And, of course, he did happen to
be one of the greatest composers of all time.

"Forget the titles," Rice said. "Where does a guy go for
some fun around here?"

AT FIRST SUTHERLAND hadn't wanted Rice at the meeting
with Jefferson. But Rice knew a little temporal physics, and
Jefferson had been pestering the American personnel with
questions about time holes and parallel worlds.

Rice, for his part, was thrilled at the chance to meet
Thomas Jefferson, the first President of the United States.
He'd never liked George Washington, was glad the man's Masonic connections had made him refuse to join the company's
"godless" American government.

Rice squirmed in his Dacron double knits as he and
Sutherland waited in the newly air-conditioned boardroom of
the Hohensalzburg Castle. "I forgot how greasy these suits
feel," he said.

"At least," Sutherland said, "you didn't wear that goddamned hat today" The VTOL jet from America was late, and
she kept looking at her watch.

"My tricorne?" Rice said. "You don't like it?"

"It's a Masonista hat, for Christ's sake. It's a symbol of antimodern reaction." The Freemason Liberation Front was another of Sutherland's nightmares, a local politico-religious group that had made a few pathetic attacks on the pipeline.

"Oh, loosen up, will you, Sutherland? Some groupie of Mozart's gave me the hat. Theresa Maria Angela something-or-other, some broken-down aristocrat. They all hang out together in this music dive downtown. I just liked the way it looked."

"Mozart? You've been fraternizing with him? Don't you think we should just let him be? After everything we've done to him?"

"Bullshit," Rice said. "I'm entitled. I spent two years on start-up while you were playing touch football with Robespierre and Thomas Paine. I make a few night spots with Wolfgang and you're all over me. What about Parker? I don't hear you bitching about him playing rock and roll on his late show every night. You can hear it blasting out of every cheap transistor in town."

"He's propaganda officer. Believe me, if I could stop him I would, but Parker's a special case. He's got connections all over the place back in Realtime." She rubbed her cheek. "Let's drop it, okay? Just try to be polite to President Jefferson. He's had a hard time of it lately."

Sutherland's secretary, a former Hapsburg lady-in-waiting, stepped in to announce the plane's arrival. Jefferson pushed angrily past her. He was tall for a local, with a mane of blazing red hair and the shiftiest eyes Rice had ever seen. "Sit down, Mr. President." Sutherland waved at the far side of the table. "Would you like some coffee or tea?"

Jefferson scowled. "Perhaps some Madeira," he said. "If you have it."

Sutherland nodded to her secretary, who stared for a moment in incomprehension, then hurried off. "How was the flight?" Sutherland asked.

"Your engines are most impressive," Jefferson said, "as you well know." Rice saw the subtle trembling of the man's

hands; he hadn't taken well to jet flight. "I only wish your political sensitivities were as advanced."

"You know I can't speak for my employers," Sutherland
said.

"For myself, I deeply regret the darker aspects of our operations. Florida will be missed."

Irritated, Rice leaned forward. "You're not really here to
discuss sensibilities, are you?"

"Freedom, sir," Jefferson said. "Freedom is the issue." The
secretary returned with a dust-caked bottle of sherry and a
stack of clear plastic cups. Jefferson, his hands visibly shaking now, poured a glass and tossed it back. Color returned to
his face. He said, "You made certain promises when we joined
forces. You guaranteed us liberty and equality and the freedom to pursue our own happiness. Instead we find your machinery on all sides, your cheap manufactured goods seducing
the people of our great country, our minerals and works of art
disappearing into your fortresses, never to reappear!" The last
line brought Jefferson to his feet.

Sutherland shrank back into her chair. "The common good
requires a certain period of—uh, adjustment—"

"Oh, come on, Tom," Rice broke in. "We didn't 'join
forces,' that's a lot of crap. We kicked the Brits out and you in,
and you had damn-all to do with it. Second, if we drill for oil
and carry off a few paintings, it doesn't have a goddamned
thing to do with your liberty. We don't care. Do whatever you
like, just stay out of our way. Right? If we wanted a lot of
back talk we could have left the damn British in power."

Jefferson sat down. Sutherland meekly poured him another
glass, which he drank off at once. "I cannot understand you,"
he said. "You claim you come from the future, yet you seem
bent on destroying your own past."

"But we're not," Rice said. "It's this way. History is like a
tree, okay? When you go back and mess with the past, another
branch of history splits off from the main trunk. Well, this
world is just one of those branches."

"So," Jefferson said. "This world—my world—does not
lead to your future."

"Right," Rice said.

"Leaving you free to rape and pillage here at will! While your own world is untouched and secure!" Jefferson was on his feet again. "I find the idea monstrous beyond belief, intolerable! How can you be party to such despotism? Have you no human feelings?"

"Oh, for God's sake," Rice said. "Of course we do. What about the radios and the magazines and the medicine we hand out? Personally I think you've got a lot of nerve, coming in here with your smallpox scars and your unwashed shirt and all those slaves of yours back home, lecturing us on humanity."

"Rice?" Sutherland said.

Rice locked eyes with Jefferson. Slowly, Jefferson sat down. "Look," Rice said, relenting. "We don't mean to be unreasonable. Maybe things aren't working out just the way you pictured them, but hey, that's life, you know? What do you want, *really*? Cars? Movies? Telephones? Birth control? Just say the word and they're yours."

Jefferson pressed his thumbs into the corners of his eyes. "Your words mean nothing to me, sir. I only want . . . I want only to return to my home. To Monticello. And as soon as possible."

"Is it one of your migraines, Mr. President?" Sutherland asked. "I had these made up for you." She pushed a vial of pills across the table toward him.

"What are these?"

Sutherland shrugged. "You'll feel better."

After Jefferson left, Rice half expected a reprimand. Instead, Sutherland said, "You seem to have a tremendous faith in the project."

"Oh, cheer up," Rice said. "You've been spending too much time with these poiticals. Believe me, this is a simple time, with simple people. Sure, Jefferson was a little ticked off, but he'll come around. Relax!"

RICE FOUND MOZART clearing tables in the main dining hall of the Hohensalzburg Castle. In his faded jeans, camo jacket, and mirrored sunglasses, he might almost have passed for a teenager from Rice's time.

"Wolfgang!" Rice called to him. "How's the new job?"

Mozart set a stack of dishes aside and ran his hands over his short-cropped hair. "Wolf," he said. "Call me Wolf, okay? Sounds more . . . modern, you know? But yes, I really want to thank you for everything you have done for me. The tapes, the history books, this job—it is so wonderful just to be around here."

His English, Rice noticed, had improved remarkably in the last three weeks. "You still living in the city?"

"Yes, but I have my own place now. You are coming to the gig tonight?"

"Sure," Rice said. "Why don't you finish up around here, I'll go change, and then we can go out for some sachertorte, okay? We'll make a night of it."

Rice dressed carefully, wearing mesh body armor under his velvet coat and knee britches. He crammed his pockets with giveaway consumer goods, then met Mozart by a rear door.

Security had been stepped up around the castle, and floodlights swept the sky. Rice sensed a new tension in the festive abandon of the crowds downtown.

Like everyone else from his time, he towered over the locals; even incognito he felt dangerously conspicuous.

Within the club Rice faded into the darkness and relaxed. The place had been converted from the lower half of some young aristo's town house; protruding bricks still marked the lines of the old walls. The patrons were locals, mostly, dressed in any Realtime garments they could scavenge. Rice even saw one kid wearing a pair of beige silk panties on his head.

Mozart took the stage. Minuetlike guitar arpeggios screamed over sequenced choral motifs. Stacks of amps blasted synthesizer riffs lifted from a tape of K-Tel pop hits. The howling audience showered Mozart with confetti stripped from the club's hand-painted wallpaper.

Afterward Mozart smoked a joint of Turkish hash and asked Rice about the future.

"Mine, you mean?" Rice said. "You wouldn't believe it. Six billion people, and nobody has to work if they don't want to. Five-hundred-channel TV in every house. Cars, helicopters, clothes that would knock your eyes out. Plenty of easy sex. You want music? You could have your own recording studio. It'd make your gear on stage look like a goddamned clavichord."

"Really? I would give anything to see that. I can't understand why you would leave."

Rice shrugged. "So I'm giving up maybe fifteen years. When I get back, it's the best of everything. Anything I want."

"Fifteen years?"

"Yeah. You gotta understand how the portal works. Right now it's as big around as you are tall, just big enough for a phone cable and a pipeline full of oil, maybe the odd bag of mail, heading for Realtime. To make it any bigger, like to move people or equipment through, is expensive as hell. So expensive they only do it twice, at the beginning and the end of the project. So, yeah, I guess we're stuck here."

Rice coughed harshly and drank off his glass. That Ottoman Empire hash had untied his mental shoelaces. Here he was opening up to Mozart, making the kid want to emigrate, and there was no way in hell Rice could get him a Green Card. Not with all the millions that wanted a free ride into the future—billions, if you counted the other projects, like the Roman Empire or New Kingdom Egypt.

"But I'm really *glad* to be here," Rice said. "It's like . . . like shuffling the deck of history. You never know what'll come up next." Rice passed the joint to one of Mozart's groupies, Antonia something-or-other. "This is a great time to be alive. Look at you. You're doing okay, aren't you?" He leaned across the table, in the grip of a sudden sincerity. "I mean, it's okay, right? It's not like you hate all of us for fucking up your world or anything?"

"Are you making a joke? You are looking at the hero of Salzburg. In fact, your Mr. Parker is supposed to make a tape of my last set tonight. Soon all of Europe will know of me! " Someone shouted at Mozart, in German, from across the club.

Mozart glanced up and gestured cryptically. "Be cool, man." He turned back to Rice. "You can see that I am doing fine."

"Sutherland, she worries about stuff like all those symphonies you're never going to write."

"Bullshit! I don't want to write symphonies. I can listen to them any time I want! Who is this Sutherland? Is she your girlfriend?"

"No. She goes for the locals. Danton, Robespierre, like that. How about you? You got anybody?"

"Nobody special. Not since I was a kid."

"Oh, yeah?"

"Well, when I was about six I was at Maria Theresa's court. I used to play with her daughter—Maria Antonia. Marie Antoinette she calls herself now. The most beautiful girl of the age. We used to play duets. We made a joke that we would be married, but she went off to France with that swine, Louis."

"Goddamn," Rice said. "This is really amazing. You know, she's practically a legend where I come from. They cut her head off in the French Revolution for throwing too many parties."

"No they didn't. . . ."

"That was *our* French Revolution," Rice said. "Yours was a lot less messy."

"You should go see her, if you're that interested. Surely she owes you a favor for saving her life."

Before Rice could answer, Parker arrived at their table, surrounded by ex-ladies-in-waiting in spandex capris and sequined tube tops. "Hey, Rice," Parker shouted, serenely anachronistic in a glitter T-shirt and black leather jeans. "Where did you get those unhip threads? Come on, let's party!"

Rice watched as the girls crowded around the table and gnawed the corks out of a crate of champagne. As short, fat, and repulsive as Parker might be, they would gladly knife one another for a chance to sleep in his clean sheets and raid his medicine cabinet.

"No, thanks," Rice said, untangling himself from the miles of wire connected to Parker's recording gear.

The image of Marie Antoinette had seized him and would not let go.

RICE SAT NAKED on the edge of the canopied bed, shivering a little in the air conditioning. Past the jutting window unit, through clouded panes of eighteenth-century glass, he saw a lush, green landscape sprinkled with tiny waterfalls.

At ground level, a garden crew of former aristos in blue-denim overalls trimmed weeds under the bored supervision of a peasant guard. The guard, clothed head to foot in camouflage except for a tricolor cockade on his fatigue cap, chewed gum and toyed with the strap of his cheap plastic machine gun. The gardens of Petit Trianon, like Versailles itself, were treasures deserving the best of care. They belonged to the Nation, since they were too large to be crammed through a time portal.

Marie Antoinette sprawled across the bed's expanse of pink satin, wearing a scrap of black-lace underwear and leafing through an issue of *Vogue*. The bedroom's walls were crowded with Boucher canvases: acres of pert silky rumps, pink haunches, knowingly pursed lips. Rice looked dazedly from the portrait of Louise O'Morphy, kittenishly sprawled on a divan, to the sleek, creamy expanse of Toinette's back and thighs. He took a deep, exhausted breath. "Man," he said, "that guy could really paint."

Toinette cracked off a square of Hershey's chocolate and pointed to the magazine. "I want the leather bikini," she said. "Always, when I am a girl, my goddamn mother, she keep me in the goddamn corsets. She think my what-you-call, my shoulder blade sticks out too much."

Rice leaned back across her solid thighs and patted her bottom reassuringly. He felt wonderfully stupid; a week and a half of obsessive carnality had reduced him to a euphoric animal. "Forget your mother, baby You're with *me* now. You want ze goddamn leather bikini, I get it for you."

Toinette licked chocolate from her fingertips. "Tomorrow we go out to the cottage, okay, man? We dress up like the peasants and make love in the hedges like noble savages."

Rice hesitated. His weekend furlough to Paris had stretched into a week and a half; by now security would be looking for him. To hell with them, he thought. "Great," he said. "I'll phone us up a picnic lunch. Foie gras and truffles, maybe some terrapin—"

Toinette pouted. "I want the modern food. The pizza and burritos and the chicken fried." When Rice shrugged, she threw her arms around his neck. "You love me, Rice?"

"Love you? Baby. I love the very *idea* of you." He was drunk on history out of control, careening under him like some great black motorcycle of the imagination. When he thought of Paris, take-out quiche-to-go stores springing up where guillotines might have been, a six-year-old Napoleon munching Dubble Bubble in Corsica, he felt like the archangel Michael on speed.

Megalomania, he knew, was an occupational hazard. But he'd get back to work soon enough, in just a few more days. . . .

The phone rang. Rice burrowed into a plush house robe formerly owned by Louis XVI. Louis wouldn't mind; he was now a happily divorced locksmith in Nice.

Mozart's face appeared on the phone's tiny screen. "Hey, man, where are you?"

"France," Rice said vaguely. "What's up?"

"Trouble, man. Sutherland flipped out, and they've got her sedated. At least six key people have gone over the hill, counting you." Mozart's voice had only the faintest trace of accent left.

"Hey, I'm not over the hill. I'll be back in just a couple days. We've got—what, thirty other people in Northern Europe? If you're worried about the quotas—"

"Fuck the quotas. This is serious. There's uprisings. Comanches raising hell on the rigs in Texas. Labor strikes in London and Vienna. Realtime is pissed. They're talking about pulling us out."

"What?" Now he was alarmed.

"Yeah. Word came down the line today. They say you guys let this whole operation get sloppy. Too much contamination, too much fraternization. Sutherland made a lot of trouble with the locals before she got found out. She was organizing the Masonistas for some kind of passive resistance and God knows what else."

"Shit." The fucking politicals had screwed it up again. It wasn't enough that he'd busted ass getting the plant up and on line; now he had to clean up after Sutherland. He glared at Mozart. "Speaking of fraternization, what's all this *we* stuff? What the hell are you doing calling me?"

Mozart paled. "Just trying to help. I got a job in communications now."

"That takes a Green Card. Where the hell did you get that?"

"Uh, listen, man, I got to go. Get back here, will you? We need you." Mozart's eyes flickered, looking past Rice's shoulder. "You can bring your little time-bunny along if you want. But hurry."

"I . . . oh, shit, okay," Rice said.

RICE'S HOVERCAR HUFFED along at a steady 80 kph, blasting clouds of dust from the deeply rutted highway. They were near the Bavarian border. Ragged Alps jutted into the sky over radiant green meadows, tiny picturesque farmhouses, and clear, vivid streams of melted snow.

They'd just had their first argument. Toinette had asked for a Green Card, and Rice had told her he couldn't do it. He offered her a Gray Card instead, that would get her from one branch of time to another without letting her visit Realtime. He knew he'd be reassigned if the project pulled out, and he wanted to take her with him. He wanted to do the decent thing, not leave her behind in a world without Hersheys and *Vogues*.

But she wasn't having any of it. After a few kilometers of weighty silence she started to squirm. "I have to pee," she said finally. "Pull over by the goddamn trees."

"Okay," Rice said. "Okay"

He cut the fans and whirred to a stop. A herd of brindled

cattle spooked off with a clank of cowbells. The road was deserted.

Rice got out and stretched, watching Toinette climb a wooden stile and walk toward a stand of trees.

"What's the deal?" Rice yelled. "There's nobody around. Get on with it!"

A dozen men burst up from the cover of a ditch and rushed him. In an instant they'd surrounded him, leveling flintlock pistols. They wore tricornes and wigs and lace-cuffed highwayman's coats; black domino masks hid their faces. "What the fuck is this?" Rice asked, amazed. "Mardi Gras?"

The leader ripped off his mask and bowed ironically. His handsome Teutonic features were powdered, his lips rouged. "I am Count Axel Ferson. Servant, sir."

Rice knew the name; Ferson had been Toinette's lover before the Revolution. "Look, Count, maybe you're a little upset about Toinette, but I'm sure we can make a deal. Wouldn't you really rather have a color TV?"

"Spare us your satanic blandishments, sir!" Ferson roared. "I would not soil my hands on the collaborationist cow. We are the Freemason Liberation Front!"

"Christ," Rice said. "You can't possibly be serious. Are you taking on the project with these popguns?"

"We are aware of your advantage in armaments, sir. This is why we have made you our hostage." He spoke to the others in German. They tied Rice's hands and hustled him into the back of a horse-drawn wagon that had clopped out of the woods.

"Can't we at least take the car?" Rice asked. Glancing back, he saw Toinette sitting dejectedly in the road by the hovercraft.

"We reject your machines," Ferson said. "They are one more facet of your godlessness. Soon we will drive you back to hell, from whence you came!"

"With what? Broomsticks?" Rice sat up in the back of the wagon, ignoring the stink of manure and rotting hay. "Don't mistake our kindness for weakness. If they send the Gray

Card Army through that portal, there won't be enough left of you to fill an ashtray"

"We are prepared to sacrifice! Each day thousands flock to our worldwide movement, under the banner of the All-Seeing Eye! We shall reclaim our destiny! The destiny you have stolen from us!"

"Your *destiny*?" Rice was aghast. "Listen, Count, you ever hear of guillotines?"

"I wish to hear no more of your machines." Ferson gestured to a subordinate. "Gag him."

THEY HAULED RICE to a farmhouse outside Salzburg. During fifteen bone-jarring hours in the wagon he thought of nothing but Toinette's betrayal. If he'd promised her the Green Card, would she still have led him into the ambush? That card was the only thing she wanted, but how could the Masonistas get her one?

Rice's guards paced restlessly in front of the windows, their boots squeaking on the loosely pegged floorboards. From their constant references to Salzburg he gathered that some kind of siege was in progress.

Nobody had shown up to negotiate Rice's release, and the Masonistas were getting nervous. If he could just gnaw through his gag, Rice was sure he'd be able to talk some sense into them.

He heard a distant drone, building slowly to a roar. Four of the men ran outside, leaving a single guard at the open door. Rice squirmed in his bonds and tried to sit up.

Suddenly the clapboards above his head were blasted to splinters by heavy machine-gun fire. Grenades whumped in front of the house, and the windows exploded in a gush of black smoke. A choking Masonista lifted his flintlock at Rice. Before he could pull the trigger a burst of gunfire threw the terrorist against the wall.

A short, heavyset man in flak jacket and leather pants stalked into the room. He stripped goggles from his smoke-blackened face, revealing Oriental eyes. A pair of greased braids hung down his back. He cradled an assault rifle in the

crook of one arm and wore two bandoliers of grenades.
"Good," he grunted. "The last of them." He tore the gag from
Rice's mouth. He smelled of sweat and smoke and badly
cured leather. "You are Rice?"

Rice could only nod, and gasp for breath.

His rescuer hauled him to his feet and cut his ropes with a
bayonet. "I am Jebe Noyon. Trans-Temporal Army" He
forced a leather flask of rancid mare's milk into Rice's hands.
The smell made Rice want to vomit. "Drink!" Jebe insisted.
"Is koumiss, is good for you! Drink, Jebe Noyon tells you!"

Rice took a sip, which curdled his tongue and brought bile
to his throat. "You're the Gray Cards, right?" he said weakly.

"Gray Card Army, yes," Jebe said. "Baddest-ass warriors
of all times and places! Only five guards here, I kill them all!
I, Jebe Noyon, was chief general to Genghis Khan, terror of
the earth, okay, man?" He stared at Rice with great, sad eyes.
"You have not heard of me."

"Sorry, Jebe, no."

"The earth turned black in the footprints of my horse."

"I'm sure it did, man."

"You will mount up behind me," he said, dragging Rice toward the door. "You will watch the earth turn black in the
tireprints of my Harley, man, okay?"

FROM THE HILLS above Salzburg they looked down on
anachronism gone wild.

Local soldiers in waistcoats and gaiters lay in bloody
heaps by the gates of the refinery. Another battalion marched
forward in formation, muskets at the ready. A handful of Huns
and Mongols, deployed at the gates, cut them up with orange
tracer fire and watched the survivors scatter.

Jebe Noyon laughed hugely. "Is like siege of Cambaluc!
Only no stacking up heads or even taking ears any more, man,
now we are civilized, okay? Later maybe we call in, like,
grunts, choppers from 'Nam, napalm the son-of-a-bitches, far
out, man."

"You can't do that, Jebe," Rice said sternly. "The poor bastards don't have a chance. No point in exterminating them."

Jebe shrugged. "I forget sometimes, okay? Always thinking to conquer the world." He revved the cycle and scowled. Rice grabbed the Mongol's stinking flak jacket as they roared downhill. Jebe took his disappointment out on the enemy, tearing through the streets in high gear, deliberately running down a group of Brunswick grenadiers. Only panic strength saved Rice from falling off as legs and torsos thumped and crunched beneath their tires.

Jebe skidded to a stop inside the gates of the complex. A jabbering horde of Mongols in ammo belts and combat fatigues surrounded them at once. Rice pushed through them, his kidneys aching.

Ionizing radiation smeared the evening sky around the Hohensalzburg Castle. They were kicking the portal up to the high-energy maximum, running cars full of Gray Cards in and sending the same cars back loaded to the ceiling with art and jewelry.

Over the rattling of gunfire Rice could hear the whine of VTOL jets bringing in the evacuees from the US and Africa. Roman centurions, wrapped in mesh body armor and carrying shoulder-launched rockets, herded Realtime personnel into the tunnels that led to the portal.

Mozart was in the crowd, waving enthusiastically to Rice. "We're pulling out, man! Fantastic, huh? Back to Realtime!"

Rice looked at the clustered towers of pumps, coolers, and catalytic cracking units. "It's a goddamned shame," he said. "All that work, shot to hell."

"We were losing too many people, man. Forget it. There's plenty of eighteenth centuries."

The guards, sniping at the crowds outside, suddenly leaped aside as Rice's hovercar burst through the ages. Half a dozen Masonic fanatics still clung to the doors and pounded on the windscreen. Jebe's Mongols yanked the invaders free and axed them while a Roman flamethrower unit gushed fire across the gates.

Marie Antoinette leaped out of the hovercar. Jebe grabbed for her, but her sleeve came off in his hand. She spotted Mozart and ran for him, Jebe only a few steps behind.

"Wolf, you bastard!" she shouted. "You leave me behind! What about your promises, you merde, you pig-dog!"

Mozart whipped off his mirrorshades. He turned to Rice. "Who is this woman?"

"The Green Card, Wolf! You say I sell Rice to the Masonistas, you get me the card!" She stopped for breath and Jebe caught her by one arm. When she whirled on him; he cracked her across the jaw, and she dropped to the tarmac.

The Mongol focused his smoldering eyes on Mozart. "Was you, eh? You, the traitor?" With the speed of a striking cobra he pulled his machine pistol and jammed the muzzle against Mozart's nose. "I put my gun on rock and roll, there nothing left of you but ears, man."

A single shot echoed across the courtyard. Jebe's head rocked back, and he fell in a heap.

Rice spun to his right. Parker, the DJ, stood in the doorway of an equipment shed. He held a Walther PPK. "Take it easy, Rice," Parker said, walking toward him. "He's just a grunt, expendable."

"You *killed* him!"

"So what?" Parker said, throwing one arm around Mozart's frail shoulders. "This here's my boy! I transmitted a couple of his new tunes up the line a month ago. You know what? The kid's number five on the Billboard charts! Number five!" Parker shoved the gun into his belt. "With a bullet!"

"You gave him the Green Card, Parker?"

"No," Mozart said. "It was Sutherland."

"What did you do to her?"

"Nothing! I swear to you, man! Well, maybe I kind of lived up to what she wanted to see. A broken man, you know, his music stolen from him, his very soul?" Mozart rolled his eyes upward. "She gave me the Green Card, but that still wasn't enough. She couldn't handle the guilt. You know the rest."

"And when she got caught, you were afraid we wouldn't pull out. So you decided to drag *me* into it! You got Toinette to turn me over to the Masons. That was *your* doing!"

As if hearing her name, Toinette moaned softly from the tarmac. Rice didn't care about the bruises, the dirt, the rips in

her leopard-skin jeans. She was still the most gorgeous creature he'd ever seen.

Mozart shrugged. "I was a Freemason once. Look, man,
they're very uncool. I mean, all I did was drop a few hints, and
look what happened." He waved casually at the carnage all
around them. "I knew you'd get away from them somehow"

"You can't just *use* people like that!"

"Bullshit, Rice! You do it all the time! I *needed* this seige
so Realtime would haul us out! For Christ's sake, I can't wait
fifteen years to go up the line. History says I'm going to be
dead in fifteen years! I don't want to die in this dump! I want
that car and that recording studio!"

"Forget it, pal," Rice said. "When they hear back in Realtime how you screwed things up here—"

Parker laughed. "Shove off, Rice. We're talking Top of the
Pops, here. Not some penny-ante refinery." He took Mozart's
arm protectively. "Listen, Wolf baby, let's get into those tunnels. I got some papers for you to sign as soon as we hit the
future."

The sun had set, but muzzle-loading cannon lit the night,
pumping shells into the city. For a moment Rice stood stunned
as cannonbails clanged harmlessly off the storage tanks.
Then, finally, he shook his head. Salzburg's time had run out.

Hoisting Toinette over one shoulder, he ran toward the
safety of the tunnels.

Under Siege

George R. R. Martin

Born in Bayonne, New Jersey, George R. R. Martin made his first sale in 1971, and soon established himself as one of the most popular SF writers of the '70s. He quickly became a mainstay of the Ben Bova *Analog* with stories such as "With Morning Comes Mistfall," "And Seven Times Never Kill Man," "The Second Kind of Loneliness," "The Storms of Windhaven" (in collaboration with Lisa Tuttle, and later expanded by them into the novel *Windhaven*), "Override," and others, although he also sold to *Amazing, Fantastic, Galaxy, Orbit*, and other markets. One of his *Analog* stories, the striking novella "A Song for Lya," won him his first Hugo Award in 1974.

By the end of the '70s, he had reached the height of his influence as a science fiction writer, and was producing his best work in that category with stories such as the famous "Sandkings," his best-known story, which won both the Nebula and the Hugo in 1980 (he'd later win another Nebula in 1985 for his story "Portraits of His Children"), "The Way of Cross and Dragon," which also won a Hugo Award in 1980 (making Martin the first author ever to receive two Hugo Awards for fiction in the same year), "Bitterblooms," "The Stone City," "Starlady," and others. These stories would be collected in *Sandkings*, one of the strongest collections of the period. By now, he had mostly moved away from *Analog*, although he would have a long sequence of stories about the droll interstellar adventures of Havalend Tuf (later collected in *Tuf Voyaging*) running throughout the '80s in the Stanley Schmidt *Analog*, as well as a few strong individual pieces such as the novella "Nightflyers"—most of his major work of the late '70s and early '80s, though, would appear in *Omni*. The late '70s and '80s also saw the publication of his memorable novel *Dying of the Light*, his only solo SF novel, while his stories were collected in *A Song for Lya*, *Sandkings*, *Songs of Stars and Shadows*, *Songs the Dead Men Sing*, *Nightflyers*, and *Portraits of His Children*. By the beginning of the '80s, he'd moved away from science fiction and into the horror genre, publishing the big horror novel *Fevre Dream*, and winning the Bram Stoker Award for his horror story "The Pear-Shaped Man" and the World Fantasy Award for his werewolf novella "The Skin Trade." By the end of that decade, though, the crash of the horror market and the commercial failure of his ambitious horror novel *Armageddon Rag* had driven him out of the print world and to a successful career in television instead, where for more than a decade he worked as story editor or producer on such shows as new *Twilight Zone* and *Beauty and the Beast*.

After years away, Martin made a triumphant return to the print world in 1996 with the publication of the immensely successful fantasy novel *A Game of Thrones*, the start of his Song of Ice and Fire sequence. A free-standing novella taken from that work, "Blood of the Dragon," won Martin another Hugo Award in 1997. Two further books in the Song of Ice and Fire series, *A Clash of Kings* and *A Storm of Swords*, have made it one of the most popular, acclaimed, and best-selling series in all of modern fantasy. His most recent book are a massive retrospective collection spanning the entire spectrum of his career, *GRRM: A Retrospective*, and a new volume in the "Song of Ice and Fire" series, *A Feast for Crows*.

In the intense and compassionate story that follows, in which an attempt is made to alter the past by a society that has

run out of future, he suggests that what really matters in such
an attempt is not so much *what* you do, but *how* you do it. . . .

ON THE HIGH ramparts of Vargön, Colonel Bengt Anttonen
stood alone and watched phantasms race across the ice.

The world was snow and wind and bitter, burning cold.
The winter sea had frozen hard around Helsinki, and in its icy
grip it held the six island citadels of the great fortress called
Sveaborg. The wind was a knife drawn from a sheath of ice.
It cut through Anttonen's uniform, chafed at his cheeks,
brought tears to his eyes and froze them as they trickled down
his face. The wind howled around the towering, gray granite
walls, forced its way through doors and cracks and gun em-
placements, insinuated itself everywhere. Out upon the frozen
sea, it snapped and shrieked at the Russian artillery and sent
puffs of snow from the drifts running and swirling over the ice
like strange white beasts, ghostly animals all asparkle, wearing first one shape and then another, changing constantly as
they ran.

They were creatures as malleable as Anttonen's thoughts.
He wondered what form they would take next and where they
were running to so swiftly, these misty children of snow and
wind. Perhaps they could be taught to attack the Russians. He
smiled, savoring the fancy of the snow beasts unleashed upon
the enemy. It was a strange, wild thought. Colonel Bengt Anttonen had never been an imaginative man before, but of late
his mind had often been taken by such whimsies.

Anttonen turned his face into the wind again, welcoming
the chill, the numbing cold. He wanted it to cool his fury, to
cut into the heart of him and freeze the passions that seethed
there. He wanted to be numb. The cold had turned even the
turbulent sea into still and silent ice; now let it conquer the
turbulence within Bengt Anttonen. He opened his mouth, exhaled a long plume of breath that rose from his reddened
cheeks like steam, inhaled a draft of frigid air that went down
like liquid oxygen.

But panic came in the wake of that thought. Again, it was
happening again. What was liquid oxygen? Cold, he knew

somehow; colder than the ice; colder than this wind. Liquid oxygen was bitter and white, and it steamed and flowed. He knew it, knew it as certainly as he knew his own name.

But *how?*

Anttonen turned from the ramparts. He walked with long, swift strides, his hand touching the hilt of his sword as if it could provide some protection against the demons that had invaded his mind. The other officers were right; he was going mad, surely. He had proved it this afternoon at the staff meeting.

The meeting had gone very badly, as they all had of late. As always, Anttonen had raised his voice against the others, hopelessly, stupidly. He was right, he *knew* that. Yet he knew also he could not convince them and that each word further undermined his status, further damaged his career.

Jägerhorn had brought it on once again. Colonel F. A. Jägerhorn was everything that Anttonen was not: dark and handsome, polished and politic, an aristocrat with an aristocrat's control. Jägerhorn had important connections, Jägerhorn had influential relatives, Jägerhorn had the confidence of Vice Admiral Carl Olof Cronstedt, commandant of Sveaborg. At the meeting, Jägerhorn had produced a sheaf of reports.

"The reports are wrong," Anttonen had insisted. "The Russians do not outnumber us. They have barely forty guns, sir. Sveaborg mounts ten times that number."

Cronstedt seemed shocked by Anttonen's tone, his certainty, his insistence. Jägerhorn simply smiled. "Might I ask how you come by this intelligence, Colonel Anttonen?" he asked.

That was the question Bengt Anttonen could never answer. "I know," he said.

Jägerhorn rattled the papers in his hand. "My own intelligence comes from Lieutenant Klick, who is in Helsinki and has direct access to reliable reports of enemy plans, movements, and numbers."

He looked to Vice Admiral Cronstedt. "I submit, sir, that this information is a good deal more reliable than Colonel Anttonen's mysterious certainties. According to Klick, the

Russians outnumber us already, and General Suchtelen will soon be receiving sufficient reinforcements to enable him to launch a major assault. Furthermore, they have a formidable amount of artillery on hand. Certainly more than the forty pieces that Colonel Anttonen would have us believe is the extent of their armament."

Cronstedt was nodding, agreeing. Even then Anttonen could not be silent. "Sir," he insisted, "Klick's reports must be discounted. The man cannot be trusted. Either he is in the pay of the enemy or they are deluding him."

Cronstedt frowned. "That is a grave charge, Colonel."

"He is a fool and a damned Anjala traitor!"

Jägerhorn bristled at that, and Cronstedt and a number of junior officers looked plainly aghast. "Colonel," the commandant said, "it is well known that Colonel Jägerhorn has relatives in the Anjala League. Your comments are offensive. Our situation here is perilous enough without my officers fighting among themselves over petty political differences. You will offer an apology at once."

Given no choice, Anttonen had tendered an awkward apology. Jägerhorn accepted with a patronizing nod.

Cronstedt went back to the papers. "Very persuasive," he said, "and very alarming. It is as I have feared. We have come to a hard place." Plainly his mind was made up. It was futile to argue further. It was at times like this that Bengt Anttonen most wondered what madness had possessed him. He would go to staff meetings determined to be circumspect and politic, and no sooner would he be seated than a strange arrogance would seize him. He argued long past the point of wisdom; he denied obvious facts, confirmed in written reports from reliable sources; he spoke out of turn and made enemies on every side.

"No, sir," he said. "I beg of you, disregard Klick's intelligence. Sveaborg is vital to the spring counteroffensive. We have nothing to fear if we can hold out until the ice melts. Once the sea lanes are open, Sweden will send help."

Vice Admiral Cronstedt's face was drawn and weary, an old man's face. "How many times must we go over this? I grow tired of your argumentative attitude, and I am quite aware of Sveaborg's importance to the spring offensive. The facts are plain. Our defenses are flawed, and the ice makes our walls accessible from all sides. Sweden's armies are being routed—"

"We know that only from the newspapers the Russians allow us, sir," Anttonen blurted out. "French and Russian papers. Such news is unrealiable."

Cronstedt's patience was exhausted. "Quiet!" he said, slapping the table with an open palm. "I have had enough of your intransigence, Colonel Anttonen. I respect your patriotic fervor, but not your judgment. In the future, when I require your opinion, I shall ask for it. Is that clear?"

"Yes, sir," Anttonen had said.

Jägerhorn smiled. "If I may proceed?"

The rebuke had been as smarting as the cold winter wind. It was no wonder Anttonen had felt driven to the cold solitude of the battlements afterward.

By the time he returned to his quarters, Bengt Anttonen's mood was bleak and confused. Darkness was falling, he knew. Over the frozen sea, over Sveaborg, over Sweden and Finland. And over America, he thought. Yet the afterthought left him sick and dizzy. He sat heavily on his cot, cradling his head in his hands. America, America, what madness was that, what possible difference could the struggle between Sweden and Russia make to that infant nation so far away?

Rising, he lit a lamp, as if light would drive the troubling thoughts away, and splashed some stale water on his face from the basin atop the modest dresser. Behind the basin was the mirror he used for shaving, slightly warped and dulled by corrosion but serviceable. As he dried his big, bony hands, he found himself staring at his own face, the features at once so familiar and so oddly, frighteningly strange. He had unruly, graying hair; dark-gray eyes; a narrow, straight nose; slightly sunken cheeks; a square chin. He was too thin, almost gaunt. It was a stubborn, common, plain face. The face he had worn all his life. Long ago, Bengt Anttonen had grown resigned to the way he looked. Until recently, he scarcely gave his appearance any thought. Yet now he stared at himself, unblinking, and felt a disturbing fascination welling up inside him, a sense of satisfaction, a pleasure in the cast of his image that was alien and troubling. Such vanity was sick, unmanly, another sign of madness. Anttonen wrenched his gaze from the mirror. He lay himself down with a will.

For long moments he could not sleep. Fancies and visions danced against his closed eyelids, sights as fantastic as the phantom animals fashioned by the wind: flags he did not recognize, walls of polished metal, great storms of fire, men and women as hideous as demons asleep in beds of burning liquid. And then, suddenly, the thoughts were gone, peeled off like a layer of burned skin. Bengt Anttonen sighed uneasily and turned in his sleep. . . .

. . . BEFORE THE AWARENESS is always the pain, and the pain comes first, the only reality in a still, quiet, empty world beyond sensation. For a second, an hour I do not know where I am, and I am afraid. And then the knowledge comes to me; returning, I am returning, in the return is always pain. I do not want to return, but I must, must. I want the sweet, clean purity of ice and snow, the bracing touch of the winter wind, the healthy lines of Bengt's face. But it fades, fades though I scream and clutch for it, crying, wailing. It fades, fades, and then is gone.

I sense motion, a stirring all around me as the immersion fluid ebbs away. My face is exposed first. I suck in air through my wide nostrils, spit the tubes out of my bleeding mouth. When the fluid falls below my ears, I hear a gurgling, a greedy sucking sound. The vampire machines feed on the juices of my womb, the black blood of my second life. The cold touch of air on my skin pains me. I try not to scream, manage to hold the noise down to a whimper.

Above, the top of my tank is coated by a thin, ebony film that has clung to the polished metal. I can see my reflection. I'm a stirring sight, nostril hairs aquiver on my noseless face, my right cheek bulging with a swollen, greenish tumor. Such a handsome devil. I smile, showing a triple row of rotten teeth, fresh new incisors pushing up among them like sharpened stakes in a field of yellow toadstools. I wait for release. The tank is too damned small, a coffin. I am buried alive, and the fear is a palpable weight upon me. They do not like me. What if they just leave me in here to suffocate and die? "Out!" I whisper, but no one hears.

Finally the lid lifts, and the orderlies are there. Rafael and Slim. Big, strapping fellows, blurred white colossi with flags sewn above the pockets of their uniforms. I cannot focus on their faces. My eyes are not so good at the best of times and especially bad just after a return. I know the dark one is Rafe, though, and it is he who reaches down and unhooks the IV tubes and the telemetry while Slim gives me my injection. Ahhh. The hurt fades. I force my hands to grasp the tank's sides. The metal feels strange; the motion is clumsy, deliberate; my body, slow to respond. "What took you so long?" I ask.

"Emergency," says Slim. "Rollins." He is a testy, laconic sort, and he doesn't like me. To learn more, I would have to ask question after question. I don't have the strength. I concentrate instead on pulling myself to a sitting position. The room is awash with a bright blue-white fluorescent light. My eyes water after so long in darkness. Maybe the orderlies think I'm crying with joy to be back. They're big but not too bright. The air has an astringent, sanitized smell and the hard coolness of air conditioning. Rafe lifts me up from the coffin, the fifth silvery casket in a row of six, each hooked up to the computer banks that loom around us. The other coffins are all empty now. I am the last vampire to rise this night, I think. Then I remember. Four of them are gone, have been gone for a long time. There is only Rollins and myself, and something has happened to Rollins.

They set me in a chair, and Slim rolls me past the empty caskets and up the ramps to debriefing. "Rollins?" I ask him.

"We lost him."

I didn't like Rollins. He was even uglier than me, a wizened little homunculus with a swollen, oversize cranium and a distorted torso without arms or legs. He had real big eyes, lidless, so he could never close them. Even asleep, he looked like he was staring at you. And he had no sense of humor. No goddamned sense of humor at all. When you're a geek, you got to have a sense of humor. But whatever his faults, Rollins was the only one left, besides me. Gone now, I feel no grief, only a numbness.

The debriefing room is cluttered but somehow impersonal. They wait for me on the other side of the table. The orderlies roll me up opposite them and depart. The table is a long Formica barrier between me and my superiors, maybe a *cordon sanitaire*. They can't let me get too close; after all, I might be contagious. They are normals. I am . . . what am I? When they conscripted me, I was classified as an HM_3. Human Mutation, third category. Or a hum-three, in the vernacular. The hum-ones are the nonviables: stillborns and infant deaths and living veggies. We got millions of 'em. The hum-twos are viable but useless, all the guys with extra toes and webbed hands and funny eyes. Got thousands of them. But us hum-threes are a fucking *elite*, so they tell us. That's when they draft us. Down here, inside the Graham Project bunker, we get new names. Old Charlie Graham himself used to call us his "timeriders" before he croaked, but that's too romantic for Major Salazar. Salazar prefers the official government term: G.C., for Graham Chrononaut. The orderlies and grunts turned G.C. into *geek*, of course, and we turned it right back on 'em, me and Nan and Creeper, when they were still with us. *They* had a terrific sense of humor, now. The killer geeks, we called ourselves. Six little killer geeks riding the timestream, biting the heads off vast chickens of probability. Heigh-ho.

And then there was one.

Salazar is pushing papers around on the table. He looks sick. Under his dark complexion I can see an unhealthy greenish tinge, and the blood vessels in his nose have burst beneath the skin. None of us are in good shape down here, but Salazar looks worse than most. He's been gaining weight, and it looks bad on him. His uniforms are all too tight now, and there won't be any fresh ones. They've closed down all the commis-

saries and the mills, and in a few years we'll all be wearing
rags. I've told Salazar he ought to diet, but no one will listen
to a geek, except when the subject is chickens. "Well?"
Salazar says to me, his voice snapping. A hell of a way to start
a debriefing. Three years ago, when it began, he was full of
starch and vinegar, very correct and military, but even the
Maje has no time left for decorum now.

"What happened to Rollins?" I ask.

Doctor Veronica Jacobi is seated next to Salazar. She
used to be chief headshrinker down here, but since Graham
Crackers went and expired she's been heading up the whole
scientific side of the show. "Death trauma," she says, profes-
sionally. "Most likely, his host was killed in action."

I nod. Old story. Sometimes the chickens bite back. "He
accomplish anything?"

"Not that we've noticed," Salazar says.

The answer I expected. Rollins had gotten rapport with
some ignorant grunt of a foot soldier in the army of Charles
XII. I had this droll mental picture of him marching the guy
up to his loon of a teenage king and trying to tell the boy to
stay away from Poltava. Charles probably hanged him on the
spot—though, come to think of it, it had to be something
quicker, or else Rollins would have had time to disengage.

"Your report," prompts Salazar.

"Right, Maje," I say lazily. He hates to be called Maje,
though not so much as he hated Sally, which was what
Creeper used to call him. Us killer geeks are an insolent lot.

"It's no good. Cronstedt will meet with General Suchtelen
and negotiate for surrender. Nothing Bengt says sways him
one damned bit. I been pushing too hard. Bengt thinks he's
going crazy. I'm afraid he may crack."

"All timeriders take that risk," Jacobi says. "The longer
you stay in rapport, the stronger your influence grows on the
host and the more likely it becomes that your presence will be
felt. Few hosts can deal with that perception." Ronnie has a
nice voice, and she's always polite to me. Well scrubbed and
tall and calm and even friendly, and above all ineffably polite.
I wonder if she'd be as polite if she knew that she'd figured

prominently in my masturbation fantasies ever since we'd been down here. They only put five women into the Cracker Box, with thirty-two men and six geeks, and she's by far the most pleasant to contemplate.

Creeper liked to contemplate her, too. He even bugged her bedroom, to watch her in action. She never knew. Creeper had a talent for that stuff, and he'd rig up these tiny little audiovideo units in his workbench and plant them everywhere. He said that if he couldn't live life at least he was going to watch it. One night he invited me into his room, when Ronnie was entertaining big, red-haired Captain Halliburton, the head of base security, and her fella in those early days. I watched, yeah; got to confess that I watched. But afterward I got angry. Told Creeper he had no right to spy on Ronnie or on any of them. "They make us spy on our hosts," he said, "right inside their fucking *heads*, you geek. Turnabout is fair play." I told him it was different, but I got so mad I couldn't explain why. It was the only fight Creeper and me ever had. In the long run, it didn't mean much. He went on watching, without me. They never caught the little sneak, but it didn't matter. One day he went timeriding and didn't come back. Big, strong Captain Halliburton died, too, caught too many rads on those security sweeps, I guess. As far as I know, Creeper's hookup is still in place; from time to time I've thought about going in and taking a peek, to see if Ronnie has herself a new lover. But I haven't. I really don't want to know. Leave me with my fantasies and my wet dreams; they're a lot better, anyway.

Salazar's fat fingers drum upon the table. "Give us a full report on your activities."

I sigh and give them what they want, everything in boring detail. When I'm done, I say, "Jägerhorn is the key to the problem. He's got Cronstedt's ear. Anttonen don't."

Salazar is frowning. "If only you could establish rapport with Jägerhorn," he grumbles. What a futile whiner. He knows that's impossible.

"You takes what you gets," I tell him. "If you're going to wish impossible wishes, why stop at Jägerhorn? Why not Cronstedt? Hell, why not the goddamned *czar*?"

"He's right, Major," Veronica says. "We ought to be grateful we've got Anttonen. At least he's a colonel. That's better than we did in any of the other target periods."

Salazar is still unhappy. He's a military historian by trade. He thought this would be easy when they transferred him out from West Point or what was left of it. "Anttonen is peripheral. We must reach the key figures. Your chrononauts are giving me footnotes, bystanders, the wrong men in the wrong place at the wrong times. It is impossible."

"You knew the job was dangerous when you took it," I say. A killer geek quoting Superchicken; I'd get thrown out of the union if they knew. "We don't get to pick and choose."

The Maje scowls at me. I yawn. "I'm tired of this," I say. "I want something to eat. Some ice cream. I want some rocky road ice cream. Seems funny, don't it? All that goddamned ice, and I come back wanting ice cream." There is no ice cream, of course. There hasn't been any ice cream for half a generation, anywhere in the godforsaken mess they call a world. But Nan used to tell me about it. Nan was the oldest geek, the only one born before the big crash, and she had lots of stories about the way things used to be. I liked it best when she talked about ice cream. It was smooth and cold and sweet, she said. It melted on your tongue and filled your mouth with liquid, delicious cold. Sometimes she would recite the flavors for us, as solemnly as Captain Todd reading his Bible: vanilla and strawberry and chocolate, fudge swirl and praline, rum raisin and heavenly hash, banana and orange sherbet and mint chocolate chip, pistachio and butter pecan. Creeper used to make up flavors to poke fun at her, but there was no getting to Nan. She just added his inventions to her list and spoke fondly thereafter of anchovy almond and liver chip and radiation ripple, until I couldn't tell the real flavors from the made-up ones anymore and didn't really care.

Nan was the first we lost. Did they have ice cream in St. Petersburg back in 1917? I hoped they did. I hope she got a bowl or two before she died.

Major Salazar is still talking, I realize. He has been talking for some time. ". . . our last chance now," he is saying. He be-

gins to babble about Sveaborg, about the importance of what
we are doing here, about the urgent need to *change* something
somehow, to prevent the Soviet Union from ever coming into
existence, and thus forestall the war that has laid the world to
waste. I've heard it all before, I know it all by heart. The Maje
has terminal verbal diarrhea, and I'm not so dumb as I look.

It was all Graham Cracker's idea, the last chance to win the
war or maybe just save ourselves from the plagues and bombs
and the poisoned winds.

But the Maje was the historian, so he got to pick all the tar-
gets, when the computers had done their probability analysis.
He had six geeks, and he got six tries. "Nexus points," he
called 'em. Critical points in history. Of course, some were
better than others. Rollins got the Great Northern War, Nan
got the Revolution, Creeper got to go all the way back to Ivan
the Terrible, and I got Sveaborg. Impregnable, invincible Sveaborg. Gibraltar of the North.

"There is no reason for Sveaborg to surrender, " the Maje
is saying. It is his own ice-cream litany. History and tactics
give him the sort of comfort that butter brickel gave to Nan.
"The garrison is seven thousand strong, vastly outnumbering
the besieging Russians. The artillery inside the fortress is superior. There is plenty of ammunition, plenty of food. If Sveaborg holds out until the sealanes are open, Sweden will
launch its counteroffensive and the siege will be broken easily. The entire course of history may change! You must make
Cronstedt listen."

"If I could just lug back a history text and let him read
what they say about him, I'm sure he'd jump through flaming
hoops," I say. I've had enough of this. "I'm tired," I announce.
"I want some food." Suddenly, for no apparent reason, I feel
like crying. "I want something to eat, damn it. I don't want to
talk anymore, you hear? I want *something to eat*."

Salazar glares, but Veronica hears the stress in my voice,
and she is up and moving around the table. "Easy enough to
arrange," she says to me, and to the Maje, "We've accomplished all we can for now. Let me get him some food."

Salazar grunts, but he dares not object. Veronica wheels me away, toward the commissary.

Over the stale coffee and a plate of mystery meat and over-cooked vegetables, she consoles me. She's not half bad at it; a pro, after all. Maybe, in the old days she wouldn't have been considered especially striking—I've seen the old magazines. Even down here we have our old *Playboys*, our old video-tapes, our old novels, our old record albums, our old funny books. Nothing *new* of course, nothing recent, but lots and lots of the old junk. I ought to know, I practically mainline the stuff. When I'm not flailing around inside Bengt's cranium, I'm planted in front of my tube, running some old TV show or a movie, maybe reading a paperback at the same time, try-ing to imagine what it would be like to live back then, before they screwed up everything. So I know all about the old stan-dards, and maybe it's true that Ronnie ain't up to, say, Bo or Marilyn or Brigitte or Garbo. Still, she's nicer to look at than anybody else down in this damned septic tank. And the rest of us don't quite measure up either. Creeper wasn't no Groucho, no matter how hard he tried; me, I look just like Jimmy Cagney, but the big green tumor and all the extra yellow teeth and the want of a nose spoil the effect, just a little.

I push my fork away with the meal only half-eaten. "It has no taste. Back then, food had *taste*."

Veronica laughs. "You're lucky. You get to taste it. For the rest of us, this is all there is."

"Lucky? Ha-ha. I know the difference, Ronnie. You don't. Can you miss something you never had?" I'm sick of talking about it though—sick of it all. "Want to play chess?"

She smiles and gets up in search of our set. An hour later she's won the first game and we're starting the second. There are about a dozen chess players down here in the Cracker Box; now that Graham and Creeper are gone, I can beat all of them except Ronnie. The funny thing is, back in 1808 I could probably be world champion. Chess has come a long way in the last two hundred years, and I've memorized openings that those old guys never even dreamed of.

"There's more to the game than book openings," Veronica says, and I realize I've been talking aloud.

"I'd still win," I insist. "Hell, those guys have been dead for centuries. How much fight can they put up?"

She smiles and moves a knight. "Check."

I realize that I've lost again.

"Someday I've got to learn to play this game," I say. "Some world champion."

Veronica begins to put the pieces back in the box. "This Sveaborg business is a kind of chess game, too," she says conversationally, "a chess game across time, us and the Swedes against the Russians and the Finnish nationalists. What move do you think we should make against Cronstedt?"

"Why did I know the conversation was going to come back to that?" I say. "Damned if I know. I suppose the Maje has an idea."

She nods. Her face is serious now. Pale, soft face, framed by dark hair. "A desperate idea. These are desperate times."

What would it be like if I did succeed, I wonder? If I changed something? What would happen to Veronica and the Maje and Rafe and Slim and all the rest of them? What would happen to *me*, lying there in my coffin full of darkness? There are theories, of course, but no one really knows. "I'm a desperate man, ma'am," I say to her, "ready for desperate measures. Being subtle sure hasn't done diddly-squat. Let's hear it. What do I gotta get Bengt to do now? Invent the machine gun? Defect to the Russkis? Expose his privates on the battlements? What?"

She tells me.

I'm dubious. "Maybe it'll work," I say. "More likely, it'll get Bengt slung into the deepest goddamned dungeon that place has. They'll really think he's nuts. Jägerhorn might just shoot him outright."

"No," she says. "In his own way, Jägerhorn is an idealist. A man of principle. It is chancy, but you don't win chess games without taking chances. Will you do it?"

She has such a nice smile; I think she likes me. I shrug.

"Might as well," I say. "Can't dance."

•   •   •

"...SHALL BE ALLOWED to dispatch two couriers to the king, one by the northern, the other by the southern road. They shall be furnished with passports and safeguards, and every possible facility shall be given them for accomplishing their journey. Done at the island of Lonan, sixth of April 1808."

The droning of the officer reading the agreement stopped suddenly, and the staff meeting was deathly quiet.

Vice Admiral Cronstedt rose slowly. "This is the agreement," he said. "In view of our perilous position, it is better than we could have hoped for. We have used a third of our powder already; our defenses are exposed to attack from all sides because of the ice; we are outnumbered and forced to support a large number of fugitives who rapidly consume our provisions. General Suchtelen might have demanded our immediate surrender. By the grace of God, he did not. Instead we have been allowed to retain three of Sveaborg's six islands and will regain two of the others should five Swedish ships-of-the-line arrive to aid us before the third of May. If Sweden fails us, we must surrender. Yet the fleet shall be restored to Sweden at the conclusion of the war, and this immediate truce will prevent any further loss of life."

Cronstedt sat down. At his side, Colonel Jägerhorn came crisply to his feet. "In the event the Swedish ships do not arrive on time, we must make plans for an orderly surrender of the garrison." He launched into a discussion of the details.

Bengt Anttonen sat quietly. He had expected the news, had somehow known it was coming, but it was no less dismaying for all that. Cronstedt and Jägerhorn had negotiated a disaster. It was foolish. It was craven. It was hopelessly doomed. Immediate surrender of Wester-Svartö, Langörn, and Oster-Lilla-Svartö, the rest of the garrison to come later, capitulation deferred for a meaningless month. History would revile them. Schoolchildren would curse their names. And he was helpless.

When the meeting at last ended, the others rose to depart. Anttonen rose with them, determined to be silent, to leave the room quietly for once, to let them sell Sveaborg for thirty pieces of silver if they would. But as he tried to turn, the compulsion seized him, and he went instead to where Cronstedt and Jägerhorn lingered. They both watched him approach. In their eyes, Anttonen thought he could see a weary resignation.

"You must not do this," he said heavily.

"It is done," Cronstedt replied. "The subject is not open for further discussion, Colonel. You have been warned. Go about your duties." He climbed to his feet, turned to go.

"The Russians are cheating you," Anttonen blurted.

Cronstedt stopped and looked at him. "Admiral, you must listen to me. This provision, this agreement that we will retain the fortress if five ships-of-the-line reach us by the third of May, it is a fraud. The ice will not have melted by the third of May. No ship will be able to reach us. The armistice agreement provides that the ships must have entered Sveaborg's harbor by noon on the third of May. General Suchtelen will use the time afforded by the truce to move his guns and gain control of the sea approaches. Any ship attempting to reach Sveaborg will come under heavy attack. And there is more. The messengers you are sending to the King, sir, they—"

Cronstedt's face was ice and granite. He held up a hand. "I have heard enough. Colonel Jägerhorn, arrest this madman." He gathered up his papers, refusing to look Anttonen in the face, and strode angrily from the room.

"Colonel Anttonen, you are under arrest," Jägerhorn said, with surprising gentleness in his voice. "Don't resist. I warn you, that will only make it worse."

Anttonen turned to face the other colonel. His heart was sick.

"You will not listen. None of you will listen. Do you know what you are doing?"

"I think I do," Jägerhorn said.

Anttonen reached out and grabbed him by the front of his uniform.

"You do *not*. You think I don't know what you are, Jägerhorn? You're a nationalist, damn you. This is the great age of nationalism. You and your Anjala League, your damned Finnlander noblemen, you're all Finnish nationalists. You resent

Sweden's domination. The czar has promised you that Finland will be an autonomous state under his protection, so you have thrown off your loyalty to the Swedish crown."

Colonel F. A. Jägerhorn blinked. A strange expression flickered across his face before he regained his composure. "You cannot know that," he said. "No one knows the terms— I—"

Anttonen shook him bodily. "History is going to laugh at you, Jägerhorn. Sweden will lose this war because of you, because of Sveaborg's surrender, and you'll get your wish. Finland will become an autonomous state under the czar. But it will be no freer than it is now under Sweden. You'll swap your King like a secondhand chair at a flea market, for the butchers of the Great Wrath, and gain nothing by the transaction."

"A . . . a market for fleas? What is that?"

Anttonen scowled. "A flea market, a flea . . . I don't know," he said. He released Jägerhorn, turned away. "Dear God, I do know. It is a place where . . . where things are sold and traded. A fair. It has nothing to do with fleas, but it is full of strange machines, strange smells." He ran his fingers through his hair, fighting not to scream. "Jägerhorn, my head is full of demons. Dear God, I must confess. Voices, I hear voices day and night, even as the French girl, Joan, the warrior maid. I know the things that will come to pass." He looked into Jägerhorn's eyes, saw the fear there, and held his hands up, entreating now. "It is no choice of mine, you must believe that. I pray for silence, for release, but the whispering continues, and these strange fits seize me. They are not of my doing, yet they must be sent for a reason, they must be true, or why would God torture me so? Have mercy, Jägerhorn. Have mercy on me and listen!"

Colonel Jägerhorn looked past Anttonen, his eyes searching for help, but the two of them were quite alone.

"Yes," Jägerhorn said. "Voices, like the French girl. I did not understand."

Anttonen shook his head. "You hear, but you will not believe. You are a patriot; you dream you will be a hero. You will be no hero. The common folk of Finland do not share your dreams. They remember the Great Wrath. They know the Russians only as ancient enemies, and they hate them. They will hate you as well. And poor Cronstedt. He will be reviled by every Finn, every Swede, for generations. He will live out his life in this new Grand Duchy of Finland, on a Russian stipend, and he will die a broken man on April 7, 1820, twelve years and one day after he meets with Suchtelen on Lonan and promised Sveaborg to Russia. Years later, a man named Runeberg will write a series of poems about this war. Do you know what he will say of Cronstedt?"

"No," Jägerhorn said. He smiled uneasily. "Have your voices told you?"

"They have taught me the words by heart," said Bengt Anttonen. He recited:

> Call him the arm we trusted in,
> that shrank in time of stress,
> call him Affliction, Scorn, and Sin,
> and Death and Bitterness,
> but mention not his former name,
> lest they should blush who bear the same.

"That is the glory you and Cronstedt are winning here, Jägerhorn" Anttonen said bitterly. "That is your place in history. Do you like it?"

Colonel Jägerhorn had been carefully edging around Anttonen; there was a clear path between him and the door. But now he hesitated. "You are speaking madness," he said. "And yet, how could you have known of the czar's promises? You would almost have me believe you. Voices? Like the French girl? The voice of God, you say?"

Anttonen sighed. "God? I do not know. Voices, Jägerhorn, that is all I hear. Perhaps I am mad."

Jägerhorn grimaced. "They will revile us, you say? They will call us traitors and denounce us in poems?"

Anttonen said nothing. The madness had ebbed; he was filled with a helpless despair.

"No," Jägerhorn insisted. "It is too late. The agreement is

signed. We have staked our honor on it. And Vice Admiral Cronstedt, he is so uncertain. His family is here, and he fears for them. Suchtelen has played him masterfully, and we have done our part. It cannot be undone. I do not believe this madness of yours, yet even if I believed, there is nothing to be done. The ships will not come in time. Sveaborg must yield, and the war must end with Sweden's defeat. How could it be otherwise? The czar is allied with Bonaparte himself, he cannot be resisted!"

"The alliance will not last," Anttonen said with a rueful smile. "The French will march on Moscow, and it will destroy them as it destroyed Charles XII. The winter will be their Poltava. All of this will come too late for Finland, too late for Sveaborg."

"It is too late even now," Jägerhorn said. "Nothing can be changed."

For the first time, Bengt Anttonen felt the tiniest glimmer of hope. "It is not too late."

"What course do you urge upon us, then? Cronstedt has already made his decision. Should we mutiny?"

"There will be a mutiny in Sveaborg, whether we take part or not. It will fail."

"What then?"

Bengt Anttonen lifted his head, stared Jägerhorn in the eyes. "The agreement stipulates that we may send two couriers to the king, to inform him of the terms, so the Swedish ships may be dispatched on time."

"Yes. Cronstedt will choose our couriers tonight, and they will leave tomorrow, with papers and safe passage furnished by Suchtelen."

"You have Cronstedt's ear. See that I am chosen as one of the couriers."

"You?" Jägerhorn looked doubtful. "What good will that serve?" He frowned. "Perhaps this voice you hear is the voice of your own fear. Perhaps you have been under siege too long and it has broken you, and now you hope to run free."

"I can prove my voices speak true," Anttonen said.

"How?" snapped Jägerhorn.

"I will meet you tomorrow at dawn at Ehrensvard's tomb, and I will tell you the names of the couriers that Cronstedt has chosen. If I am right, you will convince him to send me in the place of one of those chosen. He will agree, gladly. He is anxious to be rid of me."

Colonel Jägerhorn rubbed his jaw, considering. "No one could know the choices but Cronstedt. It is a fair test." He put out his hand. "Done."

They shook. Jägerhorn turned to go. But at the doorway he turned back. "Colonel Anttonen," he said, "I have forgotten my duty. You are in my custody. Go to your own quarters and remain there, until the dawn."

"Gladly," said Anttonen. "At dawn you will see that I am right."

"Perhaps," said Jägerhorn, "but for all our sakes, I shall hope that you are wrong."

. . . AND THE MACHINES suck away the liquid night that enfolds me, and I'm screaming so loudly that Slim draws back, a wary look on his face. I give him a broad, geekish smile, rows on rows of yellow, rotten teeth. "Get me out of here, turkey," I shout. The pain is a web around me, but this time it doesn't seem as bad. I can almost stand it; this time the pain is *for* something.

They give me my shot and lift me into my chair, but this time I'm eager for the debriefing. I grab the wheels and give myself a push, breaking free of Rafe, rolling down the corridors like I used to in the old days, when Creeper was around to race me. There's a bit of a problem with one ramp, and they catch me there, the strong, silent guys in their ice-cream suits (that's what Nan called 'em, anyhow), but I scream at them to leave me alone. They do. Surprises the hell out of me.

The Maje is a little startled when I come rolling into the room all by my lonesome. He starts to get up. "Are you . . ."

"Sit down, Sally," I say. "It's good news. Bengt psyched out Jägerhorn good. I thought the kid was gonna wet his pants, believe me. I think we got it socked. I'm meeting Jägerhorn tomorrow at dawn to clinch the sale." I'm grinning, listening to myself. Tomorrow, hey, I'm talking about 1808, but tomorrow is how it feels. "Now here's the sixty-four-thou-sand-dollar question. I need to know the names of the two guys that Cronstedt is going to try and send to the Swedish king. Proof, y'know? Jägerhorn says he'll get me sent if I can convince him. So you look up those names for me, Maje, and once I say the magic words, the duck will come down and give us Sveaborg."

"This is very obscure information," Salazar complains. "The couriers were detained for weeks and did not even arrive in Stockholm until the day of surrender. Their names may be lost to history." What a whiner, I'm thinking; the man is never satisfied.

Ronnie speaks up for me, though. "Major Salazar, those names had better not be lost to history or to us. You were our military historian. It was your job to research each of the tar-get periods *thoroughly*." The way she's talking to him, you'd never guess he was the boss. "The Graham Project has every priority. You have our computer files, our dossiers on the per-sonnel of Sveaborg, and you have access to the war college at New West Point. Maybe you can even get through to someone in what remains of Sweden. I don't care how you do it, but it must be done. The entire project could rest on this piece of in-formation. The entire world. Our past and our future. I shouldn't need to tell you that."

She turns to me. I applaud. She smiles. "You've done well," she says. "Would you give us the details?"

"Sure," I say. "It was a piece of cake. With ice cream on top. What'd they call that?"

"À la mode."

"Sveaborg à la mode," I say, and I serve it up to them. I talk and talk. When I finally finish, even the Maje looks grudg-ingly pleased. Pretty damn good for a geek, I think. "Okay," I say when I'm done with the report. "What's next? Bengt gets the courier job, right? And I get the message through some-how. Avoid Suchtelen, don't get detained, the Swedes send in the cavalry."

"Cavalry?" Sally looks confused.

"It's a figure of speech," I say, with unusual patience.

The Maje nods. "No," he says. "The couriers—it's true that General Suchtelen lied and held them up as an extra form of insurance. The ice might have melted, after all. The ships might have come through in time. But it was an unnecessary precaution. That year the ice around Helsinki did not melt until well after the deadline date." He gives me a solemn stare. He has never looked sicker, and the greenish tinge of his skin undermines the effect he's trying to achieve. "We must make a bold stroke. You will be sent out as a courier, under the terms of the truce. You and the other courier will be brought before Suchtelen to receive your safe conducts through Russian lines. That is the point at which you will strike. The affair is settled, and war in those days was an honorable affair. No one will expect treachery."

"Treachery?" I say. I don't like the sound of what I'm hearing.

For a second, the Maje's smile looks almost genuine; he's finally lit on something that pleases him. "Kill Suchtelen," he says.

"Kill Suchtelen?" I repeat.

"Use Anttonen. Fill him with rage. Have him draw his weapon. Kill Suchtelen."

I see. A new move in our crosstime chess game. The geek gambit.

"They'll kill Bengt," I say.

"You can disengage," Salazar says.

"Maybe they'll kill him fast," I point out. "Right there, on the spot, y'know."

"You take that risk. Other men have given their lives for our nation. This is war." The Maje frowns. "Your success may doom us all. When you change the past, the present as it now exists may cease to exist, and us with it. But our nation will live, and millions we have lost will be restored. Healthier, happier versions of ourselves will enjoy the rich lives that were denied us. You yourself will be born whole, without deformity."

"Or talent," I say. "In which case I won't be able to go back and do this, in which case the past stays unchanged."

"The paradox does not apply here. You have been briefed on this. The past and the present and future are not contemporaneous. And it will be Anttonen who effects the change, not yourself. He is of that time." The Maje is impatient. His thick, dark fingers drum on the table top. "Are you a coward?"

"Fuck you and the horse you rode in on," I tell him. "You just don't get it. I could give a shit about me. I'm better off dead. But they'll kill *Bengt*."

"What of it?"

Veronica has been listening intently. Now she leans across the table and touches my hand, gently.

"I understand," she says. "You identify with him, don't you?"

"He's a good man," I say. Do I sound defensive? Very well, then; I *am* defensive. "I feel bad enough that I'm driving him around the bend, I don't want to get him killed. I'm a freak, a geek, I've lived my whole life under seige, and I'm going to die here, but Bengt has people who love him, a life ahead of him. Once he gets out of Sveaborg, there's a whole world out there."

"He has been dead for almost two centuries," Salazar says.

"I was in his head this afternoon," I snap.

"He will be a casualty of war," the Maje says. "In war, soldiers die. It is a fact of life, then as now."

Something else is bothering me. "Yeah, maybe, he's a soldier, I'll buy that. He knew the job was dangerous when he took it. But he cares about *honor*, Sally. A little thing we've forgotten. To die in battle, sure, but you want me to make him a goddamned *assassin*, have him violate a flag of truce. He's an honorable man. They'll revile him."

"The ends justify the means," says Salazar bluntly. "Kill Suchtelen, kill him under the flag of truce, yes. It will kill the truce as well. Suchtelen's second-in-command is far less wily, more prone to outbursts of temper, more eager for a spectacular victory. You will tell him that Cronstedt *ordered* you to cut down Suchtelen. He will shatter the truce, will launch a furious attack against the fortress, an attack that Sveaborg, impregnable as it is, will easily repulse. Russian casualties will be heavy, and Swedish determination will be fired by what they will see as Russian treachery. Jägerhorn, with proof before him that the Russian promises are meaningless, will change sides. Cronstedt, the hero of Ruotsinsalmi, will become the hero of Sveaborg as well. The fortress will hold. With the spring the Swedish fleet will land an army at Sveaborg, behind Russian lines, while a second Swedish army sweeps down from the north. The entire course of the war will change. When Napoleon marches on Moscow, a Swedish army will already hold St. Petersburg. The czar will be caught in Moscow, deposed, executed. Napoleon will install a puppet government, and when his retreat comes, it will be north, to link up with his Swedish allies at St. Petersburg. The new Russian regime will not survive Bonaparte's fall, but the czarist restoration will be as short-lived as the French restoration, and Russia will evolve toward a liberal parliamentary democracy. The Soviet Union will never come into being to war against the United States." He emphasizes his final words by pounding his fist on the conference table.

"Sez you," I say mildly.

Salazar gets red in the face. "That is the computer projection," he insists. He looks away from me, though. Just a quick little averting of the eyes, but I catch it. Funny. He can't look me in the eyes.

Veronica squeezes my hand. "The projection may be off," she admits. "A little or a lot. But it is all we have. And this is our last chance. I understand your concern for Anttonen, really I do. It's only natural. You've been part of him for months now, living his life, sharing his thoughts and feelings. Your reservations do you credit. But now millions of lives are in the balance, against the life of this one man. This one dead man. It's your decision. The most important decision in all history, perhaps, and it rests with you alone." She smiles. "Think about it carefully, at least."

When she puts it like that and holds my little hand all the while, I'm powerless to resist. Ah, Bengt. I look away from

them, sigh. "Break out the booze tonight," I say wearily to
Salazar, "the last of that old prewar stuff you been saving."

The Maje looks startled, discomfited; the jerk thought his
little cache of prewar Glenlivet and Irish Mist and Remy Martin was a well-kept secret. And so it was until Creeper planted
one of his little bugs, heigh-ho.

"I do not think drunken revelry is in order," Sally says. De-
fending his treasure. He's homely and dumb and mean spir-
ited, but nobody ever said he wasn't selfish.

"Shut up and come across," I say. Tonight I ain't gonna be
denied. I'm giving up Bengt, the Maje can give up some
booze. "I want to get shitfaced," I tell him. "It's time to drink
to the goddamned dead and toast the living past and present.
It's in the rules, damn you. The geek always gets a bottle before he goes out to meet the chickens."

WITHIN THE CENTRAL courtyard of the Vargön citadel,
Bengt Anttonen waited in the pre-dawn chill. Behind him
stood Ehrensvard's tomb, the final resting place of the man
who had built Sveaborg and now slept securely within the
bosom of his creation, his bones safe behind her guns and her
granite walls, guarded by all her daunting might. He had built
her impregnable, and impregnable she stood, so none would
come to disturb his rest. Now they wanted to give her away.

The wind was blowing. It came howling down out of a
black, empty sky, stirred the barren branches of the trees that
stood in the empty courtyard and öut through Anttonen's
warmest coat. Or perhaps it was another sort of chill that lay
upon him: the chill of fear. Dawn was almost at hand. Above,
the stars were fading. And his head was empty, echoing,
mocking. Light would soon break over the horizon, and with
the light would come Colonel Jägerhorn, hard faced, imperi-
ous, demanding, and Anttonen would have nothing to say to
him.

He heard footsteps. Jägerhorn's boots rang on the stones.
Anttonen turned to face him, watching him climb the few
small steps up to Ehrensvard's memorial. They stood a foot
apart, conspirators huddled against the cold and darkness.

Jägerhorn gave him a curt, short nod. "I have met with Cronstedt."

Anttonen opened his mouth. His breath steamed in the
frigid air. And just as he was about to succumb to the empti-
ness, about to admit that his voices had failed him, something
whispered deep inside him. He spoke two names.

There was such a long silence that Anttonen once again
began to fear. Was it madness after all and not the voice of
God? Had he been wrong? But then Jägerhorn looked down,
frowning, and clapped his gloved hands together in a gesture
that spoke of finality. "God help us all," he said, "but I believe
you."

"I will be the courier?"

"I have already broached the subject with Vice Admiral
Cronstedt," Jägerhorn said. "I have reminded him of your
years of service, your excellent record. You are a good soldier
and a man of honor, damaged only by your own patriotism
and the pressure of the siege. You are that sort of warrior who
cannot bear inaction, who must always be doing something.
You deserve more than arrest and disgrace, I have argued. As
a courier, you will redeem yourself, I have told him to have no
doubt of it. And by removing you from Sveaborg, we will also
remove a source of tension and dissent around which mutiny
might grow. The Vice Admiral is well aware that a good many
of the men are most unwilling to honor our pact with Suchtelen. He is convinced." Jägerhorn smiled wanly. "I am nothing
if not convincing. Anttonen. I can marshal an argument as
Bonaparte marshals his armies. So this victory is ours. You are
named courier."

"Good," said Anttonen. Why did he feel so sick at heart?
He should have been full of jubilation.

"What will you do?" Jägerhorn asked. "For what purpose
do we conspire?"

"I will not burden you with that knowledge," Anttonen
replied. It was knowledge he lacked himself. He must be the
courier, he had known that since yesterday, but the why of it
still eluded him, and the future was as cold as the stone of

Ehrensvard's tomb, as misty as Jägerhorn's breath. He was full of a strange foreboding, a sense of approaching doom.

"Very well," said Jägerhorn. "I pray that I have acted wisely in this." He removed his glove, offered his hand. "I will count on you, on your wisdom and your honor."

"My honor," Bengt repeated. Slowly, too slowly, he took off his own glove to shake the hand of the dead man standing there before him. Dead man? He was no dead man; he was live, warm flesh. But it was frigid there under those bare trees, and when Anttonen clasped Jägerhorn's hand, the other's skin felt cold to the touch.

"We have had our differences," said Jägerhorn, "but we are both Finns, after all, and patriots, and men of honor, and now too we are friends."

"Friends," Anttonen repeated. And in his head, louder than it ever had been before, so clear and strong it seemed almost as if someone had spoken behind him, came a whisper, sad somehow, and bitter. *C'mon, Chicken Little*, it said, *shake hands with your pal, the geek.*

GATHER YE FOUR Roses while ye may, for time is still flying, and this same geek what smiles today tomorrow may be dying. Heigh-ho, drunk again, second night in a row, chugging all the Maje's good booze, but what does it matter, he won't be needing it. After this next little timeride, he won't even exist, or that's what they tell me. In fact, he'll never have existed, which is a real weird thought. Old Major Sally Salazar, his big, thick fingers, his greenish tinge, the endearing way he had of whining and bitching, he sure seemed real this afternoon at that last debriefing, but now it turns out there never was any such person. Never was a Creeper, never a Rafe or a Slim, Nan never ever told us about ice cream and reeled off the names of all those flavors, butter pecan and rum raisin are one with Nineveh and Tyre, heigh-ho. Never happened, nope, and I slug down another shot, drinking alone, in my room, in my cubicle, the savior at this last liquid supper, where the hell are my fucking apostles? Ah, drinking, drinking, but not with me.

They ain't s'posed to know, nobody's s'posed to know but me and the Maje and Ronnie, but the word's out, yes it is, and out there in the corridors it's turned into a big, wild party, boozing and singing and fighting, a little bit of screwing for those lucky enough to have a partner, of which number I am not one, alas. I want to go out and join in, hoist a few with the boys, but no, the Maje says no, too dangerous, one of the motley horde might decide that even this kind of has-been life is better than a never-was non-life, and therefore off the geek, ruining everybody's plans for a good time. So here I sit on geek row, in my little room, boozing alone, surrounded by five other little rooms, and down at the end of the corridor is a most surly guard, pissed off that he isn't out there getting a last taste, who's got to keep me in and the rest of them out.

I was sort of hoping Ronnie might come by, you know, to share a final drink and beat me in one last game of chess and maybe even play a little kissy-face, which is a ridiculous fantasy on the face of it, but somehow I don't wanna die a virgin, even though I'm not really going to die, since once the trick is done, I won't ever have lived at all. It's goddamned noble of me if you ask me, and you got to 'cause there ain't nobody else around to ask. Another drink now, but the bottle's almost empty. I'll have to ring the Maje and ask for another. Why won't Ronnie come by? I'll never be seeing her again, after tomorrow, tomorrow-tomorrow and two-hundred-years-ago-tomorrow. I could refuse to go, stay here and keep the happy li'l family alive, but I don't think she'd like that. She's a lot more sure than me. I asked her this afternoon if Sally's projections could tell us about the side effects. I mean, we're changing this war, and were keeping Sveaborg and (we hope) losing the czar and (we hope) losing the Soviet Union and (we sure as hell hope) maybe losing the big war and all, the bombs and the rads and the plagues and all that good stuff, even radiation-ripple ice cream, which was the Creeper's favorite flavor, but what if we lose other stuff? I mean, with Russia so changed and all, are we going to lose Alaska? Are we gonna lose vodka? Are we going to lose George Orwell? Are we going to lose Karl Marx? We tried to lose Karl Marx, actually, one of the other geeks, Blind Jeffey, he went back to take care of Karlie, but it didn't work out. Maybe vision was too damn much for him. So we got to keep Karl, although come to think of it, who cares about Karl Marx; are we gonna lose Groucho? No Groucho, no Groucho ever. I don't like that concept, last night I shot a geek in my pajamas, and how he got in my pajamas, I'll never know, but maybe, who the hell knows how us geeks get anyplace, all these damn dominoes falling every which way, knocking over other dominoes, dominoes was never my game. I'm a chess player, world chess champion in temporal exile, that's me, dominoes is a dumb, damn game. What if it don't work. I asked Ronnie, what if we take out Russia, and, well, Hitler wins World War II so we wind up swapping missiles and germs and biotoxics with Nazi Germany? Or England? Or fucking Austria-Hungary, maybe, who can say? The superpower Austria-Hungary, what a thought, last night I shot a Hapsburg in my pajamas, the geeks put him there, heigh-ho.

Ronnie didn't make me no promises, kiddies. Best she could do was shrug and tell me this story about a horse. This guy was going to get his head cut off by some old-timy king, y'see, so he pipes up and tells the king that if he's given a year, he'll teach the king's horse to talk. The king likes this idea for some reason, maybe he's a Mister Ed fan. I dunno, but he gives the guy a year. And the guy's friends say, hey, what is this, you can't get no horse to talk. So the guy says, well, I got a year now, that's a long time, all kinds of things could happen. Maybe the king will die. Maybe I'll die. Maybe the horse will die. Or maybe the horse will talk.

I'm too damn drunk, I am, I am, and my head's full of geeks and talking horses and falling dominoes and unrequited love, and all of a sudden I got to see her. I set down the bottle, oh so carefully, even though it's empty, don't want no broken glass on geek row, and I wheel myself out into the corridor, going slow, I'm not too coordinated right now. The guard is at the end of the hall, looking wistful. I know him a little bit. Security guy, big black fellow, name of Dex. "Hey, Dex," I say as I come wheeling up, "screw this shit, let's us go

party, I want to see li'l Ronnie." He just looks at me, shakes
his head. "C'mon," I say. I bat my baby blues at him. Does he
let me by? Does the Pope shit in the woods? Hell no, old Dex
says, "I got my orders; you stay right here." All of a sudden
I'm mad as hell, this ain't fair, I want to see Ronnie. I gather
up all my strength and try to wheel right by him. No cigar.
Dex turns, blocks my way, grabs the wheelchair and pushes. I
go backward fast, spin around when a wheel jams, flip over
and out of the chair.. It hurts. Goddamn it hurts. If I had a
nose, I woulda bloodied it, I bet. "You stay where you are, you
fucking freak," Dex tells me. I start to cry, damn him anyhow,
and he watches me as I get my chair upright and pull myself
into it. I sit there staring at him. He stands there staring at me.
"Please," I say finally. He shakes his head. "Go get her then,"
I say. "Tell her I want to see her." Dex grins. "She's busy," he
tells me. "Her and Major Salazar. She don't want to see you."

I stare at him some more. A real withering, intimidating
stare. He doesn't wither or look intimidated. It can't be, can
it? Her and the Maje? Her and old Sally Greenface? No way,
he's not her type, she's got better taste than that. I know she
has. Say it ain't so, Joe. I turn around, start back to my cubicle. Dex looks away. Heigh-ho, fooled him.

Creeper's room is the one beyond mine, the last one at the
end of the hall. Everything's just like he left it. I turn on the
set, play with the damn switches, trying to figure out how it
works. My mind isn't at its sharpest right at this particular
minute, it takes me a while, but finally I get it, and I jump
from scene to scene down in the Cracker Box, savoring all
these little vignettes of life in these United States as served up
by Creeper's clever ghost. Each scene has its own individual
charm. There's a gang bang going on in the commissary, right
on top of one of the tables where Ronnie and I used to play
chess. Two huge security men are fighting in the airlock area;
they've been at it a long time, their faces are so bloody. I can't
tell who the hell they are, but they keep at it, staggering at
each other blindly, swinging huge, awkward fists, grunting,
while a few others stand around and egg them on. Slim and
Rafe are sharing a joint, leaning up against my coffin. Slim

thinks they ought to rip out all the wires, fuck up everything so I can't go timeriding. Rafe thinks it'd be easier to just bash my head in. Somehow I don't think he loves me no more. Maybe I'll cross him off my Christmas list. Fortunately for the geek, both of them are too stoned and screwed up to do anything at all. I watch a half-dozen other scenes, and finally, a little reluctantly, I go to Ronnie's room, where I watch her screwing Major Salazar.

Heigh-ho, as Creeper would say, what'd you expect, really?

I could not love thee, dear, so much, loved I not honor more. She walks in beauty like the night. But she's not so pretty, not really, back in 1808 there are lovelier women, and Bengt's just the man to land 'em, too, although Jägerhorn probably does even better. My Veronica's just the queen bee of a corrupt, poisoned hive, that's all. They're done now. They're talking. Or rather the Maje is talking, bless his soul, he's not his ice-cream litany, he's just been making love to Ronnie and now he's lying there in bed talking about Sveaborg, damn him. ". . . only a thirty percent chance that the massacre will take place," he's saying, "the fortress is very strong, formidably strong, but the Russians have the numbers, and if they do bring up sufficient reinforcements, Cronstedt's fears may prove to be substantial. But even that will work out. The assassination, well, the rules will be suspended, they'll slaughter everyone inside, but Sveaborg will become a sort of Swedish Alamo, and the branching paths ought to come together again. Good probability. The end results will be the same." Ronnie isn't listening to him, though; there's a look on her face I've never seen, drunken, hungry, scared, and now she's moving lower on him and doing something I've seen only in my fantasies, and now I don't want to watch anymore, no, oh no, no, oh no.

GENERAL SUCHTELEN HAD established his command post on the outskirts of Helsinki, another clever ploy. When Sveaborg turned its cannon on him, every third shot told upon the city the fortress was supposed to protect, until Cronstedt finally

ordered the firing stopped. Suchtelen took advantage of that
concession as he had all the rest. His apartments were large and
comfortable, from his windows, across the white expanse of ice
and snow, the gray form of Sveaborg loomed large. Anttonen
stared at it morosely as he waited in the anteroom with Cronstedt's other courier and the Russians who had escorted them.
Finally the inner doors opened and the dark Russian captain
emerged. "The general will see you now," he said.

General Suchtelen sat behind a wide, wooden desk. An
aide stood by his right arm. A guard was posted at the door,
and the captain entered with the Swedish couriers. On the
broad, bare expanse of the desk was an inkwell, a blotter, and
two signed safe conducts, the passes that would take them
through the Russian lines to Stockholm and the Swedish king,
one by the southern and the other by the northern route.
Suchtelen said something, in Russian, the aide provided a
translation. Horses had been provided, and fresh mounts
would be available for them along the way; orders had been
given. Anttonen listened to the discussion with a curiously
empty feeling and a vague sense of disorientation. Suchtelen
was going to let them go. Why did that surprise him? Those
were the terms of the agreement, after all, those were the conditions of the truce. As the translator droned on, Anttonen felt
increasingly lost and listless. He had conspired to get himself
here, the voices had told him to, and now here he was, and he
did not know why, nor did he know what he was to do. They
handed him one of the safe conducts, placed it in his out-
stretched hand. Perhaps it was the touch of the paper, perhaps
it was something else. A sudden red rage filled him, an anger
so fierce and blind and all-consuming that for an instant the
world seemed to flicker and vanish and he was somewhere
else, seeking naked bodies, twining in a room whose walls
were made of pale-green blocks. And then he was back, the
rage still hot within him, but cooling now, cooling quickly.
They were staring at him, all of them. With a sudden start,
Anttonen realized he had let the safe conduct fall to the floor,
that his hand had gone to the hilt of his sword instead, and the
blade was now half-drawn, the metal shining dully in the sun-

light that streamed through Suchtelen's window. Had they
acted more quickly, they might have stopped him, but he had
caught them all by surprise. Suchtelen began to rise from his
chair, moving as if in slow motion. Slow motion, Bengt wondered briefly, what was that? But he knew, he knew. The
sword was all the way out now. He heard the captain shout
something behind him, the aide began to go for his pistol, but
Quick Draw McGraw he wasn't. Bengt had the drop on them
all, heigh-ho. He grinned, spun the sword in his hand, and offered it, hilt first, to General Suchtelen.

"My sword, sir, and Colonel Jägerhorn's compliments,"
Bengt Anttonen heard himself say with something approaching awe. "The fortress is in your grasp. Colonel Jägerhorn
suggests that you hold up our passage. I concur. Detain us
here, and you are certain of victory. Let us go, and who knows
what chance misfortune might occur to bring the Swedish
fleet? It is a long time until the third of May. In such a time,
the king might die, or the horse might die, or you or I might
die. Or the horse might talk."

The translator put away his pistol and began to translate.
Bengt Anttonen found himself possessed of an eloquence that
even his good friend Jägerhorn might envy. He spoke on and
on. He had one moment of strange weakness, when his stomach churned and his head swam, but somehow he knew it was
nothing to be alarmed at, it was just the pills taking effect, it
was just a monster dying far away in a metal coffin full of
night, and then there were none, heigh-ho, one siege was ending and another would go on and on, and what did it matter to
Bengt; the world was a big, crisp, jeweled oyster. He thought
this was the beginning of a beautiful friendship, and what the
hell, maybe he'd save their asses after all, if he happened to
feel like it, but he'd do it his way.

After a time, Suchtelen, nodding, reached out and accepted
the proffered sword.

COLONEL BENGT AUTTONEN reached Stockholm on the
third of May, in the Year of Our Lord Eighteen Hundred and
Eight, with a message for Gustavus IV Adolphus, King of

Sweden. On the same date, Sveaborg, impregnable Sveaborg, Gibraltar of the North surrendered to the inferior Russian forces.

At the conclusion of hostilities, Colonel Anttonen resigned his commission in the Swedish army and became an emigré, first to England and later to America. He took up residence in New York City, where he married, fathered nine children, and became a well-known and influential journalist, widely respected for his canny ability to sense coming trends. When events proved him wrong, as happened infrequently, Anttonen was always surprised. He was a founder of the Republican Party, and his writings were instrumental in the election of John Charles Fremont to the presidency in 1856.

In 1857, a year before his death, Anttonen played Paul Morphy in a New York chess tournament and lost a celebrated game. Afterward, his only comment was, "I could have beat him at dominoes," a phrase that Morphy's biographers are fond of quoting.

Glimpse the future with collections edited by

Jack Dann
and
Gardner Dozois

Beyond Singularity
0-441-01363-5
Some of today's most masterful practitioners of speculative fiction, present fourteen visions of a tomorrow where rapid technological and genetic breakthroughs have rendered humanity obsolete.

A.I.s
0-441-01216-7
Ten masters of speculative fiction explore the future of computerized intelligence, and how humanity interacts with machines that can outthink them—and are learning to outsmart them.

THE ULTIMATE IN
SCIENCE FICTION AND FANTASY!

From magical tales of distant worlds to stories of
technological advances beyond the grasp of man, Penguin has
everything you need to stretch your imagination to its limits.

penguin.com

ACE
Get the latest information on favorites like
William Gibson, T.A. Barron, Brian Jacques,
Ursula Le Guin, Sharon Shinn, and Charlaine Harris,
as well as updates on the best new authors.

ROC
Escape with Harry Turtledove, Anne Bishop,
S.M. Stirling, Simon Green, Chris Bunch, Jim Butcher,
E.E. Knight, and many others—plus news on the
latest and hottest in science fiction and fantasy.

DAW
Mercedes Lackey, Kristen Britain, Tanya Huff,
Tad Williams, C.J. Cherryh, and many more—
DAW has something to satisfy the cravings of any
science fiction and fantasy lover.
Also visit dawbooks.com.

Get the best of science fiction and fantasy
at your fingertips!

Penguin Group (USA) Online

What will you be reading tomorrow?

Tom Clancy, Patricia Cornwell, W.E.B. Griffin,
Nora Roberts, William Gibson, Robin Cook,
Brian Jacques, Catherine Coulter, Stephen King,
Dean Koontz, Ken Follett, Clive Cussler,
Eric Jerome Dickey, John Sandford,
Terry McMillan, Sue Monk Kidd, Amy Tan,
John Berendt…

You'll find them all at
penguin.com

*Read excerpts and newsletters,
find tour schedules and reading group guides,
and enter contests.*

Subscribe to Penguin Group (USA) newsletters
and get an exclusive inside look
at exciting new titles and the authors you love
long before everyone else does.

PENGUIN GROUP (USA)
us.penguingroup.com